"COME HERE, KATIE."

A faint smile touched Ramon's mouth. When she did not answer, he added softly, "Are you not curious about how Spaniards kiss and Puerto Ricans make love?"

Katie swallowed convulsively. "No," she whispered.

"Come here, Katie, and I will show you."

Hypnotized by that velvet voice and those mesmerizing black eyes, Katie walked willingly into his eager embrace. The moment his parted lips covered hers, the kiss was out of control. His tongue plunged into her mouth with a driving hunger and naked urgency that made Katie burst into flames in his arms. In that moment, she knew he would give her whatever she wanted. All she had to do was say, "I love you," but the words just wouldn't come.

WELCOME TO...

SUPERROMANCES

A sensational series of modern love stories
from Worldwide Library.

Written by masters of the genre, these longer,
sensual and dramatic novels are truly in keeping
with today's changing life-styles. Full of intriguing
conflicts, the heartaches and delights of true love,
SUPERROMANCES are absorbing stories—
satisfying and sophisticated reading that lovers
of romance fiction have long been waiting for.

SUPERROMANCES
Contemporary love stories for the woman of today!

JUDITH McNAUGHT

TENDER TRIUMPH

A SUPERROMANCE FROM
WORLDWIDE

TORONTO · NEW YORK · LONDON · PARIS
AMSTERDAM · STOCKHOLM · HAMBURG
ATHENS · MILAN · TOKYO · SYDNEY

For Bill Dailey,
without whose encouragement
and splendid support this novel
would never have been completed.

Published November 1983

First printing September 1983

ISBN 0-373-70086-5

Printed in Canada

CHAPTER ONE

STANDING IN BROODING SILENCE at the windows of the elegant penthouse apartment, the tall dark man gazed at the panorama of twinkling lights fanning out across the dusky St. Louis skyline. Bitterness and resignation were evident in Ramon Galverra's abrupt movements as he jerked the knot of his tie loose, then raised his glass of Scotch to his mouth, drinking deeply.

Behind him, a blond man strode quickly into the dimly lit living room. "Well, Ramon?" he asked eagerly. "What did they decide?"

"They decided what bankers always decide," Ramon said harshly, without turning. "They decided to look out for themselves."

"Those bastards!" Roger exploded. In angry frustration, he raked his hand through his blond hair, then turned and headed determinedly for the row of crystal decanters on the bar. "They sure as hell stayed with you when the money was pouring in," he gritted as he splashed bourbon into a glass.

"They have not changed," Ramon said grimly. "If the money was still pouring in, they would still be with me."

Roger snapped on a lamp, then scowled at the

magnificent Louis XIV furnishings, as if their presence in his spacious living room offended him. "I was so certain, so absolutely certain, that when you explained about the state of your father's mental health before he died the bankers would stand by you. How can they blame you for his mistakes and incompetence?"

Turning from the windows, Ramon leaned a shoulder against the frame. For a moment he stared at the remaining Scotch in his glass, then he tipped it up to his mouth and drained it. "They blame me for not preventing him from making fatal mistakes, and for not recognizing the fact of his incompetence in time."

"Not recognizing the—" Roger repeated furiously. "How were you supposed to recognize that a man who always acted like he was God Almighty, one day started believing it? And what could you have done if you'd known? The stock was in his name, not yours. Until the day he died, he held the controlling interest in the corporation. Your hands were tied."

"Now they are empty," Ramon replied with a shrug of broad, muscled shoulders on his six-foot-three-inch frame.

"Look," Roger said in desperation. "I haven't brought this up before because I knew your pride would be offended, but I'm a long way from being poor, you know that. How much do you need? If I don't have it all, maybe I can raise the rest."

For the first time, a glint of humor touched Ramon Galverra's finely sculpted mouth and arrogant dark eyes. The transformation was startling, softening the features of a face that lately looked as if it had been cast in bronze by an artist intent on portraying cold, ruthless determination and ancient Spanish nobility. "Fifty million would help. Seventy-five million would be better."

"Fifty million?" Roger said blankly, staring at the man he had known since they were both students at Harvard University. "Fifty million dollars would only help?"

"Right. It would only help." Slamming his glass down on the marble table beside him, Ramon turned and started toward the guest room he had been occupying since his arrival in St. Louis a week before.

"Ramon," Roger said urgently, "you have to see Sid Green while you're here. He could raise that kind of money if he wanted to, and he owes you."

Ramon's head jerked around. His aristocratic Spanish face hardened with contempt. "If Sid wanted to help, he would have contacted me. He knows I am here and he knows I am in trouble."

"Maybe he doesn't know. Until now, you've managed to keep it quiet that the corporation is going under. Maybe he doesn't know."

"He knows. He is on the board of directors of the bank that is refusing to extend our loan."

"But—"

"No! If Sid was willing to help, he would have contacted me. His silence speaks for itself, and I will not beg him. I have called a meeting of my corporation's auditors and attorneys in Puerto Rico for ten days from now. At that meeting I will instruct them to file bankruptcy.'' Turning on his heel, Ramon strode from the room, his long purposeful strides eloquent of restless anger.

When he returned, his thick black hair was slightly damp from a shower, and he was wearing Levi's. Roger turned and watched in silence as Ramon folded the cuffs of his white shirt up on his forearms. "Ramon," he said with pleading determination, "stay another week in St. Louis. Maybe Sid will contact you if you give him more time. I tell you, I don't think he knows you're here. I don't even know if he's in town."

"He is in town, and I am leaving for Puerto Rico in two days, exactly as I planned."

Roger heaved a long, defeated sigh. "What the hell are you going to do in Puerto Rico?"

"First, I am going to attend to the corporation's bankruptcy, and then I am going to do what my grandfather did, and his father before him," Ramon replied tautly. "I am going to farm."

"You're out of your mind!" Roger burst out. "Farm that little patch of ground with that hut on it where you and I took those two girls from. . . ?"

"That little patch of ground," Ramon interrupted with quiet dignity, "is all I have left. Along with the cottage on it where I was born."

"What about the house near San Juan, or the villa in Spain, or the island in the Mediterranean? Sell one of your houses or the island; that would keep you in luxury for as long as you live."

"They are gone. I put them up as collateral to raise money for the corporation that it cannot repay. The banks who loaned the money will be swarming over everything like vultures before the year is out.''

''Dammit!'' Roger said helplessly. ''If your father weren't already dead, I'd kill him with my own two hands.''

''The stockholders would have already beaten you to it.'' Ramon smiled without humor.

''How can you just stand there and talk as if you don't even care?''

''I have accepted defeat,'' Ramon said calmly. ''I have done everything that can be done. I will not mind working my land beside the people who have worked it for my family for centuries.''

Turning to hide his sympathy from the man Roger knew would reject it and despise him for it, he said, ''Ramon, is there anything I can do?''

''Yes.''

''Name it,'' Roger said, looking hopefully over his shoulder. ''Just tell me and I'll do it.''

''Will you loan me your car? I would like to go for a drive alone.''

Grimacing at such a paltry request, Roger dug in his pocket, then tossed his keys to his friend. ''There's a problem in the fuel line and the filter keeps clogging, but the local Mercedes dealer can't take it in for another week. With your luck the thing will probably quit in the middle of the street tonight.''

Ramon shrugged, his face wiped clean of emotion. ''If the car stops, I will walk. The exercise will help me get into condition for farming.''

"You don't have to farm that place and you know it! In the international business community you're famous."

A muscle clenched in Ramon's jaw as he made an obvious effort to control his bitter anger. "In the international business community, I have been party to a sin no one will forgive or forget—failure. I am about to become its most notorious failure. Would you have me beg my friends for a position on that recommendation? Shall I go to your factory tomorrow and apply for a job on your assembly line?"

"No, of course not! But you could think of something. I've seen you build a financial empire in a few short years. If you could build it, you could find a way to save a piece of it for yourself. I don't think you give a damn anymore! I—"

"I cannot work miracles," Ramon cut in flatly. "And that is what it would take. The Lear is in a hangar at the airport waiting for a minor part for one of the engines. When the jet mechanics have finished with it, and my pilot returns Sunday night from his weekend off, I will be flying to Puerto Rico." Roger opened his mouth to protest, but Ramon silenced him with an impatient look. "There is dignity in farming. More dignity, I think, than in dealing with bankers. While my father was alive, I knew no peace. Since he died, I have known no peace. Let me find it in my own way."

CHAPTER TWO

THE HUGE BAR at the Canyon Inn near suburban Westport was packed with the usual Friday night crowd. Katie Connelly glanced surreptitiously at her watch, then let her gaze slide over the laughing, drinking, talking groups, searching for a particular face among them. Her view of the main entrance was obscured by the profusion of lush plants suspended from macrame hangers and the tiffany lamps hanging beneath the stained-glass ceiling.

Keeping the bright smile fixed on her face, she returned her attention to the knot of men and women standing around her. "So I told him never to call me again," Karen Wilson was saying to them.

A man stepped on Katie's foot while stretching around her to get his drink from the bar. In the process of reaching into his pocket to extract some money, he jabbed her in the side with his elbow. He offered no apology, nor did Katie really expect one. It was every man, and every woman, for themselves in here. Equal rights.

Turning away from the bar with his drink in his hand, he noticed Katie. "Hello," he said, pausing to flick an interested glance over her slender, curving figure draped in a clingy blue dress. "Nice," he concluded aloud as he considered everything about her, from the shining reddish blond hair tumbling around her shoulders, to the sapphire blue eyes regarding him beneath long curling lashes and delicately arched brows. Her cheeks were elegantly curved, her nose small, and as he continued to survey her, her creamy complexion took on a becoming tint of pale rose. "*Very* nice," he amended, unaware that the reason for her heightening color was irritation, not pleasure.

Although Katie resented him for looking at her as if he had paid for the privilege, she could not really blame him. After all, she was here, wasn't she? Here in what was, despite what the owners and patrons preferred to think, nothing more than a huge singles' bar attached to a tiny dining room to give it dignity.

"Where's your drink?" he asked, lazily reexamining her beautiful face.

"I don't have one," Katie replied, stating the perfectly obvious.

"Why not?"

"I've already had two."

"Well, why don't you get yourself another one and meet me over in that corner? We can get acquainted. I'm an attorney," he added, as if that one piece of information should make her eager to snatch a drink and leap after him.

Katie bit her lip and deliberately looked disappointed. "Oh."

"Oh, what?"

"I don't like attorneys," she said straight-faced.

He was more stunned than annoyed. "Too bad." Shrugging, he turned and wended his way into the crowd. Katie watched him pause near two very attractive young women who returned his considering glance with one of their own, looking him over with blatant interest. She felt a surge of shamed disgust for him, for all of them in this crowded place, but especially for herself for being here. She was inwardly embarrassed by her own rudeness, but places like this automatically made her feel defensive, and her natural warmth and spontaneity atrophied the moment she crossed the threshold.

The attorney had, of course, forgotten Katie in an instant. Why should he bother spending two dollars to buy her a drink, then put forth the effort to be friendly and charm her? Why should he exert himself when it wasn't necessary? If Katie, or any other woman in the room, wanted to get to know him, he was perfectly willing to let her try to interest him. And if she succeeded sufficiently, he would even invite her to come to his place—in her own car, of course—so that she could indulge her equal, and much publicized, need for sexual gratification. After which he would have a friendly drink with her—if he wasn't too tired—walk her to his door, and allow her to drive herself back to wherever she lived.

So efficient, so straightforward. No strings attached. No commitments made or expected. Today's woman, of course, had equal rights of refusal; she didn't have to go to bed with him. She didn't even have to worry that her refusal might hurt his feelings. Because he had no feelings for her. He might be slightly annoyed that he had wasted an hour or two of his time, but then he would simply make another selection from the numerous willing women available to him.

Katie raised her blue eyes, again scanning the crowd for Rob, wishing she had arranged to meet him somewhere else. The popular music was too loud, adding its clamor to the din of raised voices and forced laughter. She gazed at the faces around her, all different, yet all similar in their restless, eager, bored expressions. They were all looking for something. They hadn't found it yet.

"It's Katie, isn't it?" An unfamiliar male voice spoke behind her. Startled, Katie turned and found herself looking into a confidently smiling male face above an Ivy League button-down shirt, well-tailored blazer and coordinated tie. "I met you with Karen at the supermarket, two weeks ago."

He had a boyish grin and hard eyes. Katie was wary and her smile lacked its normal sparkle. "Hello, Ken. It's nice to see you again."

"Listen, Katie," he said, as if he had suddenly devised a brilliant and original scheme. "Why don't we leave here and go somewhere quieter."

His place or hers. Whichever was closest. Katie knew the routine and it sickened her. "What did you have in mind?"

He didn't answer the question, he didn't need to. Instead he asked another. "Where do you live?"

"A few blocks from here—the Village Green Apartments."

"Any roommates?"

"Two lesbians," she lied gravely.

He believed her, and he wasn't shocked. "No kidding? It doesn't bother you?"

Katie gave him a look of wide-eyed innocence. "I *adore* them." For just a fraction of a second he looked revolted, and Katie's smile widened with genuine laughter.

Recovering almost immediately, he shrugged. "Too bad. See you around."

Katie watched his attention shift across the room until he saw someone who interested him and he left, slowly shoving his way through the crowd. She had had enough. More than enough. She touched Karen's arm, distracting her from her animated conversation with two attractive men about skiing in Colorado. "Karen, I'm going to stop in the ladies' room, and then I'm leaving."

"Rob didn't show up?" Karen said distractedly. "Well, look around—there's plenty more where he came from. Take your pick."

"I'm going," Katie said with quiet firmness. Karen merely shrugged and returned to her conversation.

The ladies' room was down a short hall behind the bar, and Katie worked her way through the shifting bodies, breathing a sigh of relief as she squeezed around the last human obstacle in her path and stepped into the relative quiet of the hallway. She wasn't sure whether she was relieved or disappointed that Rob hadn't come. Eight months ago, she had been wildly, passionately dazzled by him, by his clever mind and teasing tenderness. He had everything: blond good looks, confidence, charm and a secure future as the heir to one of St. Louis's largest stockbrokerage firms. He was beautiful and wise and wonderful. And married.

Katie's face saddened as she recalled the last time she had seen Rob.... After a marvelous dinner and dancing they had returned to her apartment and were having a drink. For hours she had been thinking of what was going to happen when Rob took her in his arms. That night, for the first time, she was not going to stop him when he tried to make love to her. During the last months he had told her a hundred times, and shown her in a hundred ways, that he loved her. There was no need for her to hesitate any longer. In fact, she had been about to take the initiative when Rob had leaned his head back against the sofa and sighed. "Katie, tomorrow's paper is going to have a story about me in the society section. Not just about me—but also about my wife and son. I'm married."

Pale and heartbroken, Katie had told him never to call her again or try to see her. He did—repeatedly. And just as tenaciously, Katie refused his calls at her office and hung up the phone at home whenever she heard his voice.

That was five months ago, and only rarely since then had Katie allowed herself the bittersweet luxury of thinking of him, even for a moment. Until three days ago, she had believed she was entirely over him, but when she answered her phone on Wednesday, the sound of Rob's deep voice had made her whole body tremble: "Katie, don't hang up on me. Everything's changing. I've got to see you, to talk to you."

He had argued vehemently against Katie's choice of this for a meeting place, but Katie held firm. The Canyon Inn was noisy and public enough to discourage him from trying to use tender persuasion, if that was his intention, and Karen came here every Friday, which meant Katie would have feminine moral support if she needed it.

The ladies' room was crowded and Katie had to wait in line. She emerged several minutes later, absently digging in her shoulder purse for her car keys as she walked down the hall, then stopped at the crowd blocking her reentry into the bar. Beside her at one of the pay telephones on the wall, a man spoke with a trace of a Spanish accent: "Pardon—could you tell me the address of this place?"

On the verge of pushing her way into the tightly packed mass of humanity, Katie turned to look at the tall, lithe male who was regarding her with faint impatience while holding the telephone to his ear. "Were you speaking to me?" Katie asked. His face was deeply tanned, his hair vitally thick and as black as his onyx eyes. In a place filled with men who always reminded Katie of IBM salesmen, this man, who was wearing faded Levi's and a white shirt with the sleeves rolled up on his forearms, definitely did not belong. He was too. . .earthy.

"I asked," the Spanish-accented voice repeated, "if you could tell me the address of this place. I have had car trouble and am trying to order a towing vehicle.''

Katie automatically named the two intersections at the corner of which the Canyon Inn was located, while mentally recoiling from the narrowed black eyes and patrician nose in a foreign, arrogant face. Tall dark foreign-looking men reeking of coarse masculinity might appeal to some women, but not to Katherine Connelly.

''Thank you,'' he replied, removing his hand from the mouthpiece of the telephone and repeating the names of the streets Katie had given him.

Turning away, Katie confronted a dark green Izod sweater stretched across the masculine chest that was blocking her way back into the bar area. Eyeball to alligator, she said, ''Excuse me, may I get by?'' The sweater obligingly moved out of the doorway.

''Where are you going?'' its wearer inquired in a friendly voice. ''It's still early.''

Katie raised her deep blue eyes up to his face and saw his smile broaden with frank admiration. ''I know, but I have to leave. I turn into a pumpkin at midnight.''

''Your *chariot* turns into a pumpkin,'' he corrected, grinning. ''And your dress turns into rags.''

''Planned obsolescence and poor workmanship, even in Cinderella's time,'' Katie sighed in mock disgust.

''Clever girl,'' he applauded. ''Sagittarius, right?''

''Wrong,'' Katie said, extracting her keys from the bottom of her purse.

"Then what is your sign?"

"Slow Down and Proceed with Caution," she flipped back. "What's yours?"

He thought for a moment. "Merge," he replied with a meaningful glance that faithfully followed every curve of her graceful figure. Reaching out, he lightly ran his knuckles over the silky sleeve of Katie's dress. "I happen to like intelligent women; I don't feel threatened by them."

Firmly repressing the impulse to suggest that he try making a pass at Dr. Joyce Brothers, Katie said politely, "I really do have to leave. I'm meeting someone."

"Lucky guy," he said.

Katie emerged into the dark, sultry summer night feeling lost and depressed. She paused beneath the canopied entrance, watching with a suddenly pounding heart as a familiar white Corvette ran the red light at the corner and turned into the parking lot, screeching to a stop beside her. "I'm sorry I'm late. Get in, Katie. We'll go somewhere and talk."

Katie looked at Rob through the open car window and felt a surge of longing so intense that she ached with it. He was still unbearably handsome, but his smile, normally so confident and assured, was now tinged with an endearing uncertainty that wrung her heart and weakened her resolve. "It's late. And I don't have anything to say to you if you're still married."

"Katie, we can't talk here like this. Don't give me a hard time about being late. I've had a lousy flight and it was delayed getting into St. Louis. Now, be a good girl and get in the car. I don't have time to waste arguing with you."

"Why don't you have time?" Katie persisted, "Is your wife expecting you?"

Rob swore under his breath, then accelerated sharply, swinging the sports car into a shadowy parking space beside the building. He got out of the car and leaned against the door, waiting for Katie to come to him. With the breeze teasing her hair and tugging at the folds of her blue dress, Katie reluctantly approached him in the darkened parking lot.

"It's been a long time, Katie," he said when she stopped in front of him. "Aren't you going to kiss me hello?"

"Are you still married?"

His answer was to snatch her into his arms and kiss her with a combination of fierce hunger and pleading need. He knew her well enough, however, to realize that Katie was only passively accepting his kiss, and by avoiding her question he had told her that he was still married. "Don't be like this," he rasped thickly, his breath warm against her ear. "I've thought of nothing but you for months. Let's get out of here and go to your place."

Katie drew an unsteady breath. "No."

"Katie, I love you, I'm crazy about you. Don't keep holding out on me."

For the first time, Katie noticed the smell of liquor on his breath and was unwillingly touched that he had apparently felt the need to bolster his courage before seeing her. But she managed to keep her voice firm. "I'm not going to have a sleazy affair with a married man."

"Before you knew I was married, you didn't find anything 'sleazy' about being with me."

Now he was going to try cajolery, and Katie couldn't bear it. "Please, please don't do this to me, Rob. I couldn't live with myself if I wrecked another woman's marriage."

"The marriage was 'wrecked' long before I met you, honey. I tried to tell you that."

"Then get a divorce," Katie said desperately.

Even in the darkness, Katie could see the bitter irony that twisted his smile. "Southfields do not divorce. They learn to live separate lives. Ask my father and my grandfather," he said with angry pain. Despite the doors opening and closing as people drifted in and out of the restaurant, Rob's voice remained at normal pitch, and his hands slid down her back caressing her, then cupping her hips, forcing her against his hardened thighs. "That's for you, Katie. Only for you. You won't be wrecking my marriage; it was over long ago."

Katie couldn't stand any more. The sordidness of the situation made her feel dirty, and she tried to pull away from him. "Let go of me," she hissed. "Either you're a liar, or you're a coward, or both, and—"

Rob's hands tightened around her arms as she struggled. "I hate you for acting like this!" Katie choked. "Let me go!"

"Do as she says," a faintly accented voice spoke from the darkness.

Rob's head snapped up. "Who the hell are you?" he demanded of the white-shirted figure that materialized from the shadows beside the building. Retaining his grip on one of Katie's arms, Rob glowered menacingly at the intruder and snapped at Katie, "Do you know him?"

Katie's voice was hoarse with mortification and anger. "No, but let go of me. I want to leave."

"You're staying," Rob gritted. Jerking his head toward the other man, he said, "And you're going. Now move, unless you want me to help you on your way."

The accented voice became extremely courteous, almost frighteningly so. "You may try if you wish. But let her go."

Pushed past all endurance by Katie's continued implacable stubbornness, and now this unwanted intrusion, Rob vented all his frustrated wrath on the intruder. He dropped Katie's arm and, in one smooth continuous motion, swung his huge fist directly at his opponent's jaw. A second's silence was followed by the terrible crack of bone connecting with bone, and then a resounding thud. Katie opened her tear-brightened eyes to find Rob unconscious at her feet.

"Open the car door," the foreign voice ordered with an insistence that brooked no argument.

Automatically, Katie opened the door of the Corvette. The man unceremoniously shoved and folded Rob inside, leaving his head lolling over the steering wheel as if he were passed out in a drunken stupor. "Which is your car?"

Katie stared at him blankly. "We can't leave him like this. He might need a doctor."

"Which is your car?" he repeated impatiently. "I have no wish to be here in the event someone saw what happened and called the police."

"Oh, but—" Katie protested, looking over her shoulder at Rob's Corvette as she hurried toward her car. She drew up stubbornly at the driver's door. "You leave. I can't."

"I did not kill him, I only stunned him. He will wake up in a few minutes with a sore face and loose teeth, that is all. I will drive," he said, forcibly propelling Katie around the front of her car and into the passenger seat. "You are in no condition."

Flinging himself behind the steering wheel, he banged his knee on the steering column and uttered what Katie thought must have been a curse in Spanish. "Give me your keys," he said, releasing the seat back into its farthest position to accommodate his very long legs. Katie handed them over. Several cars were coming in and leaving, and they had to wait before finally backing out of the space. They swooped down the rows of parked cars, past a battered old produce truck with a flat tire, which was parked at the rear of the restaurant.

"Is that yours?" Katie asked lamely, feeling that some conversation was required of her.

He glanced at the disabled produce truck, then slid her an ironic sideways look. "How did you guess?"

Katie flushed with mortification. She knew, and he knew, that simply because he was Hispanic she had assumed he drove the produce truck. To save his pride she said, "When you were on the telephone you mentioned that you needed a tow truck—that's how I knew."

They swung out of the parking lot into the stream of traffic while Katie gave him the simple directions to her apartment, which was only a few blocks away. "I want to thank you, er—?"

"Ramon," he provided.

Nervously, Katie reached for her purse and searched for her wallet. She lived so close by, that by the time she had extracted a five-dollar bill they were already pulling into the parking lot of her apartment complex. "I live right there—the first door on the right, under the gaslight."

He maneuvered the car into the parking space closest to her door, turned off the ignition, got out, and came around to her side. Katie hastily opened her own door and scrambled out of the car. Uncertainly, she glanced up into his dark, proud, enigmatic face, guessing him to be somewhere around thirty-five. Something about him, his foreignness—or his darkness—made her uneasy.

She held out her hand, offering him the five-dollar bill. "Thank you very much, Ramon. Please take this." He looked briefly at the money and then at her face. "Please," she persisted politely, thrusting the five-dollar bill toward him. "I'm sure you can use it."

"Of course," he said dryly after a pause, taking the money from her and jamming it into the back pocket of his Levi's. "I will walk you to your door," he added.

Katie turned and started up the steps, a little shocked when his hand lightly but firmly cupped her elbow. It was such a quaint, gallant gesture—particularly when she knew she had inadvertently offended his pride.

He inserted her key into the lock and swung the door open. Katie stepped inside, turned to thank him again, and he said, "I would like to use your phone to find out if the towing vehicle was sent as they promised."

He had physically come to her rescue and had even risked being arrested for her—Katie knew that common courtesy required that she allow him to use her phone. Carefully concealing her reluctance to let him in, she stepped aside so that he could enter her luxurious apartment. "The phone's there on the coffee table," she explained.

"Once I have called, I will wait here for a short while to be certain that your friend—" he emphasized the word with contempt "—does not awaken and decide to come here. By then the mechanic should have finished his repairs and I will walk back—it is not far."

Katie, who had not even considered the possibility that Rob might come here, froze in the act of taking off her slim-heeled sandals. Surely Rob would never come near her again, not after being verbally rejected by her and physically discouraged by Ramon. "I'm sure he won't," she said, and she meant it. But even so, she found herself trembling with delayed reaction. "I—I think I'll make some coffee," she said, already starting for the kitchen. And then because she had no choice, she added courteously. "Would you like some?"

Ramon accepted her offer with such ambivalence that most of Katie's doubts about his trustworthiness were allayed. Since meeting him, he had neither said nor done anything that was in any way forward.

Once she was in the kitchen, Katie realized that in the anxiety about seeing Rob tonight she had forgotten to buy coffee, and she was out of it. Which was just as well, because she suddenly felt the need for something stronger. Opening the cabinet above the refrigerator, she took out the bottle of Rob's brandy. "I'm afraid all I have to offer you is brandy or water," she called to Ramon. "The Coke is flat."

"Brandy will be fine," he answered.

Katie splashed brandy into two snifters and returned to the living room just as Ramon was hanging up the telephone. "Did the repair truck get there?" she asked.

"It is there now, and the mechanic is making a temporary repair so that I can drive it." Ramon took the glass from her outstretched hand, and looked around her apartment with a quizzical expression on his face. "Where are your friends?" he asked.

"What friends?" Katie questioned blankly, sitting down in a pretty beige corduroy chair.

"The lesbians."

Katie choked back her horrified laughter. "Were you close enough to hear me say that?"

Gazing down at her, Ramon nodded, but there was no amusement in the quirk of his finely molded lips. "I was behind you, obtaining change for the telephone from the bartender."

"Oh." The misery of tonight's events threatened to drag her down, but Katie pushed it fiercely to the back of her mind. She would think about it tomorrow when she would be better able to cope. She shrugged lightly. "I only made the lesbians up. I wasn't in the mood for—"

"Why do you not like attorneys?" he interrupted.

Katie stifled another urge to laugh. "It's a very long story, which I'd rather not discuss. But I suppose the reason I told him that was because I thought it was vain of him to tell me he was one."

"You are not vain?"

Katie turned surprised eyes up to him. There was a childlike defenselessness to the way she had curled up in her chair with her bare feet tucked beneath her; an innocent vulnerability in the purity of her features and clarity of her wide blue eyes. "I—I don't know."

"You would not have been rude to me, had I approached you there and said that I drive a produce truck?"

Katie smiled the first genuine smile of the night, soft lips curving with a winsome humor that made her eyes glow. "I would probably have been too stunned to speak. In the first place, no one who goes to the Canyon Inn drives a truck, and in the second place, if they did they'd never admit it."

"Why? It is nothing to be ashamed of."

"No, I realize that. But they would say they were in the transportation business, or the trucking business—something like that, so that it would sound as if they owned a railroad, or at least an entire fleet of trucks."

Ramon stared down at her as if the words she spoke were a hindrance, not a help, to his understanding her. His gaze drifted to the red gold hair tumbling over her shoulders, then abruptly he jerked his eyes away. Raising his glass, he tossed down half the brandy in it.

"Brandy is supposed to be sipped," Katie said, then realized that what she had meant as a suggestion sounded more like a reprimand. "I mean," she amended clumsily, "you can gulp it down, but people who are accustomed to drinking brandy usually prefer to sip it slowly."

Ramon lowered his glass and looked at her with an absolutely unfathomable expression on his face. "Thank you," he replied with impeccable courtesy. "I will try to remember that if I am ever fortunate enough to have it again."

Squirming with the certainty that she had now thoroughly offended him, Katie watched him stroll over to the living-room window and part the nubby beige curtain.

Her window afforded an uninspiring view of the parking lot and, beyond that, the busy four-lane suburban street in front of her apartment complex. Leaning a shoulder against the window frame, he apparently heeded her advice, for he sipped his brandy slowly while watching the parking lot.

Idly, Katie noticed the way his white shirt stretched taut across his broad, muscled shoulders and tapered back whenever he lifted his arm, then she looked away. She had only meant to be helpful, instead she had sounded condescending and superior. She wished he would leave. She was mentally and physically exhausted, and there was absolutely no reason for him to be guarding her like this. Rob would not come here tonight.

"How old are you?" he asked abruptly.

Katie's gaze flew to his. "Twenty-three."

"Then you are old enough to have a better sense of priorities."

Katie was more perplexed than annoyed. "What do you mean?"

"I mean, you think it is important that brandy be drunk in the 'proper' way, yet you do not worry if it is 'proper' to invite any man you meet into your apartment. You risk soiling your reputation and—"

"Invite any man I meet!" Katie sputtered indignantly, no longer feeling the slightest obligation to be courteous. "In the first place, I only invited you in here because you asked to use the phone, and I felt I had to be polite after you had helped me. In the second place, I don't know about Mexico, or whatever country you come from, but—"

"I was born in Puerto Rico," he provided.

Katie ignored that. "Well, here in the United States, we do not have such antiquated, absurd ideas about women's reputations. Men have never worried about their reputations, and we no longer worry about ours. We do as we please!"

Katie absolutely could not believe it. Now, when she *wanted* to insult him, he was on the verge of laughter!

His black eyes were warm with amusement, and a smile was hovering at the corner of his mouth. ''Do you do as you please?''

''Of course I do!'' Katie said with great feeling.

''What is it that you do?''

''Pardon?''

''What is it that you do that pleases you?''

''Whatever I want.''

His voice deepened. ''What do you want... now?''

His suggestive tone made Katie suddenly and uncomfortably aware of the raw sensuality emanating from his long muscular frame outlined in the revealing Levi's and closely fitted white shirt. A shudder ran through her as his gaze moved over her face, lingering on her soft full lips, before dropping to leisurely study the thrusting curves of her breasts beneath the clinging fabric of her dress. She felt like screaming, laughing, or weeping—or a combination of all three. After everything else that had happened to her tonight, Katie Connelly had managed to latch onto a Puerto Rican Casanova who thought he was now going to make himself the answer to all her sexual needs!

Forcing herself to sound brisk, she finally answered his question. ''What do I want now? I want to be happy with my life and myself. I want to be—to be—free,'' she finished lamely, too distracted by his dark, sensual gaze to think clearly.

"Of what do you wish to be free?"

Katie stood up abruptly. "Of men!"

As she came to her feet, Ramon started toward her with a slow deliberate gait. "You want to be free of so much freedom, but not of men."

Katie continued backing toward the door as he advanced on her. She had been crazy to invite him in here, and he was deliberately misunderstanding her reason for doing so, because it suited his purpose. She gasped as her back bumped into the door.

Ramon stopped six inches away from her. "If you wished to be free of men as you say, you would not have gone to that place tonight; you would not have met that man in the parking lot. You do not know what you want."

"I know that it's late," Katie said in a shaky voice. "And I know I want you to leave now."

His eyes narrowed on her face, but his voice gentled as he asked, "Are you afraid of me?"

"No," Katie lied.

He nodded with satisfaction. "Good, then you will not object to going to the zoo with me tomorrow, will you?"

Katie could tell that he knew she was acutely uneasy with him and that she had no desire to go *anywhere* with him. She considered saying that she had other plans for tomorrow, but she was positive he would only press her to name another time. Every instinct she possessed warned her that he could become extremely persistent if he chose. In her tired, overwrought state, it seemed more expedient to simply make the date and then not be here when he came. That rejection even he would understand and accept as final. "Okay," she feigned. "What time?"

"I will come for you at ten o'clock in the morning."

When the door closed behind him, Katie felt like a spring that was being wound tighter and tighter by some fiend who wanted to see how far she could be twisted before she snapped. She crawled into bed and stared at the ceiling. She had enough problems without having to cope with some amorous Latin who invites her to the zoo!

Rolling over onto her stomach, Katie thought of the sordid scene with Rob and squeezed her eyes closed, trying to escape her tired misery. Tomorrow she would spend the day at her parents' house. In fact, she would spend the entire Memorial Day weekend there. After all, her parents always complained that they didn't see enough of her.

CHAPTER THREE

THE ALARM'S BUZZING at eight o'clock the next morning woke her from a deep, exhausted sleep. Bewildered over why she had set it to go off on a Saturday, she groped for the button and pushed it in, silencing the insistent noise.

When she opened her eyes again it was nine o'clock and she blinked at the light flooding into her flowered bedroom. Oh, no! Ramon would be here in an hour....

Tumbling out of bed, she hurried into the bathroom and turned on the shower. Her pulse quickened with each passing minute, while everything else seemed to slow down. Her blow dryer took forever to dry her heavy hair; she kept dropping everything she touched, and she longed for a bracing cup of coffee.

Moving quickly, she opened drawers, putting on a pair of navy blue slacks and a matching top trimmed in white piping. She pulled her hair back and tied it with a red, white and blue printed silk scarf, then threw a random assortment of clothing into her overnight bag.

At 9:35, Katie closed the door of her apartment behind her and stepped into the balmy blue of a

May morning. The large apartment complex was quiet: the typical lull of a predominately singles' complex in the aftermath of Friday night dates, parties and revelry.

Katie hurried toward her car, shifting her overnight case to her left hand as she searched in her cavernous canvas shoulder bag for her keys. "Damn!" she breathed, putting her case down beside her car and rummaging frantically for her keys. She threw a nervous, apprehensive look at the traffic passing in both directions on the busy street, half-expecting to see a produce truck rattling into the entrance of the complex. "What did I do with them?" she whispered desperately. Her nerves, already strained to the breaking point, exploded in a stifled scream as a hand locked on her arm.

"I have them," a deep voice said smoothly near her ear.

Katie spun around in fright and fury. "How dare you spy on me!" she raged.

"I was *waiting* for you," Ramon emphasized.

"Liar!" she hissed, her fists clenched at her sides. "It's nearly half an hour before you're supposed to be here. Or don't you even know how to tell time?"

"Here are your keys. I put them in my pocket by mistake last night." He raised his hand and held them out to her, along with a single, long-stemmed red rose that lay across his palm.

Snatching her keys from his hand, Katie scrupulously avoided even touching the unwanted crimson flower.

"Take the rose," he told her quietly, his hand still outstretched. "It is for you."

"Damn you!" Katie raged in desperation. "Leave me alone! This isn't Puerto Rico, and I don't want your flower." Ignoring her, he continued to stand patiently. "I said I don't want it!" Katie snapped in frustrated fury and reached down for her overnight case. In the process she inadvertently knocked the rose out of his hand.

The sight of the beautiful bloom falling to the concrete sent a pang of guilt through Katie that shattered her anger and left her feeling deeply embarrassed. She glanced at Ramon; his proud face was composed, reflecting neither anger nor condemnation—only a deep, inexplicable regret.

Unable to meet his eyes Katie dropped her gaze from his, and her guilt sharpened into shame as she saw that buying her a flower wasn't the only thing he had done to try to please her—he had obviously dressed with great care for their date, too. Gone were the worn Levi's, replaced by immaculate black slacks and a short-sleeved black knit shirt; his face was freshly shaven, the scent of spicy cologne clinging to his smooth jaw.

He had only meant to please and impress her; he didn't deserve such treatment, especially after the way he had defended her last night. Katie looked at the waxy red rose lying at her feet, and she was so ashamed that tears stung her eyes and made her throat ache. "Ramon, I'm very, very sorry," she said contritely as she bent down and picked up the rose. Clutching the stem, she dragged her eyes upward and gazed pleadingly into his guarded face. "Thank you for the beautiful flower. And if—if you still want me to, I'll go to the zoo with you, because I promised I would." Pausing to pull more air into her constricted lungs, Katie plunged on. "But I want you to understand that I don't want you to get—well—*serious* about me, and start—start...." Katie trailed off in bewilderment as his eyes began to gleam with laughter.

In a dryly humorous voice he said, "I only offered you a flower and a trip to the zoo, not marriage."

Suddenly Katie found herself smiling back at him. "You're right."

"Shall we go then?" he suggested.

"Yes, but first let me put my overnight case back in the apartment." She reached for it, but Ramon was quicker. "I will carry it," he said.

When they entered her apartment, she took the case from him and started for her bedroom. Ramon's question stopped her. "Was it me you were running away from?"

Katie turned in the doorway. "Not exactly. After last night, I just felt the need to get away from everything and everyone for awhile."

"What were you going to do?"

Katie's soft lips curved into a rueful smile that brought a glow to her lovely eyes. "I was going to do what most independent, self-sufficient, adult American women do when they can't cope—run home to mother and dad."

A few minutes later they left the apartment. As they walked across the parking lot, Katie held up the expensive camera she was carrying in her left hand. "It's a camera," she told him.

"Yes, I know," he agreed with mocking gravity. "We have them even in Puerto Rico."

Katie burst out laughing and shook her head in self-deprecation. "I never realized what an 'ugly American' I am."

Stopping beside a jaunty Buick Regal, Ramon opened the passenger door for her. "You are a beautiful American," he contradicted quietly. "Get in."

To Katie's shame, she was vastly relieved that they were going in a car. Careening down the expressway in a rickety produce truck just wasn't her style. "Is your truck broken down again?" she asked as they glided smoothly out of the parking lot, turning into the stream of Saturday morning shopping traffic.

"I thought you would prefer this to a truck. I borrowed it from a friend of mine."

"We could always have taken my car," she volunteered.

The brief look he sent her made it clear that if Ramon asked someone to go somewhere with him, he expected to provide the transportation. Chastened, Katie turned on the FM radio, then stole a sideways look at him. With his superb physique and deeply tanned face and arms, he reminded her of a Spanish tennis pro.

KATIE HAD A WONDERFUL TIME with Ramon at the zoo, even though it was crowded with Memorial Day visitors. Side by side they wandered down the wide cement paths. Ramon bought her peanuts to toss to the bears and roared with laughter in the Aviary House when a toucan with an enormous beak swooped down and made Katie shriek with alarm and cover her head.

She accompanied him into the Reptile House, trying to keep her phobic aversion to snakes under control by not actually looking at anything. The hair stood up on her nape as she kept her eyes moving around the room without focusing on any of the reptilian occupants.

"Look there," Ramon said in her ear, nodding toward the huge glass enclosure right beside her.

Katie swallowed. "I don't need to look," she whispered through dry lips. "I already know there's a tree in there, which means there's probably a snake hanging from it." Her palms were beginning to perspire, and she could almost feel the reptile's sinuous slitherings on her own skin.

"What is wrong?" Ramon said sharply, noting her draining color. "Do you not like snakes?"

"Not," Katie croaked, "very much."

Shaking his head, he took her by the arm and marched her outside where Katie drew in great gulps of fresh air and sank down on a nearby bench. "I'm sure they put these benches right outside the Reptile House for people like me. Otherwise we'd be dropping like flies out here."

The slight cleft in Ramon's chin deepened as he

grinned. "Snakes are very beneficial to mankind. They eat rodents, insects—"

"Please!" Katie shuddered, holding up her hand in protest. "Do not describe their menu to me."

Regarding her with amusement, Ramon persisted, "The fact remains that they are very useful and entirely necessary to balance nature."

Katie rose a little unsteadily to her feet and gave him an arch look. "Really? Well, I've never heard of one thing that a snake can do that something less repulsive-looking can't do better."

Her delicate nose was wrinkled with distaste, and Ramon smiled thoughtfully down into the brilliant blue of her eyes. "Neither have I," he admitted.

They strolled along and Katie could not remember a more quietly enjoyable date. Ramon was always impeccably courteous, taking her arm when they walked down stairs or ramps, showing her a detached gallantry in the way he acquiesced to her slightest desire.

By the time they came to the island where monkeys and peacocks and other interesting, but not rare, small animals were kept, Katie had used most of the second roll of film. Helping herself to a handful of popcorn from the box Ramon held out to her, she leaned over the fence that isolated the little island, and tossed the kernels one at a time to the ducks. Her unintentionally provocative position caused the navy fabric of her slacks to stretch taut over the graceful contours of her hips and derriere, providing an appreciative Ramon with a delightful view, which he was thoroughly enjoying.

Unaware of where his attention was focused, Katie glanced over her shoulder. "Do you want a picture of this?" she asked.

His lips twitched. "Of what?"

"Of the island," Katie said, puzzled by his laughing expression. "This roll of film is nearly finished. I'll give both of them to you, and then when you have them developed you'll have a souvenir of your trip to the St. Louis zoo."

He looked at her in surprise. "These pictures are for me?"

"Of course," Katie replied, helping herself to another handful of popcorn.

"If I had known they were for me," Ramon grinned, "I would have wanted pictures of more than just bears and giraffes to remind me of this day."

Katie lifted her brows in inquiry. "Snakes, you mean? If you do, I'll show you how to use the camera, then you can go back into the Reptile House while I wait here."

"No," he said wryly, as he guided her from the fence. "Not snakes."

On the way home they stopped at a small market so that Katie could buy some coffee. On an impulse, she decided to invite Ramon in for a snack, and added a bottle of red wine and some cheese to her purchases.

Ramon walked her to her door, but when Katie invited him in he seemed to hesitate before finally nodding his assent.

Less than an hour later, Ramon stood up. "I have work to do tonight," he explained.

Smiling, Katie arose and went over to her camera. "There's one shot left on this roll. Stand there and I'll take a picture of you and give you both rolls to take with you."

"No, save it, and I will take a picture of you tomorrow when we go for a picnic."

Katie deliberated about accepting another date with him. For the first time in ages she had felt lighthearted and carefree, and yet.... "No, I shouldn't really. But thanks." Ramon was tall, sexy and virile, no doubt about it, but his dark features and blatant masculinity still repelled rather than attracted her. Besides, they really had nothing in common.

"Why do you look at me and then away, as if you wish you did not see me?" Ramon asked abruptly.

Katie's gaze flew to his. "I—I don't."

"Yes," he said implacably. "You do."

Katie considered lying, but changed her mind under the scrutiny of those piercing black eyes. "You remind me of someone who's dead now. He was tall and dark and, well, just very macho-looking like you."

"His death brought you great sorrow?"

"His death brought me great release," Katie said emphatically. "There were times before he died when I wished I had the courage to kill him myself!"

He chuckled. "What a dark, sinister life you have led for one so young and beautiful."

Katie, who was known and liked for her sunny disposition despite the painful memories she kept buried inside, gave him a jaunty smile. "Better a dark sinister life than a boring one, I suppose."

"But you *are* bored," he said. "I saw it as I watched you in the place where we met." With one hand on the doorknob he looked across the room at her. "I will call for you tomorrow at noon. I will provide the food." Grinning at her surprise and indecision, he added, "And you can provide a lecture on how rude I am to insist, not ask, that you go places with me."

IT WASN'T UNTIL that night, when she left a boisterous party at a friend's apartment early because she was bored, that Katie seriously considered Ramon's parting words. Was boredom the reason for this increasing restlessness, this vague, unexplainable discontent that had been growing inside of her these past months, she wondered as she changed into silky pajamas and a matching robe. No, she decided after a thoughtful pause, her life was anything but boring—at times it was almost too eventful.

Curled up on the living-room sofa, Katie traced a long, manicured fingernail absently over the cover of the novel in her lap, her blue eyes cloudy and somber. If she wasn't bored, then what *was* the matter with her lately? It was a question she'd asked herself more and more often, and with mounting frustration because the answer always eluded her. If she could just figure out what was missing from her life, then she could try to do something about it.

There was nothing missing from her life, Katie told herself firmly. Impatient with her discontent, she mentally recounted all the reasons she had to feel happy: at twenty-three, she already had her college degree and she had a wonderful, challenging job that paid very well. Even without her salary, the trust fund her father had established for her years ago provided her with more money than she needed. She had a beautiful apartment and closets full of clothes. She was attractive to men; she had good friends, both male and female, and her social life was as active as she permitted it to be. She had loving, supportive parents, she had...everything! Katie told herself firmly.

What more could she possibly want or need to make her happy? "A man," Karen would say, as she often did.

A faint smile touched Katie's lips. "A man" was definitely not the answer to her problem. She knew dozens of men already, so it was not a lack of male companionship that was responsible for this restless, waiting, empty feeling.

Katie, who positively loathed anything that even approached self-pity, caught herself up short. There was absolutely no excuse for her unhappiness—none whatsoever. She was very lucky! Women all over the world were longing for careers; fighting to be independent and self-sufficient; dreaming of financial security and she, Katie Connelly, had all of that, and at only twenty-three years old. "I have everything,'' Katie said determinedly as she opened the book in her lap. She stared at the blur of words on the page, while somewhere in her heart a voice cried out, *It's not enough. It doesn't* mean *anything.* I *don't mean anything.*

CHAPTER FOUR

THEY WENT TO FOREST PARK for their picnic, and Ramon spread the blanket Katie brought beneath a giant cluster of oaks, where they feasted on the wafer-thin delicatessen corned beef, imported ham and thick crusty French bread he had brought.

As they talked and ate, Katie was vaguely aware of his appreciative gaze on her animated face and his absorption with the shining tumble of red gold hair that spilled over her shoulders whenever she reached into the wicker picnic basket. But she was having such a lovely time, she really didn't mind.

"I believe fried chicken is customary for picnics in the States," Ramon said when there was a lull in the conversation. "Unfortunately, I cannot cook. If we have another picnic, I will buy the food and let you prepare it."

Katie almost choked on the hearty Chianti wine she was sipping from a paper cup. "What an utterly chauvinistic supposition to make," she berated him, laughing. "Why do you assume that I can cook?"

Stretching out on his side, Ramon leaned on a forearm and regarded her with exaggerated gravity. "Because you are a woman, of course."

"Are—are you serious?" she sputtered.

"Serious about your being a woman? Or about your being able to cook? Or about you?"

Katie heard the sensuous huskiness that deepened his voice as he asked the last question. "Serious about all women being able to cook," she informed him primly.

His grin widened at her evasiveness. "I did not say that all women were good cooks, merely that women should do the cooking. Men should work to buy the food for them to prepare. That is the way it ought to be."

Katie stared at him in speechless disbelief, half-convinced that he was deliberately goading her. "It may surprise you to hear this, but not all women are born with a burning desire to chop onions and grate cheese."

Ramon muffled a chuckle, then abruptly changed the subject. "What sort of job do you have?"

"I work in the personnel department of a big corporation. I interview people for jobs, things like that."

"Do you enjoy it?"

"Very much," she told him, reaching into the basket and extracting an enormous red apple. Drawing her denim-clad legs up against her chest, she wrapped her arms around them and bit into the juicy apple. "This is delicious."

"That is unfortunate."

Katie looked at him in surprise. "It's unfortunate that I like the apple?"

"It is unfortunate that you enjoy your job so much. You may resent having to give it up when you marry."

"Give it up when I—!" Katie giggled merrily, shaking her head. "Ramon, it's lucky for you that you aren't an American. You aren't even safe in this country. There are women here who could cook *you* for the way you think."

"I am an American," he said, ignoring Katie's dire warning.

"I thought you said you were Puerto Rican."

"I said I was born in Puerto Rico. Actually I am Spanish."

"You just said you were American and Puerto Rican."

"Katie," he said, using her name for the first time and sending an unexplainable thrill of pleasure through her. "Puerto Rico is a U.S. commonwealth. Everyone born there is automatically an American citizen. My ancestors, however, are all Spanish, not Puerto Rican. I am an American, born in Puerto Rico, and of Spanish descent. Just as you are—" he leisurely surveyed her fair complexion, blue eyes and reddish blond hair "—as you are an American, born in the United States, and of Irish descent."

Katie was a little stung by the tone of superiority with which he delivered this lecture. "What you are is a Spanish-Puerto Rican-American-male chauvinist—of the worst sort!"

"Why do you use that tone of voice to me? Because I believe that when a woman marries her duty is to take care of her husband?"

Katie gave him a lofty look. "No matter what you believe, the fact remains that many women need to have other interests and accomplishments outside the home, just as men do. We like having a career we can take pride in.''

''A woman can take pride in caring for her husband and children.''

Katie knew she would say anything, *anything* to wipe that insufferably complacent grin from his face. ''Luckily for us, American men who are born in the United States, don't object to their wives having careers. They are more understanding and considerate!''

''They are very understanding and considerate,'' Ramon conceded derisively. ''They let you work, permit you to hand over the money you earn, allow you to have their babies, find someone to care for their babies, clean their houses and,'' he taunted, ''still do the cooking.''

Katie was momentarily dumbstruck by this speech, then she flopped down on her back and burst out laughing. ''You're absolutely right!''

Ramon laid back beside her, linking his hands behind his head, staring up at the powder-blue sky dotted with cotton-ball clouds. ''You have a beautiful laugh, Katie.''

Katie took another bite of apple and said cheerfully, ''You're only saying that because you think you've changed my mind, but you haven't. If a woman wants a career she must be able to have one. Besides, most women want nicer homes and clothes than their husbands could provide on their salaries alone.''

''So she gets her fine house and clothes at the expense of her husband's pride, going to work herself and proving to him, and everyone, that what he can provide for her is not good enough.''

''American husbands aren't as proud as Spaniards must be.''

''American husbands have abdicated their responsibilities. They do not have anything to be proud of.''

''Baloney!'' Katie replied unarguably. ''Would you want the girl you love and marry to live in someplace like Harlem because that was the best you could give her on the money you make driving that truck; when you knew that if she worked, doing something she liked, you could both have much more?''

''I would expect her to be happy with what I could give her.''

Katie shivered inwardly at the prospect of some sweet Spanish girl having to live in a slum because Ramon's pride wouldn't allow her to work. His drowsy voice added, ''And I would not like it if she were ashamed of what I do for a living, as you are.''

Katie heard the quiet reprimand in his words, but persevered anyway. ''Don't you ever wish you did something better than drive a produce truck?''

His answer was long in coming, and Katie suspected that he was marking her down as an ambitious pushy American woman. ''I do. I grow produce too.''

Katie reared up on both elbows. ''You work on a produce farm? In Missouri?''

''In Puerto Rico,'' he corrected.

Katie couldn't decide whether she was relieved or

disappointed that he would not be remaining in St. Louis. His eyes were drifting closed, and she let her gaze wander over his thick slightly curling black hair to his face. There was Spanish nobility stamped on his bronzed features, authority and arrogance in the firm jawline and straight nose, determination in the thrust of his chin. Yet, Katie thought with a smile, the slight cleft in his chin and his long, spiky lashes laying against his cheeks, softened the overall effect. His lips were firm but sensuously molded, and with a tingle of excitement Katie wondered how it would feel to have those lips moving warmly on hers. He had told her yesterday that he was thirty-four, but Katie thought he looked younger now, with his face relaxed in sleep.

She let her gaze travel down the long, superbly fit and muscled body stretched out on the blanket beside her. The red knit shirt he was wearing hugged his wide shoulders and chest, its short sleeves exposing the corded strength of his arms. His Levi's accentuated his narrow hips, flat stomach and hard thighs. Even sleeping, he seemed to exude a raw potent virility, but this no longer repelled her. Somehow, having admitted to him that facially he reminded her slightly of David, had banished all similarity between the two men banished from her mind.

His eyes didn't open, but the mobile line of his mouth quirked in a half-smile. "I hope what you are seeing meets with your approval."

Katie's chagrined gaze flew to the rolling parkland stretching out before her. "It does. The park is beautiful today, the trees as—"

"You were not looking at the trees, *señorita*."

Katie chose not to answer that. She was glad he had called her *señorita*; it sounded alien and odd to her, emphasizing the differences between them and neutralizing the effect his blatant masculinity had been having on her. What had she been thinking of, wanting Ramon to kiss her? Getting further involved with him could only lead to disaster. They had absolutely nothing in common; they came from two completely different worlds. Socially, they were miles apart. Tomorrow, for example, she was expected to attend a barbecue at her parents' elegant home on the grounds of Forest Oaks Country Club. Ramon could never fit in with the sort of people who would be there. He would feel ill at ease if she brought him with her. He would be out of place. And the moment her parents discovered that he was a farm laborer who drove a produce truck during the spring, they would very likely make it obvious to Ramon that they didn't think he belonged in their home, or with their daughter.

She would not see Ramon again after today, Katie decided firmly. There could never really be anything between them, and her dawning sexual response to him was a solid enough reason to break off the relationship immediately. It could never lead to anything meaningful or lasting.

"Why have you drawn away from me, Katie?"

His penetrating black eyes were open, searching her face. Katie made absorbing work of smoothing the blanket beneath her, then lying back on it. "I don't know what you mean," she said, closing her eyes and deliberately shutting him out.

His voice was low-pitched and sensual. "Would you like to know what I see when I look at you?"

"Not," she said primly, "if you're going to sound like an amorous Latin lover when you tell me. And from the tone of your voice, I think that's exactly what you were going to do." Katie tried to relax, but in the charged silence that followed her words it was impossible. A few minutes later, she sat up abruptly. "I think it's time I got back home," she announced, already scrambling to her knees and beginning to re-pack the picnic hamper. Without a word, Ramon stood up and began folding the blanket.

The strained silence during the drive home was broken only twice by Katie who, in the hope of aton-ing for her earlier rudeness, made two attempts at conversation only to be rebuffed by Ramon's mono-syllabic replies. She was ashamed of her snobbish thoughts, embarrassed for the way she had spoken to him, and angry because he wouldn't let her smooth things over.

By the time he swung the Buick Regal into the parking space in front of her door, Katie wanted nothing more than to end the day, even if it was only three o'clock. Before Ramon could come around the car for her, she shoved open the door and practically leaped out.

"I will open the door for you," he snapped. "It is a gesture of common courtesy."

Katie, who realized for the first time that he was

bitingly angry, was suddenly incensed at his obstinacy. "It may surprise you to hear this," she announced as she stormed up the steps and jammed her key into the lock, "but there is nothing wrong with my hands and I am perfectly capable of opening a damned car door. And I don't see why you should be courteous to me when I have been absolutely obnoxious to you!"

The angry humor of this remark was not lost on Ramon, but it was totally eclipsed by her next one. As she flung open the door to her apartment she turned around in the doorway and said furiously, "Thank you, Ramon. I had a very nice time."

Katie, who had no idea why Ramon had burst out laughing, was relieved that he wasn't still angry, and suddenly very wary of the way he had followed her into her apartment, firmly closed the door behind him, and was now looking at her with an unmistakable expression on his face.

His smoothly spoken words were part invitation, part order: "Come here, Katie."

Katie shook her head and took a cautious step backward, but an answering quiver was tingling up her spine.

"Is it not the custom of liberated American women to show their appreciation for having 'a very nice time' with a kiss?" Ramon persisted.

"Not all of them," Katie croaked. "Some of us just say 'thank you.'"

A faint smile touched his mouth, but his heavy-lidded gaze dropped to the inviting fullness of her lips, lingering there. "Come here, Katie." When she still balked, he added softly, "Are you not curious about how Spaniards kiss and Puerto Ricans make love?"

Katie swallowed convulsively. "No," she whispered.

"Come here, Katie, and I will show you."

Hypnotized by that velvet voice and those mesmerizing black eyes, Katie went to him in a trance that was a combination of fright and excitement.

Whatever she expected when she walked into Ramon's arms, it was not to find herself crushed in an embrace of steel and swept soaring off into some thick sweet darkness where the only feeling was of his parted lips moving ceaselessly on hers; the only sensation, the waves of liquid heat that raced through her in the wake of his caressing hands. "Katie," he whispered hoarsely, dragging his mouth from hers and kissing her eyes, her temple, her cheek. "Katie," he repeated in an aching whisper as his mouth again took possession of hers.

It seemed an eternity before he finally lifted his head. Weak and trembling, Katie laid her cheek against his hard chest and felt the violent pounding of his heart. She was utterly devastated by what had just happened. She had been kissed more times than she could remember, and by men whose technique had been practiced and perfected until it was almost an art form. In their arms, she had felt pleasure— not this mindless burst of joy followed by fierce longing.

Ramon's lips brushed the shining hair atop her

head. "Now, shall I tell you what I think when I look at you?"

Katie tried to answer lightly, but her voice was nearly as husky as his. "Are you going to sound like an amorous Latin?"

"Yes."

"Okay."

His chuckle was rich and deep. "I see a beauty with red gold hair and the smile of an angel; and I remember a princess who stood in that singles' bar looking very displeased with her subjects; then I hear a witch telling a man who was making advances to her, that her roommates were lesbians." He laid his hand against the side of her face, his fingers tenderly brushing her cheek. "When I look at you, I think you are my angel-princess-witch."

The way he referred to her as "his" brought Katie's drifting spirit plummeting back to reality. Abruptly pulling free of Ramon's arms, she said with false brightness, "Would you like to walk down to the pool? It opened today, and everybody from the apartment complex will be out there." As she spoke she jammed her hands into her back pockets, caught the way Ramon's glance slipped to the straining fabric of her T-shirt across her breasts, and hastily removed her hands.

One black brow arched in mild inquiry, silently asking why she objected to having his eyes on her when he had just had his hands on her. "Of course," he said, "I would enjoy seeing your pool and meeting your friends."

Once again Katie felt uncomfortable with him. He

seemed like a dark, foreign stranger who was too intensely interested in her. Added to that, she was leery of him now, and with good reason. She knew when a man intended to maneuver her into bed, and that was where Ramon wanted her. As soon as possible.

Sliding glass doors opened off the back of her living room onto a small patio enclosed by a stockade fence that provided privacy. Two redwood loungers with thick flowered cushions were strategically placed in the center for sunbathing. Behind them, and on both sides, were scattered a profusion of Katie's lush plants, some of which were already blooming.

She stopped beside a redwood planter overflowing with red and white petunias. With one hand on the door in the stockade fence, Katie hesitated, trying to think of how to phrase what she wanted to say.

"You have a beautiful apartment," Ramon commented behind her. "The rent must be very expensive."

Katie swung around, instantly seizing on Ramon's idle comment as a perfect means of drawing attention to the differences between them, and hopefully, cooling his ardent intentions. "Thank you. As a matter of fact, the rent is very high. I live here because it's reassuring to my parents to know that my friends and neighbors are the right sort of people."

"Rich people?"

"Not rich necessarily, but successful, socially acceptable people."

Ramon's face was a mask, wiped clean of all expression. "Perhaps it would be better then, if you did not introduce me to your friends."

One look at that aloof, handsome face, and Katie again felt ashamed of herself. Raking an agitated hand through her hair, she drew a determined breath and confronted the real issue: "Ramon, despite what just happened between us in my apartment, I want you to understand that I am not going to go to bed with you. Now or ever."

"Because I am Spanish?" he asked dispassionately.

Katie's fair complexion bloomed with chagrin. "No, of course not! Because...." She smiled derisively. "To use a hackneyed phrase, 'I'm just not that kind of girl.'" Feeling much better now that everything was out in the open between them, she turned back toward the door in the fence. "Well, shall we go down and see what's happening at the pool?"

"I do not think that would be wise," he said sardonically. "Being seen with me could cause you embarrassment in front of your 'successful, socially acceptable' friends."

Katie gazed over her shoulder at the tall man who was now looking down his aristocratic nose at her, his hard eyes ironic and disdainful. She sighed. "Ramon, just because I sounded like a conceited ass, doesn't mean that you have to sound like one, too. Please come down to the pool with me?"

Laughter flickered across his features as he gazed

at her. Wordlessly, he reached over her shoulder and pushed the door open for her.

The olympic-size swimming pool was a scene of total chaos, as Katie knew it would be. Four separate games of water polo were under way with all in attendance yelling and splashing. Girls in bikinis and men in brief swimming trunks were sprawled on towels and chaise longues, their bodies slick with suntan lotion, toasting in the sun. Beer cans and portable radios were everywhere, and music was blaring over the clubhouse speakers.

Katie walked over to a nearby umbrella table and pulled out an aluminum chair. "What do you think of opening day at an American swimming pool?" she asked Ramon as he sat down beside her.

His enigmatic gaze swept the colorful pandemonium. "Interesting."

"Hi, Katie," Karen called, emerging from the pool like a graceful mermaid, her voluptuous body shining with rivulets of water. As usual, Karen was accompanied by at least two devoted males, who padded dripping beside her over to Katie and Ramon. "You know Don and Brad, don't you?" Karen said, with a perfunctory nod at the two men who were also tenants in the apartment complex. Katie knew them both almost as well as Karen did, so she was a little surprised, but then, as she soon realized, Karen didn't really care who knew whom, so long as she was introduced to Ramon.

With unaccountable reluctance, Katie performed the introductions. She tried not to notice the warm appreciation in Ramon's flashing white smile when he was presented to Karen, and the answering sparkle in Karen's green eyes as she extended her hand to him.

"Why don't you two change clothes and come back out and swim?" Karen invited, without taking her eyes off Ramon. "There's going to be a big party here at sundown. You should stay for that, too."

"Ramon doesn't have any swimming trunks with him," Katie quickly declined.

"No problem," the resourceful Karen replied, tearing her eyes from Ramon for the first time since she had climbed out of the pool. "Brad will loan Ramon a pair, won't you, Brad?"

Brad, who had been in hot pursuit of Karen for nearly a year, looked as if he would rather loan Ramon a one-way ticket out of town, but he politely seconded the offer. And how could he help it? Few men ever wanted to deny Karen anything—her looks promised so much in return. She was the same height as Katie, five feet six, but there was a ripe sexuality about her dark hair and curvaceous body that made her seem like passion fruit ready for the plucking—but only by the man of her choice. The independence that shone in her slanting green eyes made it perfectly clear that she did her own choosing. And from the way Karen was watching Ramon walk away with Brad to change into swimming trunks, it was obvious to Katie that Ramon was Karen's choice. "Where," Karen breathed almost reverently, "did you ever find him? He looks like a Greek Adonis...or was Adonis blond?

Well, anyway, he looks like a black-haired Greek god.''

Katie resisted the uncharitable impulse to cool Karen's interest in Ramon by informing her that he was a black-haired Spanish farm laborer. "I met him at the Canyon Inn, Friday night," she said instead.

"Really? I didn't see him there, and he'd be almost impossible to overlook. What does he do, beside look sexy and gorgeous?"

"He...." Katie hesitated, then to spare Ramon any possible embarrassment, she said, "He's in transportation. Trucking, actually."

"No kidding?" Karen said unanswerably, giving Katie a searching look. "Is he your private stock or can anyone sample?"

Katie couldn't help smiling at Karen's bluntness. "Would it matter?"

"You know it would. We're friends. If you say you want him, I won't take him away."

The odd thing was, Katie knew she meant it. Karen had personal ethics; she didn't steal her friends' men. Nevertheless, it rankled Katie that Karen automatically assumed she could take Ramon away, unless, out of the spirit of friendship, she chose not to do it. "Help yourself," Katie said with an indifference she didn't entirely feel. "He's all yours if you want him. I'm going to go change into my suit."

Changing into her bikini in her apartment, Katie was annoyed with herself for not telling Karen to leave Ramon alone. And she was equally annoyed for caring one way or another. She was also a little crushed by the frank admiration she had seen in Ramon's expression when he looked at Karen's lush bikini-clad figure.

Katie stood in front of the mirror in her bathing suit, critically surveying her appearance. The bright blue bikini revealed a stunning figure in all its glory, from full high breasts, narrow waist and gently curving hips, to long shapely legs. With disgust, Katie thought she must be the only woman alive who could look coolly proper when she was practically naked!

Men whistled appreciatively at girls like Karen Wilson; they stared in silence at Katie Connelly. The quiet pride in the tilt of her chin and the natural grace with which she moved always made her seem vaguely aloof, and Katie was powerless to change her image, even if she wanted to, which she normally didn't.

With the exception of singles' bars, Katie was rarely approached by men she didn't know. She didn't look approachable. As a rule, men took one look at her flawless skin and clear blue eyes and saw classic beauty rather than sex appeal. They expected her to be remote, untouchable, and they treated her with restrained admiration. By the time they knew her well enough to realize that she was basically warm and friendly with an irrepressible sense of humor, they also knew her well enough not to press her for more than she was willing to give. They talked with her and laughed with her and asked her for dates, but their sexual overtures were usually

verbal rather than physical—softly spoken innuen-
dos that Katie smilingly and pointedly ignored.

Katie pulled a brush through her tumbling mass
of waving hair, gave it a quick shake to restore it to
its casual, windblown style, and took a last dissatis-
fied look in the mirror.

When she reached the pool area she found Ramon
stretched out on a lounger beside three young
women who had spread their towels on the cement
pool deck and were sitting there, blatantly flirting
with him. Seated at the umbrella table on his other
side was Karen, along with Brad and Don.

"May I join your harem, Ramon?" Katie
quipped, standing over him with a faint smile.

A lazy, devastating grin swept across his tanned
face as he looked up at her, then he lithely rolled to
his feet, getting up to give her his coveted lounger.
Inwardly, Katie sighed. She may as well have come
out here in an overcoat. Not once had Ramon's gaze
dropped below her neck.

He sat down at the table with Karen and the other
two men.

Trying to ignore her mixed emotions, Katie began
rubbing suntan oil on her leg.

"I'm very good at that, Katie," Don grinned at
her. "Need some help?"

Katie glanced up with a plucky smile. "My legs
aren't that long," she declined. Unlike Brad, Don
was not completely obsessed with Karen, and Katie
had sensed for the last several months that if she
gave him the slightest encouragement, he would
easily shift his interest from Karen to herself. She

was in the process of spreading the oil onto her left arm when she heard Karen say, "Katie told me that you're in the transportation business, Ramon."

"Oh, she did, did she?" Ramon drawled with enough sarcasm to make Katie pause and stare at him. He was leaning back in his chair with a thin cigar clamped between his white teeth, his piercing eyes leveled on Katie. Katie flushed and hastily pulled her gaze from his.

A few moments later, Karen did her utmost to get him to go swimming with her, but was met with a firmly polite refusal.

"Do you *know* how to swim?" Katie asked Ramon when the others had left.

"Puerto Rico is an island, Katie," he replied dryly. "The Atlantic Ocean on one side, and the Caribbean on the other. There is no shortage of water in which to swim."

Katie looked at him with a puzzled frown. From the moment he had kissed her in her apartment, a subtle shift in power had been taking place. Until then she had been confident and in control of their relationship. Now she felt confused and strangely vulnerable, while Ramon seemed decisive and self-assured. Shrugging, she said, "I was only going to offer to teach you to swim if you didn't know how. There's no need for you to launch into a lecture on Puerto Rican geography."

Ignoring her cross tone, he said, "If you wish to swim, we will swim."

Katie's breath froze as he came to his feet and stood looking down at her in Brad's white swimming trunks. He was six feet three inches of splendid masculinity, wide shouldered and narrow hipped, with the firm muscles of an athlete. His chest was covered with a light furring of black hair, and as Katie arose, she kept her eyes carefully fixed on the silver medallion hanging from a chain around his neck.

Disconcerted and embarrassed by the way the sight of his bronzed body was affecting her, Katie did not look up at him until she realized that he had no intention of moving out of her way. When she finally dragged her eyes to his, he said softly, ''I think you look very nice, too.''

An unbidden smile curved Katie's lips. ''I didn't think you noticed,'' she said as they began walking over to the pool.

''I did not think you wanted me to look at you.''

''You certainly looked at Karen,'' Katie heard herself say. She shook her head bemusedly and spoke her next thought aloud as well. ''I didn't mean to say that.''

''No,'' he said with amusement. ''I am sure you did not.''

Preferring to forget the whole exchange, Katie stood poised at the deep end of the pool. She dived, cutting the water in a clean, graceful line. Ramon was right beside her, pacing himself to her strong strokes with an effortless ease that Katie had to admire. They swam twenty laps together before Katie let her feet touch bottom. She stood watching Ramon finish ten more laps before she laughingly called, ''Show off!''

Diving neatly, he disappeared from her sight. Katie let out a startled shriek as hands jerked her feet out from under her and hauled her to the bottom. When she surfaced she was gasping for air, her eyes stinging from the chlorine. "That," she said with laughing severity as Ramon raked his wet curly hair back and grinned at her, "was a very childish thing to do. Almost as childish as—this!" Slicing her hand at the water, she sent a geyser of it spraying into Ramon's face, then ducked around trying to avoid reprisal. There followed a laughing, dunking, racing session that lasted for fifteen minutes and left her breathless and exhausted.

Hauling herself over the side of the pool, Katie padded over to the lawn chair and handed Ramon the towel she had brought for him. "You play too rough," she chided him good-naturedly as she bent over and wrung out her long heavy hair.

His chest heaving from their exertions, Ramon looped the towel around his neck and put his hands on his hips. Quietly, he said, "I would be as gentle with you as you wished me to be."

Katie turned liquid inside at the meaning she read into his words. Almost certain that he had been referring to making love to her, she flopped down on the lounge on her stomach and laid her head on her arms. Her skin flinched as Ramon drizzled suntan oil onto her back, then sat down beside her. She tensed as his hands began slowly stroking up and down her back, rhythmically massaging the oil into her satiny skin. "Shall I unfasten the back?" he asked.

"Don't even consider trying it," Katie warned. By the time his hands had moved up to her shoulders and his thumbs were circling just below her nape, Katie was breathing in shallow little breaths, and every inch of her skin was vibrantly alive where his hands had touched it.

"Am I bothering you, Katie?" he asked in a husky whisper.

"You know you are," Katie murmured lethargically, before she could stop herself. She heard his satisfied chuckle and turned her head away from him. "You're doing it on purpose, and it's making me very nervous."

"In that case, I will let you relax," he said as his weight lifted from her chaise longue. When he was gone, Katie tried not to wonder what he was doing and firmly closed her eyes to the blazing late-afternoon sun.

Occasionally she heard his deep voice followed by a peal of feminine laughter, or one of the men calling something to him. He certainly fit in well here, Katie mused. But then, why shouldn't he, she though dourly. The only requirement for popularity around here with the opposite sex was having an attractive body, preferably combined with an attractive face, and if you were a man, a good job. Katie, with her small lie, had provided Ramon with the latter.

What was the matter with her, Katie wondered drowsily. She had absolutely no reason to complain. Despite her occasional bouts of discontent lately, when her world seemed populated by phony, shallow people, she enjoyed the clever bantering that she exchanged with the confident, self-assured men she knew. She liked having nice clothes, a beautiful apartment, and being the object of so much masculine admiration. She genuinely enjoyed men's company even though she carefully avoided becoming intimate with any of them, because Katie's physical desires were never stronger than her overwhelming need to retain what pride and self-respect David had left her.

Rob would have been the only other man she had ever let make love to her. Luckily she had discovered he was married before she let that happen. The right man would come along someday and she would hold nothing back. The right man, not just any man. Under no circumstances was Katie Connelly going to find herself sitting around the pool or at one of the singles' bars, with three or four men who all had intimate knowledge of her body. It happened to other women all the time, but Katie found the idea degrading and repulsive.

"Hey, Katie, wake up and roll over," Don commanded.

Katie blinked, surprised that she had fallen asleep, and obediently rolled onto her back.

"It's almost six o'clock. Brad and I are going to get some beer and pizzas for the party tonight. Do you want me to bring anything stronger for you and Ramon?" Was there a sneer in the way he said Ramon's name?

Katie wrinkled her nose at her grinning admirer. "Stronger than Mama Romano's pizzas? Heaven forbid!'' She looked around for Ramon and saw him walking toward her with Karen on one side and another woman on the other. Carefully extinguishing the ridiculous flare of jealousy she felt, Katie said to Ramon, ''There's going to be a party out here tonight—dancing and that kind of thing. Would you like to stay for it?''

''Of course he would, Katie,'' Karen said promptly on his behalf.

''Then it's fine with me,'' Katie said with a shrug. She would enjoy the party with her friends, and Ramon could enjoy it with Karen and whomever else he chose.

By nine-thirty that night the food had been devoured, along with several cases of beer and countless bottles of liquor. The pool lights were lit, giving the water an iridescent green glow, and someone had put on a disco tape to play over the loudspeakers. Katie, who loved to dance, had been doing so for nearly an hour with assorted partners when she noticed Ramon standing far away from the activity, a solitary figure leaning against the fence that surrounded the pool, staring out into the distance. Silhouetted in the night, with his swimming trunks a stark band of white in the inky darkness, he seemed very aloof, and yet, somehow, lonely.

''Ramon?'' Katie said anxiously, coming up behind him and putting her hand on his arm. He turned slowly and looked down at her, and she saw the pleasure her touch brought to his smile. Cautiously, she removed her hand. ''Why are you over here, all by yourself?''

"I needed to escape from the noise so that I could think. Do you never feel the need to be by yourself?"

"Yes," she admitted, "but not usually in the middle of a party."

"We do not have to be here in the middle of a party," he pointed out meaningfully.

Katie's heart gave a funny little lurch, which she steadfastly ignored. "Would you like to dance?"

He tipped his head in the direction of the Neil Diamond recording that was now blasting over the loudspeakers. "When I dance I like to hold a woman in my arms," he answered. "Besides, I would have to wait in line for the privilege of dancing with you."

"Ramon, do you know how to dance?" Katie persisted, certain that he probably didn't, and about to offer to teach him.

Flinging his cigar away in a glowing red arc, he said tersely. "Yes, Katie, I know how to dance. I know how to swim. I know how to tie my own shoes. I have a slight accent, which you seem to think means I am backward and ignorant, but which many women find attractive."

Katie stiffened angrily. Lifting her chin, she stared straight into his eyes and said very quietly and very distinctly, "Go to hell." Intending to walk away, she pivoted on her heel, then gasped in surprise as Ramon's hand clamped on her arm, jerking her around to face him.

In a voice vibrating with anger, he said, "Do not

ever speak to me that way again, and do not swear. It does not become you.''

"I'll talk to you any way I like,'' Katie blazed. "And if all the other women find you so *damned* attractive, they're welcome to you!''

Ramon gazed down into her stormy blue eyes and proudly beautiful face, and a reluctant smile of admiration broke across his features. "What a little spitfire you are,'' he chuckled. "And when you are angry—''

"I am not a little anything,'' Katie interrupted hotly. "I am nearly five feet seven inches tall. And if you were about to say that I'm beautiful when I'm angry, I warn you, I'll laugh my sides off. Men always say that to women because they heard it in some ridiculous old movie, and—''

"Katie,'' Ramon breathed as his firm, sensual mouth descended to hers, "You are beautiful when you are angry—and if you laugh, I will toss you into the pool.''

A jolt rocketed through Katie's nervous system as his warm lips covered hers in a lingering kiss. When he lifted his head, he slipped his arm around Katie's waist, drew her unresisting body close to his side, and led her to the crowd of dancing couples as a slow love song began to play.

Ramon's low voice murmured something in her ear as they danced, but Katie didn't understand the words he said to her. She was too preoccupied with the unbelievably arousing feel of his bare legs and thighs sliding intimately against hers as they moved in time to the music. Desire was pouring through her, melting her resolve. She wanted to lift her head and feel his mouth claim hers the way it had in her apartment; she wanted to be crushed in his strong arms and swept off into that same sweet, wild oblivion he had shown her before.

Closing her eyes in despair, Katie admitted the truth to herself. Even though she'd only known him for forty-eight hours, she wanted Ramon to make love to her tonight. She wanted it so badly that she was shaken and amazed...but at least she could understand her physical attraction to him. What she couldn't understand, and what frightened her, was this strange, magnetic pull she felt toward him emotionally. Sometimes, when he spoke to her in that deep, compelling voice of his, or looked at her with those dark penetrating eyes, Katie almost felt as if he were quietly reaching out to her and inexorably drawing her closer and closer to him.

Mentally, Katie gave herself a hard shake. Getting involved with Ramon would be disastrous. They were hopelessly incompatible. He was proud, poor and dominating, while she was also proud, wealthy by his standards, and innately independent. Any relationship between them could only end in hurt and anger.

Like the intelligent, sensible young woman she was, Katie decided the best way to avoid the danger of Ramon's attraction was to avoid Ramon himself. She would stay away from him as much as possible for the rest of the evening and firmly refuse to see him again after tonight. It was as simple as that. Except that when his lips brushed first her temple, then her forehead, Katie nearly forgot that she was sensible and intelligent, and almost lifted her mouth up to his, to receive the stirring kiss she knew he would give her.

The instant the song ended, Katie broke away from him. With a bright, smile pinned to her face she met his questioning look and said airily, "Why don't you mingle and have fun? I'll see you later."

For the next hour and a half Katie flirted with every man she knew, and several she didn't. She was her most dazzlingly sociable self, and wherever she went the men followed, each one ready to dance, swim, drink, or make love, according to her slightest preference. She laughed and drank and danced.... And every moment she was aware that Ramon had apparently taken her suggestion and was thoroughly enjoying himself with at least four other women, particularly Karen, who never left his side.

"Katie, let's get out of here and go somewhere quiet." Don's breath was hot in her ear as they danced to a throbbing disco beat.

"I hate quiet places," Katie announced, twirling away from him and draping herself across Brad who was surprised, but not displeased, to find her suddenly sitting on his lap. "Brad hates quiet places too, don't you?"

"Sure I do," Brad leered. "So let's go back to my place and make noise in private."

Katie wasn't listening. From the corner of her eye she watched Karen dancing with Ramon. Both of her arms were wound around his neck, her body swaying sensuously against his. Whatever Karen was saying to him certainly must have been amusing, because Ramon, who had been grinning down at her, suddenly threw back his head and burst out laughing. Irrationally, Katie was hurt by his easy defection. Redoubling her efforts to be gay, she stood up and pulled a reluctant Brad to his feet. "Get up, lazy, and dance with me."

Brad relinquished his can of beer, strolled into the dancers with his arm around Katie's shoulders, then caught her in a surprisingly crushing embrace. "What the hell has got into you?" he demanded in her ear. "I've never seen you act like this."

Katie didn't answer because she was frantically looking for Ramon and Karen who, as she soon realized, were nowhere in sight. Her heart plummeted. Ramon had left the party with Karen.

When they hadn't returned after thirty minutes, Katie abandoned all pretense of enjoying herself. Her stomach was twisted into sick knots and, whether she was dancing or talking, her eyes constantly scanned the shifting bodies, desperately searching for Ramon's tall form.

Katie wasn't the only one who had noted Karen's disappearance with Ramon. Katie was dancing with Brad again, ignoring him entirely while she craned her neck looking for the missing couple, when Brad hissed contemptuously, "You aren't by any wild chance hung up on that spic that Karen's taken to her apartment, are you?"

"Don't call him that!" Katie said fiercely, pulling out of his arms. There were tears in her eyes as she turned and plunged into the throngs of dancing couples.

"Where are you going?" an authoritative voice demanded right behind her.

Katie swung around and faced Ramon, her fists clenched impotently at her sides. "Where have you been?"

One dark brow lifted. "Jealous?"

"Do you know," she said, almost choking, "I don't think I even like you!"

"I do not like you very much tonight, either," Ramon replied evenly. Suddenly his gaze narrowed on her face. "There are tears in your eyes. Why?"

"Because," Katie whispered furiously, "that stupid bastard called you a spic."

Ramon burst out laughing and dragged her into his arms. "Oh, Katie," he laughed and sighed against her hair, "he is just angry because the woman he wants went for a walk with me."

Tipping her head back, Katie searched his face. "You only went for a walk?"

The laughter vanished from his expression. "Only for a walk. Nothing more." His arms tightened, holding her close as they moved in time to the music.

Katie laid her cheek against the reassuring strength of his chest and surrendered to delight as his hands caressed her bare shoulders and back, then slid lower, splaying against her spine to force her pliant body into intimate contact with every hard line of his legs and thighs. One hand lifted and curved around her nape, stroking it sensuously, then tightened in an abrupt command. Drawing an unsteady breath, Katie obediently lifted her head to receive his kiss. His hand plunged into her thick silky hair, holding her captive for the driving hunger of his mouth.

By the time he finally drew back, Ramon's breathing was harsh and Katie's pulse was racing out of control, the blood pounding in her ears. She stared up at him and shakily said, "I think I am getting very scared."

"I know, *querida*," he said gently. "Things are happening too quickly for you."

"What does '*querida*' mean?"

"Darling."

Katie closed her eyes and swallowed, swaying weakly against him. "How long will you be here before you go back to Puerto Rico?"

His answer was a long time in coming. "I can stay until Sunday, a week from today, but no longer. We will spend every day together until then."

Katie was too disappointed to even try to hide it. "We can't. I have to attend a big Memorial Day gathering at my parents' house tomorrow. I have Tuesday off work but Wednesday I have to be back at the office." She could see that he was about to argue, and since she also wanted to be with him as much as possible in the time they had left, Katie said, "Would you like to come to my parents' house with me tomorrow?" He looked uncomfortable and some sanity returned to Katie. "That probably isn't a good idea. You won't like them, and they won't like you."

"Because they are rich and I am not?" He smiled

faintly. "I may like them in spite of their wealth, who knows?"

Katie smiled at the way he deliberately misstated the problem, and his arms tightened possessively, drawing her closer to him. He had a very engaging smile that softened his virile handsomeness and could make him look almost boyish. "Shall we go back to my place?" Katie said.

Ramon nodded and Katie went to collect her things while he poured Scotch into two paper cups, added ice and water, and then crossed to where she waited.

When they got to her little enclosed patio area, Katie was surprised that, instead of going indoors, Ramon put the drinks down on the small table between the two redwood lounge chairs, then stretched out on one of them. Somehow, she expected that he would try to carry on the rest of their conversation in her bed.

With mingled feelings of disappointment and relief, she curled up on the other lounge and twisted toward him. He lit a cigar, its glowing red tip her only focal point in the darkness. "Tell me about your parents, Katie."

Katie took a fortifying swallow of her drink. "By most people's standards, they're very wealthy, but they weren't always. My father owned an ordinary grocery store until ten years ago, when he talked the bank into letting him expand it into a luxury supermarket. It did very well, and after that he opened twenty more of them. Haven't you passed any modernistic supermarkets with the name 'Connelly's' on them?"

"I believe so."

"Well, that's us. Four years ago my dad joined Forest Oaks Country Club. It isn't quite as prestigious as Old Warson or St. Louis Country Club, but the Forest Oaks members like to pretend it is, and my father built the biggest house on the club grounds, right on the golf course."

"I ask you about your parents, and you tell me about their money. What are they like?"

Katie tried to be honest and objective. "They love me very much. My mother plays golf, and my father works hard. I guess the most important thing to them, outside of their children, is having a gorgeous house, a maid, two Mercedes, and belonging to the country club. My dad is handsome for being fifty-eight, and my mother always looks terrific."

"You have brothers and sisters?"

"One of each. I'm the youngest. My sister, Maureen, is thirty, and she's married. My dad made her husband a vice-president of Connelly Corporation, and now he can't wait to take over when dad retires. My brother, Mark, is twenty-five, and he's nice. He isn't nearly as ambitious and greedy as Maureen, who spends her life worrying that Mark may get a bigger piece of the family business when dad retires than she and her husband will. Now that you know the worst, do you want to come tomorrow? A lot of my parents' friends and neighbors will be there, too, and they're pretty much like my parents."

Ramon stubbed out his cigar and wearily leaned his head back against the chair. "Do you want me to come?"

"Yes," Katie said emphatically. "But it's selfish of me, because my sister will look down her nose at you if she finds out what you do for a living. My brother, Mark, will probably go so far out of his way to show you that he isn't like Maureen, that he'll embarrass you even more."

In the deep, velvety voice she was coming to adore, Ramon asked, "What will you do, Katie?"

"Well, I'll—I don't really know."

"Then I guess I will have to come with you so that I can find out." Putting his glass down, he rose to his feet.

Katie, realizing that he intended to leave, insisted that he stay for some coffee, for the simple reason that she couldn't bear for him to go yet. She carried it into the living room on a small tray and sat down beside Ramon on the sofa. They drank their coffee in a long, increasingly uncomfortable silence, which Katie was helpless to break or to understand.

"What are you thinking about?" she asked finally, searching his somber profile in the dim light of the single table lamp.

"You." Almost harshly he asked, "Are the things that are important to your parents, important to you also?"

"Some of them, I suppose," Katie admitted.

"How important?"

"In comparison to what?"

"In comparison to this," he said in a savage whisper. His mouth came down hard on hers, his lips moving roughly back and forth, forcing her lips apart for the invasion of his tongue, while he pulled her down on the sofa and twisted his body so that it was half-covering hers.

Katie moaned in protest and instantly his mouth softened, then began a slow, unbearably erotic seduction that soon had Katie writhing beneath him in wild hunger. His tongue tangled with hers, withdrawing, then plunging deep, slowly receding as she tried to hold it, until Katie was pressing her parted lips fiercely to his, lost in the soul-destroying kiss.

When he started to raise his head she curved her hand around it, trying to keep his mouth on hers, then gasped with shocked delight as he jerked the top of her bikini down, freeing her breasts and lowering his mouth to the pink peaks. Slowly he began sucking hard on first one and then the other, until Katie was reduced to a state of mindless, aching desire.

Ramon braced his weight on his hands and lifted slightly off her, his hot eyes restlessly caressing her swollen breasts, their nipples hardened and erect from his tongue and lips and teeth. "Put your hands on me, Katie," he rasped.

Katie lifted her hands, slowly moving her sensitized fingertips over the sinewy muscles of his chest, watching them flinch reflexively and then relax. "You are beautiful," she whispered, her splayed hands drifting from the taut planes of his bronzed hair-roughened chest, along his broad shoulders, then down the corded muscles of his arms.

"Men are not beautiful," he tried to tease, but his voice was thickened from the effect her hands were having on him.

"You are. The way oceans and mountains are beautiful." Unthinkingly, she let her fingertips trace the narrowing vee of dark hair on his chest toward the place where it disappeared beneath the waistband of the low-slung white trunks.

"Don't!" he ordered hoarsely.

Katie stayed her hand and looked up at his face, dark with the passion he was fighting to keep under control. "You're beautiful and you're strong," she whispered into his burning gaze. "But you're gentle, too. I think you are the gentlest man I've ever known—and I don't even know why I think so."

His control snapped. "Oh, God!" he groaned. His mouth took hers with an unleashed passion that sent tidal waves of desire crashing over her. His hands sank into the thickness of her hair, holding her head immobile for the endless plunder of his lips. Katie gloried in the feel of his stiff throbbing manhood pressing intimately to her, then moaned with feverish longing when he began slowly circling his hips against her. "Want me," he ordered roughly. "Want me more than you want the things money can buy. Want me as much as I want you."

Katie was almost sobbing with desire when he suddenly pulled away from her, sat up, and leaned his head against the back of the sofa, closing his eyes. She watched his labored breathing even out and, after a few minutes, she straightened her clothing, ran a shaking hand through her wildly disordered hair, and sat up. Feeling discarded and hurt, she squeezed herself to the farthest end of the sofa from him and curled her legs beneath her.

"Katie." His voice was bleak and harsh.

Warily, Katie eyed him. His head was still back against the sofa, his eyes still closed as he spoke: "I did not want to say this to you while you were in my arms and we were both wild with desire for each other. I did not want to ever say this to you, yet I have known from the very first night that before I left I would still be saying it...."

Katie's heart stopped beating. He was going to tell her that he was married, and she—she was going to become hysterical.

"I want you to come back to Puerto Rico with me."

"*What*?" she whispered.

"I want you to marry me."

Katie opened her mouth, but it was several seconds before any words would come out. "I—I can't. I couldn't. I have a job here, and my family, my friends—they're all here. I belong here."

"No," he said angrily, turning his head and pinning her with his gaze. "You do not belong here. I watched you the first time I saw you in the bar, and I watched you tonight. You do not even like these people; you do not belong with them." He saw the growing apprehension widening her eyes and stretched his arm out to her. "Come," he said softly. "Now I want you in my arms."

Too dazed to do anything but obey, Katie slid across the sofa and into his comforting embrace, leaning her head on his shoulder. Gently, he continued, "There is a fineness in you that sets you apart from these people you call your friends."

Katie slowly shook her head. "You don't even know me, not really. You can't be serious about wanting to marry me."

His hand touched her chin, tipping her face up to his, and he smiled into her glazed blue eyes. "I have known what you are from the moment you knocked the flower I brought you on the ground, then nearly burst into tears with shame for what you had done. And I am thirty-four years old; I know exactly what I want." His lips clung to hers in a shattering kiss. "Marry me, Katie," he whispered.

"Couldn't...couldn't you stay in the States, in St. Louis, so that we could get to know one another better? Maybe then, after—"

"No," he said with absolute finality. "I cannot." He stood up and Katie stood with him. "Do not answer me now. There is time yet for you to decide." He glanced at the small glass clock beside the lamp. "It is late. I have to get dressed and then I have work that must be done tonight. When shall I call for you tomorrow to take you to your parents'?"

Numbly, Katie told him. "Oh, and I think my mother said it was a barbecue, so we may as well wear Levi's."

When he left, Katie wandered around, mechanically picking up coffee cups, turning off the lamp, and undressing for bed.

She lay down, stared at the ceiling, and tried to absorb what had just happened. Ramon wanted her to marry him and go to Puerto Rico with him! It was impossible, absolutely out of the question, too soon to even contemplate such a thing.

Too soon to contemplate it? Even if Ramon gave her time, would she ever really contemplate it?

She turned her head into her pillow and could still feel his hands caressing her with such violent tenderness, his mouth hungry and urgent on hers. No man alive had ever made her body come to life like that, and she doubted that anyone else ever would. It wasn't just practiced sexual technique with Ramon, it was instinct. It was natural for him to make love with such demanding, dominating sensuality; he was, by birth and culture, a dominating male.

Funny, Katie thought, she had liked being dominated by him. She had even felt a surge of excitement earlier today at the way he had ordered her into his arms with his quiet, "Come here, Katie." And yet, he was so gentle.

Katie closed her eyes, trying to think. If Ramon gave her time, was it possible that she might marry him? *Absolutely not!* her mind sensibly replied. But her heart whispered, *maybe....*

Why, Katie wondered, why would she ever consider marrying him. The answer was in that strange feeling she sometimes got when they were laughing or talking—an inexplicable feeling that, emotionally, they were almost perfectly matched; a feeling that something deep within him was reaching out to her and finding an answering response within her; this strong, magnetic pull that seemed to be slowly, inexorably, drawing them closer together.

At that thought, Katie's logical mind instantly went to battle with her emotions: If she was foolish enough to let herself marry Ramon, he would expect her to live on his income alone, yet she wasn't very happy living like an American princess the way she did now.

He was a Spanish male chauvinist; yet every instinct she possessed told her that he was a sensitive man, capable of great gentleness as well as strength. . . .

Katie almost moaned aloud at the predicament in which she found herself. She closed her eyes, and when she finally drifted into an exhausted slumber, neither logic nor emotion had won the battle.

CHAPTER FIVE

KATIE SPENT THE FOLLOWING MORNING waiting for Ramon in a state of spiraling apprehension, too worried about appearing at her parents' party with him to even contemplate the greater problem of his proposal.

The possibilities for disaster at that party were almost limitless. It wasn't important to Katie that her family like Ramon, nor would she ever let their opinion of him influence her ultimate decision about going to Puerto Rico. She loved her family, but she was old enough to make her own decisions. What she did fear was that her family might say something to humiliate Ramon. Her sister, Maureen, was an outrageous snob who had conveniently forgotten that the Connellys hadn't always been wealthy. If she discovered Ramon was a farm laborer who drove a truck, Maureen was capable of snubbing him in front of a house full of people, as a way of emphasizing her own social superiority.

Her parents, Katie knew, would treat Ramon with the same courtesy they would show any guest in their home, regardless of what he did for a living. . . as long as they had no inkling that there was anything except casual friendship between Katie and him. If they so much as suspected that Ramon wanted to marry her, they were both capable of treating him with a freezing contempt that would reduce him to the level of a social-climbing parasite, and in front of all their guests. Ramon would be disqualified as a future son-in-law the instant they discovered that he couldn't possibly support Katie in style and comfort, and they wouldn't hesitate to make their position infinitely clear if they felt it was necessary.

At precisely three-thirty, Ramon arrived. Katie let him into her apartment and greeted him with her best, cheerfully optimistic smile, which deceived him for perhaps two seconds. Drawing her into his arms, Ramon tipped her chin up, gazed into her eyes and said with grave humor, "We are not going to face a firing squad, Katie. We are only going to face your family."

The kiss he gave her was gently reassuring and, somehow, when his arms released her, Katie felt infinitely more confident. The feeling was still with her thirty minutes later when their car swept through the stone gates of Forest Oaks Country Club and pulled up in front of her parents' house.

Set back from the private road on five acres of manicured lawn, the Connellys white-pillared colonial with its sweeping circular driveway was a very imposing structure. Katie watched for some reaction from Ramon, but he only glanced casually at the house as if he had seen thousands like it, and came around to help her out of the car.

He still hadn't said anything by the time they were

halfway up the winding brick walk that led toward the massive front doors. Some devilish impulse made Katie slant a jaunty, sideways smile at him and ask, "Well, what do you think?" She jammed her hands into the back pockets of her designer jeans and took four more paces before she realized that not only had Ramon not answered, he had stopped walking entirely.

Turning, Katie found herself the object of his lazy, sweeping appraisal. With a spark of amusement in his eyes, his gaze traveled leisurely from the top of her bright head, lingered meaningfully on her lips and the thrusting fullness of her breasts, then faithfully followed the graceful curving lines of her waist, hips and thighs, drifted down her long shapely legs, stopped at her sandal-shod feet, then swept upward and returned to her face. "I think," he said with quiet solemnity, "that your smile could light the darkness, and when you laugh it is like music. I think your hair is like heavy silk shining in the sunlight."

Hypnotized by that deep voice, Katie simply stood there, warmth seeping through her system.

"I think that you have the bluest eyes I have ever seen, and I like the way they sparkle when you are happy, or darken with desire when you are in my arms." A wicked grin highlighted his lips as he glanced again at Katie's breasts, which were emphasized by her unconsciously provocative stance with her hands in her back pockets. "And I like the way you look in those pants you are wearing. But if you do not take your hands out of your pockets, I am going to take you back to the car so that I can put my hands in them, too.''

Katie slowly pulled her hands free, trying to surface from the sensuous spell he seemed able to cast over her with a few words. ''I meant,'' she said in a husky voice, ''What do you think of the house?''

He glanced up at it and wryly shook his head. ''Right out of *Gone With the Wind*.''

Katie rang the doorbell, which she could hear pealing majestically above the raised voices and laughter coming from within.

''Katie darling,'' her mother said, wrapping her in a quick hug. ''Come inside. Everyone else is already here.'' She smiled at Ramon who was standing beside Katie, and graciously extended her hand to him as Katie performed the introductions. ''We're very happy to have you here, Mr. Galverra,'' she said with perfect correctness.

Ramon replied with equal correctness that he was delighted to be here, and Katie, who had been inexplicably holding her breath, felt the tension drain out of her.

When her mother excused herself to check on the caterers, Katie led Ramon through the house and out onto the beautifully landscaped lawn where a bar had been set up for the use of the guests who were standing in small groups, laughing and talking.

What Katie had believed was to be a barbecue was, in reality, a cocktail party followed by a formal dinner for thirty people, and while it was immediately obvious that Ramon was the only man there wearing jeans, Katie thought he looked utterly fantastic.

With laughing pride, she noticed that she wasn't the only woman who thought Ramon was gorgeous; several of her mother's friends were openly admiring the tall dark-haired man who stayed by her side as they wandered sociably from group to group.

Katie introduced him to those of her parents' friends and neighbors whom she knew, watching as Ramon conquered the females with his flashing smile and relaxed charm. That she had expected. What she hadn't expected was that he would interact so well with the men who were present, all of whom were prosperous local businessmen. Somewhere in the past, Ramon had obviously acquired a social polish and smooth urbanity that positively staggered Katie when she saw it. He was utterly at ease among this gathering of the martini set, perfectly able to converse on everything from sports to national and world politics. Particularly world politics, Katie couldn't help noticing.

"You're certainly well-informed about world affairs," Katie observed when they were alone for a moment.

Ramon smiled obliquely. "I know how to read, Katie."

Chastened, Katie looked away, but as if he sensed her other question, Ramon added, "This party is not so different from any other. Whenever men gather they tend to discuss business if they are all in similar lines of work. If they are not, then they discuss sports or politics or world affairs. It is the same in any country."

Katie was not entirely satisfied with his answer, but she let the matter drop for the time being.

"I think I'm jealous!" she laughingly remarked a while later, when a forty-five-year-old matron with two grown daughters had monopolized Ramon's attention for a full ten minutes.

"Do not be jealous," Ramon said with bland amusement that made Katie think he must be accustomed to the fawning admiration of women. "They would all lose interest the moment they discovered I am only a farmer."

That, unfortunately, wasn't quite the truth, Katie discovered to her sublime discomfort two hours later. Everyone was seated in the elaborate dining room enjoying a gourmet meal, when Katie's sister inquired down the length of the long dining-room table, "What do you do, Mr. Galverra?"

Katie felt as if the clink of sterling silver flatware on English bone china stopped altogether, along with every other shred of conversation at the table. "He's in the trucking business—and groceries," Katie improvised madly before Ramon could respond.

"Trucking? In what way?" Maureen persisted.

"What possible way is there?" Katie hedged shortly, shooting a killing look at her sister.

"Groceries, did you say?" Mr. Connelly put in, his brows lifted in interest. "Wholesale or retail?"

"Wholesale," Katie interjected hastily, again cutting off Ramon's reply.

Beside her, Ramon leaned very close, smiled charmingly, and said in a low, savage voice. "Shut up, Katie, or he will think I do not know how to talk.''

"Wholesale?" Mr. Connelly mused from his position at the head of the table. He was always eager to talk about the grocery business. "What end of it—distribution?"

"No, growing," Ramon answered smoothly, clasping Katie's icy hand under the table in silent apology for the way he had spoken to her.

"A corporation operation, I imagine?" her father said. "How large?"

Calmly slicing a tender piece of veal Oscar, Ramon said, "It is a small farm, barely self-supporting."

"Do you mean you're an ordinary farmer?" Maureen demanded in subdued outrage. "In Missouri?"

"No, in Puerto Rico." Katie's brother, Mark, leaped into the breach with all the finesse of a pole-vaulter with no pole. "I was talking to Jake Masters last week and he told me he once found a spider in a shipment of pineapples from Puerto Rico that was the size of a—"

One of the guests, who apparently wasn't interested in spiders, interrupted Mark's desperate monologue to say to Ramon, "Is Galverra a common Spanish name? I've read of a 'Galverra' but I can't recall his first name."

Beside her Katie sensed, rather than saw, Ramon tense. "It is not an uncommon name," Ramon replied. "And my first name is very common."

Katie, in the act of giving Ramon an apologetic, encouraging smile, intercepted a look from her mother that could only be described as displeased and she felt the knot in her stomach tighten.

By the time they could leave, Katie's stomach was positively churning. Her parents were polite as they said goodbye to Ramon in the entrance foyer, but Katie saw the narrowed speculation in her mother's eyes when she looked at Ramon, and without actually saying anything, she managed to convey to Katie, and undoubtedly to Ramon, that she did not approve of him or of his continued association with Katie.

To make everything worse, as Ramon and Katie were leaving, Maureen's seven-year-old son jerked on her skirt and loudly announced to one and all, "Mommie, that man talks weird!"

In the car Ramon drove in thoughtful, withdrawn silence. "I'm sorry I told you to wear jeans," Katie spoke finally as they neared her apartment complex. "I could have sworn my mother told me two weeks ago this was going to be a barbecue."

"It is of no importance," Ramon said. "What people wear does not change what they are."

Katie didn't know whether he meant that better clothes wouldn't have improved his image, or that he felt his image was adequate regardless of what he was wearing. "I'm sorry about the way Maureen acted," she tried again.

"Stop saying you are sorry, Katie. One person cannot apologize for another. It is ludicrous to try."

"I know, but my sister is such a pain in the neck, and my parents—"

"Love you very much," Ramon finished for her.

"They want to see you happy, with a secure future and all the things money can buy. Unfortunately, like most parents, they believe that if your future is secure you will be happy. And if it is not, it follows that you will not be."

Katie was amazed by his defense of her parents. Inside her apartment she whirled on him, her gaze searching his dark, inscrutable face. "What sort of man are you?" she asked. "Who are you? You defend my parents, knowing that if I decided to go to Puerto Rico with you they would do everything to prevent it. If anything you were amused, not impressed, by the people you met tonight and the size of my parents' home. You speak English with an accent, but your vocabulary is better than most men I know who have college degrees. Who are you, anyway?"

Ramon put his hands on her tense shoulders and said quietly, "I am the man who wants to take you away from everything you know, and people who love you. I am the man who wants to take you to a strange country where you, not I, will have the handicap of language. I am the man who wants to take you to live in the cottage where he was born, a cottage with four rooms that are clean, but nothing more. I am the man who knows he is selfish to do these things, yet still I will try to do them."

"Why?" Katie whispered.

He bent his head and brushed his lips warmly against hers. "Because I believe that I can make you happier than you have ever dreamed of being."

Unbelievably affected by the merest touch of that

mouth, Katie tried to follow his logic. "But how could I be happy living in a primitive cottage where I don't know anyone and couldn't speak to them if I tried?"

"I will tell you later." He grinned suddenly. "For now, I have brought my own swimming trunks."

"Y—you want to swim?" Katie stuttered in disbelief.

Ramon's smile was positively wolfish. "I want to see you with as little clothing as possible, and the safest place for that, for both of us, is down at your pool."

Relief won out over disappointment as Katie went into the bedroom and quickly stripped off her clothes, pulling on a shockingly bright yellow bikini. She studied herself in the mirror with a faint smile. It was the scantiest suit she had ever owned; two extremely narrow strips of bright cloth that revealed every curving line of her body. She had never had the nerve to actually appear in it before, but today it seemed perfect. It was all well and good for Ramon to arbitrarily decide that he was going to keep his distance, but, perversely, she wanted to make it as difficult for him as possible. She brushed her hair until it was shining and emerged from her bedroom just as he came from the bathroom. He had changed into black briefs that hugged his body, displaying his magnificent physique in a way that made Katie's mouth go dry.

Ramon's response to her, however, was far less enthusiastic. His black eyes raked her all but naked body from head to toe. "Change it," he said in a hard tone that she had never heard before. Belatedly, he added, "Please."

"No," Katie said firmly. "I'm not going to change. Why should I?"

"Because I asked you to."

"You *ordered* me to, and I didn't like it."

"Now I am asking," Ramon persisted implacably. "Please change that suit."

Katie shot him a killing look. "I am wearing this suit down to that pool."

"Then I am not going with you."

Suddenly, Katie felt vulgarly naked, and she blamed Ramon for her humiliation. She went into her room, pulled off the suit and put on a green one.

"Thank you," Ramon said quietly when she walked into the living room.

Katie was too angry to speak. She shoved open the glass patio door, banged through the gate in the stockade fence, and marched down to the pool, which was nearly deserted. Most of the tenants were apparently spending Memorial Day with their families. Katie sank down gracefully on the chaise longue closest to the deep end of the pool, ignoring Ramon, who stood looking down at her with his hands on his hips.

"Are you going to swim?" he asked.

Katie shook her head, her teeth clenched together.

Sitting down on the chair across from her, Ramon lit one of those very thin cigars he seemed to like, and leaned forward, his forearms braced on his knees. "Katie, listen to me."

"I don't want to listen to you. I don't like a lot of the things you say."

"But you will listen anyway."

Katie's head swung toward him so swiftly that her long hair came spilling over her shoulder. "Ramon, that is the second time tonight that you have told me what I'm going to do and I don't like it. If I had actually been willing to marry you, which I never was, these past twenty minutes would have changed my mind." She came to her feet, enjoying the sensation of towering over him for a change. "For the sake of what's left of our evening, our *last* evening together, I will swim. Because I'm sure you're going to order me to do that next."

Three long angry strides and Katie did a shallow racing dive into the pool. A few seconds later she felt the impact of Ramon's body hitting the water behind her. Katie swam for all she was worth but she was not really surprised when Ramon easily caught her, or even when he forcibly pulled her stiff, unyielding body against his. "There are four other people in this pool, Ramon. Now let go of me before I yell for help."

"Katie, will you shut up and let me—"

"That was strike three for you," Katie snapped furiously. "You're out!"

"Dammit!" he said savagely, plunging his hand into the hair at her nape and jerking her head back as his mouth possessed hers.

More incensed then ever. Katie twisted her head away and wiped the back of her hand across her mouth. "I didn't like it!" she spat.

"Neither did I," he answered. "Please listen to me."

"I can't see where I have any choice. My feet aren't even touching the bottom."

Ramon ignored that. "Katie, it was a beautiful suit and the sight of you in it took my breath away. If you will listen I will explain why I do not want you to wear it. Last night more than one of the men who live here asked me if I was getting anywhere with their 'vestal virgin.' They call you that."

"They what?" Katie hissed in outraged disgust.

"They call you that because they have all wanted you, and not one of them has had you."

"I'll bet that amazed you," Katie said bitterly. "No doubt you thought that anyone who'd wear such a vulgar bathing suit—"

"It made me very proud," he interrupted quietly.

Katie had had all she could stand. She shoved at his immovable chest. "Well, I hate to disappoint you—knowing how 'proud' you were—but I am not a virgin."

She saw the effect of her announcement in the hardening line of his jaw, but he made no comment on it. Instead he said, "Until now, they have treated you with respect, like a beautiful little sister. But if you appear out here in the littlest bits of string and cloth I have ever seen called a bathing suit—they will be after you like a pack of dogs after a bitch in heat."

"I don't give a blessed damn what they think! And," Katie warned darkly when he opened his mouth, "if you dare tell me not to swear, I will slap you so hard your head will fall off!"

His arms fell away and Katie swam to the ladder, climbed out of the pool, stopped at the chaise longue long enough to sweep up her towel and went back to her apartment alone. Once she was inside she would have locked the door but Ramon's clothes were still there, so she locked her bedroom door instead.

Thirty minutes later, when she had showered and climbed into bed, Ramon knocked at her door.

Katie knew better than to open the door and give Ramon the opportunity to take her in his arms. Where Ramon was concerned her body refused to listen to reason, and in two minutes he'd have her melting and pliant.

"Katie, stop sulking and open this door."

"I'm sure you can find your way out," Katie said coldly. "I am going to sleep." For emphasis she turned out the lamp on her nightstand.

"Katie, for God's sake, do not do this to us."

"There is no 'us.' There never was," Katie said. And then because it hurt somehow to have said the words aloud she added, "I don't know why you want to marry me but I do know all the reasons why I can't marry you. Talking about them isn't going to change anything. Please go away. I really think it's best for both of us this way."

There was an ominous quiet in the apartment after that. Katie waited, watching the clock until forty-five minutes had elapsed, then silently, cautiously, unlocked her door and peeked around the darkened apartment. Ramon had left, turning out all the lights and locking the door behind him. She went back to bed and crawled under the cool sheets, propping the pillows up behind her and turning on the bedside lamp.

What a narrow escape she'd had! Well, not that narrow—she had never actually considered marrying Ramon. In his arms she had been swept to the brink of sexual desperation, that was all. Fortunately no woman in this day and age had to marry just to assuage her sexual needs, including Katherine Connelly! She just happened to have wanted Ramon more than she had ever wanted anyone—even Rob.

That thought sent Katie's mind into chaos. Maybe she had been closer to capitulation than she'd realized. Her job wasn't all that rewarding; the men she knew seemed shallow and self-centered. And Ramon was the antithesis of them. He catered to her every whim. At the zoo he went wherever she wanted to go. If she looked tired he insisted that she sit down and rest. If she gave more than a passing glance at any refreshment stand he was quick to ask if she was hungry or thirsty. If she wanted to swim, he swam. If she wanted to dance, he danced—so long as he could hold her in his arms, she reminded herself crossly.

He wouldn't even let her carry a small bag of groceries or her overnight case. He didn't push open a door, walk past it, and let it come banging back into her face as many men did—then glance at her with a look that said, ''Well, you women wanted equality; open your own doors.''

Katie shook her head. What was the matter with her, thinking about marrying a man because he picked up a five-pound bag of groceries and opened doors for her? But there was more to Ramon than that. He was so supremely confident of his own masculinity that he had no fear of being gentle. He was self-assured and very proud, yet where she was concerned, he seemed strangely vulnerable.

Katie's thoughts reeled onto another path. How, if he really had lived in near-poverty, had he been so thoroughly familiar with the formalities observed at her parents' elaborately laid dining table? Not once had he shown the slightest uncertainty about which piece of silver to use with which course. Nor had he been the slightest bit uneasy around her parents' affluent friends.

Why did he want to marry her and not just go to bed with her? Last night on the sofa, he had known that she was long past the point of denying him anything. "Want me as much as I want you," he had insisted and implored. And when she did want him that much, he had pulled away, sat back, closed his eyes, and unemotionally asked her to marry him. Had he asked her to marry him instead of making love to her because he thought she was a virgin? Latins still prized virginity even in this day of sexual emancipation. Would he have wanted to marry her if he had realized she wasn't a virgin? Katie seriously doubted it and that made her feel humiliated and furiously indignant. Ramon Galverra had known exactly what to do to arouse her to a fever pitch of desire last night and he hadn't learned how from books! Who did he think he was, anyway? He was no virgin!

Turning out the light Katie flopped back against the pillows. Thank heaven she'd come no closer to going to Puerto Rico with him! He would insist on being the unchallenged head of his household; he had practically said as much on their picnic. He would expect his wife to cook and clean and cater to him. He would, no doubt, keep her "barefoot and pregnant," too.

Why, no liberated American woman in her right mind would consider marrying such a classic male chauvinist...a male chauvinist who would be fiercely protective of his own...who would treat his wife as if she were made of fragile glass...who would probably work until he dropped to give her whatever she wanted...who could be so intensely passionate...and so gentle....

CHAPTER SIX

KATIE AWOKE THE NEXT MORNING to the insistent ringing of the telephone beside her bed. Groping dazedly she lifted the receiver from the cradle and pulled it across the pillow tucking it against her ear. Her mother's voice began before Katie could say hello. "Katie darling, who on earth was that man?"

"Ramon Galverra," Katie answered, her eyes still closed.

"I *know* his name, you told us that. What is he doing with you?"

"Doing with me?" Katie mumbled. "Nothing."

"Katie, don't be obtuse! The man obviously knows you have money—we have money—I have the feeling he's after something."

Katie groggily tried to defend Ramon. "He's not after money, he's after a wife."

The phone went silent. When her mother's voice sounded again, each word was iced with contempt. "That Puerto Rican farmer actually thinks he is going to *marry you?*"

"Spanish," Katie corrected, her mother's voice jarring her mind into focus.

"What?"

"I said he's Spanish, not Puerto Rican. Actually, he's American."

"Katherine," the voice demanded with terse impatience. "You are not, in your wildest imaginings, considering marrying that man are you?"

Katie hesitated as she sat up and swung her legs over the side of the bed. "I don't think so."

"You don't *think so?* Katherine, stay there and don't let that man near you until we get there. Lord, this would kill your father. We'll be there right after breakfast."

"No, don't!" Katie said, finally coming out of her sleepy stupor altogether. "Mom, listen. You woke me up and I can hardly think straight, but there's nothing for you to worry about. I'm not going to marry Ramon; I doubt if I'll ever see him again."

"Katherine, are you sure? You aren't just saying that to pacify me?"

"No, really I'm not."

"All right, darling, but if he comes near you again just call us, and we'll be there in thirty minutes."

"Mom—"

"Call us, Katie. Your father and I love you and want to protect you. Don't be ashamed to admit you can't cope with that Spaniard, or Puerto Rican, or whatever he is."

Katie opened her mouth to protest that she didn't need to be "protected" from Ramon, then changed her mind. Her mother wouldn't believe her and Katie didn't want to argue with her. "Okay," she sighed. "If I need you, I'll call. Bye mom."

What was the matter with her parents, Katie wondered angrily a half hour later as she pulled on a pair of yellow velour slacks and a matching yellow top. Why would they think that Ramon would hurt her or do anything that would make her have to call them for help? Brushing her hair back off her forehead, she secured it with a tortoiseshell clip at the crown, then added a touch of coral to her lips and mascara to her lashes. She would go shopping for something frivolous and expensive to take her mind off Ramon and her parents, she decided.

The doorbell rang, as Katie had feared it might, as she was putting her coffee mug in the dishwasher. Her parents, of course. They had finished with their breakfast; now they had come over to finish with Ramon, figuratively speaking.

Resignedly, she went into the living room, pulled open the door, then stepped back in surprise from the tall lithe figure blocking the sunlight. "I—I was just going to leave," Katie said.

Ignoring her hint, Ramon stepped inside and firmly closed the door behind him. A grim smile touched his mouth. "Somehow, I thought that was what you would do."

Katie looked at his ruggedly handsome features, which were stamped with determination, and his powerful shoulders, which were squared with purpose. Confronted with six feet three inches of potent masculinity and iron resolve, Katie chose to make a strategic retreat in order to gather her scattered wits. Turning on her heel she said over her shoulder, "I'll get you a cup of coffee."

She was pouring it into a cup when Ramon's hands settled on her waist drawing her back against his chest. His breath lightly touched her hair as he said, "I do not want coffee, Katie."

"Some breakfast?"

"No."

"Then what do you want?"

"Turn around and I will show you."

Katie shook her head, grasping the edge of the Formica counter top so hard that her knuckles turned white.

"Katie, I did not tell you the main reason why I did not want you to wear that bathing suit, because I did not like admitting it to myself. And you are not going to like it, either. But there must always be honesty between us." He paused then said with a reluctant sigh, "The whole truth is that I was jealous—I do not want anyone but me to ever see so much of your beautiful body."

Katie swallowed, searching for her voice, afraid to turn around, shaken by the feel of his hard, muscular length against her back and legs. "I accept your explanation, and you're right—I don't like it. What I wear is my decision, no one else's. But none of this really matters anymore. I'm sorry for behaving so childishly last night; I should have come out to say goodbye to you. But I can't marry you, Ramon. It wouldn't work."

She expected him to accept that. She should have known better. His hands slid up her arms to her shoulders, tightening to gently but firmly turn her around to face him. Katie kept her eyes on the tanned column of his throat above the open collar of his blue shirt.

"Look at me, *querida*."

That deep, husky voice calling her darling did it. She dragged her wide apprehensive blue eyes up to his.

"You *can* marry me. And it *will* work. I will make it work."

"There's a cultural gap between us a million miles wide!" Katie cried. "How can you possibly think you can make it work?"

His eyes held hers steadily. "Because I will come home to you at night and make love to you until you cry out for me to stop. I will leave you in the morning with the taste of my kiss on your lips. I will live my life for you. I will fill your days with gladness, and if God sends us heartbreak, I will hold you in my arms until your tears have passed and then I will teach you how to laugh again."

Mesmerized, Katie stared at the firm sensual mouth slowly descending to hers. "We'd fight," she warned shakily.

He brushed his lips against hers. "Fighting is only an angry way of caring."

"We'd—we'd disagree about everything. You're tyrannical and I'm independent."

His lips clung to hers. "We will learn to compromise."

"One person can't do all the giving. What would you want in return?"

His arms enfolded her. "No more and no less than what I offer you—everything you have to give with nothing held back. Ever.'' His mouth covered hers, coaxing her lips to part for the gentle invasion of his tongue.

What began for Katie as a warm glow kindled into a fire, then burst into raging flames, racing through her in a quivering fury. She was leaning into him returning his endless drugging kisses with helpless urgency, moaning softly as her breasts swelled to fill his caressing palms.

''We belong together,'' he whispered. ''Tell me you know it,'' he ordered thickly, his hand forcing its way under her elastic waistband to cup her bare buttocks and move her tighter against the throbbing hardness of his aroused manhood. ''Our bodies know it, Katie.''

Caught between the wildly exciting feel of his hand against her bare skin and the proud evidence of his desire pressed boldly to her, Katie's weakened defenses crumbled completely. She wound her arms tightly around his neck, running her hands over his shoulders, smoothing his thick black hair, digging her nails into the bunched muscles of his back. And when he hoarsely commanded, ''Tell me,'' she crushed her parted lips against his and almost sobbed. ''We belong together.''

The whispered words seemed to echo around the room dousing Katie's passion with cold shock. She leaned back in his arms, staring at him.

Ramon's gaze took in the hectic color tinting the smooth curve of her cheeks, the panic widening the deep blue eyes beneath their luxurious lashes. Threading his hands through the sides of her hair he cupped her face between them. "Do not be frightened, *querida*" he said gently. "I think you are not so much afraid of what is happening between us as you are of how quickly it is happening." His thumbs stroked her heated cheeks as he added, "I would do anything to be able to give you more time, but I cannot. We will have to leave for Puerto Rico on Sunday. That will still give you four full days to pack your clothing. I had intended to leave two days ago, I cannot delay my return beyond Sunday."

"But I—I have to go to work tomorrow," Katie protested distractedly.

"Yes. To tell them that you will be leaving for Puerto Rico and that this will be your last week here."

Of all the monumental obstacles to her actually marrying Ramon, Katie seized upon the lesser one of her job. "I can't just walk in there and resign with only four days' notice. I am required to give two weeks' notice, not four days. I can't"

"Yes, Katie," he said quietly. "You can."

"And then there's my parents—oh no! We have got to get out of here," she said with sudden urgency. "I forgot about them. All I need is for them to come over now and find you here. I've already had a 'Katherine' phone call from my mother this morning." In a flurry of motion, Katie broke free of his arms, hurried Ramon into the living room, grabbed her purse, and did not relax until they were in his car.

"What," Ramon asked, slanting her an amused,

sideways look as he turned the key in the Buick's ignition, "is a 'Katherine' phone call?"

Katie watched the easy competence with which he drove, admiring his long masculine fingers on the steering wheel. "When my parents call me Katherine instead of Katie, that means the battle lines have been drawn, their artillery is being moved into position, and unless I wave a white flag quickly, they are going to start firing."

He grinned at her and Katie relaxed. When he turned up the expressway ramp onto eastbound Highway 40, Katie said idly, "Where are we going?"

"To the Arch. I have never had the time to really see it up close."

"Tourist!" Katie teased.

They spent the rest of the morning and well into the afternoon outwardly behaving exactly like tourists. They boarded one of the paddle wheelers for a short trip through the murky waters of the Mississippi River. Katie absently watched the passing scenery on the Illinois side of the river, her mind whirling with disjointed thoughts.

Ramon lounged against the railing—watching Katie. "When are you going to tell your parents?"

Katie's hands actually perspired at the thought. Wiping her damp palms against her yellow slacks, she shook her head. "I haven't decided," she answered, being deliberately obscure about what she hadn't decided.

They strolled along the old brick streets of La-clede's Landing near the riverfront and stopped at a wonderful little pub where the sandwiches were masterpieces. Katie ate very little and stared out the windows at the throngs of downtown office workers coming to the Landing to eat.

Ramon leaned back in his chair, a cigar clamped between his teeth, his eyes narrowed against the smoke—watching Katie. "Do you want me to be there when you tell them?"

"I haven't thought about it."

They wandered along the parklike setting that was dominated by the soaring Gateway Arch. Katie lamely acted as tourist guide explaining that the Arch is the tallest monument in the United States rising to a height of 630 feet, then fell silent and stared blindly at the river flowing by in the foreground. With no particular destination in mind, she walked to the sweeping steps that led to the riverfront and sat down, thinking without really being able to think at all.

Ramon stood beside her, one foot propped near her thigh—watching Katie. "The longer you wait to tell them, the more nervous you will become and the harder it will be to do."

"Did you want to actually go up in the Arch?" Katie evaded. "I don't know if the tram is running, but if it is, the view is supposed to be fantastic. I can't actually say from firsthand experience...I've always been too afraid of the height to open my eyes."

"Katie, there is not much time."

"I know."

They walked back to the car and as they drove

down Market Street, Katie idly suggested that he
might like to drive down Lindell Boulevard. Ramon
automatically followed her directions. They were
driving west down Lindell when Ramon said,
"What is that?"

Katie looked up and to her right. "St. Louis
Cathedral." She was amazed when he pulled up in
front of the elaborate structure. "Why on earth are
we stopping here?"

Ramon turned in his seat and put his arm around
her shoulders. "There are only a few days before we
leave, with many decisions to be made and much to
be done. I will help you pack and do everything I
can, but I cannot tell your parents for you, nor can I
resign your job for you."

"No, I know."

His free hand touched her chin, gently lifting it,
and the kiss he gave her was filled with persuasive
tenderness.

"But why do you want to go into a church?"
Katie asked when he came around and opened her
door for her.

"Normally the finest skills the local craftsmen
possessed at the time can be found in churches, no
matter where in the world they are."

Katie didn't entirely believe that was his reason,
and her nerves, already ragged and strained, were
completely jangled by the time they had climbed the
flight of shallow stone steps leading toward the
domed cathedral. Ramon opened one of the massive
carved doors and stepped aside for her to precede
him into the vast cool interior. Instantly she was

swamped with memories of burning candles and altar flowers.

Ramon placed his hand beneath her elbow, giving her no choice but to walk beside him down the center aisle. Katie kept her eyes moving over the endless rows of pews, scanning the distant vaulted ceilings with their spectacular mosaic scenes that glittered with gold, always avoiding the marble altar. Compulsively avoiding the altar. In the front pew she knelt beside Ramon, feeling like a fraud, an unwelcome intruder. She dragged her eyes toward the altar, then closed them against the dizziness assailing her. God didn't want her here—not like this—not with Ramon. It was too poignant being here with him. And too wrong. All she wanted was his body, not his life.

Ramon was kneeling beside her, and Katie had the terrifying feeling that he was praying. She was even quite certain what he was praying for. As if she could cancel out his private appeal, Katie began to pray, quickly, incoherently, the panic beginning to mount. *Please, please don't listen to him. Don't let this happen. Don't let him care for me so much. I can't do what he wants me to do. I know I can't. I don't want to. God—* Katie cried silently. *Are you listening to me? Do you ever listen to me?*

Katie jerked to her feet, tears blinding her as she turned and collided with Ramon's hard body. "Katie?" His low voice near her ear was filled with concern, his hands gentle on her arms.

"Let me go, Ramon. Please! I've got to get out of here."

"I—I DON'T KNOW WHAT came over me in there," Katie apologized, wiping her eyes with her fingertips. They were standing in the brilliant sunlight on the church steps. Katie watched the traffic gliding down Lindell Boulevard, still too distressed and embarrassed to even look at Ramon as she explained, "I haven't been to church since I was married."

She started down the steps, halting at the sound of Ramon's stunned voice. "You have been married before?"

Katie nodded without turning. "Yes. Two years ago when I was twenty-one, the same month I graduated from college. And divorced a year later."

It still hurt her to admit that to anyone. She had descended another two steps before she realized that Ramon wasn't following her. Turning, she found him regarding her through hard, narrowed eyes. "Were you married in the Catholic church?"

The harshness of his tone, as well as the seeming unimportance of the question, surprised her. Why was he more upset about whether she'd been married in the Catholic church than he was by the actual fact of her having been married? The answer hit Katie like a bucket of ice water, revitalizing, yet sharply painful. Ramon must be a Catholic. His religion would make it difficult to marry Katie if she had been married in the Catholic church and then divorced.

God had indeed answered her prayers, Katie thought with a mixture of gratitude and guilt for the pain she was about to cause Ramon with a lie. She had been divorced, but David had been killed six

months later so there was no actual obstacle to
Ramon marrying her. On the other hand, he didn't
know that and Katie was not going to tell him.
"Yes, I was married in the Catholic church," she
said quietly.

Katie was scarcely aware that they had gotten into
the car and were driving toward the expressway. Her
mind was drifting into the painful past. David. Ruggedly handsome David, who had needed a way to silence the gossip about his association with the wife
of the law firm's senior partner, as well as several of
the firm's female clients, and had done it by becoming engaged to Katherine Connelly. She was lushly
beautiful, delightfully intelligent and suitably naive.
Those who had believed the gossip, took one look at
her and knew that they had been mistaken. After all,
what man in his right mind would bother with all
those other women when he had a woman like
Katie?

David Caldwell would. He was an attorney, an ex-
college football player. A sophisticated man of great
personal charisma, and an ego that fed itself on
women. Every woman he met was a challenge to
him. Every sexual conquest he made proved he was
better than other men. He was such a charming
man...until he was angered. Angered, he was 195
pounds of brutal, violent male.

On the six-month anniversary of their marriage,
Katie took the afternoon off from her job. She
stopped at the market for some special items and
drove to the apartment filled with excited plans to
surprise David with a celebration. When she arrived,

she discovered David was already "celebrating" with the attractive, middle-aged wife of the senior partner of his law firm. As long as she lived, Katie knew she would never forget the moment she had stood in the bedroom doorway and seen them. Even now the memory of it made her feel nauseated.

But the memory of the nightmare that followed was far more painful.

The physical bruises David inflicted on her that night had healed quickly; the emotional ones were scars now. They were healed, but they were still sensitive.

Katie remembered the phone calls that came in the middle of the night after she left him: David insisting that he would change, he loved her. David cursing her viciously and threatening her with brutal reprisals if she dared to tell anyone what he had done. Even Katie's hope for a dignified divorce had been dashed. The divorce itself was quiet, on the grounds of irreconcilable differences, but David himself was not quiet. In angry terror that Katie might tell his secret, he set to work maligning her character and even her family to anyone and everyone who would listen. The things he said were so vile, so vicious, that most of the people he talked to must have turned away in disgust or begun to question his sanity. But Katie was too humiliated and destroyed to consider that.

And then one day four months after the divorce, she dragged herself out of the pit of horror and misery where she had been dwelling, looked at herself in the mirror, and said, "Katherine Elizabeth Conneliy, are you going to let David Caldwell ruin the rest of your life? Do you really want to give him that much satisfaction?''

With some of her old spirit and enthusiasm she set to the task of putting the pieces of her life back together. She changed jobs and moved out of her parents' house and into her own apartment. Her smile returned and then her laughter. She began to live again the life that fate had given her. And she lived it with a determinedly cheerful attitude. Except occasionally when it seemed so shallow. So terribly meaningless. So empty.

''Who?'' Ramon snapped from beside her.

Katie leaned her head against the back of her seat and closed her eyes. ''David Caldwell. An attorney. We were married for six months and divorced six months after that.''

''Tell me about him,'' he said harshly.

''I hate talking about him. I hate thinking about him, as a matter of fact.''

''Tell me,'' he gritted.

Haunted by the gruesome memories of her marriage to David that were swamping her now, and panicked by Ramon's relentless pressure to marry him, Katie grasped at the only escape she could think of at the moment: even though she despised her own cowardice, she chose to deceive Ramon into believing David was still alive in order to put an end to any more talk of her going to Puerto Rico and becoming his wife. Reminding herself to talk about David as if he were still living, she said, ''There isn't a great deal to tell about him. He is thirty-two—tall dark and very handsome. He reminds me of you, in fact.''

''I want to know why you divorced him.''

''I divorced him because I despised him and because I was afraid of him.''

''He threatened you?''

''He didn't threaten.''

''He struck you?'' Ramon looked furious and revolted.

Katie was determined to sound offhand. ''David called it teaching me manners.''

''And I remind you of him?''

He sounded ready to explode and Katie hastily assured, ''Only a little bit in looks. You're both olive-skinned, dark-haired and dark-eyed. David played football in college, and you...'' she slid a covert glance at him, then recoiled in alarm from the blazing anger in his profile, ''...you look as if you should play tennis,'' she finished lamely.

As they were pulling into the parking space in front of her apartment, it dawned on Katie that this would undoubtedly be their last day together. If Ramon was as devout a Catholic as Spaniards were purported to be, he would not be able to consider marrying her.

The idea of never seeing him again was surprisingly painful, and Katie felt a little desolate and forlorn. She wanted to prolong the day, to be able to spend more time with him. But not alone—not where he could take her in his arms and in five minutes have her drowning in desire and confessing everything to him. Then she'd be right back where she was an hour ago. Trapped.

"Do you know what I'd love to do tonight?" she said as he walked her to the door. "That is, if you don't have to work."

"No, what?" he said through clenched teeth.

"I'd love to go someplace where we could listen to music and dance." Her simple statement made his face darken with rage. The hard line of his jaw tightened until a drumming pulse stood out in his cheek. He was furious, Katie thought with a jolt of fear. Quickly, apologetically, she said, "Ramon, I should have realized that you might be a Catholic and that my having been married before in the church would make it impossible for you to marry me. I'm sorry I didn't think to tell you before."

"You are so 'sorry' that you now wish to go out dancing," he said with scathing sarcasm. Then, making a visible effort to control his fury he asked tautly, "What time shall I come for you?"

Katie glanced at the afternoon sun. "In about four hours, at eight o'clock."

Katie chose a silky halter dress in royal blue that was the exact shade of her eyes and was striking against the contrast of red highlights in her hair. In the mirror, she scrutinized the slight amount of cleavage showing between her breasts to be certain Ramon wouldn't think the dress was too revealing. If this was going to be their last night together, she didn't want to spoil it with another argument about her clothing. She put gold hoops in her ears, a wide gold bracelet high on her arm, and stepped into dainty sandals that were the same blue as her dress. Giving her hair a quick toss to send it spilling back down her shoulders, she went into the living room to wait for Ramon.

Their last evening together.... Katie's spirits drooped alarmingly. She went into the kitchen and poured a tiny bit of brandy into a glass, then sat down on the corduroy sofa at a quarter to eight, slowly sipping the brandy and watching the clock on the opposite wall. When the doorbell rang at exactly eight, she jumped nervously, put her empty glass aside, and went to answer it.

Nothing in their brief acquaintance had prepared Katie for the Ramon Galverra who was standing there when she opened the door.

He looked breathtakingly elegant in a dark blue suit and vest that fit him to perfection and contrasted beautifully with his snowy-white shirt and conservative striped tie. "You look fantastic," Katie said with a beaming smile of admiration. "You look like the president of a bank," she added, stepping back to better admire his tall athletic frame.

Ramon's expression was sardonic. "As it happens, I do not like bankers. For the most part they are unimaginative men eager to reap the profit from risks, yet unwilling to take any risks themselves."

"Oh," Katie said, somewhat abashed. "Well, they're terrific dressers, anyway."

"How do you know?" Ramon replied. "Were you also married to a banker who you have forgotten to mention?"

Katie's hand froze as she reached for the silky printed shawl that coordinated with her dress. "No, of course not."

They went down to one of the riverboats and listened to Dixieland jazz, then back to Laclede's Landing where they stopped in three more places for jazz and blues music. As the evening wore on Ramon became increasingly cool and unapproachable, and the more aloof he became the more Katie drank and tried to be amusing.

By the time they had driven to a popular place out near the airport, Katie was slightly flushed, very nervous, and thoroughly miserable.

The place she had chosen was surprisingly crowded for a Tuesday night, but they were lucky enough to get a table beside the dance floor. There, however, Katie's luck ended. Ramon flatly refused to dance with her, and Katie did not know how much longer she could endure the glacial reserve that barely concealed his contempt. His hard eyes examined her with a detached, cynical interest that made Katie mentally squirm.

She looked around, more to avoid Ramon's cold eyes than because she was interested in her surroundings, and her gaze collided with a handsome man sitting at the bar watching her. He raised his brows, mouthed the word "Dance?" and Katie, in sheer desperation nodded her head.

He approached the table, eyed Ramon's obvious height and lithe build with a certain wariness, and politely asked Katie to dance.

"Do you mind?" Katie asked Ramon, eager to get away.

"Not in the least," he replied with a disinterested shrug.

Katie loved to dance; she had a natural grace and a way of moving that was very eye-catching. Her partner, it became obvious, not only loved to dance, he was a positive exhibitionist about it. The colored lights flashed overhead, the music pulsed, and Katie moved with it, giving herself to the rhythm. "Hey, you're good," her partner said, forcing her with his own movements to do a much flashier kind of dancing than she preferred to do.

"You're showing off," Katie told him as the crowd on the dance floor began to move back and give them more room, then stopped dancing altogether. At the end of the disco number there was a loud round of encouraging, insistent applause from dancers and nondancers alike.

"They want us to dance some more," her partner said, tightening his hold on her arm when Katie would have started back toward the table. Simultaneously, another disco number started reverberating through the packed room, and Katie had no choice but to give in gracefully to what she privately felt was exhibitionism. As she danced, she stole a glance at Ramon, then quickly jerked her eyes away. He had angled his chair toward the dance floor, shoved his hands into his pockets, and was watching her with the dispassionate interest of a jaded conquistador observing a paid dancing girl.

As the music wound to a close there was a gratifying thunder of applause. Her partner tried to get her to stay with him for another dance, but this time Katie firmly refused.

She sat down at the table opposite Ramon and

sipped from her drink, growing increasingly annoyed with the way they were behaving to each other. "Well?" she asked with a twinge of hostility, when he made no comment about her dancing.

One black brow rose sardonically. "Not bad."

Katie could have hit him. Another song began, this one slow and romantic. She looked around, saw two more would-be partners bearing down on their table and stiffened. Ramon, following her gaze, saw them and reluctantly stood up. Wordlessly he put his hand under Katie's elbow and led her onto the dance floor.

The love song, combined with the piercing sweetness of being in Ramon's arms again, was Katie's undoing. Moving close to him, she laid her cheek against the dark blue cloth of his suit coat. She wished his arms would tighten, that he would gather her against him and brush his lips against her temple as he had the last time they danced out by the pool. She wished... a lot of hazy, impossible things.

She was still wishing when they got back to her apartment. He walked her to the door and Katie practically had to beg him to come in for a nightcap. As soon as he had downed the brandy he stood up and without saying anything, simply started for the door.

"Ramon, please don't leave. Not like this," Katie pleaded.

He turned and looked at her, his face expressionless.

Katie started toward him, then stopped a few feet away, shaken by a surge of heartbreaking sadness and longing. "I don't want you to go," she heard herself say, and then her arms were around his neck as she pressed herself against his unyielding body, kissing him desperately. His lips were cool and unresponsive, his arms remained motionless at his sides.

Humiliated and hurt, Katie stepped back and raised blue eyes shimmering with tears to his. "Don't you even want to kiss me goodbye?" she asked with a catch in her voice.

His whole body seemed to stiffen into a taut, rigid pose of rejection, and then he jerked her into his arms. "Damn you!" he hissed furiously as his mouth came down hard, taking hers with a deliberate ruthless expertise that immediately had Katie clinging to him, responding wildly with helpless desire. His hands fondled her thoroughly, roughly molding her body to his. And then he abruptly pushed her away.

Trembling and breathless, Katie looked up at him, then backed away in alarm from the murderous rage blazing in his eyes.

"Is that the only thing you want from me, Katie?" he snapped.

"No!" Katie quickly denied. "I mean, I don't want anything. I—I just knew that you didn't have a very good time tonight and so—"

"And so," he interrupted in an insulting drawl, "you brought me in here to give me a much better time?"

"No!" Katie fumbled, "I—" Her voice choked as his black eyes raked her from head to toe. Just when Katie thought he was going to turn on his heel and leave, he turned in the other direction and strode over to the coffee table. He picked up the pencil she kept near the telephone and wrote something on the small pad beside it.

Striding back to the door, he turned with one hand on the knob. "I have written down a phone number where I can be reached until Thursday. If you want to talk, call me." His gaze lingered on her face and then he was gone, closing the door behind him.

Katie stood where he had left her, stunned and fragmented into jagged splinters of misery. That last glance before he left...it was as if he had been memorizing her face. He hated her, was furious with her, yet he had wanted to remember how she looked. Katie could not believe how shattered she was. Tears burned her eyes, and she had an aching lump in her throat.

She turned and slowly walked into her bedroom. What was the matter with her—this was the way she had wanted it, wasn't it? Well, not exactly. She wanted Ramon, she was ready to admit that to herself, but she wanted him *her* way: here in St. Louis, working at some decent job.

CHAPTER SEVEN

A DETERMINEDLY CHEERFUL Katie presented herself at her office the following morning, but the effects of her sleepless night were evident in the blue smudges under her eyes and the tightness of her normally spontaneous smile.

"Hi, Katie," her secretary greeted. "Did you enjoy your four-day weekend?"

"Very much," Katie said. She took the handful of messages her secretary handed her. "Thanks, Donna."

"Want some coffee?" Donna volunteered. "You look as though you haven't been to bed since Friday. Or," she finished with an irrepressible grin, "should I say you look as though you haven't been to *sleep* since then?"

Katie managed a wan smile in reply to Donna's banter. "I'd love some coffee." Glancing through the messages, she walked into her small office. She sat down in the chair behind her desk and looked around. Having a private office, no matter the size, was an important status symbol at Technical Dynamics, and Katie had always been proud of this external sign of her success. This morning it seemed trivial and meaningless.

How could it be that when she'd locked her desk on Friday she'd never heard of Ramon, and now the idea of never seeing him again was gnawing at her heart. Gnawing at her body not her heart, Katie corrected herself firmly. She looked up as Donna placed a white Styrofoam cup of steaming coffee on the desk.

"Miss Johnson would like to see you in her office at nine-fifteen," Donna said.

Virginia Johnson, Katie's immediate supervisor, was a brilliant, capable, attractive woman of forty, who had never married and who held the title of director of personnel. Of all the career women she knew, Katie admired Virginia more than anyone.

In contrast to Katie's small, functionally equipped office, Virginia's was spacious with lovely French-provincial furnishings and thick grass-green carpeting. Katie knew that Virginia was grooming her to take her place, that she intended Katie to be the next director of personnel—the next occupant of this office. "Did you have a nice four-day holiday?" Virginia asked, smiling as Katie entered the room.

"Very nice," Katie said, sitting down in the chair across from Virginia's desk. "I'm not having such a good 'today' though; I can't seem to get back into the swing of things."

"Then I have some news that may fire your enthusiasm." Virginia paused meaningfully and slid a familiar-looking form across the desk toward Katie. "Your raise has been approved," she beamed.

"Oh, that's very nice. Thank you, Virginia,"

Katie said scarcely glancing at the form which grant-
ed her a monumental 18-percent increase in salary.
"Was there anything else you wanted to see me
about?"

"Katie!" Virginia said with an impatient laugh.
"I had to fight tooth and nail to get you that large
an increase."

"I know," Katie said, trying to sound properly
grateful. "You've always been terrific to me and I
love the idea of the extra money."

"You're entitled to it and if you were a man you
would have been making it before now, which is
what I told our esteemed vice-president of operations."

Katie shifted in her chair. "Was there anything
else you wanted to see me about? I have an interview
scheduled now. The applicant is waiting."

"No, that's all."

Katie got up and started for the door, then
stopped at the sound of Virginia's concerned voice.
"Katie, what's wrong? Is it anything you could talk
to me about?"

Katie hesitated. She needed to talk to someone,
and Virginia Johnson was a sensible woman—in
fact, the woman Katie most wanted to emulate.
Walking over to the broad windows Katie gazed
down seven stories below, watching the endless
string of traffic. "Virginia, have you ever considered giving up your career to get married?" Turning abruptly, Katie found Virginia studying her with
penetrating interest, her forehead creased into a
frown.

"Katie, shall we be frank with each other? Are you considering marrying someone in particular or just looking toward the obscure future?"

"My future would definitely be obscure with him," Katie laughed, but she felt tense and depressed. Nervously smoothing her hand over her perfectly neat chignon Katie explained, "I met this man—very recently—and he wants me to marry him and leave Missouri. He isn't from here."

"How recently did you meet him?" Virginia asked perceptively.

Katie actually blushed. "Friday evening."

Virginia had a rich throaty laugh that was at variance with her diminutive size. "For a few minutes there you had me worried, but now I think I understand. Four days ago you met a splendid man, a man unlike any man you've ever known. You can't bear the idea of losing him. Am I getting the picture right? He's extremely handsome, of course. And charming. And he turns you on like no one else ever has. That's it, isn't it?"

"Just about," Katie admitted, mentally squirming.

"In that case, I happen to have the perfect cure: I recommend that you don't let him out of your sight unless you absolutely must. Eat with this marvelous man, sleep with him, live with him. Do *everything* together."

"Do you mean," Katie said in amazement, "that you think things could work out—that I ought to marry him?"

"Absolutely not! I'm suggesting a cure, not that

you marry the ailment! What I'm prescribing is huge doses of the man taken around the clock—just like antibiotics. The cure is very effective and the only side effect will be a mild case of disillusionment. Believe me, I know. Live with him if you want to, Katie, but give up the idea of falling in love in four days, marrying him and living happily ever after. Which brings me to the question of why we always 'fall' in love. One falls down steps, off ladders, into rivers and down mountains. If love is so wonderful, why don't we soar in love, or climb in love, or. . . ." She broke off at the sound of Katie's infectious laughter. "Good, I'm glad to see you cheerful again." Taking an interoffice memo from the stack of correspondence on her desk, Virginia smiled widely and waved Katie to the door. "Now go interview your applicant and earn that raise of yours."

Watching the disgruntled young man leave her office twenty minutes later, Katie thought disgustedly that her secretary could have done a better job of interviewing him than herself. She had asked vague, general questions, not concise, pertinent ones, and then listened to his answers with total lack of interest. But her crowning achievement had come at the conclusion of the unfortunate interview. Standing up, she had shaken hands with him across her desk and regretfully advised him she couldn't be very encouraging about his chances for a position as an engineer with Technical Dynamics.

Rather huffily, the young man had replied, "I was applying for a job as an auditor."

"Well, not as an auditor, either," Katie had mumbled tactlessly.

Still hot with embarrassment over her blunder, Katie picked up her phone and dialed Karen's office number downtown. "How're things in the newspaper business?" she asked when Karen's secretary had put her through.

"Fine, Katie. How about you? How are things in the busy personnel office of mighty Technical Dynamics?" she teased.

"Awful! I practically told an applicant that he didn't have a prayer of getting a job with us in any capacity."

"What's wrong with that?"

Sighing, Katie said, "Personnel people are supposed to have more finesse than that. Normally we say we don't have anything available commensurate with their background and experience. It means the same thing but it sounds better, and it doesn't hurt anyone's feelings." Katie ran her hand around the nape of her neck, massaging her tense muscles. "Listen, the reason I was calling was because I wondered what you're doing tonight. I don't feel like spending the evening alone." *And thinking about Ramon*, Katie silently added.

"A few of us are going to the Purple Bottle," Karen said. "Why don't you meet us there? I might as well warn you, though, it's strictly singles. But they've got a good singer and the music isn't bad."

KATIE'S EFFICIENCY, if not her enthusiasm, improved after that. She spent her day solving the usual problems and settling the usual disputes. She listened to a supervisor complain loudly and at tedious length about a file clerk; then she listened to the file clerk's tearful complaints about the supervisor. At the conclusion, Katie ignored the supervisor's demands that the file clerk be terminated, and instead, transferred the clerk to another department. After looking through the applications for employment she chose a file clerk who had impressed her during the interview as being extremely assertive and self-confident, and arranged for her to come in for an interview with the supervisor.

She calmed an irate accountant who was threatening to file a discrimination claim against the company because she had been passed over for promotion. She finished a survey on the company's compliance with governmental safety requirements.

Between all that and interviewing applicants, Katie's day flew by. At the end of it, she leaned back in her chair and somberly contemplated an entire life of days spent just like this one. This was "having a career." Virginia Johnson had devoted all her energy, her whole life, to "having a career." To this.

That restless, empty feeling that had been haunting her these past few months came over her again. Katie tried to ignore it and leaned forward to lock her desk.

KATIE HAD THE WORST TIME of her life at the Purple Bottle. She stood around pretending to listen to the music, watching the men and women making their approaches. She was uncomfortably aware of three men who were sitting at a table directly on her right and looking her over—judging her assets, measuring her possible bed-worthiness against the effort required to approach her. Privately, Katie thought that all women who were considering divorcing their husbands should first be required to spend one night in a singles' bar. After that degrading and demoralizing experience, many of them would run flying back to their husbands.

She left at nine-thirty, one hour after she had arrived, and drove back to her apartment. In the car thoughts of Ramon haunted her. She had a life to live here and he couldn't be part of it, while his life was too alien, too far away for her to even consider sharing it.

Katie went to bed at ten-thirty and after several hours, finally fell into a deep exhausted sleep.

CHAPTER EIGHT

SHE SLEPT SO DEEPLY that she didn't hear the alarm go off, had to dress in frantic haste, and still she was fifteen minutes late for work.

Thursday, June 3, her calendar boldly proclaimed as she unlocked her desk and reached for the cup of coffee Donna had brought her.

Thursday.

The last day she would ever be able to reach Ramon. How late would he be at that phone number? Until he finished working at five or six o'clock? Or would he be working late tonight? What difference did it make? If she called him she would have to be ready to leave and marry him. And that she just couldn't do.

June 3.

Katie smiled sadly as she sipped her steaming coffee. At the lightning speed with which Ramon swept her along, she probably would have been a June bride. Again.

Katie gave her head a hard shake and employed what was for her, a special talent she discovered she possessed during her divorce: By instantly forcing herself to think of something different the moment an unwanted subject entered her mind, she could totally repress the subject.

She was a positive whirlwind of productive activity all day. Not only did she handle all her scheduled interviews, she took three more applicants who had arrived without the required appointment.

She gave most of the clerical tests herself, repeating the instructions for how to type the sample copy as if it were the most interesting speech she'd ever made. She stared at the timer while they typed as if it were an absorbing masterpiece of complicated technology that utterly fascinated her.

She breezed into Virginia's office, thanked her profoundly for the marvelous raise and the wonderful advice, and then she slowly closed her office door and reluctantly went home.

It was not nearly as easy to practice her technique in the solitude of her apartment, particularly when the radio kept reminding her what time it was— "This is KMOX Radio and the time is six-forty," the announcer said.

And Ramon won't be at that number much longer, if he still is, the announcer in her mind added.

Angrily, Katie snapped off the radio and turned on the television, prowling around her apartment, unable to sit down. If she called Ramon, there could be no half-measures; she would have to tell him the truth. Even if she did, he might not want to marry her any longer. He had been furious to learn she'd been married before. Maybe the church wasn't the issue at all. Maybe he didn't want 'secondhand' goods. But if he wanted to be finished with her, why had he left her a number where she could call him?

The television screen flared to life. "It's seventy-eight degrees in St. Louis at six forty-five,'' the announcer intruded into her thoughts.

She couldn't call Ramon unless she was prepared to resign her job with one day's notice. That was all that was left. She would have to walk into Virginia Johnson's office and say to a woman who had been wonderful to her, ''Sorry to be leaving you in the lurch, but that's the way it is.''

And she hadn't even considered the problem of her parents. They would be angry, alarmed, heartbroken. They would miss her terribly if she went to Puerto Rico. Katie dialed her parents' number and was informed by their maid that Mr. and Mrs. Connelly had gone to the country club for dinner. *Damn it!* Katie thought. Why were they gone when she needed them? They should be at home, missing their little Katie, whom they only saw every few weeks. Would they miss her so much if they only saw her every few months?

Katie leaped to her feet, and in desperation to be doing something, changed into a bikini—the yellow bikini! Sitting at the dressing table in her spacious bedroom, she briskly brushed her hair.

How could she be thinking of giving all this up in exchange for the sort of home and life Ramon could offer her? She must be insane! Her own life was a modern American woman's dream. She had a rewarding career, a beautiful apartment, expensive clothes and no financial worries. She was young, attractive and independent.

She had everything. Absolutely everything.

That thought caused Katie's brush strokes to slow

as she stared soberly into the mirror. Dear God, was this really *everything*? Her eyes darkened with despair as she again contemplated a future just like her present. There had to be more to life than this. Surely this wasn't everything. It just couldn't be.

Trying to shake off her dismal thoughts, Katie snatched up a towel and marched down to the pool. There were about thirty people swimming or relaxing at the umbrella tables. Don and Brad were with some other men drinking beer. Katie waved to them when they called to her to come and join them, but she shook her head no. Putting her towel down on the most isolated lounger she could find, Katie turned and walked over to the pool. She swam twenty laps then climbed out and flopped down on the chair. Someone had a portable radio on. "It's seven-fifteen in St. Louis, the temperature a balmy seventy-eight degrees."

Katie closed her eyes trying to shut her mind off, and suddenly she could almost feel Ramon's warm firm lips moving with gentle coaxing over hers, then deepening his kiss until it was wildly erotic and she was joyously surrendering to the searching hunger of his mouth and hands. His deep voice spoke quietly to her heart: "I will live my life for you. . . I will make love to you until you cry out for me to stop. . . I will fill your days with gladness."

Katie felt as if she were slowly suffocating. "We belong together," he had said, his voice thick with desire. "Tell me that you know it. Say it." She had said it. She had even known it—as surely as she knew they *couldn't* be together.

He was so handsome, so masculine with his beautiful black hair and dazzling white smile. Katie thought of the slight cleft in his chin and the way his eyes—"Ouch!" Yelping with surprise she jack-knifed into a sitting position as icy water ran down her thigh.

"Wake up, sleeping beauty," Don grinned, sitting down on the lounge. Katie squeezed over to make more room for him, watching him warily. His eyes were glassy, his face slightly flushed; he looked as though he'd been drinking all afternoon. "Katie," he said, his eyes delving into her deep cleavage exposed by the skimpy bikini top. "You really turn me on, do you know that?"

"I don't think that's very hard to do," Katie replied with a fixed smile, pushing his hand away when his fingers started to trace the trickle of water across her left thigh.

He laughed. "Be nice to me, Katie. I could be very nice to you."

"I'm not an old lady, and you're not a boy scout," Katie quipped, hiding her uneasiness behind flippancy.

"You have a clever little tongue, redhead. But there are better things to do with it than sniping at me. Let me show you an example." His mouth started descending toward hers and Katie pulled back averting her head.

"Don," she almost pleaded, "I'm really trying not to make a scene but if you don't stop this I'm going to start screaming and we're both going to look very silly."

He jerked back and glared at her. "What the hell's the matter with you anyway?"

"Nothing!" Katie said. She didn't want to make an enemy of him, she just wanted him to go away. "What do you want?" she asked finally.

"Are you kidding? I want this woman I'm looking at—the one with the gorgeous face, a luscious body and a virginal little mind."

Katie looked him right in the eye. "Why?" she said baldly.

"Sweetheart," he teased, while his eyes made a thorough inspection of her body. "That is a stupid question. But I'll answer it the same way the man answered when they asked him why he wanted to climb the mountain. I want to climb you because you're here. Do you want me to be more blunt? I want to climb on you, or if you prefer to, you can—"

"Get away from me," Katie hissed. "You're disgusting and you're drunk."

"I'm not drunk!" he said, offended.

"Then you're just plain disgusting! Now go away."

He stood up and shrugged. "Okay. Shall I send Brad over? He's interested. Or how about Dean, he's—"

"I don't want any of you!" Katie said furiously.

Don was genuinely bewildered. "Why not? We're no worse than the next group of guys. In fact, we're better than most."

Katie was slowly straightening, staring at him as his words began sinking into her brain, pounding in her head. "What did you say?" she whispered.

"I said we're as good as the next group of guys, and better than most."

"You're right..." she breathed slowly. "You are absolutely right!"

"So what's the problem? What are you saving it for, anyway? Or, more importantly, who are you saving it for?"

And suddenly Katie knew. Oh God, she knew!

She almost stumbled over Don in her hurry to get around him. "It's not that damn Spaniard, is it?" he shouted after her.

But Katie couldn't take the time to answer, she was already running. Running down the path, bursting past the door in the stockade fence and breaking a fingernail in her urgent haste to pull open the sliding glass door.

Breathless with fear that she was already too late, she dialed the number Ramon had written on the pad beside the phone. She counted the rings, her hope dying with each one that went unanswered.

"Hello," a woman's voice said on the tenth ring when Katie was about to hang up.

"I—I'd like to speak to Ramon Galverra. Is he there?" Katie was so surprised to hear a woman's voice answering what was obviously a residential phone, that she nearly forgot to give the information the woman was obviously waiting for. "My name is Katherine Connelly."

"I'm sorry, Miss Connelly, Mr. Galverra isn't in. We expect him shortly, though. Shall I ask him to call you?"

"Yes, please," Katie said. "Would you be certain

that he gets the message that I called, as soon as he arrives?''

"Of course. As soon as he arrives."

Katie hung up the phone and stared at it. Was Ramon really out, or had he asked that friendly sounding woman to fend Katie off? He'd been furious when Katie told him she'd been married before... perhaps now that his passion had had two days to cool off, he was no longer interested in acquiring a "used" wife. What should she do if he didn't return her call? Should she assume that he didn't get her message and call him back? Or should she take the hint and realize that he didn't want to talk to her?

Twenty minutes later the phone rang. Katie snatched it up and breathlessly said, "Hello."

Ramon's voice sounded even deeper on the telephone. "Katie?"

She squeezed the receiver so tightly that her hand ached. "You said to call if I—I wanted to talk." She paused, hoping he would now say something to help her, but he remained silent. Drawing a long breath, Katie said, "I would like to talk... but I'd rather not do it on the telephone. Ramon, could you possibly come over?"

There was no emotion in his voice. All he said was "Yes."

But that was enough. Katie glanced down at the yellow bikini and flew into her room to change it. She debated over what to wear as if what she selected might make the difference between success and failure. Finally choosing a soft peach cowl-neck top and matching slacks, she dried and brushed her hair, added peach lipstick, some blusher, and then mascara. Her eyes were sparkling and her color was high as she looked in the mirror. "Wish me luck," she said to her reflection.

She went into the living room, started to sit down, then snapped her fingers. "Scotch," she said aloud. Ramon liked Scotch; she didn't have any. Leaving the front door slightly ajar, Katie raced next door and borrowed a bottle of J&B from the man who lived there.

She half-expected to find Ramon waiting for her in the apartment when she came back, but he wasn't. She went into the kitchen and fixed Ramon's Scotch the way he ordered it when they were out—on the rocks with a splash. Critically, she held the glass up to the light surveying the contents. Exactly how much was a splash, anyway? And why had she done such a stupid thing as to mix his drink so early that the ice would melt by the time he got here? She decided she would drink it. Wrinkling her nose at the taste, she carried the glass into the living room and sat down.

At a quarter to nine the shrill ring of the doorbell brought her leaping out of her chair.

Restraining herself at the last moment from flinging the door wide, she composed her features into a formal smile and opened it properly. In the mellow glow of the gaslight Ramon was framed in her doorway, looking very tall and devastatingly handsome in a light gray suit and maroon tie. His eyes looked directly into hers, his expression unreadable, neither warm nor cold.

"Thank you for coming," Katie said, stepping back and closing the door after him. She was so nervous she couldn't think where to begin. She decided to opt for a compromise. "Sit down and I'll fix you a drink."

"Thank you," he said. He walked into the living room and took off his suit jacket. Without even turning his head to glance in her direction, he tossed it carelessly over the back of a chair.

Katie was thoroughly abashed by his attitude, but at least if he was taking off his jacket he expected to stay for a little while. When she returned from the kitchen with his drink, he was standing with his back to her, his hands in his pockets, staring out her living-room window. He turned when he heard her and for the first time Katie saw the deeply etched lines of strain and fatigue at his eyes and mouth. Anxiously she scanned his features "Ramon, you look exhausted."

He loosened the knot of his tie and took the glass Katie was holding out to him. "I have not come here to discuss the state of my health, Katie," he informed her brusquely.

"No, I know," Katie sighed. He was cold, remote and, Katie sensed, still extremely angry with her. "You aren't going to help me get this over with, are you?" she said, voicing her thought aloud.

His dark eyes were impassive. "That depends entirely upon what you have to say to me. As I told you before, there was little I could offer you if you married me, but one of the things I offered you was honesty between us. Always. I expect the same from you."

Nodding, Katie turned away from him, grasping the back of a chair for physical support since it was perfectly obvious she wasn't going to get any moral support from the man behind her. Drawing a shaky breath, Katie closed her eyes. "Ramon, at the church on Tuesday, I—I realized that you are probably a devout Catholic. And then I realized that if you are, you couldn't—wouldn't marry me if I had been married in the Catholic church and then divorced. That's why I told you I was divorced. It wasn't a lie, I *was* divorced, but David is dead now."

The voice behind her was coolly unemotional. "I know."

Katie gripped the back of the chair so hard her fingers went numb. "You know? How could you?"

"You had told me once before that I reminded you of someone else, someone whose death brought you great release. When you were telling me about your former husband, you again made the remark that I remind you of him. I assumed that you probably did not know two men who remind you of me. Besides, you are an extremely transparent liar."

His complete indifference tore at Katie's heart. "I see," she said, her throat constricting with tears. Apparently Ramon didn't want another man's wife, regardless of whether she was a divorcée or a widow. As if she had to further punish herself by actually having him tell her that in so many words, Katie whispered, "Would you mind explaining to me why you are still angry with me, even after what I've just told you? I know you are, only I'm not sure why you are, and—"

His hands gripped her arms and he spun her around, his fingers pressing into her flesh. "Because I love you!" he gritted tersely. "And for two days you have put me through a living hell." His voice sounded harsh, as if it were being gouged from his chest. "I love you, and for nearly forty-eight hours I have waited for you to call, dying inside with each hour that you did not."

With a teary smile Katie laid her hand against his cheek and jaw, trying to soothe away the tautness with her fingertips. "They've been terrible days for me, too."

His arms closed around her with stunning force, his mouth opening over hers in a kiss that demanded she return the same stormy passion that he was offering her. His hands claimed her body, stroking her neck, her back, her breasts, then sweeping down, pulling her tightly to his rigidly aroused manhood. Instinctively, Katie moved her hips against him. Ramon groaned with rampaging desire and plunged his hand into her hair, holding her mouth to his as his tongue began matching her inflaming movements.

He tore his mouth from hers and lavished scorching kisses on her face, her eyes, her neck. "You are going to drive me out of my mind, do you know that?" he murmured thickly. But Katie couldn't answer. His lips had already recaptured hers and she was drowning in an ocean of pleasure, willingly sinking beneath the waves of rapture that sent her deeper with each touch of his hungry, searching mouth and hands.

Katie slowly began to surface as the pressure of his lips against hers lessened, and then was gone. Feeling deprived and bereft, she laid her cheek against his chest, her heart racing like a trip-hammer and his own thundering in her ear.

His hand cupped her cheek and Katie lifted her gaze to his, melting at the new tenderness she saw in his expression. "Katie, I would have married you if you had married that animal in every church on earth and then divorced him in every court."

Katie hardly recognized the breathy whisper that was her own voice. "I thought the reason you were furious was because I'd let things come so far between us without telling you I had been married before."

He shook his head. "I was furious because I knew you were lying to me about your husband being alive so that you would have an excuse not to marry me; furious because I knew you were terrified of what you felt for me, and yet I could not remain here longer to overcome your fear."

Katie leaned up on her toes and pressed a kiss to his warmly responsive lips, but when his arms tightened around her she drew back. Stepping away from the temptation of his nearness, she said, "I think, before I lose my nerve and it gets any later, I had better tell my parents. After tonight there are only three days left for us to try to win them over before we leave."

Katie walked over to the coffee table, picked up the telephone and started to dial her parents' number, then looked up at Ramon. "I was going to tell them we were coming over there, but I think it would be better if I had them come here—'' She gave him a nervous, rueful smile. "They can throw you out of their house but they can't very well throw you out of mine."

Waiting for her parents' phone to be answered, she raked her fingers through her rumpled hair, trying to think of how to begin. When her mother answered Katie's mind went completely blank. "Hi, mom," she said. "It's me."

"Katie, is anything wrong? It's nine-thirty."

"No, nothing's wrong." She paused. "I was hoping that, if it's not too late, you and dad might like to come over for drinks."

Her mother laughed. "I suppose we could. We just came back from dinner at the club. We'll be there right away."

Katie, searching madly for some way to keep her mother on the phone while she thought of a way to broach the subject at hand said, "By the way, better bring whatever you want to drink. All I have is Scotch."

"Okay, honey, we will. Want us to bring anything else?"

"Tranquilizers and smelling salts," Katie mumbled indistinctly.

"What, dear?"

"Nothing mom, there's something I have to tell you, but before I do, I want to ask you something. Do you remember when I was a little girl and you told me that no matter what I did, you and Dad would always love me? You said that no matter how terrible it was, you—"

"Katie," her mother interrupted sharply. "If you are trying to alarm me, you're succeeding very well."

"Not half as well as I'm about to," Katie sighed miserably. "Mom, Ramon is here. I'm going to leave with him on Sunday and marry him in Puerto Rico. We want to talk to you and dad about it tonight."

For a second the line went silent, then her mother said, "And we are going to want to talk to you, Katherine."

Katie hung up and looked at Ramon who lifted his brows in inquiry. "I'm Katherine again." Despite her attempt at joking, Katie was unhappily aware of how devastated her parents were going to be by what she was doing. She was going to stand by her decision to go to Puerto Rico, no matter what they said, but she loved them very much and she hated the unhappiness she was about to cause them.

She waited at the window with Ramon beside her, his arm comfortingly around her shoulders. She knew from the speed at which a pair of headlights made the sweeping turn into the entrance of her apartment complex that her parents had arrived.

Feeling sad and very apprehensive, Katie started to move toward the door but Ramon's voice stopped her. "Katie, if I could take the burden of what you are about to do from your shoulders and your heart, I would do it. I cannot—but I can promise you that for the next three days you will bear the only unhappiness I will ever intentionally cause you."

"Thank you," she whispered achingly, putting her hand in his outstretched palm, feeling strength in the reassuring firmness of his fingers gripping hers. "Have I ever told you how much I love the things you say to me?"

"No," he said with a faint grin. "But it is a good place to start."

There was no time for Katie to ponder his meaning because the doorbell was already ringing insistently.

Katie's father, who was famous for his charm and good manners, tore into the apartment like a whirlwind, accepted Ramon's outstretched hand and said, "Good to see you again, Galverra, enjoyed having you at the house the other day; you've got a goddamned nerve asking Katie to marry you and you're out of your goddamned mind if you think we'll permit it."

Katie's mother, renowned for her ability to maintain her composure even in times of extreme stress, stormed in right on his heels, holding the neck of a liquor bottle in each hand like a juggler. "We won't stand for this," she announced. "Mr. Galverra, we will have to ask you to leave," the bottle pointing majestically to the door. "And you, Katherine, have lost your mind. Go to your room." The other bottle swept grandly toward the hall.

Katie, watching the unfolding scene with fascinated horror, finally recovered enough to say, "Dad, sit down. Mother, you too." When they both sank into chairs, Katie opened her mouth to speak, realized that her mother was holding both liquor bottles propped erectly on her knees, and pried them from her fingers. "Here, mom, give me these before you hurt yourself."

Having relieved her mother of both weapons, Katie straightened, tried to think of how to begin, rubbed her palms against her peach-clad thighs, and cast a helpless look of appeal to Ramon.

Ramon put his arm around Katie's slim waist, ignoring her father's furious scowl at the gesture, and said calmly to him, "Katie has agreed to return to Puerto Rico with me on Sunday, where we will be married. I realize that this is difficult for you to accept, but it will mean a great deal to Katie to know that she has your support in what she is doing."

"Well, she sure as hell isn't going to get it!" her father snapped.

"In that case," Ramon said evenly, "you will be forcing her to choose between us, and we will both lose. She will still come with me, but she will hate me for causing a rift between the two of you—and she will hate you also, for not understanding and wishing her happiness. It is important to me that Katie be happy."

"It happens to be damned important to us, too," Mr. Connelly grated. "Just exactly what kind of life can you give her, living on some two-bit farm in Puerto Rico?"

Katie saw Ramon pale, and she could have strangled her father for trampling on Ramon's pride like this. But when Ramon answered, his voice was composed. "She will have only a small cottage in which to live, but the roof does not leak. She will always have food to eat and clothing to wear. And I will give her children. Beyond that, I can promise Katie nothing—except that she will awaken every single day of her life knowing that she is loved.''

Katie's mother's eyes filled with tears, the hostility was draining from her face as she stared at Ramon. ''Oh my God . . .'' she whispered.

Katie's father, however, was just warming up for battle. ''So, Katie will be a drudge, a farm wife, is that it?''

''No, she will be my wife.''

''And work like the wife of a farmer!'' her father said contemptuously.

Ramon's jaw clenched and he turned even paler. ''She will have some work to do, yes.''

''Are you aware, Mr. Galverra, that Katie has been to a farm only once in her entire life? I happen to recall the event very vividly.'' His relentless gaze swerved to his startled daughter. ''Do you want to tell him about it, Katherine, or shall I?''

''Dad, I was only twelve years old!''

''So were your three friends, Katherine. But they didn't scream when the farmer wrung the chicken's neck. They didn't call him a murderer at his own table and refuse to eat chicken for two years. They didn't find the horses 'smelly'; the process of milking a cow 'gross'; and a multimillion-dollar farm 'a great big stinking place filled with filthy animals.' ''

''Well,'' Katie shot back mutinously, ''they didn't happen to fall into a pile of manure, get bitten by a goose, or kicked by a blind horse, either!'' Turning swiftly to Ramon to try to defend herself, Katie was amazed to find him looking down at her with a crooked grin.

"You're laughing now, Galverra," Mr. Connelly said angrily, "but you won't be laughing when you discover that Katie's idea of living within a strict budget is spending everything she makes and charging anything else she wants to my account. She can't cook anything that doesn't come in a bag, box or can; she doesn't know which end of a needle to thread; she—"

"Ryan, you are exaggerating!" Mrs. Connelly unexpectedly intervened. "Katie has lived on her own income since the day she graduated from college, and she does know how to sew."

Ryan Connelly looked ready to explode. "She does petitpoint or some damn thing like that. And not well! I still don't know whether that thing she did for us is supposed to be a fish or an owl, and neither do you!"

Katie's shoulders began to shake with helpless mirth. "It's a—a mushroom," she croaked, turning into Ramon's willing arms and dissolving with laughter. "I—I made it when I was fourteen." Wiping at her tears of hilarity, she leaned back in Ramon's embrace and raised her sparkling eyes to his. "Do you know—I thought they were going to think *you* weren't good enough for *me*."

"What we think," Ryan Connelly snapped, "is—"

"Is that Katie is ill-equipped for the kind of life she would have to lead with you, Mr. Galverra," Mrs. Connelly interrupted her husband's outburst. "Katie's 'working' experience has been at college and in her job, the sort of work that is done with the mind, not the hands and back. She graduated with high honors from college, and I know how hard she works at the job she has. But Katie has absolutely no experience with backbreaking physical labor.''

''Nor will she have, being married to me,'' Ramon replied.

Ryan Connelly was evidently finished with trying to be reasonable. He jerked to his feet, took two long furious strides, then swung around glaring at Ramon with anger emanating from every pore. ''I misjudged you the other day at our house, Galverra. I thought to myself that there was pride in you, and honor, but I was wrong.''

Beside her, Katie felt Ramon go absolutely rigid as her father continued his blistering tirade. ''Oh, I knew you were poor—you said as much, but still I gave you credit for having some decency. Yet you stand here and tell us that although you can offer her nothing, you are going to take our daughter from us, take her from everything she knows, take her from her family, her friends—I ask you, is this the action of a decent honorable man? You answer me that, if you dare.''

Katie, about to intercede, took one look at Ramon's murderous expression and stepped back. In a low, terrible voice, he drawled contemptuously, ''I would take Katie away from my own brother! Is *that* answer enough for you?''

''Yes, by God, it's enough! It tells me what kind of—''

''Sit down, Ryan,'' Mrs. Connelly said sharply. ''Katie, you and Ramon go into the kitchen and fix our drinks. I would like to speak to your father privately."

Shamelessly eavesdropping in the doorway while Ramon fixed the drinks, Katie watched her mother walk over to her father and put her hand on his arm. "We've lost the battle, Ryan, and you're antagonizing the victor. That man is trying very hard not to fight you, yet you're deliberately backing him into a corner until he has no choice but to retaliate."

"He's not the victor yet, dammit! Not till Katie gets on that plane with him. Until then, he's the enemy, but he's no victor."

Mrs. Connelly smiled gently. "He's no enemy of ours. At least, he's no enemy of mine. He hasn't been since the moment he looked at you and told you that Katie will live every day of her life knowing that she is loved."

"Words! Nothing but words!"

"Spoken to us, Ryan. Spoken sincerely and without embarrassment to Katie's parents—not whispered to her in some heated moment. I can't even think of a man who would say a thing like that to a girl's parents. He'll never let her be hurt. He won't be able to give her the material things, but he'll give her everything in life that really matters. I know he will. Now give in gracefully, or you'll lose even more." When her husband looked away from her, she touched his face, turning it toward her.

His deep blue eyes, so like Katie's, were suspiciously moist. "Ryan," she said softly, "It's not really the man himself that you object to, is it?"

He sighed, a deep ragged sigh. "No," he said in a

hoarse voice. "It's not the man, not really. It's just that I—I don't want him to take my Katie away. She's always been my favorite, you know that, Rosemary. She was the only one of our children who ever gave a damn about *me*; the only one who ever saw me as something beside an open wallet; the only one who ever noticed when I was tired or worried and tried to cheer me up." He drew a long, labored breath. "Katie's been like a ray of sunlight in my life, and if he takes her away, I won't be able to see my Katie shine anymore."

Katie, unaware that Ramon had come to stand behind her, leaned her head against the doorframe, tears streaming unchecked down her cheeks.

Tipping up his wife's chin, Ryan took out his handkerchief and dabbed at the tears on her face. Mrs. Connelly managed a smile. "We should have expected this...it's exactly the sort of thing Katie would do. She was always so full of joy and love, so ready to give of herself. She always befriended the child no one would play with, and there was never a stray dog that Katie didn't fall in love with. Until now, I thought David had destroyed that beautiful, giving part of her, and I've hated him for it...but he didn't." Tears spilled over her lashes, glittering on her cheeks. "Oh, Ryan, don't you see—Katie's found another stray she loves."

"The last one bit her," Ryan chuckled sadly.

"This one won't," his wife said. "He'll protect her."

Holding his tearful wife in his arms, Ryan glanced across the room and saw that Katie was likewise crying in Ramon's arms, his handkerchief clutched in her hand. With a fleeting smile of conciliation at the tall man who held his daughter so protectively close, Ryan said, "Ramon, do you have a spare handkerchief?"

The brief flash of Ramon's smile accepted the truce. "For the women, or for us?"

WHEN HER PARENTS LEFT, Ramon asked to use the telephone and Katie went out to the patio so that he could have privacy to make his call. She wandered around, absently touching the plants growing in huge redwood containers, then perched a hip on the back of one of the lounge chairs, gazing up at the stars spilling like diamonds across the sky.

Ramon came to the open glass door and stopped, arrested by the sheer beauty of the picture she made. Lamplight from within the apartment silhouetted her against the black velvet night. With her hair falling in a loose, glorious tumble down her shoulders, there was a lush ripeness in her profile, combined with a quiet pride in the tilt of her chin that added to her allure, making her seem at once provocative and elusive.

Sensing his presence, Katie turned her head slightly. "Is something wrong?" she asked, thinking of his phone call.

"Yes," he said with tender gravity. "I am afraid that if I come any closer I will discover that you are only a dream."

A smile that was sweet yet sensual touched Katie's lips. "I'm very real."

"Angels are not real. No man can expect to reach out and take an angel in his arms."

Her smile widened delightfully. "When you kiss me, my thoughts are anything but angelic."

Stepping onto the patio he crossed to her, his eyes looking deeply into hers. "And what are your thoughts when you sit alone out here gazing up at the sky like a goddess worshiping the stars?"

Just the timbre of his deep quiet voice stirred Katie; yet now that she had committed herself to him she felt a peculiar shyness. "I was thinking how unbelievable it is that in just seven days my entire life has changed. No, not seven days, seven seconds. The moment you asked me for directions, my whole life veered onto a different course. I keep wondering what would have happened if I had walked down that hall five minutes later."

Ramon drew her gently to her feet. "Do you not believe in fate, Katie?"

"Only when things go wrong."

"And when they go beautifully?"

Katie's eyes danced. "Then, it's because of my clever planning and hard work."

"Thank you," he said with a boyish grin.

"For what?"

"For all of the times in the last seven days that you have made me smile." His lips covered hers in a warm, sweet kiss.

Katie realized that he had no intention of making love to her tonight, and she was grateful and touched by his restraint. She was emotionally spent and physically exhausted.

"What are your plans for tomorrow?" she asked a few minutes later, when he was leaving.

"My time is yours," Ramon said. "I had intended to leave for Puerto Rico tomorrow. Since we will not be leaving until Sunday, the only commitment I have here is to breakfast with your father in the morning."

"Would you like to take me to work tomorrow morning before you meet him?" Katie asked. "It will give us some time together and you could pick me up afterward."

Ramon's arms tightened around her. "Yes," he whispered.

CHAPTER NINE

KATIE SAT AT HER DESK idly rolling her pen between
her fingers. Virginia was attending the Friday morning operations meeting, which gave Katie until ten-
thirty to make up her mind. An hour and a half to
decide whether to resign her job or request two
weeks' vacation and two additional weeks' leave of
absence without pay.

She knew what Ramon wanted—no, expected—
her to do. He expected her to resign, to make the
break and sever all ties. If she merely requested a
month off instead of resigning, he would feel that
she was not committing herself wholeheartedly to
him, that she was keeping an avenue of escape open
to her.

Her mind drifted back to the way Ramon had
looked at her this morning when he arrived to take
her to work. His dark eyes had studied her face with
piercing intensity. "Have you changed your mind?"
he had asked, and when Katie replied that she
hadn't, he had gathered her into his arms and kissed
her with a mixture of violent sweetness and profound relief.

Each moment she spent with Ramon she grew
closer to him emotionally. Her heart, for whatever
reasons, kept telling her that he was right for her,

that what she was doing was right. Her mind, however, was screaming warnings at her. It told her this was happening too fast, too soon, and worse, kept tormenting her that Ramon was not what he seemed to be, that he was hiding something from her.

Katie's blue eyes clouded. This morning he had arrived wearing a beautiful loose-sleeved gold golf sweater. Twice before he had worn well-tailored business suits. It seemed so peculiar that a farmer, particularly an impoverished one, would own such clothes that Katie had bluntly asked him about it.

Ramon had smilingly informed her that farmers owned suits and sweaters just like other men. Katie had tentatively accepted that answer, but when she tried to find out more about him, he had evaded her questions by saying, "Katie, you will have many questions about me and about your future, but the answers are all in Puerto Rico."

Leaning back in her chair, Katie somberly watched the controlled bustle of activity in the personnel reception area where applicants were filling out forms, taking tests and waiting to see Katie or one of her five male counterparts who all reported to Ginny.

Perhaps she was wrong to be uneasy about Ramon. Perhaps he wasn't being deliberately evasive. Perhaps this niggling, persistent fear was simply the result of her gruesome experience with marriage to David Caldwell.

Then again, maybe it wasn't. She would have to find out in Puerto Rico, but until all her fears were resolved, she could not risk resigning her job. If she

did resign today she would be resigning without notice. If she resigned without notice, she would not be
eligible for rehire at Technical Dynamics, nor would
she get a good reference from them if she tried to go
to work for another employer. Besides, Virginia
would look like an absolute fool when she had to explain to the vice-president of operations, who had
just approved Katie's enormous raise, that Katie,
Virginia's own protégée, had resigned without notice—like the most irresponsible transient who swept
the floors.

Katie stood up, absently ran a smoothing hand
over her elegant chignon, and walked out into the
reception area, past Donna and the two other secretaries who worked in personnel. Going into one of
the cubicles where typing tests were given, she rolled
a clean sheet of paper into the electric typewriter and
stared at it, her hands poised indecisively over the
keys.

Ramon was expecting her to resign. He had said
he loved her. Equally as important, Katie sensed instinctively that he needed her; he needed her very
much. She felt disloyal merely taking a month off.
She considered lying to him about it, but honesty
mattered very much to Ramon and it was something
that mattered a great deal to Katie, too. She didn't
want to lie to him. On the other hand, after she had
agreed last night to go to Puerto Rico and marry
him, she couldn't imagine how to explain her doubts
and misgivings this morning. She wasn't even certain it would be wise to tell him how she felt yet. If
she had told David that she suspected some hidden

side to his character, he would have gone out of his way to conceal it and convince her otherwise. It seemed far better to simply go to Puerto Rico and give herself time to know Ramon better. With time, her doubts would either be resolved or her suspicions would be confirmed.

Sighing, Katie tried to think of a better excuse to give Ramon for her decision not to resign. It came to her in a flash of inspiration. It was the truth; it relieved all her feelings of disloyalty to Ramon, and it was something she would be able to make him understand. It was so obvious that Katie was amazed she had even considered resigning without notice.

Quickly and efficiently she typed out a formal request to Virginia for two weeks' vacation beginning the next day, followed by two weeks' leave of absence without pay. Tonight she would simply explain to Ramon that she could not possibly have resigned without notice in order to get married. Men did not resign without notice to get married, and if Katie did it would reflect badly on all the other women who were struggling so desperately for an equal opportunity to obtain positions in management. One of the most frequent arguments against hiring a woman in a management position was that they quit to get married or to have babies or to follow their husband when he was transferred. The director of operations was a closet male chauvinist. If Katie resigned without notice to get married, he would never let poor Virginia forget it, and he'd find some legally acceptable reason to disqualify any other female candidate Virginia wanted to hire for Katie's job. If, on the other hand, Katie resigned while on vacation in Puerto Rico, the two weeks remaining to her as leave of absence would constitute two weeks' notice. That meant she would have only two weeks to resolve her fear about marrying Ramon.

Nevertheless, Katie felt tremendously relieved. Now that she'd thought about it rationally, she decided that when and if she did resign while in Puerto Rico, she would not say that she was doing so to get married. She would say what men always said: she was resigning "to accept a better position."

Having decided that, Katie wound another sheet of paper into the typewriter, and dating it two weeks hence, formally resigned in order to accept a better position.

It was nearly eleven-thirty before Katie was finished with the applicants she was scheduled to interview. Picking up her vacation request and her postdated resignation, she walked into Virginia's office, then hesitated.

Virginia was engrossed in recording figures on a huge ledger sheet, her dark head of short-cropped hair bent over the task. She looked, as she always did, businesslike and feminine. *The Dainty Dynamo*, Katie thought with affection.

Straightening her navy blazer and smoothing the pleats of her red-and-blue-plaid skirt, Katie plunged in. "Ginny, can you spare me a few minutes?" she asked nervously, using the nickname she ordinarily used only after business hours.

"If it's not urgent, give me half an hour to finish this report first," Ginny replied without looking up.

With each second Katie's tension was mounting. She didn't think she could last another half hour. "It—it's rather important."

At the shakiness in Katie's voice, Ginny quickly raised her head. Very slowly, she laid her pen on the desk and watched Katie approach, her forehead creased with puzzled concern.

Now that the time had come, Katie couldn't think how to begin. She handed Virginia her vacation-leave-of-absence request.

Virginia scanned it, the vague alarm clearing from her forehead. "It's short notice to request a month off," Ginny said, laying the paper aside. "But you're entitled to the vacation, so I'll approve it. Why are you also requesting two weeks' leave of absence?"

Katie sank into the chair in front of Virginia's desk. "I want to go to Puerto Rico with Ramon. While I'm there I'll decide whether or not to marry him. In case I do decide to do that—here's my resignation. The two weeks' leave of absence can serve as my notice, that is, if you'll let me do it that way."

Virginia sank back in her chair and stared at Katie in astonishment. "Who?" she said.

"The man we talked about on Wednesday." When Virginia continued to stare at her incredulously, Katie explained, "Ramon has a small farm in Puerto Rico. He wants me to marry him and live there."

Virginia said "My God."

Katie, who had never seen Virginia like this, added helpfully, "He's Spanish, actually."

Virginia said "My God" again.

"Ginny!" Katie implored desperately. "I know this is sudden, but it's not that unbelievable. It's—"

"Insane," Virginia announced flatly, at last recovering her brisk composure. She shook her head as if to clear it. "Katie, when you mentioned this man two days ago I imagined him as not only handsome, but having a style and sophistication to match yours. Now you tell me that he's a Puerto Rican farmer, and you're going to be his wife?"

Katie nodded.

"I think you've lost your mind, but at least you have sense enough not to resign and burn all your bridges behind you. In four weeks, or much less, you'll regret this insanely romantic—and utterly absurd—impulse. You know I'm right or you wouldn't be asking for a leave, you'd be resigning."

"It isn't insane and it isn't an impulse," Katie said, her eyes pleading with Ginny to understand. "Ramon is different—"

"I'll bet he is!" Ginny agreed disdainfully. "Latin men are impossibly chauvinistic."

Katie ignored that because she already knew that Ramon was very Latin and very chauvinistic. "Ramon is special," she said, embarrassed at trying to put the way she felt about him into words, "He makes me feel special, too. He isn't shallow or self-centered like most of the men I've known." Seeing that Ginny was no more convinced than she was before, Katie added, "Ginny, he loves me; I can feel that he does. And he needs me. I—"

"Of course he needs you!" Ginny scoffed. "He's a small-time farmer who can't afford to pay for a cook, housekeeper and bedmate. Therefore, he needs a wife, who for the mere cost of her room and board will be all three." Instantly, Ginny held up an apologetic hand. "I'm sorry Katie, I shouldn't have said that. I shouldn't impose my own views of matrimony on you. It's just that I honestly feel you could never be content with that sort of life, not when you've had this."

"This isn't enough for me, Ginny," Katie said with quiet assurance. "Long before I met Ramon, I felt that way. I can't seem to be happy devoting all my time to me—my career, my next promotion, my future. It isn't that it's a lonely life, because I'm not lonely at all. It's an empty life; I feel useless and meaningless."

"Do you know how many women long for exactly what you have? Do you know how many women wish they had only themselves to think about?"

Katie nodded, uncomfortably aware that she was indirectly rejecting Ginny's way of life, as well as her own. "I know. Maybe it would be right for them. It isn't right for me."

Ginny glanced at her watch and regretfully stood up. "I've got to hurry, I'm due at a meeting downtown, and I won't be back until after you've left. Don't worry about calling me within two weeks. Give yourself all four of those weeks. If you decide to resign, I'll simply put this in your file and say that you gave it to me in advance. It's bending company policy, but what are friends for?'' She skimmed the letter and smiled at Katie's reason for resignation. '' 'To accept a better position,' '' she quoted. ''Very nicely done.''

Katie stood up, too, her eyes aching with sentimental tears. ''In that case, I guess this is goodbye.''

''No, Katie,'' Ginny said with a laugh as she began shoving papers into her slim briefcase. ''Two weeks from now you'll begin getting bored. Four weeks from now you'll miss the challenge of your career. You'll be back. In the meantime, have a nice vacation—that's all you really needed, anyway. You're just a little tired. I'll see you in a month—or sooner.''

At 5:05 KATIE plunged through the revolving glass doors and dashed across the pavement to where Ramon had pulled the car up at the curb to wait for her. She slid into the seat, bravely met his inquiring look and said, ''I took a month's vacation instead of resigning.''

His jaw tightened and Katie twisted in her seat to face him. ''The reason I did was that—''

''Not now!'' he snapped curtly. ''We will discuss it when we get to your apartment.''

They walked into her apartment together, neither of them having spoken a word during the thirty-five-minute ride home. Katie's frayed nerves stretched taut as she put her purse down, shrugged out of the navy blazer, and turned toward him. Aware of his smoldering anger, she asked cautiously, ''Where do you want me to begin?''

His hands shot out, gripping her arms. "Begin with why," he ordered harshly, giving her a shake. "Tell me why!"

Katie managed to keep her fear-widened blue eyes on his. "Please don't look at me this way. I know you're hurt and you're angry, but you shouldn't be." Reaching out, she ran her hands up beneath the soft material of his gold golf sweater, her palms flattened against his muscular chest, trying somehow to soothe and gentle him.

The gesture backfired. Ramon jerked her hands away. "Do not try to distract me with your touch, it will not work. This is not a game we are playing!"

"I'm not playing games!" Katie shot back, pulling her hands from his grip with a strength that was fortified by her own simmering anger. "If I wanted to play games with you, I would have lied and told you that I had resigned." Stalking away from him to the center of the room, Katie stopped and whirled around. "I decided to request four weeks off so that I could resign from Puerto Rico for several very important reasons.

"In the first place, Virginia Johnson is not only my boss, she is someone whom I like and respect immensely. If I resign without notice, I'll make Ginny look like a complete fool."

Katie's chin lifted stubbornly as she continued her angry, impassioned speech. "And what about the men? If I quit without notice, it gives them all a perfect reason to feel vindicated and superior because *men* don't run off to get married. I absolutely refuse to be a traitor to my own sex! So...when I resign from Puerto Rico *with notice* I will say that I am leaving to 'accept a better position.' Which I happen to think being your wife is!'' Katie finished defiantly.

"Thank you,'' Ramon said almost humbly. Smiling, he started walking toward her.

Katie, who had worked herself into a fine temper, began backing away. "I haven't finished yet,'' she said, her color gloriously high, her eyes stormy with hurt indignation. "You told me you wanted honesty from me at all times, and when I was honest you bullied and intimidated me. If I'm supposed to be completely truthful, I have to know that no matter how bad the truth is, you aren't going to get angry with me for telling it to you. You were unfair and unreasonable a few minutes ago, and I think you have an impossible temper!''

"Are you finished now?'' Ramon asked her gently.

"No, I'm not!'' Katie said, all but stamping her foot. "When I touched you, I was only trying to feel close to you. I wasn't playing games and I hated the way you treated me!'' Having now exhausted her complaints, Katie glowered past his shoulder, refusing to meet his gaze.

Ramon's voice was coaxing and deep. "Would you like to touch me now?''

"Not in the least.''

"Even if I say that I am very sorry, and that I want you to touch me?''

"No.''

"You no longer wish to be close to me, Katie?''

"No, I don't."

"Look at me." Ramon's fingers touched her chin, turning her face up to his. "I hurt you, and now you have hurt me back, and we both ache. We can either strike out at each other in our pain until our anger is spent, or we can stop now and begin to teach each other how to heal our hurts. I do not know which way you want it."

Gazing up into his intent eyes Katie realized that he meant that literally; he wanted her to decide whether to turn their battle into a war that would last until their tempers were exhausted, or else tell him what to do or say to soothe her. Katie stared, the gracefully feminine curves of her face vulnerable and uncertain, her eyes deep blue with confusion. Finally she swallowed and bravely said, "I—I would like you to put your arms around me."

With aching gentleness, Ramon drew her into the circle of his arms.

"And I would like you to kiss me."

"How?" he breathed softly.

"With your lips," Katie answered, confused by the question.

His mouth brushed hers sensuously, his lips warm but not parted.

"And your tongue," she clarified breathlessly.

"Will you give me yours?" he asked, beginning to tell her how he wanted his hurt soothed.

Katie nodded, and his mouth opened hungrily over hers, their tongues tangling and caressing. His hands stroked restlessly over her shoulders and back, then down her spine, forcing her hips hard against his pulsing thighs. His mouth devoured hers as he pulled her down onto the sofa to lie across his lap, his fingers fumbling with the tiny buttons on her silk blouse. Impatient with the buttons, his hand returned to her breasts. "Unfasten them," he said in a low, urgent voice.

It seemed to take Katie forever to unbutton her blouse because her hands were trembling, and Ramon never stopped kissing her. When the last one was finally undone, he pulled his mouth from hers and whispered unsteadily, "I want you to take it off for me."

Katie's heart began hammering as she pulled her arms from the sleeves, letting the white silk slide through her shaking fingers. Ramon's gaze dipped to her lacy bra. "That, too."

With fire racing through every nerve in her body, Katie unclipped her bra and slowly slid it down her arms. The ivory globes of her breasts swelled proudly beneath his possessive gaze, her nipples slowly hardening as if his fingers, rather than just his eyes, were touching them. Ramon watched them, his eyes burning with passion, his voice rough with it. "I want to see my baby at your breast."

Katie's embarrassment over her body's obvious response to him was eclipsed by the violent yearnings surging through her. Drawing a quivering breath, she said, "Right now, I would rather see you there."

"Give it to me, Katie."

An uncontrollable inner excitement shook her as she curved a hand around his nape, pulling his dark head down and simultaneously lifting her breast, offering her nipple to him. When Ramon began to suck on it, she almost screamed with the raw pleasure. By the time his lips released her, desire was running through her veins like molten steel. "Give me the other one," he ordered thickly.

Katie tremblingly cupped her other breast and lifted it to his mouth. The moment his lips covered it, flames shot through her. "Please stop," she cried softly. "I need you, I can't stand any more."

"You can't?" he breathed, swiftly lowering her to lie on the sofa, his mouth exquisitely exploring her ear, the curve of her neck and cheek, as he lay down beside her. Lost in a frenzy of rampaging desire, Katie felt his hands sliding up under her skirt, pulling the elastic lace band of her panties down from her hips to her lower thighs.

Ramon groaned softly as his fingers traced between her thighs. "You *want* me," he corrected. "You want me but you do not need me yet," he breathed, plundering her mouth with demanding insistence.

Katie was almost sobbing with desire for his possession, her hands feverishly rushing over the taut muscles of his back and shoulders. "I need you," she whispered fiercely, crushing her parted lips to his. "Please—"

Ramon raised his head and said almost gruffly, "You do not need me." Taking one of her hands from around his neck, he pressed it tightly against his rigid arousal. "*That* is need, Katie."

Opening her desire-glazed eyes, Katie focused on

his strained face as he said, "You *want* me when I take you in my arms, but I *need* you every moment of every hour. It is an ache that never leaves me; a longing to make you mine that ties me into knots." Abruptly he asked, "Do you know what fear is?"

Bewildered by his sudden change of subject, Katie searched his handsome somber features, but did not attempt to reply.

"Fear is knowing that I have no right to want you, and knowing that I cannot stop myself. Fear is dreading the moment when you will see the small cottage where you will have to live and decide you do not want me enough to live there."

"Don't think that way," Katie pleaded, her fingers smoothing the short hair at his temple. "Please don't."

"Fear is lying awake at night, wondering if you will decide not to marry me, and wondering how I will bear the pain." Gently, he brushed away the tear that trickled from the corner of Katie's eye. "I am afraid of losing you, and if it makes me 'unreasonable' and bad-tempered, then I humbly apologize. It is only because I am afraid."

Melting with tenderness, Katie laid her hand against his jaw and gazed deeply into his dark eyes. "In my whole life," she whispered, "I have never known a man with enough courage to admit he's afraid."

"Katie...." Her name was a hoarse groan that tore from his chest as his mouth came down hard and hungry on hers, his lips and hands fiercely urgent now, guiding her toward the peak of fulfillment, driving her as close to the edge as she was deliberately driving him. And then the doorbell rang.

"Don't answer it!" Katie implored when he immediately pulled out of her arms and sat up. "They'll go away."

Slanting her a rueful smile, Ramon combed his hand through the side of his thick hair, restoring it to order. "No, they will not. In the...excitement...I forgot to tell you that your parents were coming over to help us pack and then have dinner with us."

Katie jackknifed to her feet, scooping up her clothing as she dashed to the bedroom. "Hurry and let them in or they'll guess what we were doing," Katie told him when she saw that Ramon was merely standing near the sofa, his hands on his hips.

"Katie," he said with a wicked grin, "if I let them in too quickly, they will *see* what we were doing."

"What?" she asked, standing in the doorway to her room, her perplexed gaze sweeping over the sofa for incriminating evidence, then the floor, then over Ramon. "Oh!" she said, blushing like a schoolgirl.

Katie pulled off her clothes in mad haste, telling herself that she was being absolutely absurd. She was twenty-three years old, she had been married before, and she was going to marry Ramon. No doubt her parents assumed they had already made love many times. After all, her parents were modern, sensible people. Very modern and sensible—except where their children's behavior was concerned.

Exactly four minutes after the doorbell rang,

Katie strolled out of her room wearing tan slacks and a soft cream jersey turtleneck, her hair brushed into a shining mantle around her shoulders. She managed to give her mother a cheery greeting, but her face was still slightly flushed, her eyes suspiciously languorous, and inwardly she was trembling with little aftershocks of desire.

She found Ramon, who appeared to be feeling none of her sensual sensitivity, fixing drinks for the four of them in the kitchen, laughing about something with her father. "I'll bring these drinks into the living room," Ryan Connelly said, picking up two glasses. Turning, he discovered his bemused daughter staring at her fiancé's profile. "Honey, you look radiant," he said, planting an affectionate kiss on Katie's forehead. "Ramon must be good for you."

Hot color ran up under Katie's cheeks as she smiled helplessly at her father. Waiting until he vanished into the living room, Katie turned to Ramon who was putting ice into two more glasses. A smile tugged at the corner of his mouth. Without looking at her, he said, "You are blushing, *querida*. And you do look radiant."

"Thank you," Katie said in exasperated amusement. "I look as though I've been ravished, and you look as though you've been reading the newspaper! How can you be so calm?" She started to reach for the drink Ramon had just fixed her, but he put it on the counter beside his. Turning, he drew her tightly into his arms for a long, drugging kiss. "I am not calm, Katie," he whispered against her mouth, "I am starving for you."

"Katie?" her mother called from the living room, causing Katie to pull awkwardly out of Ramon's embrace. "Are you two coming in here, or should we wait out on the patio?"

"We're coming in there," Katie answered hastily. With a laughing look at Ramon, Katie said, "I once read a novel where every time the man and woman began to make love, the phone rang; someone came to the door; or something happened to stop them."

Ramon's grin was lazily amused. "It will not happen to us. I will not permit it."

CHAPTER TEN

SUNLIGHT GLINTED ON the big jet as it streaked southeastward, thirty thousand feet above the earth.

Careful not to disturb Katie who was asleep, her shining head resting against his shoulder, Ramon reached across her and pulled the shade down over the window, shielding her beautiful face from the glare of the sun. The flight had been extraordinarily rough, and many of the passengers were showing distinct signs of alarm. But not Katie, Ramon thought with a tender smile at her sleeping form. Beneath her delightfully soft, feminine exterior, Ramon was discovering that she possessed tremendous courage, strength and determination.

Even yesterday and today, when her parents' obvious sadness over her impending departure had placed a terrible burden of guilt on Katie's slim shoulders, she had borne their unhappiness with calm understanding and smiling resolve, despite the emotional strain Ramon could see she was feeling.

On Friday night Katie's parents had volunteered to handle the subletting of her apartment and to pack the rest of her belongings for shipment to Puerto Rico. Then they had insisted that she spend the weekend at their home instead of her apartment.

Although he had also stayed there over the weekend, Ramon had not had either the opportunity or the excuse to be alone with her since Friday.

As the hours had passed, he had watched Katie's tension mounting, bracing himself for the time when she would weigh her uncertain future with him against the love and security her parents and job still offered, and tell him she had changed her mind about going to Puerto Rico. Selfishly, he had longed to get her back to her apartment and into his arms where, with time and privacy, he knew he could make her passion overwhelm her mind. Yet, even without the physical stimulus of desire, Katie hadn't wavered in her brave resolve to leave with him.

Her long curly lashes made shadows on her creamy cheeks, and he pleasured himself with the sheer beauty of her profile. He was glad he had booked first-class seats for them because they were roomier. Katie had mistakenly assumed that the reason they were "lucky enough" to fly first class was that the airline had oversold the coach seats and had automatically offered them vacant first—class seats for the same price, and Ramon had let her believe it.

Bitterness seeped through him, hardening his jaw, and Ramon turned his head to stare out the window across the aisle. A few months ago he could have taken Katie to Puerto Rico in Galverra International's private Boeing 727 jet, with its splendid bedroom, dining room and spacious living room, all furnished in magnificent antiques and carpeted in white. Katie would have enjoyed that, Ramon thought. But she would have been more thrilled with his own sleek Lear jet, which he had flown into St. Louis and which was now in a hangar at the St. Louis airport.

The Lear was his plane, not the corporation's, but like everything else he owned, including the houses, the island and the yacht, he had put the small jet up as collateral against loans the corporation had needed and now could not repay. What would have been the point of flying Katie to Puerto Rico in the Lear today, of giving her a taste of the luxurious life he could have offered her—when doing so would only make the life he was now able to afford appear even more drab and impoverished by comparison?

Wearily, he leaned his head against the back of his seat and closed his eyes. He had no right to ask Katie to share his exile, to take her from her fashionable apartment, her career, and ask her to live on a farm in a renovated cottage. It was selfish and wrong of him, but he couldn't bear to think of life without her. Once he could have given her everything, now he could give her nothing—not even honesty. Not yet.

Tomorrow he was scheduled for several meetings, one of which was with his accountant, and he was clinging to the slender hope that his personal financial situation might not be as disastrous as it now seemed. After the meeting he would know exactly where he stood, and then he would have to find some way to explain to Katie who he was and what he had been. He had insisted on honesty between them, and although he had not actually lied to her, he now owed her the truth—the whole truth. The thought of telling Katie that he was a failure twisted his insides into knots. He didn't care if the whole world thought of him that way, but it hurt unbearably to know he would be a failure in Katie's eyes.

It had been bad enough explaining the situation to Katie's father at breakfast Friday morning. Fondness for his future father-in-law softened Ramon's taut features as he recalled the unexpectedly hostile beginning of that meal.

When Ramon had walked into the private men's club where they had agreed to meet, Ryan Connelly had been waiting for him with suppressed anger radiating from his entire body. "What the hell kind of game are you playing, Galverra?" the older man had demanded in a low, furious voice as soon as Ramon sat down. "You're no more a small-time Puerto Rican farmer than I am. It's been driving me crazy why you looked so familiar to me. It wasn't just your name that seemed familiar, it was your face. Last night I remembered the article about you in *Time* Magazine, and—"

As Ramon had explained to Katie's father about the impending collapse of Galverra International, Ryan Connelly's fury had given way first to amazement and then to compassionate understanding. Ramon had tried not to smile when Katie's father volunteered financial help. Ryan Connelly was a wealthy man, but as Ramon had explained to him, it would take one hundred investors like Ryan to shore up Galverra International. Otherwise it would still collapse beneath its own weight and take everyone who had invested in the corporation with it.

The big jet dropped sickeningly into a powerful downdraft, then soared upward with a stomach-tightening lurch. "Are we landing?" Katie mumbled.

"No," Ramon said. He brushed his lips against her fragrant hair. "Go back to sleep. I will awaken you when we begin our final approach at Miami." Obediently, Katie closed her eyes and snuggled closer to him.

The cockpit door opened and the pilot started down the aisle toward the rest room. The passenger seated in front of Ramon stopped him with some questions and as the pilot bent down to reply, Ramon watched his eyes rove appreciatively over Katie's face, lingering there as he answered. Ramon felt a flash of annoyance that he immediately recognized as jealousy.

Jealousy—another new emotion with which he must learn to cope because of Katie. After bestowing a glacial look on the unfortunate pilot, Ramon reached for Katie's hand and laced his fingers through hers. He sighed. At this rate, jealousy was going to be his constant companion.

Just walking through the airport with her and watching the men who turned to stare as she passed had set his teeth on edge. Dressed in a turquoise silk dress that showed off her long, shapely legs in their high heels, she looked like a model. No—the models he had known did not have Katie's lush curves or elegant perfection of features. They had glamour. Katie had beauty.

Katie flexed his fingers, and Ramon realized that

he'd been possessively tightening his grip on her hand. Lightly, sensuously, he stroked his thumb against her palm. Even in her sleep Katie responded to his touch and moved closer against him. God, how he wanted her! Just having her nestled against his shoulder made him throb with desire and ache with tenderness.

Leaning his head back, Ramon closed his eyes and sighed with profound pleasure. He had done it! He had actually gotten Katie on this plane with him! She was coming to Puerto Rico. She was going to be his. He admired her independence and intelligence, and he adored the vulnerability and softness within her. She was the embodiment of everything he liked in women: she was feminine without being vapid or helpless; proud without being haughty; assertive without being aggressive. Sexually, she was liberated in her thinking but not her actions, which pleased him immensely. He knew he would have hated it if Katie had casually given her beautiful body to other men. She was infinitely more special, more precious to him because she had chosen not to indulge in casual sex. Which, he supposed, made him guilty of applying the double standard for men and women's morality, considering the number of women from St. Moritz to St. Croix he'd had in the last decade.

Ramon smiled inwardly, thinking of how irate Katie would be if she knew he felt this way about her morals. She would accuse him of being everything from outrageously old-fashioned to hopelessly Latin, which was rather humorous, because he suspected that the reason Katie was drawn to him was—

The brief pleasure he'd been feeling was promptly strangled by the same doubt that had been winding tighter and tighter within him for the past several days. He didn't know why Katie was drawn to him. He didn't know why she thought she should marry him, had no idea what reasons she was giving herself for doing so. The only valid reason would be that she loved him.

But she didn't.

Mentally, Ramon recoiled from that truth, yet he knew he had to face it and come to terms with it. Not once had Katie so much as mentioned the word *love*. Three nights ago, when he had told her that he loved her, the words had burst out of him, yet Katie had chosen to act as if she hadn't heard him. How ironic that when, for the first time in his life, he told a woman he loved her, she hadn't even been able to say she loved him, too.

Grimly, he wondered if this was fate's way of repaying him for all the times women had said they loved him and he had responded with silence, or a noncommittal smile, because he refused to claim an emotion he didn't feel.

If Katie didn't think she loved him, why was she on this plane? Sexually, she wanted him, he knew that. From the first moment he had taken her into his arms he had been forcing her to want him more, relentlessly fanning the flames of her body's desire for his. Apparently passion was the only thing she felt for him; desire her only reason for being on this plane.

No, dammit! That couldn't be true. Katie was too

intelligent to consider marrying him solely for sexual gratification. She must feel something else for him. After all, there had always been a tremendous magnetic pull between them, and it was emotional as well as physical. If she didn't love him, could he possibly bind her to him with her body alone? Even if he was able to, could he bear to live with her, knowing his feelings for her were so much deeper than hers for him?

CHAPTER ELEVEN

RETURNING FROM THE LADIES' ROOM in San Juan airport, Katie made her way toward the baggage claim area where the luggage was arriving from their Miami–San Juan flight.

A thrill of anticipation danced up her spine as she listened to the tide of incomprehensible rapid-fire Spanish interspersed with English, being spoken all around her. To her left, a group of distinguished, fair-haired men were speaking what Katie was certain must be Swedish. Behind her was a large cluster of tourists conversing in flowing French. Puerto Rico, she realized with surprised delight, must be a vacation place for more than just Americans.

She scanned the throngs of people and saw Ramon nod toward a porter who immediately changed direction, wheeled his trolley over to Ramon, and began loading Katie's six Gucci suitcases onto it. Katie smiled to herself because everyone else was waving frantically and calling to the busy porters, trying to attract their attention, but Ramon merely had to incline his head. And no wonder, she thought with pride. Dressed in a dark business suit and conservative tie, Ramon was the most impressive-looking man Katie had ever seen. There was an aura of implacable authority and calm purposefulness about him that even a porter couldn't miss. Looking at him, Katie thought he resembled an affluent business executive, not a struggling local farmer. She supposed the porter must have thought so, too, and was probably expecting a handsome tip for his services. Uncomfortably, Katie wondered if Ramon realized that.

Why hadn't she suggested that they carry their own luggage? Between them, they could have managed in two or three trips since Ramon was traveling with only one large suitcase and a smaller one. She was going to have to learn to be thrifty, to remember that Ramon had very little money, that he even drove a truck to earn extra.

"Ready?" Ramon asked, placing his hand beneath Katie's elbow and guiding her through the crowded airport.

Taxis were lined up outside waiting for fares. The porter started for the first one at the head of the line with Katie following beside Ramon. "Is the weather always this beautiful?" she asked, lifting her face to the azure sky decorated with fluffy white clouds.

The pleasure in Ramon's smile told her how much he wanted her to like her future home. "Usually it is. The temperature generally remains in the upper seventies, and the easterly trade winds provide a breeze that—" Ramon glanced up to see how far ahead the porter was, and whatever he'd been about to say was left unfinished.

Following his angry gaze, Katie was shocked to see their luggage being loaded into a gleaming maroon Rolls-Royce, which was waiting at the curb ahead of the line of taxis. A chauffeur wearing an immaculate black uniform and visored cap was standing at attention beside the Rolls. As they neared the car he swept open the back door with a flourish, stepping aside for them to enter.

Katie stopped short and looked inquiringly at Ramon, who snapped questions at the chauffeur in Spanish. Whatever the man replied seemed to make Ramon positively furious. Wordlessly, he put his hand against the small of Katie's back and forced her off the curb and into the cool luxury of the Rolls' white leather interior.

"What is going on?" Katie asked as soon as Ramon slid in beside her. "Whose car is this?"

Ramon waited until the chauffeur had closed the passenger door before replying. His voice was tight with the strain of controlling his inexplicable anger. "The car belongs to a man who has a villa on the island, but is rarely here. Garcia, the chauffeur, is er, an old friend of my family. When he found out we were arriving today, he decided to meet us."

"What a thoughtful thing for him to do!" Katie said brightly.

"I specifically said I did not want him to do it."

"Oh," Katie faltered. "Well, I'm sure he meant well."

Turning his attention to the chauffeur who was now seated behind the steering wheel looking expectantly into the rearview mirror, Ramon pressed a button that opened the glass partition separating the driver from his passengers. In a clipped Spanish voice he issued instructions, then the glass partition glided back into place and the Rolls slid smoothly away from the curb.

Katie had never been in a Rolls-Royce, and she was enchanted with the car. She ran her fingertips over the seat, luxuriating in the feel of unbelievably soft, white glove leather. "What's this?" she asked, leaning forward and pressing a button in the back of the driver's seat. She laughed as a small rosewood writing desk lifted electronically out of the seat and flipped down over her lap. Raising the top, she looked inside and found it equipped with thick parchment writing paper, gold pens and even a tiny gold stapler. "How do I put it back?" she asked, after trying unsuccessfully to push it into place.

"Press the same button again."

Katie did. With a faint mechanical whir the rosewood desk lifted off her lap, flipped up, and retracted into place as the concealing panel of white leather slid down to cover it. "What does that one do?" She smiled, nodding toward the button above Ramon's knees.

Ramon was watching her, his face completely expressionless. "It opens a liquor cabinet concealed in the seat in front of me."

"Where's the television set and stereo?" Katie joked.

"Between the desk and the liquor cabinet."

The delighted smile faded from her lips. Ramon, she realized, was not sharing her enjoyment of the luxury car's unique equipment. After an uncertain pause, she said hesitantly, "Whoever owns this car must be extraordinarily wealthy."

"He was."

"Was?" she repeated. "Is he dead?"

"Financially, he is dead." With that curt, inscrutable reply, Ramon turned his head away and stared out the window.

Bewildered and hurt by his coldness, Katie looked out her own window. Her dismal musings were interrupted as her hand, which was lying limply on the seat between them, was suddenly enclosed in Ramon's warm, firm grasp. With his head still averted, he said harshly, "I wish that I could give you a dozen cars like this one, Katie."

Comprehension dawned, and for a moment Katie was too stunned to speak. Relief washed over her, followed by unabashed amusement. "I wish you could afford to give me just *one* like it. After all, an expensive car is a guarantee of happiness, isn't it?" Ramon's sharp gaze veered toward her, and Katie widened her blue eyes with exaggerated innocence. "David gave me a Porsche for a wedding present, and look how happy my life was with him!"

The stern line of Ramon's mouth relaxed into a faint smile as she continued. "Now, if David had given me a Rolls-Royce, I would have been perfectly content with our marriage. Although," she said as Ramon's arm went around her shoulders, drawing her close to him, "the only thing that would have made my life absolutely ecstatic was—" Her sentence was smothered by the abrupt descent of Ramon's mouth as he covered her lips with his, kissing her deeply...kissing her, Katie realized, with gratitude.

When he finally lifted his head she basked in the tenderness of his smile. "What would have made your life absolutely ecstatic?" he teased huskily.

Katie's eyes danced as she snuggled closer to him. "A Ferrari!"

Ramon burst out laughing and Katie felt the tension leave his powerful body. Now things were in their proper perspective, out in the open where they could be laughed about, which was exactly what she had intended.

PUERTO RICO TOOK KATIE completely by surprise. She had not expected a mountainous tropical paradise with lush green valleys and tranquil blue lakes sparkling in the sunlight. The Rolls climbed steadily along smooth, curving roads bordered with spectacular flowering trees, their branches covered thickly in pink and yellow blossoms.

They passed through picturesque villages nestled between the mountains; each village with its own town square in the center of which was the church with its spire pointing heavenward. Katie craned her neck, her eyes delighting in the vivid colors nature had splashed over hills and meadows, her voice happy as she exclaimed over everything from ferns to farmhouses. Throughout it all, she could feel Ramon's piercing eyes on her, watching her beneath their heavy lids, observing her every reaction. Twice she had turned abruptly to make some enthusiastic comment, and had glimpsed the anxiety in his expression before he could cover it with one of his bland smiles. He desperately wanted her to like his homeland, and for some reason, he seemed unable to believe that she really did.

Nearly an hour after they left the airport, the Rolls passed through another small village and turned off the paved road onto a dirt track, continuing to climb. Katie gasped in speechless wonder; it was as if they were driving through a red silk tunnel illuminated with gossamer sunbeams. Blossoming royal poinciana trees marched along both sides of them, their laden branches meeting overhead, their fallen scarlet petals literally carpeting the road beneath the tires in deep red. "It's absolutely unbelievable," she breathed, turning to Ramon. "Are we getting close to your home?"

"About a mile and a half farther up this lane," he said, but the tension was back in his features, and his smile was nothing more than a slight curving of his tight lips. He was staring straight ahead as if he were as intent upon discovering what was at the end of the drive as she was.

Katie was about to ask him if the pretty flowers with the scarlet cups were a variety of tulip, when the Rolls emerged from the poinciana's two-mile-long red canopy and pulled into an ugly overgrown yard surrounding a run-down white brick cottage. Trying to hide her appalled disappointment, Katie turned to Ramon who was staring at the house with an expression of such murderous fury that she unconsciously pressed back into the seat cushions.

Before the car had come to a complete stop in the

yard, Ramon had flung open his door, lunged out of
the vehicle, slammed the door violently behind him
and was striding across the pitiful lawn with rage in
every step.

The elderly chauffeur helped Katie out of the car,
and they both turned in time to see Ramon rattle the
cottage door, then throw his shoulder against it with
so much explosive power that it flew off its hinges
and crashed onto the floor of the cottage.

Katie stood frozen to the spot, looking at the gaping black hole where a door had been a moment
before. Her gaze moved over the shutters hanging at
drunken angles over the windows and the paint peeling off the wood trim.

In a flash, all of Katie's optimism and courage
deserted her. She missed her beautiful apartment
complex with its gas lamps and enclosed patios. She
could never live in a place like this; she had been a
fool to try to deny her own love of luxury, her own
upbringing.

The breeze tugged a few silken strands of hair
loose from her elegant chignon. Katie lifted her
hand to brush them out of her eyes, trying at the
same time to brush away the vision of herself standing in this overgrown weed patch, looking as shabby
and unkempt as this awful hovel. In a year or two
she would become as slovenly as her surroundings,
because living like this would corrode anyone's personal pride until they just didn't care anymore.

Reluctantly she began picking her way along what
was left of a brick walk leading to the door of the
cottage. Red tiles had blown off the roof, shattering

when they hit the walk, and Katie carefully avoided stepping on them with the thin soles of her expensive Italian sandals.

She walked hesitantly through the doorway, blinking her eyes to adjust to the gloom. Revulsion swelled in her throat. The inside of the empty cottage was covered in layers of dirt, filth and cobwebs. Where the sun streamed through the broken slats of the shutters dust floated in the air. How could Ramon live like this, she wondered in horror. He was always so immaculately well-groomed, she couldn't imagine him existing in this. . . this squalor.

With a supreme effort, Katie brought her frantic emotions under control and forced herself to think logically. In the first place, no one had been living here—the dirt hadn't been disturbed for years. Or the mice either, she thought with a shudder as scratching sounds emanated from the walls.

Ramon was standing in the middle of the room, his rigid back to her.

"Ramon?" Her voice was an apprehensive whisper.

"Get out of this place," he gritted in a low voice vibrating with fury. "The filth will cling to you, even if you do not touch anything."

There was nothing Katie wanted to do more than leave here—unless it was to leave for the airport, then home, then her beautiful modern apartment. She started to go, realized that Ramon wasn't following her, stopped and turned toward him again. He was still standing with his back to her, either unwilling—or unable—to turn around and face her.

With a stab of compassion Katie realized how much he must have been dreading the moment when she would see this place. No wonder he had seemed so tense when they drove up the lane. Now he was angry because he was embarrassed and ashamed that this run-down cottage was the best he could offer her. She spoke to break the uneasy silence. "You—you said you were born here."

Ramon slowly turned and stared through her as if she didn't exist.

Braving his mood, Katie continued. "I assumed that you meant you had lived here since you were born, but no one has lived here for years, have they?"

"No," he snapped.

Katie winced at his tone. "Has it been long since you were here last?"

"Yes," he bit out.

"Places—houses that haven't been lived in for a while always seem dreary and ugly, even when they're really nice." She was trying desperately to console him, even though she knew he really ought to be consoling her. "It probably doesn't look the way you remember it."

"It looks exactly the way I remember it!"

His scathing sarcasm sliced into Katie's highly sensitized emotions like a razor blade, but still she tried. "If—if it looks exactly as you remember it, why, are you so furio...so upset," she amended hastily.

"Because," he said in a terrible voice, "I sent a telegram four days ago asking that as many men as necessary be sent to clean and make repairs to this place.''

"Oh," Katie breathed in relieved surprise.

Her evident relief made Ramon's whole body go rigid. His eyes became twin black daggers that impaled her. "Do you have such a low opinion of me that you think I would bring you to live in this—this filthy shack? Now that you have seen it like this, I would not permit you to live here. You would never be able to forget the way it looks now."

Katie stared at him in anger and bewilderment. Only minutes ago she'd been certain of her future and that she was wanted, secure and loved. Now she was certain of nothing, and she was furious with Ramon for unfairly venting his frustration on her.

A dozen indignant rejoinders sprang to mind, only to lodge in her throat behind a lump of sympathetic tenderness that swelled unbearably as she regarded him. Standing there in the middle of the shabby empty house where he was born, Ramon seemed so utterly defeated, and so proudly determined not to show it, that her heart twisted. "I think you have a low opinion of me if you believe that," she said into the charged silence.

Turning away from his narrowed gaze, Katie walked to the two arched doorways leading off the right side of the living room and peeked inside—two bedrooms, one large one at the front of the house, and a smaller one at the rear. "There's a lovely view from both bedroom windows," she announced.

"Neither of which have glass in the frames," Ramon responded tersely.

Katie ignored him and went to another doorway. A bathroom, she surmised with a mental grimace at the rusted sink and tub. An unwelcome image of her parents' sunken marble bath paraded across Katie's mind, followed immediately by the memory of her own modern bathroom at the apartment. Bravely, she banished both from her mind and flipped on a light switch. "There's electricity right to the house," she enthused.

"Which is not turned on," Ramon snapped.

Katie knew she was sounding like a real-estate saleswoman trying to make a sale, but she couldn't help herself. "And this must be the kitchen," she said, walking over to an antiquated porcelain sink standing on steel legs. "Which has hot and cold running water." To prove it, she reached for the taps.

"Do not bother," Ramon said in a tight voice, watching her from the doorway. "They do not work."

Katie's chin lifted as she tried to summon the courage to turn around and face him. In the process she found herself staring out a wide grimy window above the sink. "Ramon," she breathed, "whoever built this house must have loved a view as much as I do." Verdant green hills spread out in a panorama in front of her, their slopes covered in blooming yellow and pink blossoms.

When she swung away from the sink there was genuine pleasure in her expression. "It's beautiful, absolutely beautiful! I would wash dishes for a living if I could look out at that while I washed them." Eagerly, her gaze moved over the large rectangular kitchen. At the opposite end, one entire wall of windows was joined at the corner with another large expanse of windows. Situated in front of them was a crude wooden table and chairs. "It would be like eating on a terrace—you can see for miles in two different directions," she announced, watching a slight uncertainty flicker across Ramon's frozen features. "Why, this kitchen could be made to look bright and spacious!"

Studiously avoiding looking at the peeling linoleum on the uneven floor, Katie turned and marched back into the living room. She walked over to the large panes of glass that extended across two walls and rubbed away a bit of the grime. Peering out through the patch she had cleared, she gazed at the view. "I can see the village!" she exclaimed in awe. "I can even pick out the church. From up here it's like a little white toy village with green hills all round it. Ramon, it's like looking at a—a picture postcard. These windows must have been placed so that no matter where you look there will always be something beautiful to see. Do you know what—?" Unaware that Ramon had walked up behind her, Katie whirled around and collided with his tall, powerful body. "This house has real possibilities!" She met his cynical expression with a bright smile. "All it needs is a fresh coat of paint and some new curtains."

"And an exterminator and an army of carpenters," Ramon replied acidly. "Or better yet, a competent arsonist."

"All right—fresh paint, new curtains, an exterminator and you with a hammer and nails.'' She bit her lip as a disquieting thought occured to her. ''You *do* know about carpentry, don't you?''

For the first time since they had arrived at the house, Katie saw a glimmer of humor touch his handsome face. ''I imagine that I know as much about carpentry as you know about making curtains, Katie.''

''Wonderful!'' bluffed Katie who hadn't the foggiest notion how to make a curtain. ''Then you won't have any trouble fixing things here, will you?''

He seemed to waver, then he swept the shabby room with a contemptuous glance. His features hardened until his face seemed to be carved out of stone. Katie, realizing that he was about to refuse, put her hand on his arm. ''This could be a cozy, cheerful home. I know you're embarrassed because I've seen it looking this way, but that will only make it more rewarding and exciting when it finally looks the way it should. I'll really enjoy helping you restore it—honestly I will. Ramon,'' she whispered beseechingly when he simply stared at her, ''please, please don't spoil it for me like this.''

''Spoil it for you?!'' he exploded, raking his hand through the side of his hair. ''Spoil it for you?'' Without warning he reached for her, and Katie found herself crushed against him, his arms wrapped tightly around her. ''I knew I should not have brought you to Puerto Rico, Katie,'' he said in an agonized whisper. ''I knew it was selfish of me, but I did it anyway. Now that I have, I know I

should send you back home, where you belong. I
know it," he said, drawing a ragged breath. "But—
God forgive me—I cannot bear to do it!"

Katie wound her arms around his waist and pressed
her cheek against the solid hardness of his chest. "I
don't want to go home; I want to stay here with you."
And—at least for the moment—she was certain she
did.

She heard his breath catch and felt the sudden tensing of his muscles. He drew back slightly and tenderly
cradled her face between his hands. "Why?" he
whispered, his black eyes intently searching hers.
"Why do you want to stay here with me?"

A beaming smile lit Katie's features. "So that I can
prove to you that this house can become the home of
your dreams!"

Her answer caused an unexplainable sadness to
shadow his eyes. It lingered there as Ramon slowly
bent his head to her. "This is the real reason you want
to stay with me, Katie." His lips brushed over hers,
warm and tantalizing, while his hands drifted down
her shoulders and over her back in an enticing, ever-
changing caress.

Every nerve in Katie's body began to quiver in anticipation. It seemed like weeks, not days, since
Ramon had kissed and caressed her with stormy passion. Now he was intentionally taking his time, making her wait, teasing her. Katie did not want to be
teased and tantalized. Wrapping her arms around his
neck, she pressed herself into his muscular body. She
kissed him deeply, trying to break his iron control.
Against her, she felt the rising hardness tightening his

thighs, but as if to retaliate for her having deliberately aroused him, Ramon slid his lips from hers and began kissing the corner of her mouth, trailing his lips over her cheek, down the sensitive column of her neck, then up again to her ear, his tongue sensuously exploring each curve, each crevice.

"Don't!" Katie pleaded with a throbbing ache in her voice. "Don't tease me, Ramon. Not now." She half-expected him to ignore her. Instead, his mouth claimed hers with a fierce hunger and raw urgency that surpassed her own. His hands rushed over her, sliding up her nape and over her shoulders, possessively cupping her aching breasts, then sweeping low to press her tightly against his rigid, pulsing thighs.

Shuddering with pleasure, Katie dug her fingers into the bunched muscles of his shoulders and back, joyously fed the insatiable hunger of his mouth, willingly arched herself against the demanding, rhythmic thrusts of his hardened, aroused manhood.

An eternity later, the pressure of his lips lessened and then was gone as Ramon slowly raised his head. Even in her dazed state, Katie recognized the passion blazing in his eyes and knew he saw it in hers, too. Still shaking with quick, piercing stabs of desire, she watched his sultry gaze dip to her softly parted lips. His arms tightened convulsively as he started to bend his head to her, then hesitated, trying to fight the temptation. "Oh, God!" he groaned, and his mouth hungrily covered hers once more.

Time after time he began to pull away, only to

change his mind and bury his lips in hers for another series of long drugging kisses.

When they finally stopped, Katie was shattered. Helplessly, mindlessly, joyously shattered by the combined force of their exchanged passion and pleasure. He rested his cheek against her bright head, his hands gently caressing her back, holding her close against the violent hammering of his heart, while Katie leaned weakly against him, her arms still around his neck.

Several minutes had passed when Katie thought she heard Ramon murmur something. She managed to lift her head, open her languorous blue eyes and look at him. Lost in her dreamy euphoria, she admired the masculine face looking back at her. He really was incredibly handsome, she thought; so utterly masculine with those hard, sculpted features. She liked his firm jawline, his determined chin with its attractive cleft, and the sensuality in the mold of his mouth. And he had the most compelling, riveting eyes—eyes that could melt her or freeze her. His hair was so thick and glossy black, beautifully styled and shaped to lie flat at the sides, yet just long enough for her to run her fingers through it at the nape.

Katie reached up and smoothed the hair at his temple, then rested her hand against his cheek, her thumb idly tracing the cleft in his chin.

Ramon's dark eyes had been watching her. They captured her gaze, holding it, while he turned his head and slid his lips back and forth against her sensitive palm. He spoke, and his deep voice was raw, hoarse with an intense emotion that wasn't passion. "You make me very happy, Katie."

Katie tried to smile, but the painful quality she heard in his voice made her eyes burn with tears. And after three days of emotional turmoil culminating in the last tumultuous hour, she was too weakened to stop them. "You make me happy, too," she whispered, as two tears spilled over her lashes.

"Yes," Ramon said with solemn amusement as he watched the shimmering tears. "I can see that."

Katie gaped at him, feeling as if she were teetering on the brink of insanity. Ten seconds ago she could have sworn there were tears in his voice, but now *he* was smiling and *she* was crying. Except she wasn't crying, she was starting to laugh. "I—I always cry when I'm happy," she explained wiping away the two tears.

"Surely not!" he exclaimed in mock horror. "Do you then laugh when you are sad?"

"I probably will," Katie admitted, her face wreathed in a brilliant smile. "I've been all mixed-up ever since I met you." Impulsively, she reached up and pressed a kiss on his warmly responsive lips, then leaned back in his encircling arms. "Garcia will be wondering what we've been doing. I suppose we'd better go."

She sighed with such regret that Ramon grinned at her. "Garcia is a man of great dignity; he would never stoop to speculating about our activities." Nevertheless, Ramon obligingly released her. With his arm around her waist, they walked through the doorway into the sunlight.

Katie was about to ask when they could start working on the house, but Ramon's attention was riveted on a man about sixty years old who was walking into the yard.

When he saw Ramon, his tanned, leathery face broke into a slow smile. "Your telegram only arrived an hour ago—just before I saw the Rolls pass through the village. Do these old eyes of mine trick me, Ramon, or is it really you I see standing here?"

Grinning, Ramon held out his hand. "Your eyes are as sharp as the night you saw smoke coming through a window and caught me in the shed with a pack of cigarettes, Rafael."

"They were my cigarettes," the man named Rafael reminded him, simultaneously shaking Ramon's hand and affectionately clapping him on the arm.

Ramon winked at Katie. "Unfortunately, I had none of my own to smoke."

"Because he was only nine years old, and too young to buy them," Rafael explained, flashing a conspiratorial smile at Katie. "You should have seen him, *señorita*. He was lying on his back on a bale of hay with his hands behind his head, looking like a very important man who was enjoying his leisure. I made him eat three of the cigarettes."

"Did that cure you?" Katie laughed.

"It cured me of cigarettes," Ramon admitted. "I switched to cigars after that."

"And then to girls," Rafael said with humorous severity. He turned to Katie. "When Padre Gregorio read your banns at mass this morning, the *señoritas* all wept with disappointment, and Padre

Gregorio sighed with relief. Praying for Ramon's immortal soul had been Padre Gregorio's most time-consuming task.'' Pausing in this good-natured monologue to enjoy Ramon's visible discomfort, he added, "But you are not to worry, *señorita*. Now that he is engaged to you, Ramon will no doubt mend his wicked ways and ignore those fast women who have been chasing him all these years.''

Ramon shot a quelling look at the older man. "If you are through assassinating my character, Rafael, I will introduce you to my fiancée—assuming Katie is still willing to marry me after listening to you.''

Katie was stunned that marriage banns—the formal proclamation of an intended marriage—were already being read in church here. How had Ramon accomplished that from St. Louis? Somehow, Katie managed a weak smile while Ramon introduced Rafael Villegas as the man who had been "like a second father'' to him, but it was several minutes before she could pull herself together and pay attention to their conversation.

"When I saw the car heading in this direction,'' Rafael was saying, "I was glad that you are not ashamed to bring your *novia* here and show her where your roots are, even though you now—''

"Katie,'' Ramon interrupted abruptly. "You are not accustomed to this sun yet. Perhaps you would rather wait in the car where it is cool.''

Surprised by this politely worded dismissal, Katie said goodbye to Rafael and obediently returned to the air-conditioned Rolls. Whatever Ramon was telling Señor Villegas had the man looking almost comically bewildered, then stunned, then extremely grim. She was relieved that when they finally shook hands and parted they were both smiling again.

"Forgive me for asking you to leave like that," Ramon said, sliding into the car. "Among other things, I needed to discuss some work I need done to the cottage, and it would embarrass Rafael if you were present when we talked about money." Pressing the button that opened the glass between the chauffeur and themselves, Ramon issued instructions in Spanish, then shrugged out of his suit jacket, pulled off his tie, loosened the top buttons of his cream-colored shirt, and stretched his legs out. He looked, Katie thought, like a man who had just been through an ordeal, but was relatively pleased with the outcome.

Questions tumbled over in her mind, and she started with the least important first. "Where are we going now?"

"We are going to the village where we will have a quiet meal." Ramon put his arm around her shoulders, his fingertips playing with the little turquoise stud in her earlobe. "While we are dining, Rafael will have his married daughter prepare her spare bedroom for you. I had intended for you to stay at the house but it is not habitable. Besides, I had not considered the need for a chaperon for you until Rafael reminded me."

"A chaperon! You can't mean it," Katie sputtered. "It's—it's—"

"Necessary," Ramon provided for her.

"I was going to say Victorian, archaic and silly."

"True. But in our case it is still necessary."

Katie's delicate brows rose. "Our case?"

"Katie, this village is like a small town where very little happens, so everyone watches what everyone else does, and they gossip about it. I am a bachelor, therefore, an object of interest."

"So I gathered from what Señor Villegas said," Katie retorted primly.

Ramon's lips twitched, but he made no comment. "As my fiancée, you too are an object of interest. What is more important, you are also an American, which makes you a target for criticism. There are many here who believe that American women all have loose morals."

Mutiny was written on Katie's beautiful face. Her high cheekbones were tinted with pink and her blue eyes were sparkling dangerously. Ramon, correctly interpreting the danger signals, swiftly pulled her close and pressed his lips to her temple. "By 'chaperon' I did not mean someone to follow you around, Katie. I only meant that you could not live alone. If you do, the moment I set foot through your door the gossips will say that you let me share your bed, and because you are an American, everyone else will believe it. You may think you do not care, but this is going to be your home. You will not like it if, even years from now, you cannot walk through the village without having people whisper about you."

"I still object to the idea, on principle," Katie said, but without much conviction because Ramon was sensuously exploring her ear.

His muffled laugh sent thrills racing down her spine. "I hoped you were objecting to the idea because you thought a chaperon would make it more difficult for us to...be alone together."

"That, too," Katie admitted with breathless candor.

Ramon's chuckle was rich and deep. "I am going to stay with Rafael's family. Gabriella's house, where you will be staying, is only a mile away." Smoothing his hand from her silken cheek back to the coil of her chic chignon, he said huskily. "We will find the time, and the places, to share ourselves with each other."

Katie thought that was a beautiful way to describe making love; two people sharing their bodies with each other so that each could derive pleasure from the other. She smiled, wondering if she would ever understand him. He was such a unique combination of gentleness and strength; of raw, potent virility overlaid with smooth sexual expertise and tender restraint. No wonder she'd been confused since the day she met him. She'd never known anyone even remotely like him in her entire life!

At the edge of the village square Garcia pulled over and stopped. "I thought you might prefer to walk," Ramon explained, helping Katie to alight. "Garcia will deliver your things to Gabriella's house, then go back to Mayagüez where he lives."

The sun was beginning its descent in a blaze of pink and gold against the blue sky as they strolled across the plaza in the center of which was a stately old Spanish church. "This is where we will be married,'' Ramon told her. Katie's gaze roamed appreciatively over the church and the small buildings that surrounded it on all four sides, creating the village square. The Spanish influence was evident in the arched doorways and windows, and the black wrought-iron trim on the shops that sold everything from fresh bakery goods to small, intricately carved religious figurines. Flowers bloomed everywhere, hanging from balconies and windows, and in huge urns in front of the shops, adding their vibrant splashes of color to the picturesque little square. Tourists with cameras ambled across the plaza, stopping to peer into shop windows or sit at the little sidewalk café, sipping cool rum drinks as they watched the villagers.

Katie glanced at Ramon who was walking beside her with his suit jacket hooked on a thumb over his shoulder. Despite his outwardly casual appearance, Katie could almost feel his anxiety as he waited for her first reaction to his village. ''It's beautiful,'' she said honestly. ''Very picturesque and charming.''

The sideways look he slanted her was dubious. ''But tiny, and not what you expected?''

''Prettier and more convenient than what I expected,'' Katie argued stubbornly. ''It even has a general store. And,'' she added with a teasing glance, ''It has two hotels! I'm very impressed.''

Her joking succeeded where her sincere compliments had not. Grinning, he put his arm around her waist and drew her close against his side for a brief, tight hug. ''The Casa Grande,'' he said, nodding toward a quaint, three-story hotel with wrought-iron balconies, "boasts ten guest rooms. The other has only seven, but it has a small dining room and the food used to be good. We will dine there."

The restaurant had five tables, four of which were occupied with tourists who were laughing and talking. Katie and Ramon were given the remaining table. The waiter lit the candle in the center of the red-and-white-checked tablecloth and took their order. Ramon leaned back in his chair and smiled at Katie who was watching him with puzzled eyes. "What are you thinking about?" he asked.

"I was wondering where you lived before now, and what you've been doing. You couldn't have been working at your farm, or you wouldn't need to stay with Rafael."

Ramon answered slowly, almost cautiously. "I have lived near Mayagüez in the past, and until now I have been working for a company that is going out of business."

"Is the company in the farming business?" Katie asked.

Ramon hesitated and then he nodded. "Among other things, it is a canning operation. Instead of going to work for another company, I had already decided when I met you that I would prefer to work on my own farm rather than pay someone else to do work that I could be doing. During the next two weeks, I will still devote some time to the company; the rest I will spend working with the men who will be repairing our house."

Our house. The phrase made Katie's stomach clench. It sounded so strange. So final. Averting her eyes, she played with her glass, slowly turning it in her fingers.

"What frightens you about that, Katie?" he asked after a pause.

"Nothing. I—I was just wondering what I would be doing while you're gone."

"While I am working you can shop for things we will need for our house. Many items you will be able to buy in the villages. Furniture will have to be purchased in San Juan. Gabriella will take you to the shops and act as translator for you where one is needed."

"Furniture?" Katie stared. "Don't you have furniture in your place in Mayagüez?"

"I am going to sell it. It would not be appropriate for the cottage, anyway."

Katie, seeing the way his mouth tightened, assumed that his furniture would be an embarrassment to him, as the cottage had been, and that he didn't feel it was good enough for her. She knew perfectly well Ramon was having her stay with Rafael's daughter because he couldn't afford the expense of putting her in a hotel for three weeks; his explanation about wanting to forestall gossip didn't deceive her in the least. He couldn't afford a hotel, and he certainly couldn't afford a houseful of new furnishings, either. Yet he was going to buy them for her—to please her. Knowing that made her feel acutely uneasy.

What if something happened to convince her she shouldn't marry him after all? How could she possibly face him with an announcement like that, after she let him spend so much of his money trying to give her what he thought she wanted? She felt as if she were caught in a trap, a cage into which she had willingly placed herself, but as the doors began swinging closed on her, panic was setting in. Marriage in all its awesome finality suddenly loomed ahead of her, and Katie knew that somehow she had to feel free to leave if she changed her mind at any time during the next weeks.

"I want to pay for part of the furniture," Katie blurted suddenly.

Ramon waited for the man who was serving their meal to leave before replying. "No," he said succinctly.

"But—"

"I would not have suggested we buy it if I could not pay for it."

He meant that to end the discussion once and for all, but Katie was desperate. "That isn't the point!"

"No?" he asked. "Then exactly what is the point?"

"The point is that you're already spending a great deal of money renovating the cottage, and furniture is very expensive."

"Tomorrow I will give you three thousand dollars to spend on things for the house—"

"Three thousand dollars?" Katie interrupted, astonished. "How can you possibly afford to spend so much? Where will you get it?"

There was an imperceptible hesitation before Ramon answered. "The company that is going out of business owes me several months' back pay. I will get it from there.''

"But—" Katie started to argue.

Ramon's jaw hardened into an uncompromising line. With cool finality he said, "As a man, it is my responsibility to provide a home for you and the furnishings for it. You will not pay for anything.''

Katie's long lashes flickered down as she carefully concealed her rebellious blue eyes from his penetrating gaze. Ramon, she decided, was about to discover she was a brilliant bargain hunter. His furnishings were going to cost him exactly one-half of what they were worth—because she was going to pay for the other half!

"I meant that, Katie.''

His authoritative tone froze her hand in the act of slicing her meat.

"I forbid you to use any of your money either now or after we are married. It is to remain untouched in your bank in St. Louis.''

So determined was she to make her point that Katie forgot to be rankled by his use of the word "forbid." "You don't understand. . .I wouldn't even miss the money. Besides the money I saved from my job, I have a trust fund my father established for me years ago, and some sort of profitsharing account from his business. Both of those have huge balances. I wouldn't have to touch the principal, I could just draw out some of the interest and—''

"No," he said implacably. "I am not destitute. Even if I were, I would not accept your money. You have known my feelings on that from the beginning, have you not?''

"Yes," Katie murmured.

He sighed, a harsh sound that was filled with an anger that Katie sensed was directed more at himself than her. "Katie, I have never tried to live on the income from the farm alone. I do not know yet how much money will be required to make the necessary improvements to the land so that every acre can become productive again. Once it is fully operational it will support us in reasonable comfort, but until then, whatever money I can spare must go into the land. That farm is the only security I can offer you; its needs must come before luxuries. It is humiliating for me to be explaining this to you now, after I have already brought you here. I thought you understood what sort of life I could offer you before you came."

"I did, and I'm not worried about doing without luxuries."

"Then what are you worried about?"

"Nothing," Katie lied, more determined than ever to use her money to help pay for the furnishings. Ramon was carrying the issue of pride too far! His attitude was unreasonable, unrealistic and positively antiquated—particularly if they were going to be married. But since he felt so deeply about the matter of her money, she simply would never tell him what she had done.

His expression gentled. "If you wish, you could put your money into trust for our children. I believe there are tax advantages to doing so."

Children? Katie thought with a quickening of her heart that was part pleasure, part panic. At the rate Ramon was rushing her, she would undoubtedly have a baby within a year. Why did everything have to be happening so quickly? She remembered Rafael's remark about hearing the banns read in church this morning, and her panic grew. She knew that banns had to be read on three consecutive Sundays before they could be married. By somehow arranging to have them begin today, Ramon had smoothly eliminated one week of the precious time Katie was counting on having before she had to make a final decision. She tried to concentrate on her meal, but she could hardly swallow. "Ramon, how did you manage to have the banns read here this morning, when we didn't arrive until this afternoon?"

Something in her voice seemed to alert him to her inner turmoil. He shifted his plate aside, no longer bothering to make even a pretense of eating. Watching her with an intent, speculating gaze that was utterly unnerving, he said, "On Friday, while you were at work, I phoned Padre Gregorio and told him that we wished to be married here as soon as possible. He has known me since I was born; he knows there is no obstacle to my being married in the church. I assured him that there was no obstacle for you, either.

"When I had breakfast with your father earlier that morning, he gave me the name of his pastor, who also knows you. I gave that information to Padre Gregorio so that he could assure himself, if he wished to do so. It was as simple as that."

Katie hastily looked away from his piercing stare, but not in time.

"Something about that displeases you," he concluded dispassionately. "What is it?"

After a tense silence, Katie shook her head. "Nothing, really. I'm just a little surprised that it was all handled without my knowing anything about it."

"It was not handled that way intentionally. I assumed your father had mentioned it, and he evidently assumed that you already knew."

Katie's hand trembled as she pushed her own plate aside. "Won't Padre Gregorio need to meet with me—us, I mean—before he agrees to marry us?" she asked.

"Yes."

Ramon lit a thin cigar, then leaned back in his chair, regarding her attentively.

Katie ran a nervous hand over her red gold hair, smoothing nonexistent strands into place. "Please stop staring at me like that," she whispered imploringly.

Turning to glance over his shoulder, Ramon nodded briefly at their waiter, signaling for the check. "It is difficult not to look at you, Katie. You are very beautiful. And very frightened."

He said it so coolly, so unemotionally, that it was a long moment before Katie was certain she'd heard him correctly. By then it was too late for her to react; Ramon was already tossing money on the table, standing up, and coming around to assist her out of her chair.

In silence they walked out into a black satin night studded with brilliant stars, and crossed the deserted square. After the warmth of the afternoon sun, the evening breeze was surprisingly chilly as it teased the silken folds of Katie's turquoise dress. She shivered, more from her bewildering emotions than from the cold. Ramon swung his jacket off his shoulder and draped it over her back.

As they passed the lovely old Spanish church, Ramon's words echoed in Katie's mind: ''This is where we will be married.''

Fourteen days from today, it was possible that she would be walking out of that church as a bride.

Once before she had emerged from a church as a bride. . . except it had been a huge gothic edifice with limousines lined up on the street blocking Saturday traffic while they waited for the bridal party. David had stood beside her on the steps in the sunlight while the photographers took pictures; he in his splendid tuxedo and she in her magnificent white gown and veil. Then they had dashed through the throngs of cheering well-wishers, laughing as they dodged the showers of rice. David had been so handsome, and she had loved him so much that day. She had loved him so damned much!

Lights twinkled from the windows of the houses they passed as Katie walked beside Ramon down the little country road, her mind suddenly haunted by memories she had thought were buried.

David.

During the six months of their marriage he had kept her in a state of bewildered humiliation, and

later, fear. Even during their short engagement,
Katie had occasionally noticed his speculative glances
at other women, but the times were few, and she managed her painful jealousy by reminding herself that
David was thirty; he would think she was being childishly possessive. Besides, he was only looking at
them. He would never actually be unfaithful.

They had been married for two months before
Katie finally criticized him, and then it was only
because she was so hurt and embarrassed that she
couldn't stop herself. They had been at a formal
dinner-dance for the members of the Missouri Bar
Association, where the attractive wife of a prominent
Kansas City attorney captured David's interest. The
flirtation began over predinner cocktails, gathered
force when they sat together at dinner, and burst into
full bloom on the dance floor. Shortly thereafter,
they vanished for nearly an hour and a half, and
Katie was left to endure not only the pity of the
people she knew, but the glowering fury of the
woman's own husband.

By the time David and she returned to their apartment, Katie's insides were churning with resentment.
David listened to her tearfully indignant outpouring,
his hand clenching and flexing, but it was another
four months before Katie discovered what that convulsive flexing of his hand presaged.

When she was finished, she expected him to either
deny that he had done anything wrong, or else
apologize for his behavior. Instead he stood up,
passed a look of withering contempt over her, and
went to bed.

His retaliation began the next day. Her punishment was meted out with the refined cruelty of a man who, on the surface, seemed to be simply tolerating her unwanted presence in his life, but who was really succeeding in mentally torturing her.

No real or imagined flaw in her face, figure, posture or personality escaped his notice or went unremarked. "Pleated skirts make your hips look even broader," he observed impersonally. Katie protested that she didn't have broad hips, but she enrolled in an exercise class just to be sure. "If you cut your hair short, your chin wouldn't seem so prominent." Katie protested that her chin wasn't prominent, but she had her hair cut. "If you tightened up your knees, your rear end wouldn't wiggle so much when you walk." Katie tightened up her knees and wondered if she was still "wiggling."

His eyes were never still, they followed her everywhere until Katie became so self-conscious she could hardly cross the room without bumping into a table or banging into a chair. That too, did not escape his notice. Neither did the meal she burned, nor the clothes she forgot to take to the cleaners, nor the dust she overlooked on the bookshelf. "Some women can handle a career and run a house," David observed one night while she was polishing furniture. "Obviously you aren't one of them. You're going to have to give up your job."

Looking back, Katie could not believe how easily he had manipulated her. For two weeks, David "worked late at the office." When he was home, he shut her out completely. When he spoke to her at

all, it was with cold ridicule or polite sarcasm. Katie
tried repeatedly to patch their quarrel in every way
she could think of, but David viewed her obvious efforts with freezing contempt. In two short weeks, he
managed to reduce her to a piteous bundle of teary
tension, and had her believing that she was clumsy,
stupid and inept. But she had been only twenty-one
then, and fresh out of college, while David was nine
years older, very sophisticated and authoritative.

The thought of giving up her job broke her control. "But I love my job," she had said, tears streak-
ing down her cheeks.

"I thought you 'loved' your husband," David
had retorted coldly. He looked at her hands feverishly polishing the table. "I'm very fond of that
Steuben bowl," he drawled insolently. "Move it,
before you knock it over."

"I'm not going to knock it over," Katie burst out,
rounding on him in a tearful fury and knocking the
valuable glass bowl off the table. It hit the floor with
a sickening crash and broke. Katie was as broken as
the bowl. She flung herself into David's arms and
burst into racking sobs. "I love you, David—I don't
know what's wrong with me, lately. I'm so sorry.
I'll give up my job, and I'll—"

David was avenged. All was forgiven. He patted
her consolingly, told her that as long as she loved
him that was all that mattered, and of course she
didn't have to give up her job. The sun beamed
down upon her marriage again, and David was his
thoughtful, considerate, charming self once more.

Four months later, Katie left her office early intending to surprise David with a special dinner to celebrate their six-month anniversary. She surprised him. He was in bed with the wife of his law firm's senior partner, leaning back against the headboard casually smoking a cigarette, with the naked woman cradled in his free arm. Deadly calm washed over Katie, even though her stomach was twisting. "Since you've obviously finished," she said quietly in the doorway, "I'd appreciate it if you'd get out of here. Both of you."

She walked into the kitchen in a daze, took mushrooms out of the grocery bag and began slicing them for dinner. She sliced her finger twice without noticing the blood. Minutes later, David's low, savage voice hissed behind her, "You little bitch, before tonight is over you're going to learn some manners. Sylvia Conners' husband happens to be my boss. Now get out there and apologize to her."

"Go to hell," Katie said in a voice strangled with pain and humiliation.

His hands dug viciously into her hair, snapping her head back. "I'm warning you, do as I say or it will only go harder on you when she leaves."

Tears of tormented anguish filled Katie's eyes, but she met his glittering gaze without flinching. "No."

David let go of her and strolled into the living room. "Sylvia," she heard him say, "Katie is sorry that she upset you, and she'll apologize for her rudeness tomorrow. Come on, I'll walk you down to your car."

When they left the apartment, Katie walked

woodenly into the bedroom she had shared with David and pulled her suitcases out of the closet. She was mechanically opening drawers and removing her clothing when she heard him return.

"You know, darling," David said in a soft, silky voice from the doorway, "four months ago, I thought you learned never to make me angry. I tried to teach you the easy way, but evidently it didn't work. I'm afraid this lesson will have to be a little more memorable."

Katie looked up from her mindless packing and saw him calmly unbuckling his belt and sliding it out of its loops. Even her vocal cords froze with stark terror. "If you dare to touch me," she said in a suffocated voice, "I'll have you arrested for assault."

David stalked her slowly across the bedroom, watching with malicious enjoyment as Katie backed away. "No you won't. You're going to cry very hard, and say you're sorry, and tell me that you love me."

He was right. Thirty minutes later, Katie was still screaming "I love you" into the pillow when the apartment door closed behind him.

She had no idea how much time passed before she dragged herself off the bed, pulled a coat on, picked up her purse and left the apartment. She had no recollection of driving to her parents' house that night, nor did she ever return to the apartment.

David called her day and night, alternately trying to cajole and threaten her into coming back. He was deeply sorry; he had been under tremendous tension at the office with his case load; it would never happen again.

The next time she saw him she was with her lawyer in divorce court.

Katie glanced up as Ramon turned into a narrow dirt driveway. Straight ahead in the distance she could see light glowing against the hillside. Gabriella's house, she assumed. She looked around at the surrounding hills, which were sprinkled with the twinkling lights from the other houses, some high, some low, some much farther away than others. It made the hills seem welcoming, like a safe harbor on a dark night. She tried to enjoy the sight, to concentrate on the present and the future, but the past refused to let go of her. It clutched at her, warning her. . . .

David Caldwell had not completely deceived her; she had *let* herself be deceived. Even at a naive, virginal twenty-one, she had sensed that he was not entirely the charming man he seemed to be. Subconsciously she had registered the controlled rage in his eyes when a waiter didn't scurry fast enough in a restaurant; she had seen the clenching of his hands on the steering wheel when another driver didn't move out of his way; she had even seen the veiled speculation in his eyes when he looked at another woman. She had suspected that he was not the man he wanted her to believe he was, but she had been in love and she had married him anyway.

Now she was on the verge of marrying Ramon, and she couldn't shake the creeping suspicion that he wasn't the man he wanted her to believe he was, either. He was like a puzzle whose pieces didn't quite fit together. And he seemed so hesitant, so uninformative when she asked questions about him and his past. If he had nothing to hide, why was he so reluctant to talk about himself?

That brought a storm of argument from Katie's heart. Just because Ramon didn't like to talk about himself didn't necessarily mean that he was concealing some sinister personality trait from her. David had loved talking about himself, so in that respect the two men were very different.

They were very different in every respect, Katie told herself firmly. Or were they?

She just needed some time to adjust to the idea of marrying again, she decided. Everything had happened so fast that she was panicking. In the next two weeks her irrational fear would leave her. Or would it?

Gabriella's house was clearly in sight when Ramon abruptly stepped in front of her, blocking her path. "Why?" he demanded in a terse, frustrated voice. "Why are you so frightened?"

"I—I'm not," Katie denied, startled.

"Yes," he said harshly, "You are."

Katie stared up at his moonlit face. Despite his harsh tone, there was gentleness in his eyes and calm strength in his features. David had been neither gentle nor strong. He had been a vicious coward. "I think it's because everything seems to be happening so quickly," she said with partial honestly.

His brows drew together into a frown. "Is it only the haste that worries you?"

Katie hesitated. She could not explain the source of her fear to him. She didn't entirely understand it herself, at least not yet. "There's so much to be done, and so little time to do it," she prevaricated.

He sighed with relief as his hands slid up her arms, drawing her close against his heart. "Katie, I always intended for us to be married two weeks from today. Your parents will be here for the ceremony, and I will handle all the necessary arrangements. All you have to do between now and then is meet with Padre Gregorio."

His velvety voice, his breath stirring her hair, the musky, masculine scent of his body, were all combining to work their magic on Katie. "Meet with Padre Gregorio to discuss the ceremony, you mean?" she asked, leaning back to look at him as his arms encircled her.

"No, to convince him of your suitability to become my wife," Ramon corrected.

"Are you serious?" she breathed, her attention absorbed in the sensuous male lips slowly coming nearer and nearer to hers. Desire was beginning to course through Katie's veins, sweeping aside her doubts and fears.

"Serious about you? You know I am," he murmured, his mouth so close now that his warm breath mingled with hers.

"Serious about having to convince Padre Gregorio that I'd make a good wife for you?" she told his descending mouth.

"Yes," he whispered huskily. "Now convince me."

A hazy smile touched her lips as she curved a hand behind his head, bringing his mouth even closer to hers. "Are you going to be hard to convince?" she teased.

Ramon's voice was hoarse with burgeoning passion. "I am going to try."

Katie's other hand glided up his chest in a deliberately tantalizing caress that made his muscles tense and his breath catch. "How long do you think it will take me to convince you?" she whispered seductively.

"About three seconds," he murmured hotly.

CHAPTER TWELVE

KATIE ROLLED OVER onto her back and opened her eyes, emerging from her deep, exhausted sleep with a queer sensation of unreality. The room in which she had slept was sunny and immaculately clean, spartanly furnished with an old maple dresser and nightstand that had been polished to a mirror shine.

"Good morning," Gabriella's soft voice spoke from the doorway. Katie's memory snapped into focus as Gabriella crossed the room and placed a steaming cup of coffee on the nightstand beside the bed. At twenty-four, Gabriella was strikingly lovely. Her high cheekbones and luminous brown eyes were a magazine photographer's dream. Last night, she had confided to Katie that she had been asked to pose by a famous photographer who had seen her one day in the village, but her husband, Eduardo, had refused to permit it. That, Katie thought irritably, was exactly what she would have expected from that taciturn, handsome man she had met last night. Katie thanked her for the coffee and Gabriella smiled. "Ramon came to see you this morning before he left, but when he learned you were sleeping, he said not to disturb you," Gabriella explained. "He asked me to tell you that he will see you this evening when he returns."

"From Mayagüez," Katie put in, merely to keep the conversation going.

"No, from San Juan," Gabriella corrected. A look of almost comic horror crossed her face. "Or perhaps it was Mayagüez. I am sorry I do not recall."

"It doesn't matter," Katie assured her, puzzled over her obvious distress.

Gabriella brightened with relief. "Ramon left much money for you. He said we should begin our shopping today if you feel ready for it."

Katie nodded and glanced at the plastic alarm clock beside her bed, surprised to see that it was already ten o'clock. Tomorrow she would be sure to be up when Ramon came to see her before he left for work at the failing farm in Mayagüez.

SILENCE HUNG LIKE A PALL over the seven men seated at the conference table in the boardroom at Galverra International's San Juan headquarters—a silence that was shattered as the baroque grandfather clock began ominously tolling the hour of ten—marking the final, gasping breaths of a dying corporation that had once been a thriving world conglomerate.

From his position at the head of the long table, Ramon's glance raked over the five men on his left who were Galverra International's board of directors. Each man had been carefully selected by his father, and each possessed the three qualities that Simon Galverra required of his board members: intelligence, greed and spinelessness. For twenty years, Simon had drawn on their intelligence, exploited their greed, and ruthlessly taken advantage of their inability to contradict his opinions or challenge his decisions.

"I asked," Ramon repeated in a cold clipped voice, "if any of you can suggest a viable alternative to filing corporate bankruptcy." Two directors nervously cleared their throats, another reached for the Waterford pitcher of ice water in the center of the table.

Their averted gazes and continued meek silence ignited the rage he was keeping under such tenuous control. "No suggestions?" he asked with silky menace. "Then perhaps one of you who is not incapable of speech altogether will explain to me why I was not informed of my father's disastrous decisions or his erratic behavior during the last ten months."

Running a finger between his shirt collar and his throat, one of the men said, "Your father said you were not to be bothered with matters here. He specifically said that to us, didn't he, Charles?" he asked, nodding for confirmation at the Frenchman seated beside him. "He told us all 'Ramon is going to be overseeing the operations in France and Belgium for six months, then he is addressing the World Business Conference in Switzerland. When he leaves there, he will be busy entering into negotiations with people in Cairo. He is not to be bothered with the little decisions we are making here.' That is exactly what he said, isn't it?" Five heads nodded in unison.

Ramon looked at them as he slowly rolled a pencil between his fingers. "So," he concluded in a dangerously soft voice, "not one of you 'bothered' me. Not even when he sold a fleet of oil tankers and an airline for half their worth...not even when he decided to donate our South American mining interests to the local government as a gift?"

"It—it was your money, and your father's, Ramon." The man on the end held up his hands in a gesture of helplessness. "All of us combined own only a small percentage of stock in the corporation. The rest of the stock is your family's. We knew what he was doing wasn't in the best interest of the corporation, but your family *owns* the corporation. And your father said he wanted the corporation to have some tax write-offs."

Fury boiled up inside of Ramon, pouring through his veins; the pencil in his hand snapped in two. "Tax write-offs?" he bit out savagely.

"Y—yes," another said. "You know—tax deductions for the corporation."

Ramon's hand crashed down on the table with the impact of an explosion as he surged to his feet. "Are you trying to tell me that you thought it was rational for him to give away the corporation's assets so we would not have to pay taxes on them?" A muscle rioted in his clenched jaw as he passed a final murderous look over them. "I am sure you will understand that the corporation will not be able to reimburse you for your travel expenses to attend this meeting." He paused, maliciously enjoying their stunned looks. "Nor will I approve the payment of your annual retainer fees for your services as 'directors' during this past year. This meeting is adjourned!"

Unwisely, one of them chose that moment to become assertive. "Er, Ramon, it is in the bylaws of the corporation that directors are paid the annual sum of—"

"Take me to court!" Ramon spat. Turning on his heel, he stalked through the doorway into his adjoining office, followed by the man who had been seated on his right, silently observing the proceedings.

"Fix yourself a drink, Miguel," Ramon gritted as he stripped off his suit coat. Jerking his tie loose, he walked over to the windows.

Miguel Villegas glanced at the elaborate drinks cabinet against the paneled wall, then quickly sat down in one of the four gold velvet armchairs facing the baronial desk. His brooding eyes were dark with suppressed sympathy as he looked at Ramon, who was standing at the windows with his back to him, one arm braced high against the frame, his hand clenched into a fist.

After several tense minutes, the hand unclenched and the arm came down. In a gesture of weary resignation, Ramon flexed his broad shoulders, then ran his hand around the back of his neck, massaging the taut muscles. "I thought I had accepted defeat weeks ago," he said on a bitter sigh as he turned. "Apparently I had not."

Moving over to the desk he sat down in the massive, high-backed chair behind it and looked at Rafael Villegas's eldest son. With an expressionless face, he said, "I take it that your search turned up nothing encouraging?"

"Ramon," Miguel almost pleaded, "I am an accountant with a local practice; this was a job for your corporate auditors—you cannot rely on my findings."

Ramon was undeterred by Miguel's evasiveness. "My auditors are flying in from New York this morning, but I will not give them the access to my father's personal records that I gave you. What were your findings?"

"Exactly what you expected," Miguel sighed. "Your father sold off everything the corporation owned that was making a profit, and kept only those companies that are currently operating at a loss. When he couldn't find anything else to do with the proceeds from the sales, he donated millions to every charity imaginable." He took several ledger sheets out of his briefcase and reluctantly slid them across the huge desk to Ramon. "The item that is the most frustrating to me is the high-rise office towers you were building in Chicago and St. Louis. You have twenty million dollars invested in each one. If the banks would just loan you the rest of the money so you could finish them, you could sell them, get your investment back, and make a sizable profit besides."

"The banks will not cooperate," Ramon said tersely. "I have already met with them in Chicago and St. Louis."

"But why, dammit?" Miguel burst out, abandoning all pretense of being the impersonally professional accountant. His face was agonized as he looked at the coolly impassive features of the man he loved like a brother. "They loaned you part of the money to get them completed this far, why won't they loan you the rest to finish them?"

"Because they have lost faith in my judgment and my ability," Ramon said, looking at the figures on the ledger sheets. "They do not believe I can be relied upon to see that the buildings are finished and their loans repaid. From their point of view, while my father was alive they received their one-million-dollar interest payments every month. He died, I took control of the corporation, and suddenly we are almost four months delinquent in our payments."

"But it is your father's fault the corporation has no money coming in to make the payments!" Miguel gritted between his teeth.

"If you explain that to the banks, they reverse their original opinion and point out that while he was chairman of the board, I was still the president, and I should have taken steps to stop him from making these mistakes."

"Mistakes!" Miguel exploded. "They were not mistakes. He planned it this way so that you would have nothing left. He wanted everyone to think that when he died, the corporation fell apart without him."

Ramon's eyes turned hard and cold. "He had a

brain tumor; he was not responsible for his actions."

Miguel Villegas stiffened in his chair, his dark, Spanish face glowering. "He was a miserable bastard, an egotistical petty tyrant, and you know it! Everybody knew it. He resented your success and he hated your fame. All that tumor did was make him finally lose control of his jealousy." Seeing the mounting anger in Ramon's expression, Miguel softened his voice. "I know you do not want to hear it, but it is the truth. You came into the corporation and in a few short years, you created a worldwide financial empire worth three hundred times what your father had made it. You did it, not him. You were the one the magazines and newspapers wrote about; you were the one they called one of the world's most dynamic entrepreneurs; you were the one who was asked to address the World Business Conference in Geneva. I was having lunch in a hotel at a table near your father's the day he found out about that. He was not proud, he was furious! He was trying to convince the men he was with that the conference had taken you as a second choice because he could not spare the time to go to Switzerland."

"Enough!" Ramon said sharply, his face white with angry pain. "He was still my father, and he is dead now. There was little love between us while he was alive; do not destroy what little feeling I have left for him." In grim silence, Ramon concentrated on the ledger sheets Miguel had given him. When his eyes swept over the last entry, he glanced up. "What is this three-million-dollar asset of mine you list at the end?''

"Not really an asset at all," Miguel said glumly. "I found the file among your father's private things at the house in Mayagüez. As far as I could tell, it is a loan you made to a Sidney Green in St. Louis, Missouri, nine years ago. He still owes you the money, but you cannot sue him or take any legal action to try to get it back now; under the law you have only seven years to file a lawsuit—that time has already elapsed.

"The loan was repaid," Ramon said with a shrug.

"Not according to the records I found."

"If you dig deeply enough you will discover it was repaid, but do not waste any more of your time looking through the files. You have enough to do." There was a brief knock on the door, followed immediately by the appearance of Simon Galverra's elegantly groomed secretary.

"The auditors from New York are here. Also, there are two local newspaper reporters asking to schedule interviews, and an urgent telephone call from Zurich."

"Send the auditors into the conference room, and tell the reporters I will give them an interview next month; that will keep them out of our way. I will return the Zurich call later." Nodding, she retreated, her skirt swirling around long shapely legs.

Miguel watched Elise leave, his brown eyes admiring. "At least your father had good taste in secretaries. Elise is beautiful," he observed in a tone of impersonal aesthetic appreciation.

Ramon unlocked the massive, carved desk and did not reply as he extracted three heavy files marked "Confidential."

"Speaking of beautiful women," Miguel went on with studied nonchalance as he gathered up his papers, preparing to leave. "When am I going to be able to meet the grocer's daughter?"

Reaching for the intercom on his right, Ramon pressed the button and issued instructions to Elise: "Have Davidson and Ramirez come up. When they arrive, send them into the conference room with the auditors." With his attention still on the files before him, Ramon said, "What grocer's daughter?"

Miguel rolled his eyes in amusement. "The one you brought back from the States. Eduardo says she is reasonably attractive. Knowing how he dislikes American women, that means she must be extraordinarily beautiful. He said she is a grocer's daughter."

"A grocer's—?" For a moment Ramon looked irritated and blank, then the uncompromising line of his jaw slowly relaxed. His eyes, which had been cold and harsh, kindled with warmth, and his stern mouth was touched by an unexplainable smile. "Katie," he breathed aloud. "He is talking about Katie." Leaning back in his chair, Ramon closed his eyes. "How could I possibly have forgotten I have Katie here?" Regarding Miguel through half-closed eyes, Ramon said with wry humor, "Katie is the daughter of a wealthy American who owns a large chain of supermarkets. I brought her back from the States with me yesterday. She is staying with

Gabriella and Eduardo for two weeks until we are married.''

While Ramon briefly explained that he was misleading Katie, and why, Miguel was slowly sinking back into the chair he had just vacated. He shook his head. ''*Dios mio*, I thought she was going to be your mistress.''

''Eduardo knows she is not. He mistrusts all American women, and he prefers to think I will change my mind about marrying her. When he learns to know Katie, he will like her. In the meantime, out of respect for me he will treat her as a guest in his home, and he will not discuss my past with her.''

''But your return is undoubtedly the talk of the village. Your Katie will be bound to overhear some village gossip.''

''I am certain she will, but she will not understand a word of it. Katie does not speak Spanish.''

Heaving himself out of his chair, Miguel shot a worried look at Ramon. ''What about the rest of my family—they all speak English—and the younger ones may inadvertently give you away.''

''Only your parents and Gabriella and her husband remember their English,'' Ramon said dryly. ''As of yesterday, your brothers and sisters know only Spanish.''

''Ramon, after this, nothing you ever do or say will surprise me.''

''I want you to be my best man.''

Miguel smiled somberly. ''That does not surprise me. I always expected to be your best man, just as you flew back from Athens to be mine." He put his hand out across the desk. "Congratulations, my friend." His firm handshake conveyed his pleasure as well as his unspoken regret for Ramon's staggering financial losses. "I will go back to work on your father's files."

The intercom buzzed, and the secretary's voice announced that the corporation's two attorneys, whom Ramon had instructed her to summon, were now in the conference room waiting with the auditors.

Still seated behind the desk, Ramon watched Miguel cross the broad expanse of thick gold carpet. When the door clicked shut behind him, Ramon let his gaze roam over his office as if he were seeing it for the last time, unconsciously memorizing it in all its quiet splendor.

The Renoir landscape he had purchased for an exorbitant sum from a private collector was framed beneath a portrait light, its colors a vibrant contrast to the rich, walnut-paneled walls. He had put all his personal possessions up as collateral to obtain loans for the corporation before he discovered the full extent of his father's destructiveness. Along with everything else he owned, the Renoir would soon be auctioned off to the highest bidder. He hoped whoever bought it would love it as much as he always had.

Leaning his head back against the chair, Ramon closed his eyes. In a minute he was going to walk into the conference room, turn the auditors loose on the records, and instruct the corporation's attorneys to file the legal documents that would announce to the courts and the business world that Galverra International was crippled. Broken.

For four months he had fought to save it, trying to transfuse it with his own money—doing anything just to keep it alive. He had failed. Now all he could do was make certain that it died swiftly and with dignity.

Night after night he had lain awake, dreading this moment. Yet now that it was finally here, he was facing it without the wrenching agony he would have felt two weeks ago.

Because now he had Katie.

He had given his life to the corporation. Now he was going to give the rest of it to Katie. Only to Katie.

For the first time in many years, Ramon felt deeply religious. It was as if God had decided to take away his family, his possessions, his status, and then, realizing that Ramon had absolutely nothing left, He had taken pity and given him Katie instead. And Katie made up for everything he had lost.

KATIE BRUSHED HER LIPS with a tawny lipstick that matched the shiny polish on her long tapered fingernails. She checked her mascara, then combed her fingers through the sides of her hair, restoring the glossy mane to its windblown style. Satisfied, she turned away from the mirror above the dresser and glanced at the clock. At five-thirty it was still broad daylight, and Ramon had told Gabriella he would be here between five-thirty and six to take Katie to dinner at Rafael's.

On an impulse, Katie decided to walk out and meet him. After changing into a pair of white slacks and a jaunty navy silk shirt trimmed in white, she slipped out the front door, relieved to escape the rather oppressive presence of Gabriella's disapproving husband, Eduardo.

Overhead, the powder-blue sky was heaped with piles of whipped cream clouds. The hills rose around her, carpeted in emerald green and splashed with pink and red flowers. With a contented sigh, Katie lifted her face to the balmy breeze and started across the front yard toward the dirt driveway that led through the trees out to the main road.

She had felt a little lost being among strangers all day, and she had missed Ramon's reassuring presence. She hadn't seen him since he introduced her to Gabriella and her husband last night, then left an hour later to go back to Rafael's house.

"Katie!" The familiar voice stopped her in her tracks. Turning her head, Katie saw Ramon about fifty yards away on her left. He was cutting across the hillside from Rafael's house, and she had obviously just crossed directly in his path as she walked toward the road. He stopped, waiting for her to come to him. With a cheery wave, Katie turned and started up the hill.

Ramon forced himself to stay where he was, to luxuriate in the sheer pleasure of knowing she had come out to meet him. His gaze moved over her in a tender caress, watching the way her hair was blow-ing across her shoulders in a shining tumble of red gold. Her deep blue eyes were laughing up at him, and a welcoming smile was curving the inviting fullness of her lips. She moved with a natural, unaffected grace, her slim hips swaying just enough to be exquisitely provocative.

His heart pounded with the yearning to snatch her into his arms and crush her against him, to absorb her into himself. He wanted to cover her mouth with his and whisper over and over, I love you, I love you, I love you. He wanted to say that to her, but not enough to risk the possibility that Katie's response—or lack of it—would tell him that she did not love him. That he could not bear.

A few yards from him Katie stopped, immobilized by a strange combination of happiness and shyness. Ramon's dark blue shirt was open halfway to his waist, revealing an expanse of tanned chest covered with curling black hairs; his dark pants hugged his lean hips and hard thighs, faithfully following every line of his long legs. The raw, potent sexuality he was exuding made Katie feel strangely fragile and vulnerable. She swallowed, searching for something to say, and finally said with soft uncertainty, "Hello."

Ramon's arms opened wide to her. Huskily he replied, "Hello, *mi amor*."

Katie hesitated, and then flung herself into his welcoming embrace. His arms closed around her, holding her to him as if he would never let her go.

"Did you miss me?" he whispered thickly, when his mouth at last released hers.

Katie pressed her lips to the base of his throat, inhaling the heady scent of warm, masculine skin and spicy after-shave. "Yes. Did you miss me?"

"No."

Leaning back, Katie looked up at him, her smile quizzical. "You didn't?"

"No," he said with quiet gravity. "Because since ten o'clock this morning I have kept you with me; I have not let you leave my side."

"Since ten o'clock—?" Katie started to ask, then something in his voice made her look at him more closely. Intuitively she recognized the ravaged emotions hidden in the depths of those onyx eyes. Reaching up, she took his chin between her thumb and forefinger, turning his surprised face first to the left, then the right. Keeping her expression bright, she asked teasingly, "How do the other men look?"

"What other men?"

"The ones who tried to beat you up."

"You mean I look as if I have been in a fight?" Ramon said.

Slowly, Katie nodded, her smile widening. "With at least six armed men and a demented bulldozer."

"That bad?" he grinned wryly.

Katie nodded again, then sobered. "It must be very hard, very depressing working for a company that you know is going out of business."

His stunned look told Katie that her conclusion was correct. "Do you know," he said with a bemused shake of his head, "I have been told by many men from many countries that I have a face that is absolutely unreadable when I wish it to be."

"And you wanted it to be unreadable tonight, with me?" Katie guessed. "Because you didn't want me to see that you're tired and depressed?"

"Yes."

"Did you have any of your own money invested in the company?"

"Virtually all of my money and most of my life," Ramon admitted smiling at her in amazement. "You are very perceptive. But there is no need for you to worry. After today it will be much easier, and I will not have to be there for so many hours each day. Tomorrow afternoon I can begin helping the men who are working on our home."

Dinner at Rafael's house was a relaxed affair with much joking and laughing around the table. Señora Villegas, Rafael's wife, was a stout, bustling woman who treated Ramon with the same solicitude she lavished on her husband and children—two boys in their early twenties and a girl of about fourteen. For Katie's benefit most of the conversation was in English, which the young members could not speak but apparently understood a little, because several times Katie saw them smile at something Rafael or Ramon said.

After dinner the men went into the lounge while the women cleared the table and did the dishes. When they were through, they joined the men for coffee. As if he had been watching for her, Ramon's gaze lifted and he held out a beckoning hand to her. Katie slid her hand into his firm grasp, and he exerted just enough pressure to pull her down beside him. She listened to Rafael Villegas talking to Ramon, making suggestions about the farm, but every moment she was vitally aware of Ramon's hard thigh pressing against hers. His arm was resting along the back of the sofa, his hand imperceptibly caressing her shoulder, his thumb moving idly against her nape beneath the cloak of her heavy hair. Except there was nothing idle about what he was doing—he was deliberately keeping her fully aware of his nearness. Or was he, Katie wondered suddenly. She thought about what he had said earlier about keeping her beside him, implying that he had needed her to get through his day. Was he keeping her physically close now, touching her this way because he needed her to get through the evening as well?

Katie stole a glance at his chiseled profile and, with a pang of sympathy, she recognized the preoccupation in his features.

Katie delicately faked a yawn behind her fingers, and Ramon's eyes were instantly on her. "Are you tired?"

"A little," Katie lied.

In three minutes, Ramon had seized on her comment, made their excuses to the Villegases, and whisked her out the front door. "Do you feel up to walking back, or would you rather I drove you?"

"I feel up to almost anything," Katie smiled softly, "but you looked tired and distracted, so I used that as a way of excusing you from being there."

Ramon didn't deny it. "Thank you," he said tenderly.

Gabriella and her husband had already gone to bed, but they had left the front door unlatched.

Katie stopped to turn on a mellow lamp while Ramon walked over and sat down on the sofa. As she neared him, he reached out and captured her arms, starting to pull her down onto his lap. Firmly disentangling herself from his grip, Katie went around behind him.

Beneath her ministering hands his broad shoulders were taut as she began to massage the tenseness from his thick muscles. She felt so strange with him in this mood. There was a relaxed closeness between them that had never been present before; Ramon always seemed to have a leashed sexual energy that kept her senses in a state of trembling anticipation. Tonight that energy was a quiet magnetism. "How does that feel?" she asked, kneading the tendons at the base of the neck.

"Better than you can imagine," he said, bending his dark head forward to give her better access to his neck. "Where did you learn to do that?" he asked a few minutes later as Katie began quickly chopping the sides of her hands over his shoulders and back.

Katie's hands froze. "I don't remember," she lied.

Something in her voice made Ramon turn around sharply. He saw the haunted expression in her eyes, caught her arms and brought her around in front of him, pulling her down onto his lap. "Now I will make you feel better," he stated, his hands unfastening the buttons of her shirt, delving into the lacy cups of her bra, and pushing her breasts up and out of them.

Before Katie could gather her wits, his mouth was

at her breasts, obliterating her thoughts, driving her into a state of hot need. With one arm around her shoulders and the other around her waist, he shifted her down onto the sofa, his body half covering hers. "He is dead," he reminded her fiercely. "And I do not want his ghost between us." Despite the harshness of his tone, his kiss was filled with sweetness. "Bury him," he implored in a whisper. "Please."

Katie wrapped her arms around his shoulders, arching her lower body to his, and immediately forgot the world.

CHAPTER THIRTEEN

THE NEXT DAY, Miguel strode past the startled secretary, opened the door to Ramon's office, and shut it firmly behind him. "Tell me all about your good friend Sidney Green in St. Louis," Miguel said, with sarcastic emphasis on the word *friend*.

Ramon, who was leaning back in his chair, engrossed in some legal documents he was reading, glanced distractedly at Miguel. "He is not a friend of mine, he is merely a man who knew a friend of mine." Returning his attention to the documents, he said, "He approached me at a cocktail party at this friend's house nine years ago, and described a new formula for paint that he had worked out. He said that using his formula he could produce paint that would wear better and last longer than any other paint on the market. The next day he brought me an analysis of his paint, which was performed by an independent testing laboratory, and proved his claims.

"He needed three million dollars to begin to manufacture and market it, and I arranged for Galverra International to lend it to him. I also put him in touch with several of my friends who owned companies that bought paint for use on the products they manufacture. You will find the information in a closed file somewhere. It was as simple as that.''

''Part of the information was in the file, I got the rest from the treasurer of the corporation this morning. It was not quite as simple as you think. Your father had Green investigated, found out he was a small-time chemist, and decided as such, he would never have the business acumen to market his product, and the the three million would be wasted. Being the 'kind, loving father' that he was, your father decided to teach you a lesson. He instructed the treasurer to advance three million dollars into your personal account and make the loan from you personally to Green. One year later, when the loan was to be repaid, Green wrote and said he wanted an extension. According to the treasurer, you were in Japan at the time, and he took Green's letter to your father. Your father said to ignore the letter, and not to make any attempt to collect the loan; collecting it was your problem.

Ramon sighed irritably. ''Nevertheless, the loan was repaid. I remember my father telling me that it had been.''

''I don't give a damn what that devil told you—it wasn't. Sidney Green told me so himself.''

Ramon's head snapped up, his jaw clenched in anger. ''You called him?!''

''Well. . .yes. . .you told me not to waste any more time going through the files, Ramon,'' Miguel reminded him, flinching under Ramon's furious glance.

''Damn you! I gave you no authority to do that,''

Ramon exploded. Leaning back in his chair, he briefly closed his eyes, obviously struggling with his rampaging temper. When he spoke again his voice was controlled. "Even when I was in St. Louis, I did not call him. He knew I was in trouble; if he had wanted to help he would have contacted me there. He will interpret your phone call about an old loan as a pitiful ploy on my part to try to get money from him. He was an arrogant bastard nine years ago when he had nothing but the shirt on his back; I can imagine what he must be like now that he is success-ful."

"He is still an arrogant bastard," Miguel said, "And he never repaid one dime of the money. When I explained that I was trying to locate the records of the repayment of the money you loaned him, he said that you are too late to take him to court over it."

Ramon listened to this with cynical amusement. "He is right, of course. It was my responsibility to see that the money was repaid, and when it wasn't, to take appropriate legal action within the allowable time limit."

"For God's sake! You gave the man three million dollars and he is refusing to pay you after you made him rich! How can you just sit there like that?"

Ramon shrugged ironically. "I did not 'give' him the money, I loaned it to him. I did not do it out of kindness or charity, I did it because I felt there was a need for the superior product he could manufacture, and because I hoped to make a profit. It was a busi-ness investment, and it is the investor's responsibili-ty to look after his money. Unfortunately, I did not realize that I was the investor, and I assumed the corporation's auditors would oversee it. To Green, his refusal to repay it now, when he does not have to, is nothing personal—he is merely looking out for his own interests. That is business."

"It is theft!" Miguel said bitterly.

"No, it is merely good business," Ramon said, regarding him with dry amusement. "I suppose that after telling you he would not repay the money, he sent me his regards and his 'deep regrets' for my sad state of affairs."

"Like hell he did! He told me to tell you that if you were half as smart as everyone always said you were, you would have demanded your money years ago. He said if you, or anyone else representing you, contacted him again to try to collect it, he would have his legal staff file suit against you for harassment. Then he hung up on me."

All of the amusement vanished from Ramon's expression. He put his pen down. "He what?" he asked with deadly softness.

"He—he said those things, and then he hung up on me."

"Now that was very bad business," Ramon said in a silky, ominous voice.

He leaned back and was thoughtfully silent, his mouth quirked in a faint, ironic smile. Abruptly, he reached over and punched the intercom button. When Elise answered his buzz, he gave her seven names and seven phone numbers to call in seven different cities all over the world.

"If I recall the terms of the loan correctly,"

Ramon said, "I loaned him three million at whatever interest rate was being charged on the day of repayment."

"Right," Miguel said. "If he had repaid the loan in one year, the interest rate then was eight percent, and he would have owed you about $3,240,000."

"Today the interest rate is seventeen percent, and he has owed it for nine years."

"Technically he owes you more than twelve million dollars," Miguel said, "but it does not matter. You cannot possibly collect it."

"I have no intention of trying," Ramon said affably. His gaze shifted to the telephone on the desk, waiting for the first of the transatlantic calls to go through.

"Then what are you going to do?"

Ramon's brow lifted with amusement. "I am going to teach our friend Green a lesson he should have learned long ago. It is a variation on an old saying."

"What old saying?"

"The saying that when you are climbing up the ladder of success, you should never deliberately step on anyone's hands, because you may need them to help you when you are on your way down."

"What variation are you going to teach him?" Miguel asked, his eyes beginning to gleam with delighted anticipation.

"Never make unnecessary enemies," Ramon answered. "And the lesson is going to cost him twelve million dollars."

When the calls came through, Ramon pressed a

button on his telephone that activated a speaker system so that both sides of the conversation were clearly audible to Miguel. Several of the conversations took place in French and Miguel struggled desperately to follow them, hampered by his rudimentary knowledge of a language Ramon spoke fluently. After the first four calls, however, Miguel had gathered enough of what was taking place to be utterly staggered.

Each of the men Ramon talked to were major industrialists whose companies either used or had used paint manufactured by Green's company. Each man treated Ramon with warm friendliness and listened with amusement as he briefly explained what he was trying to do. When each call was completed, Miguel was a little surprised to hear everyone of them ask if there was anything they could do to help Ramon in his "difficult circumstances," and in every case Ramon politely declined.

"Ramon!" Miguel burst out when the fourth call was over at four-thirty in the afternoon. "Any one of those men could bail you out of this financial disaster you are in, and they all offered to help."

Ramon shook his head. "It is a polite formality, nothing more. They offer to help, and it is understood that I will decline their offer. That is good business. You see," he said with a shadow of a smile, "we have all already learned the lesson Mr. Green is being taught."

Miguel could not suppress a chuckle. "If I followed those calls correctly, tomorrow the Paris press is going to report that their major automobile manufacturer had a problem with Green's paint fading on their test car, and has decided to use something else.''

Ramon went over to the liquor cabinet and poured drinks for himself and Miguel. ''It is not quite as lethal to Green as it sounds to you. My friend in Paris had already told me he'd decided against using Green's paint because it was too expensive; I was the one who had put him in touch with Green nine years ago. The problem with the fading paint was because it was incorrectly applied by his factory personnel, but of course he has no intention of mentioning that to the press.''

He carried the glasses over to Miguel and handed him his. ''The farm-equipment manufacturer in Germany will wait one day after the Paris press announcement before calling Green and threatening to cancel his order because of what he saw in the Paris press.''

Ramon shoved his hands in his pockets and grinned at Miguel, a cigar clamped between his white teeth. ''Unfortunately for Green, his paint is no longer superior; other American manufacturers have since produced an equally good product. My friend in Tokyo will respond to the Paris press announcement by stating to the Tokyo press that they have never used Green's paint so they have no trouble with their automobiles' finish fading.

''On Thursday, Demetrios Vasiladis will call from Athens and cancel all orders for marine paint for all of his shipyards.''

Ramon took a swallow of his drink, sat down behind his desk and began loading papers into his briefcase that he would go over tonight after he left Katie.

Intrigued, Miguel leaned forward on the edge of his chair. "And then what?"

Ramon glanced up as if the matter had lost its interest. "Then it is anyone's guess. I expect that the other American paint manufacturers who make an equally good product will take up the sword and do their best to demolish Green in the American press. Depending upon how effective they are, the adverse publicity will probably drive down the value of Green's stock on the stock exchange."

CHAPTER FOURTEEN

EARLY THURSDAY MORNING, Miguel was going over the financial statement he had prepared with Ramon, when Elise entered Ramon's office without her customary knock.

"Excuse me," she said, her face pale and stony. "There is a man—a very rude man—on the telephone. I have told him twice that you cannot be interrupted, but as soon as I hang up the telephone he calls back and starts shouting at me again."

"What does he want?" Ramon said impatiently.

The secretary swallowed apprehensively. "He—he wants to talk to the dirty bastard who is trying to put some green paint down his drain. Do you—is that you?"

Ramon's lips twitched. "I believe so. Put him through."

Eagerly, Miguel leaned forward. Ramon flipped on the phone's external speaker, then relaxed back in his chair, picked up the financial statements he had been reading, and calmly continued to study them.

Sidney Green's voice exploded through the room. "Galverra, you bastard! You're wasting your time, do you hear me? No matter what you do, I'm not paying one dime of that three million. Have you got that? No matter what you do!'' When there was no response, Green shouted, ''Say something, damn you!''

''I admire your courage,'' Ramon drawled.

''Is that your way of telling me you plan more guerrilla tactics? Is it? Are you threatening me, Galverra?''

''I am certain I would never be so crude as to 'threaten' you, Sid,'' Ramon replied in a bland, preoccupied voice.

''Damn you, you are threatening me! Who the hell do you think you are?''

''I think I am the bastard who is going to cost you twelve million dollars,'' Ramon said and, with that, he reached out a hand and disconnected the call.

KATIE QUICKLY SIGNED HER NAME to the charge slip for one-half the cost of the furniture she had just purchased, then paid for the rest with some of the money Ramon had left for her. The salesclerk gave her an odd look when she asked for two receipts, each for one-half the actual amount of the purchase. Katie firmly ignored it, but Gabriella blushed and looked away.

Outside, the temperature was deliciously warm, and tourists were strolling along the sun-drenched streets of Old San Juan. The car was parked at the curb; a battered but reliable old automobile that belonged to Gabriella's husband, and which he was allowing them to use for their shopping expeditions.

''We're doing great,'' Katie sighed, rolling down

her window to let the breeze into the stuffy car. It was Thursday already, the fourth day of their frenetic, but successful shopping spree, and she was happily exhausted. "I wish I could get over this feeling that there's something I'm forgetting, though," she mused, glancing over her shoulder at the two lamps and an end table that were crammed into the back seat.

"There is." Gabriella's pretty face was concerned as she turned the key in the ignition and shot Katie a rueful smile. "You are forgetting to tell Ramon the truth about how much this is costing." She pulled into the stream of downtown San Juan traffic. "Katie, he will be very angry with you when he discovers what you have done."

"He isn't going to discover it," Katie announced cheerfully. "I'm not going to tell him and you promised you wouldn't."

"Of course I will not!" Gabriella said with a hurt look. "But Padre Gregorio has spoken many times on Sundays about the need for truth between a husband and—"

"Oh, no!" Katie moaned aloud. "That's what I forgot." She leaned her head back and closed her eyes. "Today is Thursday, and at two o'clock this afternoon I was to meet with Padre Gregorio. Ramon made the arrangements on Tuesday and reminded me this morning, but I completely forgot about it."

"Do you want to see the padre now?" Gabriella offered an hour later as their car rattled into the village. "It is only four o'clock. Padre Gregorio will not be having his evening meal yet."

Katie quickly shook her head. She had been thinking all day about the picnic she and Ramon were
going to have up at the cottage tonight. She was to
bring the food up there where he was working with
the other men. When the men left, Katie and Ramon
were going to have a few hours alone—their first in
the four days since she had arrived.

When they reached Gabriella's house, Katie slid
behind the steering wheel, waved goodbye to Gabriella, and turned the dilapidated old car back toward
the village where she could stop in the general store
for food and a bottle of wine for the picnic.

These past four days had a strange, unreal quality
for her. Ramon had been working at the farm in
Mayagüez in the mornings, and at the cottage in the
afternoons until it was dark, so she only saw him in
the evenings. She spent her days shopping and planning and choosing color schemes for Ramon's house
with only her idea of Ramon's tastes to guide her.
She felt as if she were on a vacation, earning her way
by redecorating his house—rather than planning for
her own home. Perhaps it was because he was so
busy and she saw so little of him, and when they
were together there were always other people nearby.

Rafael and his sons were also working up at the
cottage with Ramon, and at dinner every night the
four men were cheerful, but plainly worn-out. Although Ramon lavished her with his attention in the
evening, keeping her near him while they sat in the
friendly atmosphere of Rafael's living room with
the rest of his family, the "time and place to share

ourselves with each other" so far had not presented itself.

Each evening, Ramon walked her back to Gabriella's darkened house, led her over to the sofa, and drew her down beside him.

By now, Katie could hardly pass that sofa in the daylight without feeling her face grow warm. For three nights in a row, Ramon had tenderly stripped her of most of her clothing, aroused her until she could hardly stand it, gently dressed her again, walked her back to the bedroom, and silently bade her good-night with a final, passionate kiss. And each night Katie crawled beneath the cool sheets of her temporary bed in a state of aching, unfulfilled desire, which she was beginning to think was precisely what Ramon intended her to feel. Yet there was no doubt in her mind that he was always more aroused then even she was, so it made no sense for him to put them both through this torture.

Last night, in a welter of confusion and desire, Katie had taken matters into her own hands and volunteered to get the blanket from her bed so that they could go outdoors where there would be privacy and no fear of interruption.

Ramon had gazed down at her with eyes like fiery black coals, his face hard and dark with passion. But he had reluctantly shaken his head. "The rain will interrupt us, Katie. It has been threatening for the last hour." Even as he spoke a flash of heat lightning cast an eerie glow through the room. But it had not rained.

Tonight, no doubt, was the "time and place" he

had been waiting for, Katie decided, and she was charged with anticipation. Katie pulled the car over in front of the general store and climbed out. Pushing open the heavy door, she walked into the crowded interior of the ancient building, blinking her eyes to adjust to the light.

Besides doubling as the village post office, the general store stocked everything from flour and canned goods to bathing suits to inexpensive pieces of furniture. Stacks of merchandise covered the wooden floors with only a narrow aisle between them for customers to walk through. The counters were heaped with goods, as were the shelves high along all the walls. Without the assistance of someone who worked there, it would have taken Katie and Gabriella weeks to dig their way through everything.

The Spanish girl to whom Gabriella had introduced Katie before as Ramon Galverra's *novia*, saw Katie, beamed a bright smile at her, and hurried over. With her help on Monday, Katie had discovered thick, fluffy towels in solid colors of red, white and black beneath a stack of men's work pants. Katie had bought all six of them and ordered a dozen more in assorted sizes. Evidently the girl thought Katie had come to see if the rest of the towels were here yet, for she picked up a towel, held it up, and regretfully shook her head, relying on pantomime since she spoke no English.

Katie grinned and pointed to the shelves of groceries interspersed with shovels and rakes, then went over to make her selections. Carrying the fresh fruit, bread and packaged meat she had selected over to the crowded counter, Katie dug in her purse for her money. When she glanced up, the little Spanish girl smilingly presented her with two bills, each for one-half the amount of her purchase. The girl was so proud of having remembered that Katie always asked for the bills in this way, that Katie didn't bother trying to explain that it wasn't necessary for groceries.

The scene that greeted Katie when the car bumped past the canopy of scarlet poinciana trees took her completely by surprise. The yard was filled with battered old trucks, two horses and another truck loaded with debris, which had obviously been removed from the house and was being hauled away. Two men were replacing tiles on the roof, and two more were stripping all the peeling paint from the wood trim. The shutters had been repaired and were open beside windows with crystal-clear panes of glass. This was the first time Katie had been here since Sunday, and she was eager to see what progress had been made inside. She took a quick look in the car's rearview mirror, freshened her lip gloss, and smoothed her hair back into place.

She climbed out of the car and brushed a piece of lint from her designer jeans, then tucked her plaid shirt into her waistband. The constant staccato sounds of hammering that had been coming from inside ceased abruptly. The men on the roof scampered down as Katie walked up the brick path, which was no longer missing bricks or strewn with broken tiles. She glanced at her watch: it was exactly six, and apparently the men were finished for the day.

The front door, which Ramon had broken on Sunday, had been rehung, and the peeling paint stripped down to smooth bare wood. Katie stepped aside as eight men came through the doorway carrying their wooden toolboxes. Rafael and his two sons were behind them. There was an army working up here, Katie thought with amazement. "Ramon is in the kitchen with the plumber," Rafael said with one of his warm, fatherly smiles. His sons both grinned at her as they passed.

The living-room walls, which were made of grooved boards, had been sanded already, as had the planked floors. It took Katie a moment to understand why the house seemed so cheerful and sunny. Then she realized that all of the windows were sparkling clean, and some of them were open, letting the balmy breeze in to mingle with the pungent scent of fresh sawdust. An elderly man carrying a huge wrench in each hand shuffled out of the kitchen, tipped his hat politely to Katie, then vanished through the living room and outside. The plumber, Katie guessed.

With a last appreciative glance around her, Katie wandered into the kitchen. Like every other wooden surface, the kitchen cabinets had been stripped, and the ugly peeling linoleum had been taken up. The sharp clang of metal on metal drew her attention toward the sink. A pair of long, muscular legs were stretched out on the floor, the torso belonging to them hidden beneath the sink. Katie smiled, recognizing those long legs and slim hips even without seeing the head and shoulders that were blocked from view by the convoluted plumbing pipes.

Apparently Ramon didn't realize the plumber had left, because his familiar Spanish voice issued a muffled order in a sharp tone. Katie hesitated uncertainly, then, feeling like a child playing a trick on an adult, she picked up the wrench lying on the counter and passed it beneath the newly installed stainless steel sink to Ramon. She almost laughed aloud when the wrench was rudely shoved back at her, and the same order was irritably repeated, this time accompanied by an impatient bang on the bottom of the sink.

Making a calculated guess, she leaned forward and turned on both taps. The torrent of water brought a string of savage curses that erupted from below the sink at the same time Ramon did, with water streaming from his face, his hair and his bare chest. Snatching a towel from the floor, he came to his feet in one lithe, furious movement, drying his head and face while Katie frantically dived for the taps and turned them off. In appalled fascination she listened to the scathing Spanish remarks coming from behind the towel, then jumped when he flung it down and glared at her.

His expression turned to blank shock. "I—I wanted to surprise you," Katie explained, biting her lower lip to control her laughter. Water was dripping from his curling hair, his eyebrows and his eyelashes, and sparkling on the crisp hairs on his broad chest. Katie's shoulders began to shake.

A gleam entered Ramon's eyes. "I think one 'surprise' deserves another." His right hand shot out and turned on the cold water tap. Before Katie could do more than squeal a protest, her head was being forced down into the sink a bare inch from the rushing water.

"Don't you dare!" she shrieked, laughing. The water was turned up harder, and her head forced even closer to the spout. "Stop it!" she howled, her laughter echoing in the stainless-steel sink. "The water is running all over the floor!"

Ramon released her and turned off the tap. "The pipes leak," he remarked without concern. He arched an eyebrow at her and added ominously, "I will have to think of some better way to 'surprise' you."

Katie laughingly ignored the threat. "I thought you said you knew about carpentry," she teased, plunking her hands on her slim hips.

"I said," Ramon corrected dryly, "that I know as much about carpentry as you know about making curtains."

Katie choked back a giggle and managed to look comically indignant. "My curtains are progressing far better than your plumbing." *Because Gabriella and Señora Villegas are doing the sewing,* Katie added silently.

"Oh, is that right?" Ramon mocked. "Go into the bathroom."

Katie was surprised when he didn't follow her, but instead reached for the towel and the clean shirt hanging on a nail. Outside the bathroom door she paused, mentally bracing herself to face again the crawling insect population that had inhabited the rusty bathtub on Sunday. When she hesitantly opened the door her eyes widened.

Gone were the old bathroom fixtures. In their place was a modern vanity with a sink, and a large fiberglass shower stall with sliding glass doors. Experimentally, she pushed one of the doors aside, noting with approval that it slid smoothly on its track. The shower spout was dripping, however, and Katie shook her head in amusement at Ramon's lack of concern about leaking water. Cautiously, she stepped inside, avoiding the slippery puddle on the fiberglass floor, while reaching out for the tap to turn it off. Her mouth opened in a silent scream as a deluge of freezing water hit her in the face. Blinded, she turned to leap out of the shower and the leather sole of her shoe slid from beneath her, sending her sprawling on all fours beneath the icy downpour.

She crawled out of it on her hands and knees, her soaked clothing clinging to her skin, water streaming from her hair and face. Awkwardly, she struggled to her feet and lifted the hair out of her eyes. Ramon was standing in the doorway, visibly struggling to keep his face straight. "Don't you dare laugh," Katie warned darkly.

"Would you like some soap?" he offered solicitously. "A towel, perhaps?" he volunteered deadpan, handing her the towel he had been holding in his hand. He pulled the clean shirt he had just put on from his waistband and began unbuttoning it, con-

tinuing conversationally. "Would you allow me to
offer you the shirt off my back, then?"

Katie, who was on the verge of laughing herself,
was about to make some sheepish retort when Ramon added, "Strange, is it not, the way one 'surprise' can lead to another?"

Outrage burst within her at the realization that he
had actually done this to her on purpose. Shivering,
she snatched the shirt from his hand and slammed
the door in his grinning face! He must have watched
her step into the shower and then turned on the main
valve, she thought furiously as she pulled off her
freezing wet jeans. So this was how a Latin male re-
taliated for being made the recipient of an uninten-
tional dousing! This was the sort of retribution their
monstrous male egos demanded! She flung open the
bathroom door, clad only in her wet underpants and
Ramon's white shirt, and stalked out of the empty
house.

Ramon was in the front yard, calmly spreading
the blanket she had brought in the trunk of the car,
beneath a tree. Of all the monumental arrogance...! He actually believed she would meekly
tolerate this sort of treatment. He truly expected her
to stay here and have a cozy little picnic with him!

Ramon paused in his crouching position and
looked up at her, his expression impassive. "Do not
ever slam another door in my face," he said evenly.
And then, as if that was supposed to conclude the
entire episode, his expression warmed admiringly.
Seething inwardly, Katie folded her arms beneath
her breasts, leaned her shoulder against the door-

frame, and crossed one trim ankle over the other, letting him look his fill. Because looking at her was all he was going to do. In another few seconds she was going to pick up that blanket, wrap it around her and drive back to Gabriella's!

Ramon's gaze moved from the cascade of reddish hair hanging in damp waves down her shoulders, over her thrusting breasts revealed by the clinging shirt, paused at the place where his shirt ended at mid-thigh, then continued down her long, shapely legs. "Have you seen enough?" she asked him, not bothering to hide her hostility. "Are you quite satisfied?"

His head lifted sharply, his eyes assessing her face as if he could not quite fathom her mood. "Is 'satisfying' me what you have in mind, Katie?"

Ignoring the sexual innuendo, Katie straightened and strolled over to the blanket where he was sitting back on his heels. "I'm leaving," she said, looking down at him with stony hauteur.

"There is no need to go for more clothes. Yours will dry, and in the meantime, I have already seen you wearing far less."

"I'm not going for more clothes. I have no intention of staying here for a picnic after you purposely soaked me to get even."

Ramon came slowly to his feet, towering over her, and Katie angrily kept her eyes on the bare expanse of his bronzed chest. "I need the blanket to put around me so that I can go back to Gabriella's, and you're standing on it."

"So I am," he said softly, stepping back.

Katie snatched it up, wrapped it around her toga-style and headed for the car, aware that Ramon was leaning casually against a tree, watching her every step. She slid behind the steering wheel and reached for the keys she had left in the ignition. They were gone. She didn't need to search the seat, she knew exactly who had them.

She glowered at him through the open car window, and he reached into his pocket, extracted the keys and held them out to her in his open palm. "You will need these."

Katie climbed out of the car and marched toward him with as much dignity as her trailing blanket would allow. Warily, she searched his face when she came within arm's reach. "Give them to me," she said, thrusting out her hand.

"Take them," he replied indifferently.

"Do you swear you won't touch me?"

"I would not dream of it," Ramon replied with infuriating calm. "But I see no reason why I should not make you touch me." In angry stupefaction Katie watched him shove the keys into the deep pocket of his Levi's, and cross his arms over his chest. "Go ahead and take them."

"Are you enjoying this?" Katie hissed furiously.

"I am planning to."

Katie was now so angry she'd have knocked him down and wrestled him for the damned keys. She strode up to him, jammed her hand down into his side pocket ignoring the intimacy, and jerked them out. "Thank you," she said snidely.

"Thank you," he replied suggestively.

She whirled around and took a step, only to have her blanket come loose and fall to the ground—with the aid of Ramon's booted foot, which was firmly planted on the end of it. With her fists clenched impotently at her sides, Katie swung around on her heel.

"How could you think I would deliberately do a thing like that to you?" he asked her quietly.

Katie scanned his handsome, composed face, and her anger evaporated, leaving her deflated. "Didn't you?"

"What do you think?"

Katie bit her lip, feeling utterly foolish and thoroughly obnoxious. "I—I don't think you did," she admitted, glancing at her bare feet in dejected shame.

His voice was tinged with amusement. "Now what are you going to do?"

Katie's blue eyes were warm with laughter and apology when she raised them to his. "I am going to show you how sorry I am by waiting on you hand and foot for the rest of the night!"

"I see," he said with an answering grin. "In that case, what should I do now?"

"Just stand there while I arrange the blanket, then I'll pour you some wine and fix you a sandwich." With amused satisfaction, Ramon allowed her to fix him three roast beef sandwiches, keep his wineglass filled, and provide him with slices of cheese whenever he requested one.

"A man could get used to this," he chuckled when Katie insisted on not only peeling his apple but cutting it into wedges and feeding it to him.

Katie looked at him in the deepening twilight, her senses alive to his nearness. He was stretched out on his back, his hands linked behind his head, looking like a lithe, powerful jungle cat who knows that his prey is within reach and not going to escape.

"Katie," he murmured in a sensuous voice. "Do you know what I want now?"

Katie's hand stilled as she lifted her glass of wine to her lips, her pulse quickening. "What?" she asked softly.

"One of your back rubs," he announced, rolling onto his stomach, presenting his back for his ministrations.

Katie put her glass aside and came up on her knees beside him. His broad, muscled shoulders and tapered back felt like bunched satin, smooth and warm beneath her stroking fingers. She continued kneading and rubbing his hard flesh until her hands tired, then she sat back down and picked up her wineglass.

"Katie?" he said again, turning his dark head away from her.

"Hmm?"

"I did it on purpose."

In one lightning movement, Katie dumped her wine on his bare back, scampered to her feet and sprinted toward the house. Ramon grabbed her by the waist when she was halfway across the dark living room, his whole body shaking with laughter as she kicked backward at him. "You beast!" she gasped, caught somewhere between hilarity and hostility. "You are the most treacherous, arrogant—"

"Innocent person you know," he chuckled. "I give you my word."

"I could murder you!" she laughed, wriggling and writhing ineffectually in his unbreakable hold.

Behind her, his deep voice suddenly became very husky. "If you continue to do that, *I* am going to need a cold shower."

Katie stilled, becoming aware of the stirring hardness pressing against her rounded bottom, while desire began to pour through her veins. His lips brushed her ear, then slid sensuously down the curve of her neck, tasting and exploring every inch of her exposed skin. His hands caressed her breasts with the same possessive mastery that always made her knees weak.

"Your nipples are hard," he told her in a low, throbbing voice, his thumbs brushing over the hardened, sensitized nubs. "And your breasts are swelling to fill my hands. Turn around, *querida*," he murmured hotly, "I want to feel them against my chest."

Shivering with anticipation, Katie turned in his arms. He stared at the cleft between her full, aching breasts, then lifted his burning gaze to hers. Mesmerized, Katie watched his mouth slowly descending, as his hand slid up her nape and his fingers sank into her heavy hair.

The moment his parted lips covered her lips the kiss was out of control. His tongue plunged into her mouth with a driving hunger and naked urgency that made Katie burst into flames in his arms. His free hand swept down her spine, fusing her melting body

to the scorching heat of his thighs, holding her there
as he kissed her into absolute insensibility. He lifted
his mouth from hers. "Come outside with me,"
he ordered hoarsely, and when Katie whispered
"yes," he groaned and buried his lips in the moist
softness of hers for one more endless, shattering
kiss.

A blinding flash of light exploded behind Katie's
closed eyelids at the same instant a voice demanded,
"May I ask who performed the wedding that pre-
cipitated this honeymoon, Ramon?"

Katie's eyes snapped open, her shocked gaze flew
to the peculiarly garbed man who was standing in
the now brightly lit room, then ricochetted to Ramon whose head was thrown back, his eyes tightly
shut, his expression a combination of utter disbelief,
irritation and amusement. Sighing, Ramon finally
opened his eyes and looked over his left shoulder at
the intruder. "Padre Gregorio, I—"

Katie's knees buckled.

Ramon's arms tightened, his gaze swerving from
the priest to Katie's white face with its huge, stricken
eyes. "Katie, are you all right?" he asked anxiously.

"I am certain that Señorita Connelly is not all
right," the old priest snapped. "She would undoubtedly like to go and clothe herself."

Embarrassed antagonism brought bright flags of
color to Katie's pale cheeks. "My clothes are soak-
ing wet," she said. Unfortunately at that moment
she became conscious that with Ramon's arms
around her, his shirt was hiked up above the lace
band at the leg of her underpants. Self-consciously

she jerked the shirt down and pulled away from Ramon's supporting arms.

"Then perhaps you would like to put that blanket I saw outside, to the use for which it was intended, and cover yourself with it."

Ramon said something in sharp Spanish to the priest and reached out to stop Katie, but she sidestepped and stalked outside. She was humiliated, intimidated and furiously angry with herself for feeling like a naughty fifteen-year-old. That hateful, domineering old man was the priest whose approval she had to win before he would perform their marriage, she raged inwardly. Never, never in her life had she despised anyone more! In ten seconds he had made her feel dirty and cheap. She who was practically a virgin by today's standards!

Ramon was speaking to the priest in a calm voice when Katie entered the cottage wrapped in the blanket. He held his arm out to her and drew her comfortingly close to his side, but his first words were laced with reproof. "Why did you not keep your appointment with Padre Gregorio, Katie?"

Katie's chin lifted defensively as she looked at the priest. Bald at the crown, his head was circled with a wide rim of white hair. His bushy white eyebrows slanted up at the ends, giving him a satanic look, which Katie thought was entirely appropriate for an old devil! Nevertheless, her eyes wavered when they collided with his piercing blue ones. "I forgot it."

Katie could actually feel Ramon's narrowed gaze aimed at her head.

"In that case," Padre Gregorio said in a cool, uncompromising voice, "Perhaps you would care to make another—for four o'clock tomorrow afternoon."

Katie agreed to this command performance with an ungracious, "Very well."

"I will drive you back to the village, Padre," Ramon said.

Katie nearly dropped through the floor when, after nodding his acceptance, the priest directed a meaningful look at her over the rim of his wire spectacles. "I am certain that Señorita Connelly wants to return to Gabriella's now. It is growing late."

Without waiting for Ramon to reply, Katie turned abruptly and walked into the bathroom, closing the door. In a state of suffocating humiliation, she struggled into her damp clothing and combed her fingers through her hair.

Pulling open the door, she walked right into Ramon who was standing in the doorway, his hands braced high against the frame on either side of her. The wry amusement in his expression chafed against her already lacerated emotions. "Katie, he thinks he is protecting your virtue from my lecherous intentions."

Katie, who was suddenly perilously close to tears, stared at the cleft in Ramon's chin. "He doesn't believe for one minute that I have any virtue! Now please let's go, I want to get out of here. I—I'm tired."

As Katie stalked toward Padre Gregorio who was standing at the car, her soaked canvas shoes made a loud, squishing noise and her denim Levi's slapped wetly against her legs. This indisputable proof that her clothes had truly been soaked brought a flickering smile of approval to the priest's lips, but Katie merely gave him a frosty look and slid into the car. On the way to the village, he made two attempts to converse with her, which Katie discouraged by replying in monosyllables.

After leaving the priest in the village, they pulled up at Gabriella's house. Fifteen minutes later, when Katie emerged from her bedroom in dry clothes, Ramon was standing in the living room talking with Gabriella's husband, Eduardo. The moment he saw her, Ramon excused himself and invited Katie outside. Most of the ill effects from her encounter with Padre Gregorio had evaporated, but Katie was vaguely uneasy about Ramon's mood.

In heavy silence, they strolled through the neat little backyard. At the far end of it, Katie stopped and leaned her shoulders against a tree trunk. Ramon's hands came down on either side of her, imprisoning her. Katie saw the determination in his jaw and the cool speculation in his intent gaze. "Why did you not go to see Padre Gregorio this afternoon, Katie?"

Completely taken aback, Katie stammered. "I—I told you, I forget."

"I reminded you this morning when I came to see you, before I left for work. How could you forget it a few hours later?"

"I forgot it," she said defensively, "because I was busy doing what I've been doing for four days—trying to buy everything you need for your house."

"Why do you always refer to it as my house instead of our house?" he persisted relentlessly.

"Why are you suddenly asking me all these questions?" Katie burst out.

"Because when I ask myself the questions, I do not like the answers that occur to me." Moving back a step, he calmly extracted a thin cigar and lighter from his pocket. With his hands cupped over the flame he lit it, watching an uncomfortable Katie through the haze of aromatic smoke. "Padre Gregorio is the only possible obstacle to our getting married in ten days, is he not?"

Katie felt as if he were verbally stalking her, backing her into a corner. "I suppose so, yes."

"Tell me something," he said with casual curiosity. "Are you planning to keep your appointment with him tomorrow?"

Katie raked her hair off her forehead in an agitated gesture. "Yes, I'm going to keep it. But you may as well know right now that he doesn't like me, and I think he's nothing but a tyrannical busybody."

Ramon dismissed this with a noncommittal shrug. "I believe it is customary, even in the States, for a priest to assure himself that an engaged couple is reasonably suited to each other and has a good chance of making a successful marriage. That is all he wishes to do."

"He's not going to believe that about us! He's already decided the opposite."

"No, he has not," Ramon stated implacably. He moved closer and Katie unconsciously pressed back against the rough bark of the tree. His gaze roamed her face, calculating her answer to his next question before he even asked it. "Do you *want* him to decide we are not suited, Katie?"

"No!" Katie whispered.

"Tell me about your first marriage," he commanded abruptly.

"I will not!" Katie flung back, her whole body stiffening with anger. "Don't ever ask me to do that, because I won't. I try never to think about it."

"If you had truly recovered from it without scars," Ramon continued, "you should be able to talk about it without pain."

"Talk about it?!" Katie exploded in stunned rage. "Talk about it?" The violence of her own reaction momentarily shocked Katie into silence. Drawing a deep breath, she gained control of her stampeding emotions. With an apologetic smile at Ramon who was studying her like a specimen under a microscope, she said, "It's only that I don't want the ugliness of the past to spoil the present, and it would. Surely you can see that?"

The ghost of a reluctant smile touched Ramon's face as he gazed down at the smooth perfection of her glowing features. "I can see," he sighed softly. His hands slid up her arms in a gentle caress, tightening to draw her close against his heart. "I can see that you have a beautiful smile, and that you look tired."

Katie twined her arms around his neck. She knew he wasn't satisfied with her explanation, and she was grateful beyond words that he wasn't going to pursue it further. "I am a little tired. I think I'll go to bed."

"And when you are lying in bed, what do you think about?" he asked, his voice husky and teasing.

Katie's eyes held an answering sparkle. "A color scheme for the kitchen," she lied.

"Oh, is that right?" he breathed softly.

Katie nodded, a slow smile touching her lips. "What do you think about?"

"The wholesale price of pineapples."

"Liar," she whispered, her gaze on the sensual mouth that had moved tantalizingly close to hers.

"Yellow," he breathed against her lips.

"You mean the pineapples?" Katie murmured absently.

"I mean the kitchen."

"I thought green," she said, her heart pounding with anticipation.

Ramon drew back abruptly, his entire expression friendly and thoughtful. "Perhaps you are right. Green is a lively color, and one rarely becomes tired of it." He turned her and headed her toward the house with an affectionate pat on her derriere. "You think about it in bed tonight."

Katie took a few surprised steps, then turned to look at Ramon with puzzled disappointment.

His even white teeth flashed in a lazy grin as he quirked a brow at her. "Did you want something more? Something better to think about in bed, perhaps?"

Katie felt the sexual magnetism he was exuding as if it were some primitive force against which she had no resistence.

Even his velvet voice seemed to reach out and touch her. "Come here, Katie, and I will give it to you."

Katie's whole body felt flushed as she walked into his crushing embrace. The turmoil of the last hour, the wild fluctuations of mood from desire to humiliation to anger and now to teasing, had twisted Katie into a mass of raw emotion that exploded the instant Ramon's arms closed around her.

Driven by a desperate need to somehow reassure Ramon—and herself—that everything was going to be all right, she kissed him with an unleashed urgency, a deep passion that sent a tremor through his powerful frame and made his arms tighten convulsively.

Ramon pulled his lips from hers and kissed her face, her forehead, her eyes, her neck.

And just before his mouth sought hers for one last stormy kiss, she thought he whispered, "Katie, I love you."

CHAPTER FIFTEEN

KATIE AND GABRIELLA spent the morning and most of the afternoon combing through shops in two neighboring villages. Katie liked Gabriella immensely. Besides being a wonderful companion, she was a tireless shopper. At times she was more enthusiastic about what Katie was doing than Katie was. But then, endless shopping with hundreds of things to buy and no time to do it was not Katie's idea of pleasure.

Katie paid for the sheets and coverlet she had just bought, while Gabriella delicately removed herself from the procedure that involved Katie's requesting duplicate bills, each for one-half the amount of her purchase, then paying for it using equal parts of Ramon's money and her own.

"I think Ramon will like the colors I chose for the bedroom, don't you?" Katie asked gaily as they slid into the car.

"He should," Gabriella said, turning in the seat to look at Katie with a smile. Her thick black hair was beautifully windblown and her eyes were bright. "Everything you buy is to suit him and not yourself. I would have bought the coverlet with the ruffles."

Katie, who was driving, glanced in the rearview

mirror before pulling into the slow traffic, then she fired a wry look at Gabriella.

"Somehow I can't quite see Ramon surrounded by dainty ruffles with pastel flowers."

"Eduardo is as manly as Ramon and he would not object if I chose to make our bedroom feminine."

Katie had to admit to herself that what Gabriella said was true; Eduardo would probably acquiesce to Gabriella's wishes with one of those faint, amused smiles he frequently gave her. In the last four days, Katie had revised her opinion of Eduardo. He didn't look at the world with stern, disapproving eyes—he only looked at Katie that way. He was always unfailingly courteous to her, but the moment she walked into the room the warmth left his expression.

It might not have been so uncomfortable for Katie if he were small and homely or big and slow-witted, but the truth of the matter was that Eduardo was a very impressive man, which immediately made Katie feel that she was somehow lacking. At thirty-five, he was extremely handsome in a darkly Spanish way. He was three inches shorter than Ramon, with a powerful build and an attitude of confident male supremacy that alternately annoyed and intrigued Katie. He was not Ramon's equal in either looks or polish, but when the two men were together there was an easy comradery between them that made Katie acutely aware that she, and only she, failed to meet some unknown standard of Eduardo's. He treated his wife with indulgent affection; Ramon with an odd combination of friendship and admiration. . . and Katie with nothing more than courtesy.

"Have I done something to offend Eduardo?" Katie asked aloud, half-expecting Gabriella to deny anything unusual in his attitude.

"You must not pay any attention to him," Gabriella said with amazing candor. "Eduardo mistrusts all American girls, especially wealthy ones such as you. He thinks they are spoiled and irresponsible, among other things."

Katie assumed that "other things" probably included promiscuous. "What makes him think I'm wealthy?" she asked cautiously.

Gabriella flashed an apologetic smile at her. "Your luggage. Eduardo used to work at the desk of a fancy hotel in San Juan while he was going to school. He says your luggage costs more than all the furniture in our living room."

Before Katie could recover, Gabriella turned grave. "Eduardo likes Ramon very much for many reasons, and he is afraid that you will not adjust to being a Spanish farmer's wife. Eduardo thinks, because you are a wealthy American woman, that you lack courage, that you will leave when you discover that your life here is sometimes hard; that when the crop is poor or prices are low you will flaunt your money in front of Ramon."

Katie flushed uncomfortably and Gabriella nodded sagely. "That is why Eduardo must never discover that you are paying for part of the furniture. He would condemn you for disobeying Ramon and he would think you are doing this because what Ramon could buy wasn't good enough for you. I do not know why you are paying for things, Katie, but I

do not think it is because of that. Someday you can
tell me if you wish to do so, but in the meantime
Eduardo must not find out. He would tell Ramon
immediately.''

"Neither of them will find out unless you say
something," Katie reassured with a smile.

"You know I will not." Gabriella glanced up at
the sun. "Do you want to go to the auction at that
house in Mayagüez? We are very close."

Katie readily agreed, and three hours later she was
proud owner of a dining set for the kitchen, a sofa
and two chairs. The house had been owned by a
wealthy bachelor who, before his death, had obviously developed an appreciation for fine wood, excellent craftsmanship and solid comfort. The chairs
were wing-backed, deeply tufted in a nubby cream
cloth with rust threads. There were two ottomans to
match. The sofa was rust with wide rolled arms and
deep thick cushions. "Ramon will love it," Katie
said as she paid the auctioneer and arranged to have
the furniture delivered to the cottage.

"Katie, will you love it?" Gabriella asked anxiously. "You are going to live there, too, yet you have not
bought one thing just because you want it."

"Of course I have," Katie said.

At ten minutes to four, Gabriella stopped the car
in front of Padre Gregorio's little house. It was on
the east side of the village square, directly across the
street from the church, easily identified by its white
paint and dark green shutters. Katie took her hand-
bag off the seat, threw a nervous smile at Gabriella,
and slid out of the car.

"Are you certain you don't want me to wait for you?" Gabriella asked.

"Positive," Katie said. "It isn't a long walk to your house from here, and I'll have plenty of time to change clothes afterward and go to see Ramon at the cottage."

Reluctantly Katie walked up to the front door. She paused to smooth the skirt of her pastel green cotton shirtwaist dress and run a shaky hand over her light red hair, which was caught into a soft chignon with tendrils at her ears. She looked, she hoped, very prim proper and composed. She felt like a nervous wreck.

An elderly housekeeper answered Katie's knock and admitted her into the house. Following her down the dim hall, Katie felt like a condemned prisoner walking the last steps to meet the executioner— though why she felt so upset was something that baffled her.

Padre Gregorio stood up when she entered his study. He was thinner and shorter than she had thought last night, which was absurdly reassuring considering that they weren't going to engage in physical combat. Katie took the seat he indicated across the desk from him, and he sat down.

For a moment they regarded one another with polite wariness, then he said, "Would you care for some coffee?"

"Thank you, no," Katie replied with a fixed, courteous smile. "I haven't a great deal of time to spare." That was the wrong thing to say, Katie realized as his bushy white brows snapped together over his nose.

"No doubt you have more important things to do," he said curtly.

"Not for myself," Katie hastily explained, by way of a truce. "For Ramon."

To her immense relief, Padre Gregorio accepted the truce offering. His tight lips relaxed into something that was almost a smile as he nodded his white head. "Ramon is in a great hurry to have everything finished, and he must be keeping you extremely busy." Reaching into his desk, he pulled out some forms and picked up his pen. "Let us begin by completing these forms. Your full name and age, please?"

Katie told him.

"Marital status?" Before Katie could answer, he glanced up and sadly said, "Ramon mentioned that your first husband died. How tragic for you to have been widowed in the first bloom of your marriage."

Hypocrisy had never been one of Katie's faults. Politely but firmly she said, "I was 'widowed' in the first bloom of our divorce, and if there was a tragedy, it was that we were ever married at all."

Behind the spectacles the blue eyes narrowed. "I beg your pardon?"

"I divorced him before he died."

"For what reason?"

"Irreconcilable differences."

"I did not ask you for the legal grounds, I asked you the reason."

His prying struck sparks of rebellion in Katie's breast, and she expelled a slow, calming breath. "I divorced him because I despised him."

"Why?"

"I would rather not discuss it."

"I see," Padre Gregorio said. He shoved the papers aside, laid down his pen, and Katie felt the fragile truce begin to crumble. "In that case, perhaps you would not object to discussing Ramon and yourself. How long have you known each other?"

"Only two weeks."

"What an unusual answer," he remarked. "Where did you meet?"

"In the States."

"Señorita Connelly," he said in a chilling tone, "would you consider it an invasion of your privacy if I asked you to be a little more specific?"

Katie's eyes flashed militantly. "Not at all, Padre. I met Ramon at a bar—a *cantina*, I think you call it here."

He looked stunned. "Ramon met you in a *cantina*?"

"Actually, it was outside."

"Pardon?"

"It was outside, in the parking lot. I was having some trouble and Ramon helped me."

Padre Gregorio relaxed in his chair and nodded his complete approval. "Of course. You were having automobile trouble, and Ramon assisted you."

As if she had taken an oath to tell the whole truth and nothing but, Katie corrected him. "Actually, I was having trouble with a man who was, ah, kissing me in the parking lot, and Ramon hit him. He was a little intoxicated I think."

Behind his gold wire spectacles, the priest's eyes

turned into icicles. "*Señorita*," he said with contempt, "are you trying to tell me that Ramon Galverra engaged in a drunken brawl in a public parking lot of a *cantina* over some woman he did not know—namely, you?"

"Of course not! Ramon hadn't been drinking, and I certainly wouldn't call it a brawl—he only hit Rob once, and that knocked him unconscious."

"And then what?" the priest demanded impatiently.

Unfortunately, Katie's wayward sense of humor chose that moment to assert itself. "Then we stuffed Rob in his car, and Ramon and I drove away in mine."

"Charming."

A genuine smile drifted across Katie's features. "Actually, it wasn't quite as terrible as it sounds."

"I find that hard to believe."

Katie's smile faded. Her eyes turned a deep, rebellious blue. "Believe whatever you wish, padre."

"It is what *you* wish me to believe that astounds me, *Señorita*," he snapped, rising from behind his desk. Katie stood up, her emotions so tangled by this unexpectedly abrupt conclusion to their interview that she scarcely knew whether she felt relieved or worried. "What do you mean by that?" she asked, puzzled.

"You think about it, and we will meet again on Monday morning at nine."

AN HOUR LATER, Katie had changed into slacks and a white knit shirt. She felt angry, bewildered and guilty as she began the hike up the long hill from

Gabriella's house to the cottage where Ramon was working.

On the first plateau, she turned to look out over the hills splashed with wild flowers. She could still pick out the roof of Gabriella's house, and Rafael's house, and of course, the village itself. Ramon's cottage was so much higher than the surrounding houses—two more plateaus up, in fact—that Katie decided to sit down and rest. Drawing her legs up against her chest, she wrapped her arms around them and perched her chin on her knees.

"It is what *you* wish me to believe that astounds me, *Señorita*," the old priest had said. He actually made it seem as if she were *trying* to give him a bad impression, Katie thought angrily, when in actuality she had shopped all day in a shirtwaist and heels so that she would be appropriately and respectfully dressed when she kept her appointment!

She had merely told him the truth about how she and Ramon had met, and if that outraged his old-fashioned morality it was certainly not her fault. If he didn't want his questions answered, he shouldn't ask so many of them, Katie thought wrathfully.

The more she thought about it, the more blameless Katie felt for the hostile tone of her first meeting with Padre Gregorio. In fact, she was feeling quite justifiably indignant about the whole thing until Ramon's words floated through her mind. "How could you forget your appointment with Padre Gregorio only a few hours after I reminded you of it? . . . Padre Gregorio is the only possible obstacle to our getting married in ten days.... Do you *want* him to decide we are not suited, Katie?''

Uncertainty promptly cooled Katie's ire. How could she have forgotten that appointment? Her first wedding had required months of preparation and countless appointments with dressmakers, florists, caterers, photographers, printers and a half-dozen other people. Not once had she ever ''forgotten'' an appointment with any of them.

Had she subconsciously wanted to forget yesterday's appointment with Padre Gregorio, Katie wondered a little guiltily. Had she deliberately tried to make a bad impression on Padre Gregorio today? That question made Katie squirm inwardly. No, she hadn't tried to impress him either way—bad or good, she admitted to herself. But she *had* let him form a distorted and unflattering image of her meeting with Ramon at the Canyon Inn, without trying to correct it.

When he tried to probe into her divorce she had practically told him it was none of his business. With innate honesty, Katie conceded that it was very much his business. On the other hand, she felt she had a right to resent anyone—anyone at all—who tried to force her to discuss David. Still, she could have been less hostile about the subject. She could have simply told Padre Gregorio that her reason for divorcing David was adultery and physical brutality. Then, if he tried to delve further into the subject, she could have explained that the details were impossible for her to discuss and she would rather forget about it.

That's what she should have done. Instead she had been uncooperative, flippant and coldly defiant. In fact, she could not remember ever being so brazenly discourteous to anyone in her life. As a result, she had antagonized the only man who could stand in the way of her marrying Ramon in ten days. What a foolish, irrational thing for her to have done.

Katie picked up an African tulip that had fallen beside her and began idly stripping it of its scarlet petals. Unbidden, Gabriella's words came to mind. "You have not bought one thing just because *you* want it." At the time, Katie had disregarded that as being untrue. But now that she really thought about it, she realized that she had unconsciously avoided choosing one single item that would put the stamp of her femininity, or her personality, on Ramon's house. Because that would obligate her to marry him and live there.

The closer their wedding day came, the more alarmed and hesitant she was becoming. There was no point in denying it, but admitting it didn't help either. When she left St. Louis with Ramon she had been so certain that coming here was the right thing to do. Now, she was certain of nothing. She couldn't understand her fear or her uncertainty; she couldn't even understand some of the things she was doing! For someone who prided herself on her logical thinking, she was suddenly behaving like a complete neurotic. There was absolutely no excuse for her behavior, Katie thought angrily.

Or perhaps there was. The last time she had committed herself to a man, to marriage, her world had fallen apart. Few people knew better than she what an agonizing, humiliating experience a bad marriage could be. Perhaps marriage was not worth the risk. Perhaps she should never have considered remarrying and—no! Absolutely not!

She would not let the emotional scars David left her with ruin her life and destroy her chance to have a warm and happy marriage. She would not give David Caldwell that much satisfaction—dead or alive!

Katie jumped up and brushed off her slacks. On the second plateau, she turned again and looked down on the village. She smiled softly, thinking that it looked like a page from a travel brochure; tiny white toy buildings nestled in green hills, with the church in the center. The church where she would be married in ten days.

Her stomach instantly clenched into knots at the thought, and Katie could have wept in desperation. She felt as if she were being torn to pieces. Her mind pulled her one way and her heart tugged another. Fear coiled in her chest, desire pulsed through her veins, and her love for Ramon burned like a steady, glowing fire in the center of it all.

And she did love him. She loved him very much.

She had never actually admitted that to herself before, and the admission sent a fierce jolt of pleasure and panic through her. Now that she acknowledged her feelings, why couldn't she just accept her love for this beautiful, tender, passionate man, and follow wherever it led her?

Follow love wherever it led her, Katie thought with bitter despair. She had done that once before, and it had led her into a living nightmare. Biting her lip, Katie turned away and started up the hill again.

Why was she suddenly thinking of David and her first marriage all the time, she wondered miserably. The only similarity between David and Ramon, other than their height and coloring, was that they were both intelligent. David had been an ambitious, talented attorney; a polished, worldly man. While Ramon....

While Ramon was an enigma, a puzzle: a well-spoken, widely read, intelligent man with an intense interest in, and staggering grasp of, world affairs. A man who could mingle with effortless ease among her parents' sophisticated friends—a man who chose, nevertheless, to be a farmer. A man who chose to be a farmer, yet had no deep feeling, no real pride, in his land. He had never offered to take Katie into the fields, even though she had asked to see them, and when he discussed improving the farm with Rafael, Ramon spoke with resolute determination—but never any real enthusiasm.

Katie had been so surprised by his attitude that earlier this week she asked him if he had ever wanted to do something besides farm. Ramon had answered with an uninformative "Yes."

"Then why are you going to do it?" Katie had persisted.

"Because the farm is here," he had replied unanswerably. "Because it is ours. Because I have found more peace and joy being here with you than I have ever known.''

Peace from what, Katie wondered desperately. And if he was really happy, he didn't always look it. In fact, there were many times this past week when Katie had glanced at him and glimpsed a grim tautness in his face, a ravaged harshness in his eyes. The instant he realized she was watching him, the expression would vanish. He would smile at her—one of his warmly intimate smiles.

What was he hiding from her? Some deep sadness? Or something much worse? A streak of viciousness like David's or—

Katie shook her head in denial. Ramon was nothing like David. Nothing like him. She stopped in her climb to break off a branch of a small flamboyant tree. It was covered with yellow blossoms and she raised the branch to her nose, trying to chase away the tormenting uncertainties that pursued her everywhere.

As she came to the top of the hill, Katie heard the sounds of hammers and saws coming from the cottage. Four painters were working on the outside applying a fresh coat of white paint to the bricks and wood trim, another was painting the shutters black.

Her spirits lifted when she compared the rundown hovel it had seemed to be on Sunday, with the way it looked now. In five days, with the help of an army of carpenters, Ramon was transforming it into the picturesque little house he must have remembered visiting in the days when his grandfather lived here.

"Flower boxes," Katie said aloud. She tipped her head to the side, trying to visualize the boxes blooming with flowers below the wide windows on either side of the front door. That was exactly what the cottage needed, she decided. That would make it a storybook cottage in a storybook setting on a storybook island. But would her life be a storybook life here?

She found Ramon stepping off a ladder on the far side of the house where he had also been painting. At the sound of her softly spoken "Hi" he turned in surprise; a slow, devastatingly attractive smile sweeping across his tanned features. He was so obviously pleased to see her that Katie felt suddenly, absurdly happy, too.

"I brought you something," she joked, taking the blossom-covered branch from behind her back and thrusting it toward him like a bouquet.

"Flowers?" Ramon teased, accepting the branch with grave formality. "For me?"

Though his tone was light, Katie caught the warmth kindling in his expressive eyes. She nodded, a provocative smile curving her lips. "Tomorrow it will be candy."

"And the next day?"

"Oh, jewelry is customary. Something tastefully expensive, but small—nothing ostentatious that might alert you to my true intentions."

He grinned. "And the next day?"

"Lock your doors and guard your virtue, because that's collection day," she laughed.

His broad chest was bare, gleaming like oiled

bronze, and he smelled like soap and sweat, a combination that Katie found strangely stimulating as he pulled her into his arms. "For you," he said as his hands moved lazily over her back and his mobile mouth came nearer to hers, "I will be an easy conquest: my virtue for the flowers alone."

"Shameless hussy!" Katie teased a little breathlessly.

His eyes darkened. "Kiss me, Katie."

CHAPTER SIXTEEN

KATIE'S HEAD JERKED up as Padre Gregorio said her name from the altar, followed by Ramon's. He was reading the banns, she realized. Everyone in the crowded church seemed to turn in unison toward the pew near the back where Katie and Ramon were seated between Gabriella and her husband, and Rafael's family.

The villagers certainly knew who Ramon Galverra Vicente was, Katie thought, which wasn't surprising, since he had been born here. But what was surprising was their peculiar attitude toward him. From the moment he had walked into church at her side, they had been watching him with open curiosity. A few of the villagers nodded or smiled at him, but there was curiosity in their expressions, too, mixed with uncertainty and even awe.

Of course, Ramon's demeanor before the service began had definitely discouraged anyone who might have wanted to make a friendly overture. With an aloof, coolly courteous smile, he had passed one glance over the inquisitive occupants of the church, sat down beside Katie, and completely ignored them.

Katie shifted uncomfortably in the hard pew, her

expression one of rapt attention as she listened to
Padre Gregorio's sermon, of which she understood
not one word. She was beginning to wonder if the
fates were all conspiring to prevent Ramon and her
from being alone together for any appreciable
length of time. In the last seven days there had been
no occasion for the "sharing of each other" that
Ramon had predicted there would be.

On Friday, while Katie was still wrapped in
Ramon's arms joyously receiving his drugging kisses
of gratitude for his "bouquet," a bank of dark
clouds had rolled across the sky, blotting out the
sun. What began as a sprinkle soon became a downpour. They spent a pleasant, if very unsatisfactory,
evening playing cards with Gabriella and her husband.

Saturday it cleared, and the men worked all day at
the cottage. Now that the electricity was on, Ramon
was keeping them working inside when darkness
fell, which eliminated the cottage as a trysting place.
Early Saturday evening, Gabriella's husband,
Eduardo, suggested to Ramon that Katie might enjoy a trip to Phosphorescent Bay.

Katie had been amazed that Eduardo, of all
people, would suggest a romantic outing for them,
as well as offer his car for the drive to the south-
western coast of the island. She couldn't imagine
Eduardo in the role of Cupid, when she knew he
heartily disapproved of her. The mystery was solved
the moment Ramon consulted Katie and she eagerly
agreed to the trip. "Then it is settled," Eduardo
said. "Gabriella and I will be pleased to have you

accompany us.'' That effectively prevented Ramon and her from being alone in the house while Eduardo took Gabriella to the bay. Beneath Ramon's expression of bland surprise, Katie could tell that he was very annoyed with his friend.

Despite that, the evening was an unexpected success. At the beginning of the fifty-mile drive over well-maintained island roads, Ramon was silent and thoughtful as he sat beside Katie in the back seat. Realizing that Eduardo was the cause, Katie put on her brightest smile and soon had Ramon grinning at her while he tried to answer her endless questions about the passing landscape.

Phosphorescent Bay was a magical experience for Katie. The same heavy clouds that had brought the rain and kept most of the tourists away from the Bay, also obliterated the moon. With Gabriella and Eduardo in the front of the rented motorboat and Katie and Ramon in the rear, Katie alternately turned her face up to Ramon's for a lingering stolen kiss, then twisted in her seat to watch the shimmering green lights that swelled in the wake of the boat. At Ramon's suggestion, she leaned over the side and dipped her arm into the water. When she lifted it, a veil of the same shimmering green lights clung to her arm. Even the fish that leaped from the water left a shower of light behind them.

For his part, Ramon relaxed in the boat, looking like an indulgently amused native who was humoring three tourists. If there was anything he enjoyed more than watching Katie enjoy herself, it was thwarting Eduardo's wish to have some romantic privacy with his wife in the back of the boat. Each time Eduardo suggested Ramon and Katie take the front seat, Ramon declined with a good-natured, "We are perfectly comfortable back here, Eduardo."

By the end of the evening, it was Eduardo who looked annoyed and Ramon who was grinning with satisfaction.

Thunder boomed, echoing through the dim church, followed by a triple flash of lightning that illuminated the splendid stained-glass windows. Katie smiled wryly, accepting what was apparently going to be another day when the weather drove them indoors, another day and evening when Ramon and she would not even be able to talk alone.

"WE HAVE A PERFECT DAY for shopping," Gabriella announced at eight-thirty the next morning as she carried her cup of coffee into Katie's bedroom. "The sun is out," she added gaily, sitting down on the bed. She sipped her coffee, watching Katie who was getting ready for her appointment with Padre Gregorio.

"Do I look demure enough, do you think?" Katie asked, straightening the gold chain at the waist of her mandarin-collared white dress.

"You look perfect," Gabriella smiled. "You look the way you always look—beautiful!"

Katie rolled her eyes, laughingly accepting the compliment as she left the house, and promised to come back for Gabriella as soon as she was finished with Padre Gregorio.

Fifteen minutes later, Katie was not laughing. She was pinned to her chair, flushing under Padre Gregorio's piercing scrutiny.

"I asked," he repeated ominously, "if Ramon knows that you are using your money, your credit cards, to pay for the furnishings for that house?"

"No," Katie admitted apprehensively. "How did you find out?"

"We will get to that in a minute," he said in a low, angry voice. "First I want to know if you are aware that Ramon is returning to this village after an absence of many years? That he left it long ago for something better?"

"Yes—to work for a business that failed."

Her admission made Padre Gregorio look even angrier. "Then you understood that Ramon has come back here to start over again, with nothing?"

Katie nodded, feeling as if the ax were about to fall, though she wasn't certain from which direction.

"Do you have any idea, *señorita*, how much strength and courage it takes for a man to return to his birthplace, not as a success, but as a failure? Do you realize what it does to his pride when he must face people who all believed he had left them and achieved success—and who will now see that he has come back defeated?"

"I don't think Ramon feels defeated or disgraced," Katie protested.

Padre Gregorio's hand hit the desk with a crash. "No, he was not disgraced—but he is going to be, thanks to you! Thanks to you, everyone in this village is going to be saying that his rich *novia* from the United States had to pay for the towels so he could wipe his hands!"

"No one knows that I've been paying for half of everything!" Katie burst out. "Except you, and— no one," she amended quickly, protecting Gabriella.

"No one, except you and I," he mocked scathingly. "And Gabriella Alverez, of course. And half the village who are this minute gossiping about it to the other half! Do I make myself clear?"

Miserably, Katie nodded.

"Gabriella has obviously kept it secret from Eduardo, or he would have told Ramon. You have forced her to deceive her own husband for you!"

Apprehensively, Katie watched him trying to get control of his temper. "Señorita Connelly, is there the remotest, the slightest possibility that you thought Ramon would not object to what you are doing?"

More than anything, Katie longed to snatch at this excuse, but her pride prevented her from cowering. "No, I had mentioned to Ramon that I wanted to share the cost of things, and he—he wasn't pleased with the idea." She saw the priest's eyes narrow. "All right, he was adamantly opposed to it."

"So," he said in an awful voice. "Ramon told you not to, but you did it anyway, only slyly, is that it? You disobeyed him."

Katie's temper flared. "Do not use the word *disobey* to me, Padre. I am not a trained dog. Secondly, I would like to remind you that I have been 'slyly' spending a great deal of *my* money for Ramon which I think comes under the heading of charity, and is hardly a crime.

"Charity!" he exploded furiously. "Is that what Ramon is to you—a charity case, an object of pity?"

"No! Of course not!" Katie's eyes were huge with genuine horror.

"If you are paying for half of everything, then you are spending twice what he can afford. Are you so spoiled that you must have exactly what you want right now, this minute?"

Compared to this, Katie thought the Spanish Inquisition must have been a breeze. She couldn't avoid his question, and she certainly couldn't tell him she'd paid for half of everything so she wouldn't feel obligated to marry Ramon.

"I am waiting for an answer."

"And I would like to give you one," miserably. "Only I can't. I didn't do it for any of the reasons you think. It's too hard to explain."

"It is even harder to understand. In fact, *señorita*, I do not understand *you*. Gabriella is your friend, yet you do not hesitate to involve her in your treachery. You are staying under Eduardo's roof, yet you feel no remorse for repaying his hospitality by forcing his wife to mislead him. You want to marry Ramon, yet you disobey him, deceive him and disgrace him. How can you do that to someone you love?"

The color began draining out of Katie's face and Padre Gregorio, noting her stricken expression, shook his head in frustration. When he spoke again his voice was strained, but gentler. "*Señorita*, despite everything, I cannot believe that you are either selfish or heartless. You must have had some good reason for doing what you have; tell me so that I can understand."

Speechless with misery, Katie could only look at him.

"Tell me!" he said, his face angry and bewildered. "Tell me that you love Ramon, and that you did not realize the village would gossip. I would believe that; I would even help you explain it to Ramon. Just say that, and we will finish making the arrangements for your marriage right now."

Katie's stomach was cramping painfully, but her pale face was composed. "I don't owe you any explanations, padre. And I will not discuss my feelings about Ramon with you, either."

His bushy white eyebrows knitted together into a thunderous scowl. Leaning back in his chair, he subjected Katie to a long penetrating stare. "You will not speak of your feelings for Ramon, because you have no feelings for him. . . . Is that it?"

"I didn't say that!" Katie denied, but the convulsive clenching of her hands in her lap betrayed her inner turmoil.

"Can you say you love him?"

Katie felt as if she were being torn to pieces by raging emotions she could neither understand nor control. She tried to say the words he was waiting to hear, to give him the assurance he had a right to expect, but she could not. All she could do was look at him in frozen silence.

Padre Gregorio's shoulders drooped. When he spoke, the terrible despair in his voice made her feel like bursting into tears. "I see," he said quietly. "Feeling as you do, what kind of wife could you possibly be to Ramon?"

"A good one!" Katie whispered fiercely.

The intensity of her emotion seemed to stun him. He stared at her again, as if he were truly trying to understand her. His gaze moved over her pale face, searching her blue eyes and discovering something in their agonized depths that brought a puzzled gentleness to his voice. "Very well," he said softly. "I will accept that."

This astonishing announcement had an equally astonishing effect on Katie, who suddenly began to shake from head to toe with an unexplainable mixture of relief and alarm.

"If you tell me that you are prepared to fulfill your duties as Ramon's wife, I will believe you. Are you willing to put his needs before your own, to honor and respect his—"

"Authority?" Katie provided tersely. "Don't forget 'obey' him," she added mutinously as she stood up. "Isn't that what you were going to ask?"

Padre Gregorio also arose. "Suppose that I was?" he queried in a tone of cool curiosity. "What would you say?"

"Exactly what any other woman with a brain, a mouth and a backbone should say to such an outrageous insulting suggestion! I will not, *will not* promise obedience to any man. Animals and children obey, not women!''

"Are you quite through, *señorita*?"

Katie swallowed and nodded firmly.

"Then allow me to tell you that I was not going to mention the word 'obey.' I was about to ask you if you were willing to respect Ramon's wishes, not his authority. And for your information, I would have asked Ramon for exactly the same commitments I asked you to make.''

Katie's lashes shadowed her pale cheeks, hiding her acute embarrassment. "I'm sorry," she said in a small voice. "I thought—"

"There is no need to apologize," Padre Gregorio sighed wearily. He turned and walked over to the window that looked out on the little square and the church. "And you will not need to come back here again," he added without looking at her. "I will let Ramon know what I have decided."

"Which is?" Katie managed.

His jaw was set as he shook his head. "I want to think about it quietly for a while before I decide anything."

Katie ran her hand through her hair. "Padre Gregorio, you can't prevent us from being married. If you don't marry us, someone else will."

His back stiffened. Turning slowly, he gave her a look that was both angry and amused. "Thank you for reminding me of my limitations, *señorita*. I would have been very disappointed in you if you had not found some new way to antagonize me just before you leave, so that I will have the worst possible opinion of you.''

Katie looked at him in frustrated fury. "You are the most self-important, self-righteous—!'' She drew a long, deliberate breath, trying to steady herself. ''I don't happen to care what your opinion of me is.''

Padre Gregorio inclined his head in an exaggerated bow. ''Thank you again.''

KATIE PULLED UP a handful of grass and irritably flung it away. She was sitting on a large flat rock, her back supported against a tree, looking blindly out across three miles of gently rolling hills and valleys. The sun was setting in streaks of red and gold, but the view hadn't soothed her temper after this morning's meeting with Padre Gregorio. Neither had six hours of shopping with Gabriella. A hundred yards off to her right, the men working in the cottage were putting down their tools and leaving for dinner at their homes, after which they would return to finish their remaining tasks.

Idly, Katie wondered where Ramon had been all day, but she was too frustrated and annoyed with herself and that prying priest to give it much thought. How dare that man question her motives and emotions, she thought, glowering ferociously at the looming mountains.

''I hope,'' drawled a deep, amused voice, ''that you are not thinking of me with that expression on your face.''

Katie's head swung around in surprise, sending

her glossy hair spilling over her right shoulder. Ramon was standing less than a yard from her, his tall, broad-shouldered frame blocking the golden sunset. He looked as if he had spent the day in the office of the cannery, and had merely removed his suit coat, unbuttoned the collar of his crisp white shirt, and turned the cuffs up on his tanned forearms. His black brows were lifted slightly in inquiry, his gaze unwavering on her face.

Katie gave him a plastic smile. "Actually, I was—"

"Plotting a murder?" Ramon suggested dryly.

"Something like that," Katie muttered.

"Is the intended victim anyone I know?"

"Padre Gregorio," she admitted as she came to her feet.

Gazing down at her from his daunting height, Ramon shoved his hands into his pants pockets. The action stretched his white shirt over his muscular chest and wide shoulders, and Katie felt her pulse give a little leap in answer to the sheer, powerful masculinity he emanated. However, his next words snapped her attention back to the issue at hand.

"I saw him in the village a few minutes ago, Katie. He does not want to marry us."

Katie was perversely crushed that Padre Gregorio's contempt for her actually went that deep. Her beautiful face flushed with indignation. "Did he tell you why?"

Unexpectedly, Ramon smiled; one of those sudden, devastating smiles that always took her breath away. "Padre Gregorio seems to think that you lack certain attributes that he feels are necessary to make me a good wife.''

"Such as?'' Katie demanded mutinously.

"Meekness, docility and a respect for authority.''

Katie was torn between antagonism and guilt. "What did you say?''

"I told him that I wanted a wife, not a cocker spaniel.''

"And?''

Ramon's black eyes glinted with laughter. "Padre Gregorio thinks I would be better off with a cocker spaniel.''

"Oh, is that right!'' Katie retorted heatedly. "Well if you ask me, that interfering old tyrant shows an unnatural concern for your welfare!''

"Actually, he is concerned about *your* welfare,'' Ramon said wryly. "He greatly fears that after we have been married a short time, I may be tempted to murder you.''

Katie turned her back to him to hide her confusion and hurt. "Is what he thinks so important to you?''

Ramon's hands settled on her shoulders, gently but firmly drawing her back against him. "You know it is not. But any delay in our marriage is important to me. If Padre Gregorio will not change his mind, I will have to find a priest in San Juan to marry us, and the banns will probably have to be read again. I want to marry you on Sunday, Katie, and Padre Gregorio is the only one who can make that possible. You know that. Everything else is in readiness. Work in the cottage will be finished tonight, your parents already have plane reservations for Saturday, and I have reserved a suite for them at the Caribe Hilton.''

Katie was vibrantly aware of his warm breath stirring her hair; of the intimate feeling of his hard, muscular body pressing against her back and legs as he continued: "Padre Gregorio has just left for Vieques Island. When he returns on Thursday I want you to talk to him and give him whatever reassurance he needs.''

Katie's resistance began to crumble as he turned her into his arms and covered her mouth with his. "Will you do that for me?'' he murmured huskily when he broke the contact.

Katie gazed at his strong, sensual mouth. She raised her eyes and looked into those dark compelling eyes of his, and the rest of her defenses disintegrated. He wanted her so badly, his thighs were already hardening against her. And she wanted him too—just as badly. "Yes,'' she whispered.

His arms tightened fiercely as he claimed her mouth in a hungry searching kiss. When her lips parted eagerly to admit his tongue, he groaned with pleasure, and the sound struck some primitive response in Katie. Unashamedly she met his passion with her own, wanting to give him the same pleasure he was giving her. She kissed him as erotically as he kissed her, her hands convulsively sliding over his back and shoulders, her body arching to his.

She gasped with dismay when he ended the kiss and raised his head. Still shuddering with aftershocks of desire, Katie opened her slumberous eyes.

In the deepening dusk, his gaze held hers. "I love you," he said.

Katie opened her mouth to speak and couldn't. Her stomach churned wildly, then clenched into an agonizing knot. She tried to say "I love you" but the words she had screamed again and again to David on that hideous night long ago, stuck in her throat now, paralyzing her vocal cords. With a low, anguished moan, she wrapped her arms around his neck and began kissing him with frenzied desperation, while every muscle in his body was tensing to reject her.

Pain ripped through Ramon like a hot jagged knife. She didn't love him. God damn her! She didn't love him.

"I—I can't say it," she wept brokenly, clinging tightly to him, her body molded to his. "I can't say the words you want to hear. I just can't."

Ramon stared at her, hating her and hating himself for loving her. Reaching up, he started to pull her arms from around his neck, but Katie wildly shook her head, tightening her hold, pressing even closer to him. Tears rushed from her beautiful blue eyes, sparkling on her long lashes, wetting her smooth cheeks. "Don't stop loving me," she pleaded fiercely, "just because I can't say the words yet. Please don't!"

"Katie!" he said harshly. Her soft lips trembled at the cold rejection in his voice, and he gripped her shoulders. He intended to free himself from her arms, to push her firmly away.

Katie knew it. "Please don't," she whispered, and her voice broke.

So did Ramon's restraint. With a groan, he drew her into his passionate embrace and smothered her lips with his. She melted against him, the fire in her response igniting the flames deep within him. "Katie," he whispered achingly, tightening his arms as she kissed him with a blazing ardor beyond anything she had ever shown him before. "Katie... Katie...Katie."

She loved him, he knew it! He could feel it. She might not be able to say the words, but her body was telling him she loved him. No woman alive could give her body to a man the way Katie was giving him hers, unless she had already given her heart.

He moved her down into the grass, and even while he did, Katie's lips clung to his, her hands feverishly caressing him. She was setting him on fire, and Ramon unbuttoned his shirt and pulled it off, willing to let himself be burned to ashes, so long as Katie went up in flames with him.

His hands dispensed with her blouse and bra, then luxuriated in the feel of her naked breasts swelling eagerly against his palms. Bending over her, he captured her mouth, the driving rhythmic plunging of his tongue boldly telling her what he wanted to do to her. And Katie welcomed the possessive invasion.

His body felt like a furnace as he pulled her up to lie on top of him, his eyes devouring the sight of her pale breasts crushed against the dark hair on his chest. "I'm starving for you," he whispered thickly. "I want you so much that I ache for you."

He curved his hand around her nape, pulling her

mouth down to his, and said thickly. "Make me ache more, Katie."

She did. She kissed him with all her heart and body, wringing a low, animal groan of pleasure from him as she moved sinuously against his rigid arousal. Ramon clutched her tighter to him, wanting to absorb her body into his, letting her drive him into agonies of desire before he finally rolled onto his side, taking her with him.

Katie's lashes flickered open. Ramon was breathing fast, his face hard and dark with passion. She lifted her lips to his, and he started to bend toward her, then checked himself. "Before this is over," he sighed hoarsely, "you are going to drive me out of my mind."

Katie expected him to finish what they had begun. Instead he laid back and stretched out beside her, cradling her head in the curve of his arm and shoulder, keeping her close against his side while he stared up at the night sky. Katie laid there, bewildered. She couldn't imagine why Ramon had suddenly stopped, unless he somehow thought it was what she wanted. But it wasn't what she wanted at all! How could he think that when her whole body was yearning for his, when she wanted more than anything to give him pleasure? She rolled onto her side, fully intending to take matters into her own hands. "If I do drive you out of your mind, it's your own fault," Katie said, and before he could reply she began leisurely and seductively tracing the outline of his ear with her tongue.

His free hand crossed over to lightly grip her

waist, caressing it. His hand gripped her tighter and he shuddered with pleasure when she put her tongue into the hollow crevice and sensuously explored it. "Katie, stop it," he warned in a throaty growl. "Or I am going to do that to you."

Undaunted, Katie continued her arousing exploration. "You already did," she breathed into his ear, "And I like it."

"I like it too, that is why I want you to stop."

Katie gathered all her courage together and leaned up on an elbow. For a moment she stared thoughtfully at the shining silver chain and medal lying in the dark mat of hair on his chest, then she lifted her wide, questioning eyes to his. "Ramon," she said, tracing her fingertips down the chain, oblivious to the stirring effect this was having on him. "Has it occurred to you that we don't have to stop?"

Ramon captured her wayward hand, holding it to prevent its further tantalizing descent. "It has occurred to me—" he murmured dryly, "—about two hundred times in the last ten minutes."

"Then why are we? Stopping, I mean?"

He turned his head and looked at the tiny stars twinkling shyly in the inky blue sky. "Because the men will soon be returning from their evening meal." It was the truth, of course, but it wasn't the reason he was holding back. If he could be absolutely certain Katie loved him, he would simply take her somewhere else where they could have privacy now. If he had been certain she loved him, he would have been making love to her every day since they arrived to Puerto Rico. If Katie loved him, then the physical

union of their bodies would strengthen and deepen
that love.

But if all she felt for him was intense physical desire, if that was the only reason she was willing to
marry him, then satisfying that desire before they
were actually wed, would relieve the pressure that
was driving her to the altar. And that he would not
risk doing. Particularly not, he thought with bitter
self-recrimination, when for nine days he had been
deliberately arousing her passion to a fever pitch
and keeping it there, without any intention of fulfilling her desire and giving her release. He was
purposely feeding her sexual appetite without ever
satisfying her hunger. For that, she would have to
marry him first.

From the moment he had taken her into his arms
in St. Louis, there had been a tremendous physical
chemistry between them. He had recognized it then,
and he had been exploiting it ever since. He was
ashamed of what he was doing to her. Katie trusted
him, and he was using her own desire as a weapon to
force her to marry him. But the weapon was a
double-edged sword, because he was physically torturing himself by kissing and caressing her until they
were both wild, and then drawing back. Every time
he held her it was sheer torment knowing that she
was sweet and warm and willing to be taken, and
then not taking her.

What sort of man was he to stoop to this sexual
blackmail, Ramon wondered contemptuously. The
answer was as humiliating as the question: He was
the sort of man who deeply loved a woman who ap-

parently did not love him. Fiercely, his mind rejected that. Katie loved him! He could taste it on her lips. By God, before they were married, she would admit it! He would make her tell him she did.

Or what?

Closing his eyes, Ramon drew a deep, ragged breath. Or he would have to let her go. His pride and self-respect would never let him live with her, loving her like this, knowing that she didn't love him. He couldn't bear the shame, or the pain, of an unrequited love.

Beside him, Katie snuggled closer, rousing him from his reverie. "It is time to leave," he told her, reluctantly sitting up. "Gabriella and Eduardo are expecting us for dinner. They will wonder where we are."

Katie flashed a wry smile at him as she pulled on her blouse and combed her fingers through her rumpled hair. "Gabriella knows where we are. Eduardo will automatically assume that I've dragged you off somewhere to try to seduce you. Where I'm concerned, Eduardo suspects the worst."

Ramon eyed her with glinting amusement. "Eduardo is not worried that you might steal my virginity, Katie. I lost it long ago—on the same night he lost his, as I recall."

Katie's pretty chin lifted in an attitude of well-bred disinterest, but her voice was tinged with jealousy, which delighted Ramon, who had hoped for just such a reaction. "How old were you then?"

"None of your business," he laughed.

CHAPTER SEVENTEEN

"Thank you again," Katie called gaily, two days later. She wiped a smudge off her cheek, then waved goodbye to Rafael, his wife and his sons, who had been helping her clean the cottage, arrange furniture and hang curtains all day yesterday and today. She watched Rafael's old truck clatter down the drive, then turned to Gabriella who was tiredly pushing herself out of a chair.

They had been working since dawn and it was now late afternoon. "Do you think Ramon will be surprised?" Katie asked, her face wearing the same expression of happy exhaustion that she saw on Gabriella's.

"Will he be surprised?" Gabriella repeated, her dark eyes shining with merriment. "Two days ago, there were workmen in here and the place was bare. Tonight when he sees it, every piece of furniture is in place, the bed is made and there are even candles and linen placemats on the kitchen table. Ramon will not be able to believe his eyes!" Gabriella predicted.

"I hope you're right," Katie said with a touch of pride. "I told him this house could be pretty, but he wouldn't believe me."

"Pretty?" Gabriella said with a shake of her head as she picked up her purse and trailed to the front door. "It is beautiful. You have a great talent for decorating, Katie."

Looking at her, Katie thought of the endless miles they had driven together, the frenetic shopping expeditions, the exhausting hours of searching through shops. Through it all Gabriella had been cheerful and supportive. "Gaby," Katie said softly, shaken by a deep surge of affection and gratitude, "you have a great talent for being a friend."

A smile lit Gabriella's features. "Strange, is it not—this kinship between us? We have known each other for only eleven days, yet you are almost like a sister to me."

The two women, who had been sharing a bottle of wine while they worked, smiled sheepishly at each other, their faces flushed with drink and pleasure, then Gabriella turned and left.

Katie picked up Gabriella's wineglass, drained the last drops from her own, and glanced at her wristwatch; it was five o'clock. Last night she had made Ramon promise to come here straight from work, which meant he ought to be arriving any time during the next half hour. In the kitchen she washed both glasses and set them on the new white Formica counter top so they would be ready when Ramon came.

Humming, she opened a cupboard and took out the other bottle of red wine and the corkscrew. Actually, she had already had enough wine. *A little more than enough*, she thought wryly. She was feeling rather warm and overexhilarated. But, she reminded herself gaily, the completion of the house was a very good reason for celebration.

She glanced around the kitchen. Cheerful and inviting, just as she had told Ramon it could be, she decided proudly. Above the wainscoting, the walls were covered in a bright green-and-white wallpaper. One wall displayed a collection of native wicker and straw baskets of every size and shape, which Katie had purchased for a fraction of what their price would have been in the States. All the cupboards had been stripped and repainted white, with an inset of wallpaper that matched the green and white on the walls.

She left the kitchen and wandered from room to room. In the bedroom, she paused to needlessly smooth the handmade coverlet on the bed. It was sewn in large squares, each square a different pattern, but each incorporating the basic colors of gold, white and brown. Gold curtains hung at the wide windows, harmonizing and complementing the dark oak dresser and headboard, and the thick gold carpet that partially covered the polished oak floor. She straightened the folds of the curtains so that they hung gracefully on either side of the windows. The room was perfect, she decided.

And masculine.

Katie pushed the unwanted thought aside and sauntered into the living room. She had spent about three thousand dollars of her own money, but it was worth it, she thought proudly. The rust-colored sofa with its rolled arms and thick tufted back was positioned opposite two chairs upholstered in nubby cream and rust threads. A broad expanse of sculptured cream carpeting stretched between them on the polished floor. The huge coffee table with its burl-wood inlays and narrow brass trim had been her biggest extravagance, but when she had seen it she couldn't resist it, or the matching lamp table between the two chairs. Or was the antique hammered brass lamp her biggest extravagance? Katie couldn't recall, but it didn't matter anyway. The room, with its rough-textured cream curtains and long windows, was rich and inviting and perfect.

And masculine, a little voice whispered.

Katie studiously ignored it and went into the bathroom where she washed her face and brushed her hair. Her eyes were shining with expectation when she looked at herself in the mirror above the new vanity. Or were her eyes just glassy from too much wine? Katie shrugged and glanced around the bathroom. Had she gone too ultramodern here, she wondered apprehensively. Since the bathroom fixtures were white, she had carried the theme into the wallpaper, using a shiny white paper with bold reprints of newspapers printed on it. At the time she had thought herself clever; if Ramon got tired of the black and red towels he could substitute another color for the red and it would seem like a whole new bathroom. She dried her hands on a red hand towel, then carefully refolded it and placed it on the vanity atop the black one. The rest of the towels should have arrived at the store in the village by now. Tomorrow she would stop and pick them up after she saw Padre Gregorio.

She cast a last glance over the bathroom, her head tipped consideringly to the side. It might be a little too modernistic for the rest of the house, but it was certainly vivid.

And masculine.

Katie finally admitted it—but if it were true, then surely Ramon would be pleased. After all, he was very masculine. She went over to the coffee table in the living room and began rearranging the bright yellow and orange flowers in the center.

The maroon Rolls-Royce glided to a purring stop on the shoulder of the road a few feet beyond the dirt track that led up to the cottage. Ramon glanced impatiently at the long red canopy of blossoming flamboyant trees, deliberating over having Garcia drive him to the front door of the cottage. He was eager to see Katie, and he didn't want to take the time to walk the two miles up the track. On the other hand, if Katie realized the chauffeur took him to and from work in the Rolls every day, she would naturally ask further questions. Questions he would have to either refuse to answer, or answer with blatant lies. Out of necessity he had misled her, but he would not lie to her.

"Wait for me at the usual place tomorrow morning," he instructed Garcia. Ramon opened his door and climbed out of the car, without waiting for the chauffeur to reply. He knew that tomorrow morning at seven-thirty Garcia would be pulled over at the side of the road, waiting around a blind curve a half-mile from the village square. No questions asked, no explanations expected. Even though Garcia was no longer being paid, the old man still insisted on driving Ramon. "We have been together a long time, you and I," Garcia had told Ramon at the airport the day Katie had come to Puerto Rico. With somber dark eyes and great dignity he had added, "Until this car is sold, I will do for you what I have always done."

Walking up the track, Ramon thought of Garcia with mingled fondness and regret. If Ramon asked him to keep the motor running in front of a bank while he went in and robbed it, Garcia would do so without hesitation. His reward for twenty years of faithful service was going to be unemployment— and a letter of recommendation. Ramon wished he could give him more than that. He deserved more.

In the doorway of the cottage, Ramon stopped dead; the day's worries and problems slipping away, forgotten. Katie was here, in his house, waiting for him. Sunlight streamed in the window, bathing her in a golden halo of light as she bent over something in the living room, rearranging sprigs of vibrant wild flowers in an earthenware bowl.

A feeling of deep contentment seeped through him, spreading its warmth through his veins. How strange that he had supposedly been one of the "richest" men in the world, yet he had never had this to come home to, never experienced this feeling before. He had come home to mistresses and servants, in mansions, penthouse apartments and villas by the sea. But he had never found this exquisite feeling of peace waiting for him—because he had never really come "home" at all. Katie was home.

People had envied him before; now they would pity him because he had lost his wealth. How incredibly stupid! Now he had Katie, and Katie made him very rich. This beautiful angel with the red gold hair and laughing blue eyes was going to bear his children and share his days and nights. She was everything that had always been missing from his life. She was joy.

Very quietly and without emphasis, Ramon said, "I love you, Katie."

She whirled around, a smile lighting up her face. "Well?" she beamed at him. "What do you think?" Arms outstretched she turned in a circle, watching him expectantly over her shoulder.

Ramon knew she had heard him, and his heart sank at her lack of response, but he let it pass. "I think you are beautiful," he said running his appreciative glance over the bright green velour top that left her midriff bare, and the matching shorts that revealed her long shapely legs.

Katie rolled her eyes. "Not about me! About the house, the furniture, everything. . . ."

For the first time, Ramon looked at something besides Katie. What he saw dumbfounded him. "How did you manage to buy all this with the money I gave you? I never meant for you to have to stretch it so far. I intended to give you more when you said you were ready to look for furniture."

Her face fell. "Don't you like it?"

"Like it?" he grinned. "I have not even looked at it yet. But how—"

"Stop thinking about the money. I happen to be a

terrific bargain hunter,'' Katie said, linking her hand through his arm, and leading him from room to room.

Ramon's reaction puzzled Katie. She could tell that he liked what she had purchased, and that he was pleased. He was lavish with his praise and his praise was genuine, yet something was bothering him.

She did not have long to wait to discover what it was. The kitchen was the last room on her guided tour. When Ramon had finished inspecting it, he walked over to the counter top where she had put out the wine. Katie watched him, admiring the way his long, capable fingers dealt with the corkscrew, deftly uncorking the bottle. ''Well?'' she said expectantly. ''Now that you've seen the whole house, what do you think?''

''I think it is extremely attractive,'' he said, pouring wine into both glasses. He handed one to her. ''Are you planning to live here?''

The question stunned her into momentary silence, then she said, ''Yes.''

''For how long?'' he asked dispassionately.

The wine she had drunk was making her feel foggy. ''Why are you asking me these questions?''

''Because there are two bedrooms in this house,'' he said, watching her intently. ''The second one, as I am sure you know, is meant for children. Yet you went to a great deal of trouble to furnish it with a handsome desk for me, bookcases and one overstuffed chair. Not two chairs. You intended that room to be used by me alone, not by both of us and not by our children. Your apartment was filled with plants, yet there is not one plant in this house. Your bedroom was extremely feminine, yet—''

''Plants?'' Katie blinked at him, her emotions veering from alarm to mirth. ''I didn't even think of plants! I'll give you plants for a wedding present!'' she decided promptly.

''And will you give me children?'' he asked, his face impassive.

''Not,'' Katie quipped, ''for a wedding present. Think of the gossip!''

Ramon's gaze swerved from the faint flush on her high cheekbones to the empty wine bottle beside the one he had just opened. ''How much of that bottle did you drink?''

''A little more than half,'' she declared rather proudly. ''Gabriella drank the rest.''

Ramon felt like shaking her. Instead, he walked over to the wide windows at the corner of the kitchen. Tipping his glass up, he drank deeply, then stared out at the panoramic view. ''Why do you want to marry me, Katie?''

Katie saw the tension in his shoulders, the tautness in his profile, and desperately tried to keep things light. ''Because you're tall dark and handsome!'' she teased.

The brief, sidelong smile he sent her was without humor. ''Why else do you want to marry me?''

''Oh, the usual reasons people get married these days,'' she joked. ''We like the same movies, we—''

''Stop playing games with me!'' he snapped. ''I asked you why you want to marry me.''

Panic jolted through Katie's entire nervous system; her heart began to race wildly. "I—" She tried to speak and couldn't. She knew Ramon wanted her to say she loved him, and that he wanted to hear her make a final, irrevocable commitment to marry him. Katie could do neither. Afraid not to speak, yet unable to say anything that would satisfy him, Katie could only look at him in mute misery.

In the electrified silence that crackled between them, she could feel Ramon mentally withdrawing from her, and when he finally spoke there was a harsh bitter finality in his words that thoroughly alarmed her: "We will not speak of it again," he said.

In heavy silence they walked back to Gabriella's. Katie tried to cloak herself in the comforting glow of the wine she had consumed, but she was feeling more apprehensive with every step. Instead of coming in for dinner, Ramon stopped at the front door, briefly touched his lips to her forehead, and said "Good night."

There was an ominous ring to that, Katie thought. It sounded more like goodbye than good-night. "Are—are you coming over to see me before you leave for work in the morning?"

He turned on the step and looked at her, his face utterly unreadable. "I am not going to work tomorrow."

"Then will I see you after I meet with Padre Gregorio? I thought I'd go over to his house first thing in the morning. Then I was going to go up to the cottage to take care of some things that need to be done."

"I will find you," he said.

"Ramon," she said, afraid to let him leave in this mood, "I don't think you were very enthusiastic about—about the cottage. Didn't you like it?"

"I apologize," he said politely. "You did an excellent job. It suits me perfectly."

Although he'd put no emphasis on the word *me*, Katie noticed he avoided using the word *us*. She didn't know what to say to him in this distant, coolly courteous mood. She opened the door. "Well, good night."

Ramon stared at the door she had just closed, while bitterness and pain rose like bile in this throat. He walked aimlessly for hours thinking about the past two days. For two days he had waited for her to say she loved him. He had teased her and laughed with her and made her moan with passion in his arms, but not even in her most heated moment had she responded to his "I love you." She would kiss him or smile at him, placate him like an infatuated little boy, but she would not say it back.

The moon was high in the sky when he returned to his temporary room in Rafael's house. He stretched out on the bed and stared at the ceiling. He had asked her for honesty, and she was being honest. She was refusing to claim an emotion that she didn't feel. It was as simple as that.

God! How could she not love him, when he loved her so damned much.

Katie's image danced before him: Katie coming up the hill toward him with that graceful leggy walk of hers and the breeze teasing her glorious hair;

Katie looking at him, her deep blue eyes sparkling with laughter or dark with concern because he looked tired.

Ramon closed his eyes, trying to postpone the moment when he would have to make a decision, but it was no use. The decision had already been made. He was going to have to send her home. He would send her home tomorrow. No, not tomorrow, the next day. He had to keep her with him one more day... and one more night. Just one more. One more day to watch her moving around the cottage, to memorize the way she looked in each room—so that he could remember her there when she was gone. One more night to make love to her in the bedroom she had decorated for him, to join his ravenous body with hers and lose himself in her. He would lavish her senses with every exquisite pleasure a man could give a woman, make her moan with delight and cry out with rapture, and then bring her again and again to shuddering ecstasy.

One day and one night to accumulate memories: memories that would bring him as much torment as they would pleasure, but it didn't matter. He had to have them.

And then he would send her home. She would be relieved, he knew that now. He had always known it. Whatever her reasons for agreeing to marry him had been, she was never entirely committed to the idea. If she were, she would not have decorated her future home as a handsome bachelor retreat without a trace of her own personality.

CHAPTER EIGHTEEN

Padre Gregorio greeted Katie with polite reserve when the housekeeper showed her into his office the next morning. He waited for her to take a seat, then sat down behind his desk.

Katie tried to match his composed expression. "Ramon said that you feel I lack meekness, docility and respect for authority."

"I said that, yes." He leaned back in his chair. "Do you disagree?"

Katie slowly shook her head, a smile touching her lips. "Not at all. In fact, I consider it a great compliment." When his expression didn't alter, she hesitated, and then continued. "Obviously you don't see it that way. You told Ramon that was the reason you didn't want to marry us."

"Would you have preferred that I tell him the main reason—that the woman he loves does not love him?"

Katie's long, tapered fingernails dug into her palms. "I didn't say—"

"Señorita Connelly!" he interrupted in a low, controlled voice. "We are not going to waste any more time waltzing each other around in circles that more time waltzing each other around in circles that go nowhere. You are looking for a way to avoid this marriage, and I have given it to you.''

Katie was stricken. ''How can you possibly say a thing like that?''

''Because it is true. I sensed it from our first meeting. When I asked you how long you have known Ramon, you told me 'only' two weeks. You deliberately led me to think you are the sort of woman who frequents *cantinas* in the hope of meeting men, men whom you let publicly caress you in parking lots. You are nothing of the kind, *señorita*, and we both know it.''

He held up an imperious hand to silence Katie's outburst. ''It is too late for that now. There are other reasons I believe what I do: I told you that if you would simply say you love Ramon, we would finalize the marriage plans. If you really wanted to marry him, you would have said it whether it was true or not, so that I would agree to the ceremony.

''When I told you that, instead, I would accept your word that you intended to make Ramon a good wife, your face turned as white as a sheet. Ten seconds later you jumped up and accused me of trying to make you promise to respect his authority and obey him.''

Katie's gaze dropped to her lap. She rubbed her moist palms against her knees. ''There's nothing I can say to prove you're wrong, is there?''

''You do not want to prove I am wrong, *señorita*. In your heart, you want to avoid this marriage.'' He took off his glasses and wearily rubbed the bridge of his nose. "Perhaps you are afraid of commitment, of giving your love. I do not know. But I do know this—when Ramon realizes that you can give him only your body, and not your heart, he will not be satisfied. No man with any pride will let himself continue to care deeply for someone who does not care for him. Ramon's love for you will wither and die, because he will make certain that it does; he will kill it himself. When that happens, he must be free to find another, and to marry if he chooses. Knowing all of this, I cannot, I will not bind him to you for the rest of his life with the unbreakable ties of Holy Matrimony."

Katie's eyes were burning with tears she refused to shed, and there was a lump in her throat the size of a boulder as he finished: "It would be best for both of you if you went back to the States immediately. If you lack the courage and decency to do that, then live with him in sin or marry him in a civil ceremony. I cannot stop you. I have given you a way out of this, I expect you to give Ramon a way out, too—do not bind him to you in the church."

Katie stood up stiffly. "And that's your final decision?"

It seemed to take Padre Gregorio forever to rise to his feet. "If you must phrase it that way, yes, it is my final decision. I will leave it to you to tell Ramon." His blue eyes turned almost sympathetic. "Do not feel guilty because you cannot love him, *señorita*. Ramon is the sort of man who is attractive to women. Many have loved him in the past; there will be many who will love him in the future, and be more than eager to be his wife.''

Katie's head was proudly erect, but her eyes were swimming with tears. ''I don't feel guilty, I feel furious!'' Turning on her heel she walked to the door.

Padre Gregorio's voice sounded incredibly sad. ''*Señorita*....''

Katie kept her face averted, unwilling to give him the satisfaction of seeing her cry. ''Yes?''

''God bless you.''

The tears clogging her throat prevented Katie from answering. She opened the door and walked out.

Katie drove up to the cottage, half-blinded with tears of humiliation and fear. Padre Gregorio was right. She had been looking for a way out—no, not a way out, a way to gain more time. ''Damn you, David!'' she whispered thickly. This awful mess she was making of her life was his fault. Even dead he was haunting her; literally haunting her. It was because of him that she couldn't overcome this slumbering panic that she might be making the same mistake twice.

Once before she had married a man who her own instinct had warned her wasn't what he appeared to be. Now she wanted to marry another man and she felt that way again. She couldn't shake that feeling.

She pulled up in front of the little storybook cottage and let herself inside, relieved that Ramon wasn't there. She didn't want to have to explain her ravaged face. How would she? How could she say, there is something about you that is scaring me, Ramon.

Katie wandered into the kitchen and methodically spooned coffee into the new percolator she had purchased. When it was made she poured it into a mug and carried it over to the kitchen table. With her hands wrapped around the hot mug, she gazed out at the terraced hills stretching in two directions, letting the magnificent view quiet her rioting emotions.

She thought back to the way she had felt about David before they were married. Some intuition, some instinct, had warned her that David Caldwell was not the man he wanted her to believe he was. She should have listened to herself.

And now she wanted to marry Ramon—and every instinct she possessed was telling her that he was not the man he wanted her to believe he was, either.

Katie rubbed her fingertips against her temples. Never had she felt so afraid and confused. There was no time left to stall. Either she was going to ignore her instinctive fears and marry Ramon, or she had to go back to the States.

The thought of leaving him made her almost physically ill. She adored him!

She loved his dark eyes and dazzling smile, the reassuring strength in his firmly chiseled features, and the quiet authority in the line of his jaw. He was six feet three inches of taut, powerful muscle, yet he was gentle and tender with her. In height, he dwarfed her own five feet six inches, yet being with him made her feel protected and cherished, not threatened and insignificant.

By nature, he was a dominating male, virile and self-assured, while she was stubborn and independent. She ought to resent him for wanting to confine her to the role of wife and mother, but she didn't. The idea of being his wife filled her with joy, and the thought of bearing his children thrilled her. She would gladly clean his house and cook his meals in return for being held in those strong arms of his at night.

He wanted her to accept a form of sexual bondage, commit her body and her life into his keeping. In return, he would be her lover, provider and father to her children. Katie shamefully admitted to herself that it was what she wanted, too. It might be un-American and unemancipated, but it seemed so right, so fulfilling. At least for her.

Katie stared at her hands lying limply in her lap. Ramon was everything she could ever want: an intelligent, sensitive, sexy man who loved her.

Except he wasn't real.

He wasn't what he wanted her to believe he was. She didn't know why she felt that way, or what was wrong, but the feeling wouldn't leave her.

RAMON PULLED RAFAEL'S CAR to a stop in front of the general store and climbed out. Eduardo opened the passenger door. "I will go in with you. Gabriella asked me to buy some milk."

"What?" Ramon said absently.

"I said—" Eduardo shook his head in exasperation. "Never mind. You have not heard a word I have said all morning. Getting married is affecting your hearing, my friend."

"I am not getting married," Ramon said grimly, leaving Eduardo gaping at him as he shoved open the door and walked into the store. In contrast to the heat outside, the crowded little store was cool. Ignoring Eduardo's staggered look, as well as the ten customers who were all staring at him with avid curiosity, Ramon selected several cigars, then carried them over to the counter where two salesclerks were waiting on customers. Eduardo put the container of milk on the counter beside Ramon's cigars and said in a low voice. "Are you joking?"

Ramon glanced at him. "I am not joking."

A pretty little Puerto Rican girl waiting on a huge woman who was exchanging an apron, saw Ramon and her face brightened. She asked the other clerk, a middle-aged man, to take care of the refund and stepped over to the line that had formed behind Ramon and Eduardo. "Señor Galverra," she beamed, speaking in Spanish. "Do you remember me? I am Maria Ramirez. I used to have pigtails when I was little and you used to pull them and tell me that I was going to be pretty when I grew up."

"I was right," Ramon said with an effort at a smile.

"I am engaged to be married to Juan Vega now," she said, still smiling as she reached beneath the counter and pulled out a large package wrapped in white paper and tied with strings. "These are the towels Señorita Connelly ordered for you. Do you want to take them with you?"

"Fine," Ramon said with a curt nod. Reaching into the back pocket of his Levi's, he pulled out his wallet and glanced at the sales slip. "You only charged me for the cigars, Maria. How much are the towels?"

"Señorita Connelly has already paid for them with her credit card," she reassured him.

Ramon tried not to sound as impatient as he felt. "There must be some mistake."

"Mistake?" Maria repeated. "I do not think so, but I will look." She cut the string and tore open the white paper. A pile of thick, fluffy red and black towels spilled onto the counter. Behind him and beside him, Ramon felt the villagers pressing imperceptibly closer to get a better view of the contents of the package. "Here is the charge-account receipt and these are the sales tickets," Maria said as she pulled them from between two towels. "No, there is no mistake. Señorita Connelly paid for these towels with her charge account at the same time she paid for everything she took with her a week ago. See, it is all here on the sales slips, included in the five-hundred-dollar total. She paid for a toaster, percolator, dishes, pots and pans, glasses in several sizes, a blender, a rotary mixer, kitchen utensils and all these other items."

The old man beside Ramon poked him slyly in the ribs. "You are a lucky man, Ramon. Your *novia* wants you to have only the best. Not only is she beautiful, she is very generous, too, eh?"

"Wrap up the towels," Ramon snapped at Maria in a low, savage voice.

Maria paled at the look on his face and began

clumsily and hastily pulling the edges of the paper together. "Here—here are Señorita Connelly's duplicate bills, each for one-half the amount she spent," she stammered, her eyes recoiling from Ramon's murderous expression as she handed him the slips. "Señora Alverez," she glanced apprehensively at a furious Eduardo as she spoke his wife's name, "explained that I do not have to prepare duplicate bills this way, unless Señorita Connelly pays in cash, but I—I do it anyway."

She shoved the package toward Ramon as if it were hot, and her voice dropped to a panicked whisper. "That way, I never forget."

Ramon's tone was glacial. "I am certain that Señorita Connelly has appreciated your help, Maria." Everyone hastily backed out of his path as he strode out of the store with fury raging in every purposeful stride.

Eleven villagers watched the door slam behind Ramon and then Eduardo. In unison they turned to stare at each other, their faces reflecting a variety of reactions from alarm to satisfaction. Only one occupant of the store was oblivious to what had just taken place—an Englishman who did not understand Spanish. He cleared his throat politely and shifted the parcels in his arms, but he was ignored.

Maria was the first to speak. She looked around at the others, her soft brown eyes wide and stricken as she whispered, "What did I do wrong?"

The middle-aged man, who was the other salesclerk, regarded her dryly. "Maria, you have just given Señorita Connelly more 'help' than I think she wanted.''

The old man who had gibed Ramon about his *novia*'s generosity slapped his thigh and cackled gleefully. "I told you Galverra didn't know what the girl was doing. I told you!'' His weathered face creased into a satisfied grin as he looked at his neighbors. "Told you he'd never live off a woman even if he was starving.'' Smugly he added, "He ought to take a stick to her!''

"I will come back for the other apron," the enormous woman said as she headed for the door.

"Where are you going, Rosa?'' her friend called after her.

"To offer up a prayer in church.''

"For the American girl?'' one of the ladies asked, laughing.

"No, for Gabriella Alverez.''

"Ought to take a stick to her, too," the old man announced.

WHEN SHE HEARD RAMON come in, Katie stood up and made a great pretense of rearranging the straw place mats on the kitchen table. It was crazy how her spirits soared at the mere sound of his voice calling her name.

"Here are the rest of the towels you ordered," he said, dropping the package carelessly on the table. "The girl at the store said they had already been paid for. Is this coffee still fresh?" he asked as he went over and poured some into a mug.

Katie smiled at him over her shoulder and nodded

as she pulled the bunched towels out of the wrapping and began refolding them.

"I still cannot imagine how you managed to buy all this with the money I gave you," he remarked.

"I told you," Katie said brightly. "I'm a fantastic bargain hunter."

"You are also a liar."

Katie spun around, feeling a prickling of fear that escalated to panic the moment she looked at him. In contrast to the deadly quiet of his voice, Ramon's face was a mask of savage fury.

"How much of your money have you spent?"

Katie's mouth went dry. "Very little. A—a hundred dollars."

His eyes slashed her like razors. "I asked you how much!" he repeated in a terrible voice.

"Two—two hundred."

"Lie to me just once more," he warned silkily, "and I will make your first husband seem like a saint."

The threat made Katie almost sick with fright. "About three thousand dollars."

The next question hit her like a whip. "Why?"

"Because I...didn't want to feel obligated to marry you."

Naked pain sliced across his features in the instant before his whole body went rigid, tensing against it. "Garcia will take you to the airport at two o'clock tomorrow afternoon. He will have a check with him to reimburse you for what you have spent. There is no need for you to make any explanations to Gabriella and Eduardo; they already know you are leaving."

Katie was breathing in shallow, suffocated breaths. "You're actually going to send me back just because I bought some things for the house?"

"Because I told you not to do it," he corrected her scathingly.

"And just—just for that? For—for disobeying you?" Katie felt as if she had been physically beaten. Her mind couldn't seem to absorb the shock. He must be insane; the man she had thought she knew could never, never do this. Not for such a small thing.

She started slowly toward the door on legs that felt wooden. As she passed Ramon, she glanced at him, her eyes dark with pain and disillusionment. "Just for that," she murmured and numbly shook her head. "Don't!" she cried out as his hands spun her around and brought her crashing into the wall of his chest.

His eyes glittered down at her from a face that was white with rage. "You are nothing but an eager body and an empty heart," he gritted viciously. "Did you think I was so desperate for your body that I would accept the temporary loan of it and call it a marriage?" He flung her away from him as if he couldn't bear to touch her, and strode to the doorway, where he turned, his voice murderous. "If you have not cashed the check Garcia gives you within fourteen days, I will have everything in this house carried outside and set on fire."

KATIE SNAPPED THE LOCKS SHUT on the last piece of her luggage and carried it to the open bedroom door, setting it down beside the other five pieces.

There was nothing more to do tonight except sleep.

She sat down on her bed in Gabriella's spare bedroom and listlessly looked around. She had wanted time—now she had it. She had the rest of her life ahead of her to wonder whether she had thrown away her chance for glorious happiness, or escaped from another nightmare of a marriage. Katie glanced up at the mirror, and the grief-stricken face that looked back at her was a perfect reflection of her inner feelings.

Gabriella was asleep, and Eduardo had gone out immediately after dinner. Katie shuddered just remembering that ominous meal. Not one word had been spoken by anyone. Eduardo had eaten in furious silence and Gabriella, who was as pale as death, kept giving Katie pitiful little smiles of sympathy and reassurance in between muffled sniffling noises. Katie, who was incapable of swallowing past the lump in her throat, had carefully avoided Eduardo's thunderous gaze and looked with helpless apology at poor Gabriella. When the meal was over, Eduardo had shoved his chair back, stood up and glared wrathfully at Katie. "I congratulate you," he said between clenched teeth. "You have managed to destroy a very great man. Not even his own father succeeded when he tried, but you did." Then he turned on his heel and stalked out.

Katie glanced automatically at the plastic clock beside the bed when she heard the front door open and close. Eduardo's heavy footsteps were coming toward her bedroom. Hastily she swiped at her cheeks with her fingertips, then glanced up to see Eduardo looming in the doorway Her chin came up in weak defiance as he stalked over to the bed where she was sitting.

Thrusting a large leather-bound photograph album at her, he said coldly, "This is the man whom you have reduced to the level of a beggar in the eyes of this village."

Numbly Katie took the album from him.

"Open it," he snapped. "It belongs to Rafael and his wife. They want you to see it before you leave."

Katie swallowed. "Is Ramon there with them?"

"No," Eduardo said curtly.

When he left, Katie opened the album. It was not filled with snapshots: it was filled with dozens and dozens of magazine and newspaper clippings. Her eyes riveted on the first one, and her hand began to tremble violently as she lifted the plastic-covered page. It was a newspaper photograph of Ramon standing in front of a dozen microphones as he addressed the World Business Conference in Geneva, Switzerland. "Oh, God," she whispered. "Oh, my God."

Snatches of copy flew out of her; pictures of Ramon in a hundred different poses assailed her senses. Ramon, his handsome face very grave as he spoke to a gathering of Arab oil sheikhs; Ramon, lounging back in his chair at a conference table with international business leaders; Ramon, with his briefcase in hand, boarding a jet airliner with the name "Galverra International" emblazoned on the side.

Katie tried to read the articles, but her whirling mind could only absorb phrases:

Noted for his genius as a negotiator, Galverra was responsible for the acquisitions that elevated Galverra International to the status of a financial empire...Fluent in Spanish, French, Italian, English and German...Graduate of Harvard University...Master's degree in business administration...Masterminded mergers all over the globe...An innately private man who resents the intrusion of the press into his personal life....

There were shots of Ramon in a tuxedo, gambling at a casino in Monte Carlo while a dazzling blonde smiled adoringly at him, Ramon leaning against the railing of his huge ocean-going yacht, the breeze ruffling his hair.

Many of the other pictures testified to his reported refusal to admit the press into his personal life, for they were fuzzy and obviously taken from very far away with some sort of special lens.

It was all there, including the beginning of the end. There were pictures of half-completed skyscrapers in Chicago and St. Louis, along with stories about the corporation suffering staggering financial losses in Iran.

Katie closed the album and wrapped her arms around it, clutching it protectively to her heart.

She laid her cheek against the binding, and her body shook with harsh wracking sobs. "Oh, darling, why didn't you tell me?" she choked brokenly.

CHAPTER NINETEEN

GARCIA CARRIED THE LAST two pieces of her luggage out to the Rolls, and Katie turned to Gabriella, who was hovering despondently in the living room. "I am so sorry," Gabriella whispered as Katie hugged her goodbye. "So very sorry."

Eduardo stepped forward and stiffly offered his hand. "Have a good flight," he said, his attitude more coldly aloof than it had ever been.

Garcia opened the door to the Rolls, and Katie got in. She looked at the sumptuous white leather interior with its gold-trimmed gadgetry that had once delighted her. This was Ramon's car, of course, Katie realized with a fresh stab of sorrow. No wonder he had looked so bleak when she had been enchanted with it—he was losing the car. He was losing everything—even her.

Realizing that Garcia hadn't closed the door yet, she glanced up at him. He reached into the pocket of his black uniform and extracted a bank draft. Katie stared at it in dumb misery. It was for thirty-five hundred dollars—five hundred dollars more than she had spent. Apparently Ramon hadn't even believed her when she was telling the truth.

Katie felt sick. Most of what she was being blamed for wasn't even her fault! If only Ramon hadn't tried to pass himself off to her as an ordinary farmer, she wouldn't have been so suspicious and afraid to marry him. She wouldn't have felt she had to pay for half of everything. None of this would have ever happened. But it had happened. She had shamed and humiliated him, and he was sending her away.

Sending her away, she thought as the car pulled down Gabriella's driveway. What was the matter with her, letting Ramon send her away like this! This wasn't the time to start being obedient. It wasn't the time to be frightened and intimidated, either, but she was. With a shiver of terror Katie remembered the raging fury in his expression yesterday, the murderous wrath in every carefully enunciated word he said to her. But most of all, she remembered his threat: "Lie to me one more time, and I will make your first husband look like a saint!" In that moment, he had looked enraged enough to do it.

Katie bit her lip, desperately trying to find enough courage to ask Garcia to take her to Ramon so that she could explain. She *had* to go to him. Frantically, she told herself that Ramon wouldn't do the things to her David had. Ramon didn't know what he was threatening her with when he said that. Anyway, she was not going to lie to him, so he would have no reason—

It was no use, Katie realized. She wanted to go to him, to explain, but she couldn't face his rage alone.

Irrational or not, she was terrified of physical violence.

She needed someone to go with her to confront him. Katie's hands began to tremble with a combination of panic and determination. There was no one here to help her, and it was already too late. Ramon hated her for what she had done. No, he *loved* her. And if he did, he couldn't possibly stop loving her this easily.

He had to listen to her, Katie thought feverishly as the maroon Rolls glided through the village and stopped to allow a group of tourists to cross the street. Dear God, someone had to make him listen! Just then, Katie saw Padre Gregorio crossing the square from his little house to the church, his dark robes billowing in the gentle afternoon breeze. He glanced toward the car, saw her face through the window, and slowly turned away. Padre Gregorio would never help her. . . . Or would he?

The Rolls was already picking up speed. Katie couldn't find the button to open the communicating window. She knocked on it and called "Stop—¡Parese!" but only the merest flicker of Garcia's eyes in the rearview mirror told her he had even heard her. Obviously, Ramon had instructed Garcia to put her on a plane, and he meant to do just that. She tried the door handle but it was electronically locked.

In inspired desperation, she covered her mouth with her hand and cried, "Please stop, I am going to be sick."

That got results! In a flash Garcia was out of the car, opening her door and helping her out.

Katie jerked her arm loose from the amazed old man who thought he was helping her. "I'm better now," she called, running across the square toward the church, toward the one man who had once offered to help her explain to Ramon. She darted a glance over her shoulder, but Garcia was waiting beside the car, apparently under the impression that she was having some seizure of religious fervor.

At the top of the stone steps Katie hesitated, her stomach tightening with dread. Padre Gregorio had nothing but contempt for her now; he would never help her. He had told her flatly to go back to the States. She made herself push open the groaning oak door and step into the cool candle-lit darkness.

She scanned the altar and the little decorative alcoves where candles flickered in small red glass holders, but the priest wasn't there. And then she saw him, not performing some task as she had expected, but sitting all alone at the front of the church in the second pew. His white head was bent, even his shoulders were bent, in a posture of abject despair, or devout prayer, Katie wasn't certain which.

Her footsteps faltered, and her meager reservoir of courage went dry. He would never help her. In his way, Padre Gregorio disliked her as much as Eduardo did, and for more and better reasons. Turning, Katie started back down the aisle.

"*Señorita!*" Padre Gregorio's sharp, imperative voice cracked out like a whip, making her whole body stiffen.

Slowly, Katie turned and faced him. He was standing in the center of the aisle now, looking more stern than she had ever seen him.

Katie swallowed past the raw ache in her throat, and tried to drag air through the thick ropes of tension in her chest. "Padre Gregorio," she said in a ragged, pleading voice. "I know what you must think of me, and I don't blame you, but I never understood until last night why it would be so humiliating for Ramon to have me paying for things, especially in the village. Yesterday, Ramon discovered what I have been doing, and he was furious. I—I've never seen anyone so furious in my life." Her voice dropped to a suffocated whisper. "He's sending me back home."

She searched his austere face, hoping for some sign of empathy or compassion, but he was staring at her with narrowed piercing eyes. "I—I don't want to go," she choked. She lifted her hand in a helpless, beseeching gesture, and to Katie's utter horror, tears flooded her eyes and began racing down her cheeks. Too humiliated to even look at him, Katie tried unsuccessfully to brush away the torrent of tears streaming down her face. "I want to stay here with him," she added fiercely.

The priest's voice was a gentle whisper. "Why, Katherine?"

Katie's head snapped up in amazement. He had never called her "Katherine" before, and she was almost as stunned by that as she was by the incredible tenderness in his voice. Through a haze of tears she stared at him. He was walking toward her, a smile slowly dawning across his features and illuminating his whole face.

He stopped in front of her and prodded gently, "Tell me why, Katherine."

The warmth and approval in his smile began to melt the icy misery in Katie's heart. "I want to stay because I want to marry Ramon—I don't want to avoid the marriage anymore," Katie admitted with childlike candor. Her voice gained strength as she continued, "I promise you I'll make him happy. I know I can. And he—he makes me very happy."

Padre Gregorio's smile positively beamed, and to Katie's profound joy and relief he began asking her the same questions he had tried to ask her on Monday. "Will you put Ramon's needs before your own?"

"Yes," Katie whispered.

"Will you commit yourself entirely to this marriage, putting its success ahead of all other priorities in your life?"

Katie nodded emphatically.

"Will you honor Ramon and respect his wishes?"

Katie nodded vigorously and added, "I'll be the most perfect wife you've ever seen."

Padre Gregorio's lips twitched. "Will you obey him, Katherine?"

Katie looked at him accusingly. "You said you weren't going to ask me to promise that."

"And if I did ask you?"

Katie briefly weighed the beliefs of a lifetime against her entire future. She looked right into Padre Gregorio's eyes and said, "I would promise."

His eyes lit with laughter. "Actually, I was only inquiring about that."

Katie breathed a sigh of relief. "Good, because I'd never have kept the promise." Imploringly she said, "Now will you marry us?"

"No."

He said it so kindly that for a moment Katie thought she had misunderstood him. "No?" she repeated. "Why—why not?"

"Because you have not yet told me the one thing I need to hear you say."

Katie's heart flung itself against her ribs with a sickening thud, and the color drained from her face. She closed her eyes, trying to shut out the memory of herself screaming those words, willing herself to say the words again, now. "I—" Her voice broke. "I can't. I can't say it. I want to, but I—"

"Katherine!" Padre Gregorio said in bewildered alarm. "Here, sit down," he said quickly, gently pushing her into the nearest pew. He sat down beside her, his kindly face a study of anxiety and concern. "You do not have to say you love him, Katherine," he hastily reassured her. "I can see perfectly well that you do. But can you at least tell me why you find it so painful to admit, and so impossible to say?"

White-faced, Katie turned her head and looked at him in helpless consternation and shuddered. In a voice that was a raw whisper, she said, "I keep remembering the last time I said it."

"Child, whatever happened, you cannot carry it around inside of you like this. Have you never told anyone?"

"No," Katie said hoarsely. "No one. My father would have tried to kill David—my husband. By the time my parents came back from Europe the bruises were healed, and Anne, their maid, promised never to say how I looked the night I came back to their house."

"Can you try to tell me what happened?" he asked softly.

Katie looked at her hands lying limply in her lap. If talking about it would finally exorcise David from her mind, from her life, she was ready to try. She spoke haltingly at first, and then the horror came pouring out in a torrent of choked, anguished words.

When she was finished, Katie leaned against the back of the pew, emotionally exhausted, drained of everything—even, she realized with a jolt of surprise—the pain. Hearing herself talking about David out loud had made her realize that there was no similarity between Ramon and David; none at all. David had been a selfish, egotistical, sadistic monster, while Ramon wanted to love and protect and provide for her. And even when she had defied, humiliated and infuriated Ramon, he had not physically abused her. What had happened in the past, belonged there.

Katie glanced at Padre Gregorio and realized that he seemed to have shouldered her whole burden. He looked positively shattered. "I feel much better," she said softly, hoping to cheer him up.

Padre Gregorio spoke for the first time since she had begun her story. "Is Ramon aware of what happened to you that night?"

"No. I couldn't talk about it. And anyway, I didn't really think it was bothering me anymore. I hardly ever think of David."

"It was bothering you," Padr⸱ Gregorio contradicted. "And you have been thinking of him, whether you realized it or not. Otherwise, you would have simply confronted Ramon with your suspicion that he was not entirely what he said he was. You did not confront him because in your heart you were afraid of what you might learn. Because of your terrible experience, you automatically assumed that whatever secret there was in Ramon would be as frightening as the secrets you discovered in this other man."

He was quietly thoughtful for several minutes, then he seemed to snap out of his pensive reverie. "I think it would be best if you confided in Ramon before your wedding night. There is always the possibility that, because of your memories, you will experience some understandable revulsion when you are again faced with the intimacy between a man and wife. Ramon should be prepared for that."

Katie smiled and confidently shook her head. "I won't feel any revulsion at all with Ramon, so there's no need to worry."

"You're probably right." Unexpectedly, Padre Gregorio's expression darkened to an irritated, thoughtful scowl. "Even if you do react to the marital intimacies with fright, I am certain that Ramon has enough experience with women to be able to handle any problems of that sort."

"I'm absolutely certain he can," Katie assured, laughing at Padre Gregorio's grumpy, censuring expression. The old priest's narrowed gaze swerved to Katie's laughing face. "Not *that* certain," she corrected hastily.

Approvingly, he nodded. "It is good that you have made him wait."

To her mortification, Katie felt her cheeks pinken. Padre Gregorio saw it, too. His bushy white brows lifted and he peered at her over the rim of his gold spectacles. "Or that Ramon has made *you* wait," he amended astutely.

They both glanced over their shoulders as some tourists entered the church. "Come, we can finish this discussion better outside," he said. They walked down the steps and stood on the plaza surrounding the church. "What are you going to do now?" he asked.

Katie bit her lip and glanced toward the general store. "I suppose," she said with obvious reluctance, "I could bring back the things I bought there and say in front of everyone that Ramon wouldn't... wouldn't..." she choked on the word, "*permit* me to keep them."

Padre Gregorio threw back his head and the plaza rang with his laughter. Across the street several villagers turned to stare as they emerged with parcels from the shops. "Permit and obey...that is most encouraging," he chuckled. Then he shook his head at her suggestion. "I do not think Ramon would want you to do that. He would not want to buy back his pride at the cost of your own. You might offer to do it, however. That would help convince him you are truly repentant.''

Katie slanted him a jaunty, teasing look. "Do you still think I lack meekness, docility and a respect for authority?''

"I sincerely hope so," he said with a warm smile at her sparkling face. "As Ramon rather bluntly informed me, he has no desire to marry a cocker spaniel.''

Katie's smile faded. "He has no desire to marry me, either, right now.''

"Do you want me to come with you when you speak to him?''

Katie shook her head after a moment's thought. "When I came into the church, that was what I was going to ask you to do. I was terrified of his anger yesterday, and he actually threatened to make David seem like an saint.''

"Did Ramon raise his hand to you?''

"No.''

Padre Gregorio's lips twitched. "If he did not strike you with the provocation he had yesterday, I am certain he never will.''

"I suppose I always knew that," Katie admitted. "It was probably just thinking about David that made me so afraid of Ramon yesterday and today.''

Clasping his hands behind his back, Padre Gregorio beamed his general approval upon the mountains, the sky, the village and the villagers. "Life can be so good if you let it, Katherine. But you must trade with life. You give something and you get something, then you give something of yourself

again and you receive something again. Life goes
bad when people try to take from it without giving.
Then they came away empty-handed, and they grab
harder and more often, growing more disappointed
and disillusioned each time.'' He grinned at her.
''Since you are not afraid of Ramon doing physical
violence to you, I assume you do not need me?''

''Actually I do,'' Katie said with a wry look at
Garcia who was standing sentry beside the Rolls, his
arms crossed over his chest, his eyes following her
every move. ''I think Ramon instructed Garcia to
get me off this island, and if I've missed my plane
that man will put me in a boat, a box or a bottle, but
he'll do what Ramon told him to do. Do you think
you could convince him to take me back to Gabriella's, and also tell him I want to surprise Ramon, so
he shouldn't mention that I didn't leave?''

''I think I can handle that,'' he said, putting his
hand under her elbow and walking with her toward
the car. ''A 'self-important, self-righteous' man
such as myself ought to be able to intimidate one
chauffeur.''

''I'm terribly sorry about the things I said,'' Katie
said contritely.

Padre Gregorio's blue eyes laughed at her. ''One
has a tendency to acquire those rather unattractive
traits after wearing these robes for forty years. I
confess that since you said that to me, I have done
some serious soul-searching trying to discover if you
were right.''

''Is that what you were doing when I interrupted
you in church a while ago?''

His face shadowed. "It was a moment of deepest sorrow, Katherine. I had seen you passing by the church in Ramon's car, and I knew you were leaving. I had hoped and prayed that before it came to that you would realize what was in your heart. Despite everything you said and did, I felt that you loved him. Now, shall I see if I can convince the loyal Garcia that it is in Ramon's best interest for him to disobey Ramon's instructions?"

When the Rolls pulled into Gabriella's yard, Katie debated about having Garcia take her up to the cottage instead. The problem was that Ramon might not come back to the cottage for days, and Katie had no idea how to find him. Gabriella would help her, so long as Eduardo could be kept from finding out.

She lifted her hand to knock on the door, but it was flung open. Instead of Gabriella, Eduardo was standing there, his face uncompromising and forbidding. "You are not leaving?"

"No, I—" Katie began pleadingly, but the rest of her sentence was cut off by Eduardo's crushing bear hug.

"Gabriella said I was wrong about you," he whispered gruffly. With an arm thrown around her shoulders, he drew her into the living room to face Gabriella's shining countenance. "She told me you had courage." He sobered abruptly. "You are going to need a great deal of it to face Ramon.... He will be twice as angry at being twice defied."

"Where do you think he'll go tonight?" Katie asked bravely.

RAMON SAT WITH ONE HIP perched on his desk, his weight braced on the opposite foot. His expression betrayed no emotion as he listened to Miguel and the four auditors who were seated on the luxuriously upholstered sofa at the far end of his office, discussing the bankruptcy papers that they were preparing to file.

Ramon's gaze was turned toward the windows of his high-rise San Juan office as he watched a jet climbing in a wide arc into the blue afternoon sky. Based on the time, he knew it was Katie's plane. His eyes followed it, clinging to it as it diminished to a silver speck on the horizon.

"As far as you personally are concerned, Ramon," Miguel spoke up, "there is no need to file bankruptcy. You have enough to cover your outstanding debts. The banks that loaned you the money, which you in turn loaned to the corporation, will foreclose on the island, houses, plane, yacht, art collection, etc., and recover their money by selling them to others. The only other personal debts you have are for the two office buildings you were constructing in Chicago and St. Louis."

Miguel reached across the large coffee table in front of him and picked up a sheet of paper from one of the stacks. "The banks that loaned you part of the construction money are preparing to sell the buildings to other investors. Naturally, those investors will make the profit when they finish the buildings and sell them. Unfortunately, they will also be able to keep most of the twenty million dollars of your own money that you put into each building." He glanced apologetically at Ramon. "You probably knew this already?"

Ramon nodded impassively.

Behind him, the buzzer on his desk sounded and Elise's agitated voice burst over the intercom. "Mr. Sidney Green is calling from St. Louis again. He is very insistent about speaking with you, Señor Galverra. He is swearing at me," she added tersely. "And shouting."

"Tell him that I said to call me another time when he feels more composed, and then disconnect the call," Ramon said curtly.

Miguel smiled. "No doubt he is somewhat distressed about the rumors his competition is now spreading that his paint is defective. It is all over the *Wall Street Journal* and the business sections of the American papers."

One of the auditors glanced at Miguel with wry amusement for his naiveté. "I imagine he's a hell of a lot more upset about his stock. Green Paint and Chemical was selling for twenty-five dollars a share two weeks ago; it was down to thirteen dollars this morning. There seems to be something of a panic."

Miguel leaned back into the sofa and folded his arms complacently. "I wonder what could be wrong?" He straightened immediately at Ramon's sharp frown, however.

"Are you talking about Sidney Green from St. Louis?" The thin, bespectacled auditor on the right end of the sofa looked up for the first time from his ledger sheets. "That's the name of the man who heads the group who is planning to take over the office building you were constructing in St. Louis, Ramon. They've already made the bank an offer to buy it and finish it.''

''That vulture!'' Miguel hissed, and launched into a string of savage expletives.

Ramon didn't hear him. All of the roiling pain and fury he felt over losing Katie was exploding inside of him in a volcanic surge of pure rage that now had a target he could strike: Sidney Green. ''He is also on the board of directors of that same bank, and it refused to extend my construction loan so that I could finish the building,'' he said in a low, threatening voice.

Behind him the buzzer went off on his desk. Ramon answered it automatically while the auditors gathered up their papers, preparing to leave. ''Señor Galverra,'' Elise said. ''Mr. Green is on the line. He says he feels more composed now.''

''Put him on,'' Ramon said softly.

Green's voice exploded over the speaker system. ''Bastard!'' he screamed. Ramon nodded a curt dismissal to the auditors, and flicked a look at Miguel that invited him to say. ''You dirty bastard, are you there?'' Green shouted.

Ramon's voice was quiet, controlled and very dangerous. ''Now that we have exhausted the topic of my legitimacy, shall we get down to business?''

''I don't have any business with you, you—''

''Sid,'' Ramon said in a silky voice, ''You are annoying me, and I become very unreasonable when I am annoyed. You owe me twelve million dollars.''

''I owe you three million,'' he thundered.

"With interest it is now over twelve million. You have been drawing interest on my money for nine years; I want it back."

"Go to hell!" he hissed.

"I am in hell," Ramon replied with no expression in his voice. "And I want you with me. Beginning today, it is going to cost you one million dollars for each day the money remains unpaid."

"You can't do that, you don't have that much influence, you arrogant son of a—"

"Just watch me," Ramon bit out, then he broke the connection.

Miguel leaned forward eagerly, "Do you have that much influence, Ramon?"

"No."

"But if he believes you do—"

"If he believes it, he is a fool. If he is a fool, he will not want to risk 'losing' another million today, and he will call back within three hours so that he can get the money into my bank in St. Louis before it closes tonight."

Three hours and fifteen minutes later, Miguel was slumped morosely in his chair, his tie loose, his jacket open. Ramon glanced up from the papers he was signing and said, "I know you did not stop to have lunch. Now it is dinnertime. Call downstairs and order some food to be sent up from the restaurant. If we are going to work late, you should have something to eat."

Miguel paused with his hand on the phone. "Don't you want anything, Ramon?"

The question brought an image of Katie, and

Ramon closed his eyes against the wrenching pain. "No."

Miguel called down to the restaurant and ordered sandwiches. When he hung up the phone, it rang again.

"Elise has gone home for the day," Ramon said, answering it himself. For a moment he was very still, then he reached out and pressed the speaker button.

Sidney Green's strangled voice filled the elegant office. ". . . need to know which bank."

"No bank," Ramon said curtly. "Deliver it to my St. Louis attorneys." He gave the name and address of the firm, then added, "Have them call me at this number when the check is in their hands."

Thirty minutes later, Ramon's attorney called. When Ramon replaced the phone he looked at Miguel whose eyes were feverish with excitement. "How can you just sit there like that, Ramon? You've just made twelve million dollars."

Ramon's smile was ironic. "Actually, I have just made forty million. I will use the twelve million to buy stock in Green Paint and Chemical. Within two weeks I will be able to sell it for twenty million. I will take that twenty million and use it to finish the building in St. Louis. When I sell the building in six months, I will get back the twenty million I originally invested, plus this twenty million."

"Plus whatever profit you make on the building."

"Plus that," Ramon agreed flatly.

Miguel was eagerly pulling on his suit coat. "Let's go out and celebrate," he said, straightening his tie.

"We'll call it a combination bachelor and success party."

Ramon's eyes turned enigmatic. "There is no need for a 'bachelor' party. I forgot to mention that I am not getting married on Sunday. Katie... changed her mind." Ramon pulled open the large file drawer on his right, carefully avoiding the astonished regret he knew he would see on his friend's face. "Go out and celebrate my 'success' for both of us. I want to look over the file on that building."

A short time later, Ramon glanced up to see a boy standing in front of his desk, holding two white paper sacks. "Someone phoned downstairs and ordered sandwiches, sir," he said, looking around in awe at the palatial office.

"Just leave them there," Ramon nodded toward the coffee table across the room and absently reached into the inside pocket of his suit coat. He took out his wallet and rifled through it looking for some one-dollar bills to give the boy as a tip.

The smallest he had was a five-dollar bill—Katie's five-dollar bill. He had never intended to part with it, and had folded it in half, then half again, to distinguish it from other money he would ever carry; a memento he'd treasured from a red-haired angel with laughing blue eyes.

Ramon felt as if he was shattering into a thousand pieces as he slowly pulled Katie's money out of his wallet. His fingers tightened convulsively around it, and then he forced himself to let it go. Just as he had forced himself to let Katie go. He opened his hand and gave the crumpled bill to the eager boy.

When the boy left, Ramon looked down at his wallet. Katie's money was gone. Katie was gone. He was an extremely wealthy man again. Bitter rage boiled up inside of him, and his hand clenched into a fist with the savage urge to smash something.

CHAPTER TWENTY

EDUARDO RAN HIS HAND through his rumpled dark hair and glanced at Katie whose pale face was reflecting her mounting tension. "The security guard said he left the building three hours ago, at nine o'clock. Garcia picked him up in the Rolls, but neither Garcia nor Ramon returned to the villa in Mayagüez, nor is Ramon at his house in Old San Juan."

Katie bit her lip apprehensively. "Do you think Garcia might have told Ramon that I didn't leave, and Ramon is just refusing to answer the phone?"

Eduardo's look was filled with derisive scorn. "If Ramon knew you were still here, he would not be hiding from you—he would have descended on this house like forty devils, believe me."

"Eduardo," Gabriella said with an exasperated sigh, "you are petrifying Katie, and she is nervous enough without that."

Jamming his hands into his back pockets, Eduardo stopped pacing and stood looking down at Katie. "Katie, I do not know where he could be. He is not at either of his houses, nor is he staying with Rafael's family. I cannot think where else he would choose to spend the night."

Katie tried to ignore the painful stab of jealousy she felt at the possibility that Ramon might well have decided to spend the night in the arms of the beautiful woman he was often pictured with in the local magazine clippings. "I was so certain he would go to the cottage," she said. "You're positive he wasn't there?"

Eduardo was emphatic. "I told you, I went there. It was only ten-thirty, too early for him to go to sleep, but there were no lights on inside."

Katie bent her head abjectly, twisting her fingers in her lap. "If things had been reversed, I would have gone there—where I could feel closest to him."

"Katie," Gabriella said with sympathetic determination. "I know where you are thinking he is, but you are wrong. He would not turn to another woman tonight."

Katie was too preoccupied to see the dubious look Eduardo tossed at his wife. "You knocked when you went to the cottage, didn't you?" Katie said.

Eduardo's head swung to her. "Why should I knock on the door of a dark, empty house? Besides, Ramon would have seen the car lights coming up the driveway. He would have come out to see who was there."

Katie's smooth brow furrowed. "I think you should have knocked." She stood up more out of restlessness than anything else, and then said, "I think I'll go up to the cottage."

"Katie, he is not there, but if you insist on going, I will go with you."

"I'll be fine," Katie reassured.

"I do not want you to confront Ramon alone," Eduardo persisted. "I saw how furious he was yesterday, I was with him, and—"

"I was with him, too," Katie reminded him gently. "And I'm positive I'll be fine. He can't be much angrier than he was yesterday."

Eduardo dug in his pocket and pulled out the car keys, handing them to her. "If I believed for a minute he is there now, I would come with you, but he is not. You are going to have to wait until tomorrow to talk to him."

"My parents are arriving tomorrow," Katie said desperately. She looked at the clock ticking ominously on the wall. "It's after midnight—technically this is Saturday morning. I'm getting married on Sunday—that's tomorrow."

Remembering what Eduardo had said about Ramon seeing the car lights coming up the driveway, Katie drove the last hundred yards without them. If Ramon was there, she thought it would be best to have the element of surprise on her side. Particularly because she didn't relish the idea of confronting a furious Ramon on the doorstep.

Up ahead a faint light was visible through the swaying branches of the trees and Katie's heart gave a wild leap of joy as she stopped the car. She walked up the moonlit brick path, her knees shaking harder with each step. The bedroom lamp was on!

She reached for the door handle, mumbling a disjointed prayer that it wouldn't be locked because she had no key, and breathed a sigh of relief when it opened easily. She closed it cautiously, then turned around. The living room was in shadow, but there was the mellow glow of lamplight streaming into it through the open doorway from the bedroom.

This was it. She pulled the sweater off her shoulders and dropped it on the floor. She ran shaky hands over the clingy cinnamon dress she had deliberately chosen hours ago with the specific intention of tantalizing Ramon and hopefully weakening his resistance. It scooped very low in the front, exposing a glimpse of deep cleavage, had narrow shoulder straps, no sleeves and virtually no back. She combed her fingers through her long hair, then started walking very quietly.

In the bedroom doorway, Katie stopped to steady her rioting nerves—Ramon was lying on the bed, his hands clasped behind his head, staring at the ceiling. His white shirt was unbuttoned nearly to his waist, and he hadn't bothered to take off his shoes. His profile was so bitter and desolate that Katie's chest filled with remorse. She gazed at the dark, austere beauty of his face, the power and virility stamped in every line of his long body, and her pulse raced with a mixture of excitement and trepidation. Even lying down, Ramon seemed like a very formidable opponent.

She took one step into the room, throwing a shadow on the ceiling across his line of vision.

Ramon's head twisted toward her, and Katie froze.

He stared at her, his stark black eyes piercing through her as though he wasn't really seeing her at all.

"I didn't leave," Katie whispered inanely.

At the sound of her voice, Ramon shot up and off the bed in one lithe, terrifying lunge.

His granite features were an impenetrable mask, and Katie was too nervous to notice anything about his mood except that he was tensed, ready to spring at her. "I—I didn't want to go," she stammered. He stepped forward and Katie stepped back. "Padre Gregorio says he'll marry us," she told him quickly.

"Oh, is that right?" Ramon said in a low voice.

He started toward her and Katie started backing away. "I—I'll take back everything I paid for," she volunteered as he stalked her through the bedroom doorway and into the living room.

"Will you, now?" Ramon breathed softly.

Katie nodded vigorously, backing into the sofa and moving around it. "I—I saw Rafael's scrapbook," she explained breathlessly. "If you'd only told me who you really are, I would have understood why you didn't want me to pay for anything. I would have obey—" she choked on the word "—obeyed you."

"I see you have learned a new word," Ramon mocked.

Katie bumped into the lamp table and scooted sideways around it. "I'll fill the whole house with plants and ruffles and children," she promised desperately. The backs of her legs hit the chair, blocking any further retreat, and uncontrollable panic welled in Katie's throat. "You have to listen to me! I was afraid to marry you because I knew that you were hiding something from me, but I didn't know what it was, and David had—''

Ramon closed the distance and Katie put her hand out trying to fend him off. "Please listen to me," she cried out. "I love you!"

His hands gripped her shoulders pulling her against him with enough force to snap Katie's head back. For the first time she was close enough to see the expression in those smouldering eyes, and what she saw was not anger. It was love—a love so intense that she was humbled by it.

"You love me," he repeated in a strangely gruff voice. "And I suppose you thought that if you told me you love me, I would forget everything else and forgive you?"

"Yes," Katie whispered. "I thought you might. J—just this once."

"Just this once," he murmured in tender amusement, and his hand trembled as he laid it against her cheek, slowly running it back to smooth her hair. He made a sound that was half groan, half laugh as his fingers sank into her hair. "Just this once?" he repeated as if it were the greatest of understatements, and his other arm crushed her to him, his mouth capturing hers in a deep devouring kiss.

With joy and relief bursting like fireworks in her heart, Katie slid her hands up his hard chest, around his neck, and welcomed his tongue into her mouth. She arched herself against his rigid thighs, and Ramon shuddered with pleasure, his hands rushing over her shoulders and back, then lower, pulling her hips tighter to him.

He tore his mouth from hers and brushed scorching kisses over her temple, her forehead, her eyes and her cheek. "Say it again," he ordered hoarsely.

"I love you," Katie told him with a throbbing ache in her voice. "And I need you...and I want you...and I...."

Ramon's mouth opened ravenously over hers, silencing her words and sending her spinning off into a world where nothing existed but the fiery demands of his hands and mouth and body. He kissed her again and again, until Katie was moaning and moving against him, her body racked with fierce, wild jolts of desire.

He took his mouth from hers, and gazed down into her glorious, sultry eyes. "Come to bed, *querida*," he murmured hotly.

Katie spread her flattened hands inside the open front of his shirt, her fingers moving over his hair-roughened chest, but to Ramon's frustrated disappointment, the beautiful woman in his arms said very softly, "No."

"Yes," he whispered, already bending his head with every intention of kissing away her objections, but this time she shook her head.

"No," she repeated. Smiling with wistful regret, she explained. "Eduardo didn't want me to confront you alone. The only reason he let me come was because he was positive you weren't here. I didn't come right back, so he's bound to have started up here on foot—to defend me from your wrath." Ramon's brows drew together in annoyance, and Katie smoothed her fingers over his heart, her smile widening. "And there are two other reasons why I'd like to wait. One is that we need to talk. You asked me for honesty, insisted on it, and then you deliberately misled me. I would like to understand why you did."

Ramon's arms loosened slightly, reluctantly. "What is the other reason?" he asked gently.

Katie ruefully looked away from him. "Tomorrow is our wedding day. We've waited this long already, and, well, Padre Gregorio—"

Ramon burst out laughing and swept her up into his arms. "When we were young, Eduardo, Miguel and I believed that if we did something wrong, Padre Gregorio would look into our eyes and he would know it." He carried her over to the sofa and settled her on his lap, his arm around her waist.

"Did it keep you from doing anything wrong?" Katie teased.

"No," Ramon admitted with a grin. "But it kept us from enjoying it."

In the dimly lit quiet of the living room she had decorated for him, Ramon explained to Katie why he had misled her and then, as simply as he could, he explained how the events of the day had drastically altered the prospects for their future. She listened to the story of Sidney Green, her face alight with laughter, her quick, intelligent mind easily comprehending the pressure Ramon had brought on Sidney Green and the havoc he had wrought on Green Paint and Chemical. Yet when he was finished, Katie's excited elation faded slightly.

"Katie, what is wrong?" he asked her softly.

Katie looked around at the cozy room where they sat. "Nothing really. It's just that I'll miss this house; I could have been very happy here."

Ramon touched her chin, turning her face up to his. "You will like your other houses much better."

Katie frowned in puzzlement. "I thought you said the houses and the island were going to be taken away by the banks."

"It is still possible," Ramon said, "but it is not likely. Banks are like scavengers. When they scent a failure, they are quick to close in to ensure that they get their share of what is left. But if the 'failure' suddenly shows signs of recovery, they are just as quick to back away. They will wait and watch. They will consider how much more they have to gain if I should prosper, as I have in the past. My St. Louis lawyers tell me that Sidney Green has been crying to everyone from St. Louis to New York that I have been manipulating his stock and driving him out of business. The banks will hear that, and they will wonder if perhaps they have underestimated my influence. They will continue to circle, and to watch, but they will begin backing further away. When I resume construction of the St. Louis high rise, the Chicago bank will scent a profit and they will decide to reconsider loaning me the money to finish the Chicago high rise.

"So you see," he concluded, "you will have your houses and servants and—"

"—and nothing to do," Katie finished with a wan smile. "Because you think a woman's place is at home."

Ramon's eyes narrowed. "A moment ago, you said you could have been very happy here. Why can you not be happy in a more luxurious home?"

Katie, bracing for an argument, moved off his lap and walked over to the windows. She could feel Ramon's eyes on her back as she parted the curtains and stared out into the darkness, trying to think of a way to make him understand. "I said I could have been happy living here," she said quietly, "and I *could* have been—because we would have been working to build a life together. I would have felt useful and needed. I could still feel useful and needed, but you won't let me," she said.

Behind her, she heard Ramon get up and start toward her, and her voice gained determination. "You're going to begin rebuilding Galverra International, and my background is in personnel. I'm familiar with hiring practices and wage scales and government regulations and payroll procedures—I could help you, but you won't let me!"

His hands settled on her shoulders, but Katie refused to turn as she continued. "I know how you feel about a woman working outside the home— you made that very clear the day of our picnic. You said that when a woman takes a job, it shows the world that what her husband can provide isn't good enough for her. You said that it hurts his pride and—"

Ramon's hands tightened on her shoulders. "Turn around and look at me," he interrupted gently.

Katie turned, half-expecting him to try to pacify her with a kiss. Instead he looked down at her with quiet gravity. "Katie, a man is always most sensitive about his pride when he knows in his heart that he has little of which to be proud." He tipped her chin up and gazed somberly into her eyes. "Telling a woman what her 'place' is, is a man's way of trying to make a woman settle for less than she has a right to expect. I was ashamed of how little I could offer you then, but I believed that I could make you feel happy and contented here, living simply as my wife. I was trying to convince you of the rightness of it, because that was the only argument, and the only future, I could offer. I would be very proud, and very pleased, to have you working with me now."

His head turned abruptly, and Katie followed his gaze. A small beam of light was tracing its way slowly up the long hill to the cottage. Eduardo, carrying a flashlight, was "coming to her rescue."

She glanced at Ramon, but instead of being irritated by Eduardo's impending arrival, he was grinning thoughtfully at her.

"What are you thinking about?" she asked him softly.

Ramon gazed down at her, his eyes dark with love. "I have just decided what to give you for a wedding present. A Ferrari," he announced, pulling her into his arms. "You said once that a Ferrari would make your life 'absolutely ecstatic.'"

"I think I'd rather have a title," Katie twinkled, wrapping her arms tightly around his neck.

"Manager of personnel, Galverra International," she clarified.

Ramon buried his face in her fragrant hair, and he laughed. But he knew he was going to give her both.

CHAPTER TWENTY-ONE

On a balmy June Sunday, Katherine Elizabeth Connelly walked slowly up the aisle of a stately old Spanish church, past the rows of shyly smiling villagers, to willingly and proudly meet her fate.

With sunlight streaming in rainbows through the stained-glass windows, she placed her hand in the hand of the tall, darkly handsome man who was waiting for her at the altar, and standing before a solemn priest with smiling blue eyes, she became Katherine de Galverra.

Ramon gazed down at the beautiful woman beside him, her shining hair entwined with flowers. He heard her saying her marriage vows, while other visions of her danced through his mind: Katie looking somberly beautiful and regally aloof in the singles' bar where they had met three weeks ago. . . .

Katie, handing him a five-dollar bill. "Please take it, Ramon. I'm sure you can use it."

Katie, her eyes glowing with merriment on their picnic as she accused him of being a male chauvinist. "It may surprise you to hear this, but not all women are born with a burning desire to chop onions and grate cheese."

Katie, dancing in his arms at the pool party, her

lips still warm from their passionate kiss, her eyes dark and apprehensive.... "I think I am getting very scared."

And now, Katie, standing beside him in church. Katie, turning her face up to him: "I, Katherine, take you to be my lawfully wedded husband....

Ramon looked down at her and joy exploded in his chest, pouring through his veins until it was almost past bearing.

Her glowing face was a picture he knew he would remember as long as he lived; her softly spoken words a benediction that lingered in his heart.

The memory was still vibrantly alive many hours later, when his wife finally came to him, the naked splendor of her body bathed in moonlight streaming through the bedroom window of the cottage. He watched her, aching to give her the world and everything in it, because she had already given him so much.

Love tightened his throat as her arms drew him to her, and he covered her body with his. Tenderness burst within him when she unashamedly welcomed him into her incredible warmth.

They moved together, two people making wild beautiful love to each other, until Katie finally cried out in shivering ecstasy; then he gathered her into his arms and, whispering her name, Ramon gave her the only gift that was his alone to give. He gave her himself.

ABOUT THE AUTHOR

Judith McNaught brings to her characters the kind of enthusiasm and energy she herself possesses.

Her background is exciting and colorful. From producer at a major network radio station to assistant director for a motion picture company—from the single life to marriage and motherhood. And through it all, Judith maintains a delightful sense of humor that happily comes across in her writing.

Now living in Missouri with her husband and the youngest of their seven children, Judith tends to her favorite occupation—writing. We don't know where she finds the time, but we're certainly glad she does!

ROBERTA LEIGH

A specially designed collection of six exciting love stories by one of the world's favorite romance writers—Roberta Leigh, author of more than 60 bestselling novels!

1 **Love in Store**
2 **Night of Love**
3 **Flower of the Desert**
4 **The Savage Aristocrat**
5 **The Facts of Love**
6 **Too Young to Love**

Available now wherever paperback books are sold, or available through Harlequin Reader Service. Simply complete and mail the coupon below.

Harlequin Reader Service

In the U.S.
P.O. Box 52040
Phoenix, AZ 85072-9988

In Canada
649 Ontario Street
Stratford, Ontario N5A 6W2

Please send me the following editions of the Harlequin Roberta Leigh Collector's Editions. I am enclosing my check or money order for $1.95 for each copy ordered, plus 75¢ to cover postage and handling.

☐ 1 ☐ 2 ☐ 3 ☐ 4 ☐ 5 ☐ 6

Number of books checked_____ @ $1.95 each = $_____

N.Y. state and Ariz. residents add appropriate sales tax $_____

Postage and handling $_____.75_____

                                                          TOTAL $_____

I enclose_____

(Please send check or money order. We cannot be responsible for cash sent through the mail.) Price subject to change without notice.

NAME_____
(Please Print)
ADDRESS_____ APT. NO._____

CITY_____

STATE/PROV._____ZIP/POSTAL CODE_____

Offer expires May 31, 1984   31156000000

RL-N

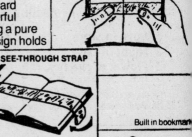

Enter a uniquely exciting new world with

Harlequin American Romance ™

Harlequin American Romances are the first romances to explore today's love relationships. These compelling novels reach into the hearts and minds of women across America... probing the most intimate moments of romance, love and desire.

You'll follow romantic heroines and irresistible men as they boldly face confusing choices. Career first, love later? Love without marriage? Long-distance relationships? All the experiences that make love real are captured in the tender, loving pages of **Harlequin American Romances.**

What makes American women so different when it comes to love? Find out with **Harlequin American Romance!**

Send for your introductory FREE book now!

Get this book FREE!

Mail to:

Harlequin Reader Service

In the U.S.
2504 West Southern Avenue
Tempe, AZ 85282

In Canada
649 Ontario Street
Stratford, Ontario N5A 6W2

YES! I want to be one of the first to discover
Harlequin American Romance. Send me FREE and without
obligation *Twice in a Lifetime.* If you do not hear from me after I
have examined my FREE book, please send me the 4 new
Harlequin American Romances each month as soon as they
come off the presses. I understand that I will be billed only $2.25
for each book (total $9.00). There are no shipping or handling
charges. There is no minimum number of books that I have to
purchase. In fact, I may cancel this arrangement at any time.
Twice in a Lifetime is mine to keep as a FREE gift, even if I do not
buy any additional books.

Name _____ (please print)

Address _____ Apt. no. _____

City _____ State/Prov. _____ Zip/Postal Code _____

Signature (If under 18, parent or guardian must sign.)

This offer is limited to one order per household and not valid to current Harlequin
American Romance subscribers. We reserve the right to exercise discretion in
granting membership. If price changes are necessary, you will be notified. Offer
expires May 31, 1984

154-BPA-NAJS

Now's your chance to discover the earlier books in this exciting series.

Choose from this list of great

SUPERROMANCES!

SUPERROMANCE

Complete and mail this coupon today!

Worldwide Reader Service

In the U.S.A.
1440 South Priest Drive
Tempe, AZ 85281

In Canada
649 Ontario Street
Stratford, Ontario N5A 6W2

Please send me the following SUPERROMANCES. I am enclosing ▮
check or money order for $2.50 for each copy ordered, plus 75¢
cover postage and handling.

☐ # 26   ☐ # 32   ☐ # 38
☐ # 27   ☐ # 33   ☐ # 39
☐ # 28   ☐ # 34   ☐ # 40
☐ # 29   ☐ # 35   ☐ # 41
☐ # 30   ☐ # 36
☐ # 31   ☐ # 37

Number of copies checked @ $2.50 each = $_____
N.Y. and Ariz. residents add appropriate sales tax $_____
Postage and handling $_____
                                          TOTAL $_____

I enclose_____
(Please send check or money order. We cannot be responsible for ca
sent through the mail.)
Prices subject to change without notice.   Offer expires May 31, 1▮

NAME_____
                    (Please Print)
ADDRESS_____APT. NO.____
CITY_____
STATE/PROV._____
ZIP/POSTAL CODE_____
                                          311560000